'Christopher Golden has reinvented the vampire myth into non-stop
ction, suspense, and fascinating dark fantasy. [He's] an imaginative
ıd prodigious talent who never lets genre boundaries hold him
ack'
Jouglas Clegg, author of the *Vampirycon* series

illed with tension, breathtaking action . . . and a convincing
piction of worlds existing unseen within our own'
ience Fiction Chronicle*

Iarrowing, humorous, overflowing with characters and plot
ntortions, abundantly entertaining . . . a portent of great things to
me'
Jouglas E. Winter, *Cemetery Dance*

olden combines quiet, dark, subtle mood with Super-Giant
onster action. Sort of M.R. James meets Godzilla!'
ike Mignola, creator of *Hellboy*

breathtaking story that succeeds in marrying gore and romance,
x and sentiment. A brilliant epic'
irk News (Paris)

he most refreshing books in the vampire genre since Anne Rice
ote *Interview with a Vampire*, [Golden's novels] are completely
a class by themselves'
thway to Darkness

Passionate . . . excellent . . . and a surprise explanation for vampires.
3rilliant'
LitNews Online

Wildly entertaining . . . like mixing Laurell K. Hamilton with the
lark ambivalence of an H. P. Lovecraft story. The pacing is always
dal-to-the-floor, the main characters are larger than life and the
mons and other assorted monstrosities give Lovecraft's Cthulu
thos a run for their money'
Barnes & Noble Online

ABOUT THE AUTHOR

CHRISTOPHER GOLDEN is the bestselling author of such novels as *The Myth Hunters*, *The Boys Are Back in Town*, and *Strangewood*. He co-wrote the lavishly illustrated novel *Baltimore*, or, *The Steadfast Tin Soldier and the Vampire* with Mike Mignola, and the comic book series spin-off. With Tim Lebbon, he has co-written the *Hidden Cities* series, the latest of which, *The Shadow Men*, hits in 2011. With Thomas E. Sniegoski, he is the co-author of the book series *OutCast* and the comic book miniseries *Talent*. With Amber Benson, Golden co-created the online animated series *Ghosts of Albion* and co-wrote the book series of the same name. He is also known for his many media tie-in works, including novels, comics, and video games, in the worlds of *Buffy the Vampire Slayer*, *Hellboy*, *Angel*, and *X-Men*, among others.

Golden was born and raised in Massachusetts, where he still lives with his family. His original novels have been published in more than fourteen languages in countries around the world. Please visit him at www.christophergolden.com

The Shadow Saga

Of Saints and Shadows
(July 2010)

Angel Souls and Devil Hearts
(October 2010)

Of Masques and Martyrs
(December 2010)

The Gathering Dark
(February 2011)

Waking Nightmares
(May 2011)

ANGEL SOULS
— AND —
DEVIL HEARTS

Christopher
Golden

POCKET
BOOKS

LONDON • SYDNEY • NEW YORK • TORONTO

First published in the USA by Berkley, 1995 and by Ace Books, 1998
First published in Great Britain by Pocket Books, 2010
An imprint of Simon & Schuster UK Ltd
A CBS COMPANY

1 3 5 7 9 10 8 6 4 2

Simon & Schuster UK Ltd
1st Floor
222 Gray's Inn Road
London
WC1X 8HB

www.simonandschuster.co.uk

Simon & Schuster Australia
Sydney

A CIP catalogue record for this book is available from the British Library

ISBN 978-1-84739-925-0

Printed in the UK by CPI Cox & Wyman, Reading, Berkshire RG1 8EX

For my son, Nicholas James Cody Golden.
I now have a measure by which to judge myself:
his eyes.

Nothing will ever mean so much.

Acknowledgements

As always, thanks to my lovely wife, Connie, whose understanding truly baffles some people, and whose enthusiasm for the work often equals my own. Thanks, also, to . . .

Lori Perkins, who worked tirelessly to prepare me, emotionally and financially, for fatherhood.

Ginjer Buchanan, who *asked* for a sequel.

Everyone who read the first book, and still wanted to read this one.

And finally, of course, to my family and friends, who have continued to support and encourage me, often against their better judgement, and some of whom believed from the beginning.

"The world is full of other things. Some are friendly, some aren't."

— JONATHAN CARROLL, *Outside the Dog Museum*

"While the camp fire held out to burn, the vilest sinner might return."

— WILLIAM F. CODY, *The Life of Buffalo Bill*

Prologue

The cruel war was over—oh, the triumph was so sweet!
> We watched the troops returning, through our tears;

There was triumph, triumph, triumph down the scarlet glittering
> street,
> And you scarce could hear the music for the cheers.

And you scarce could see the house-tops for the flags that flew
> between;
> The bells were pealing madly to the sky;

And everyone was shouting for the soldiers of the Queen,
> And the glory of an age was passing by.

And then there came a shadow, swift and sudden, dark and drear;
> The bells were silent, not an echo stirred.

The flags were drooping sullenly, the men forgot to cheer;
> We waited, and we never spoke a word.

The sky grew darker, darker, till from out the gloomy rack
> There came a voice that checked the heart with dread:

"Tear down, tear down your bunting now, and hang up sable black;
> They are coming—it's the Army of the Dead."

—ROBERT SERVICE, "The March of the Dead"

Humanity is jaded, that is true. At the dawn of the twenty-first century, the capacity of human society to accept the extraordinary, the incredible, the fantastic, has reached almost infinite proportions. Less than five years ago, aided by a nearly omniscient media, the world discovered the existence of the Defiant Ones, known in the western lexicon as vampires.

Of course, humanity's initial reaction was fear, and rightly so in many cases. But one of the Defiant Ones is a master showman, a legend named Will Cody, known to millions around the world as Buffalo Bill. Cody's natural rapport with the media, and the CNN news reports and video footage clearly showing the vampires as victims in the terrible conflict that destroyed the city of Venice, turned things around. Though these beings continue to refer to themselves as vampires, Cody has engendered within the world press the use of the term "shadow." Once used by the Church to describe all supernatural beings, the word is now the politically correct referent for a vampire.

A United Nations probe guided by myself and the de facto leader of the shadows, Meaghan Gallagher, exposed to the public eye an ancient Roman Catholic conspiracy to destroy the shadows, as well as Catholic control of other supernatural elements through the use, incredibly, of magic. Rome, of course, denied all charges, putting the blame on international terrorists and a small sect within the church. But that was mere fantasy. In the wake of the Pope's murder and the Venice Jihad, human governments and religions had no choice but to ignore Vatican claims. The UN ordered its own investigation.

Vatican City shut its doors. Threats of force were empty, and Rome knew that. Regardless of what might have been suspected, the Roman Catholic Church was a monolithic figure, against which any open aggression would have been reviled the world over. Military solutions were, of course, ruled out.

Still, the damage was done. The first to splinter, to nobody's surprise, was the United States. Declaring themselves the American Christian Church, the formerly Catholic U.S. clergy avoided the use of the word "Catholic" altogether. Around the world, diplomatic ties were cut, Vatican ambassadors sent home. In time, Vatican City became an island unto itself, impregnable yet alone. By the time the smoke rose declaring a new Pope, few noticed. The church will have to build itself anew, drag itself kicking and screaming into the twenty-first century, or die an excommunicant dinosaur.

Religions that worshipped the shadows themselves sprang up around the world, many quite naturally based on blood rituals, many rising from the ashes of the worldwide network of volunteers who had given their lives for centuries in a fanatical worship of some of the darkest elements of vampiric society.

It was a PR nightmare.

Alexandra Nueva, one of the heroes of Venice, testified in Congress and before international governments, spearheading efforts to create a justice system to control errant shadows. Today, all shadows must obey the laws of the countries in which they declare primary residence. Many of them are excessively wealthy, but those that are not must make a living, and all must pay taxes and take responsibility for their actions.

What little analysis has been allowed by the shadows has shown that some of them are nearly indestructible, making it very difficult, and often nearly impossible, for human authorities to apprehend a shadow alone. Though loyalty to one another had prevented such things in the past, the necessity of living in the sunlit world of humanity requires that the law be enforced upon shadows by their own kind. The force charged with this mission is, of course, the Shadow Justice System. In the days before Venice, when the checks and balances of myth still held sway, a simple stake through the heart may have done the trick. Today, the more time that passes, the more invulnerable the vampires become, the more truth there is in the word "immortal."

Murder is not tolerated under any human legal system, but many shadows once survived through the murder of human beings. Fortunately that is no longer a necessity. As news of the shadows spreads, and more information becomes available about the effects of their bite, there seems to be no end to the number of new volunteers, new donors. Many seek the "gift" of death under the fang, to become shadows themselves, but apparently very few have received it. Of course, certain shadows were determined to live as they had in ages past, but in the new century, with satellite tracking and instant media, these rebels, criminals now, cannot avoid justice.

Those were the developments of the first year after Venice, and it is easy to see how much they have affected us already. In the four years since, shadow culture has adapted to its new strictures, woven itself into the fabric of human society, and moved from front-page news to the Lifestyles section. As they used to say, back when I was a very young man, they're all the rage.

Will Cody said to me that "humanity has slowed its vehicle down as if to observe a terrible car wreck and now it's moving on." In truth, the squabbles are incessant on Capitol Hill and in the laboratories on every continent. Humanity has learned a new excitement, a new fascination. We've been wishing for centuries for such a revelation, and now that it has come true, we have thrown wide the door to the unknown with a sense of daring adventure born of fear and fear alone.

And the politics continue.

Lazarus shut the book from which he had been reading aloud, Allison Vigeant's *Jihad*, a first-hand account of the battle between Roman assassins and the vampires who had gathered that year for the Venice Carnival. The selection he'd read was the afterword, by Dr. George Marcopoulos, a human who had become the shadows' ambassador to the U.N. Lazarus thought Vigeant had scored quite a coup by including the ambassador's contribution. The Stranger, on the other hand, was less than impressed.

"No matter the uncertain tone of his words," the Stranger said, tapping the arm of his chair, "it is clear Marcopoulos believes we will continue to be integrated, that left to our own devices, we will blend into the world until one day we become as invisible as before. Also clear however, is that he fears this will not happen, that the future will be far less, hmm, ordered.

"I would like to tell this man that his worst nightmares, his most unsettling fears *are* true. Though he whistles in the dark with his words of caution, he does not believe them. But the time for invisibility has passed, for better or for worse. No matter our name, we have returned to the sunlight at last. We'll never be able to hide in the shadows again. If chaos is our get, then so be it."

The Stranger had been speaking almost to himself, staring at nothing, but now he looked to where Lazarus stood in the door to the useless kitchen, awaiting a response.

"So now what?" Lazarus obliged. "Do we sit back and watch time go by?"

The Stranger stood and went to the window, where the hot Greek sun was finally beginning to sink back into the sea.

"Gallagher, Cody and Nueva," the Stranger said and shook his head. "Even Hannibal in his twisted way. Despite the burden that this . . . integration has laid upon their shoulders, they still find time to pursue Octavian's quest, to search for an answer to his final question. *Find out what we are*, Octavian instructed them before he went through the portal to Hell."

"He was beginning to suspect," Lazarus said as he joined the Stranger by the window.

"Oh, yes," the other said, the corners of his mouth turning up slightly. "He would never have made the final connection, though. Even with the assistance of every scientist in the world, there is no way our brother and sister shadows will ever discover their heritage on their own."

"You plan to tell them, then?"

"When they're ready, Lazarus. When they're ready."

"And what do we do in the meantime, my friend, now that we have joined the world, now that our hunters hunt no longer?"

The smile disappeared from the Stranger's lips. The burning light died in his eyes, and another, colder light grew there.

"You are mistaken, Lazarus," the Stranger said. "The struggle of our people is far from over. And as quickly as the humans opened their arms to us, on the day our existence puts them in danger they will strike a match to the pyre of our kind.

"And believe me, that day is coming."

The Stranger turned and threw open the doors to the balcony. In the dying sunlight, he underwent a most fluid, graceful change, and took wing. Lazarus had been given instructions, but the Stranger kept his destination a mystery even to his one true friend. The words floated, a ghostly whisper in the air, and Lazarus could not brush them away.

They will strike a match to the pyre of our kind.

Lazarus knew that could mean only one thing.

Human and vampire would become hunters again.

---------------------------------- ✳ ----------------------------------

1

"It's actually quite intimidating," Allison said. "I mean, the way it just sits up there, observing the city. Ominous, really."

"Oh, I don't know," Will answered. "I'm certain when it was built it was quite reassuring. A fortress of that size and strength must have allowed people to sleep much better at night."

They walked through Mirabell Gardens, in the city of Salzburg, Austria, hand in hand. Allison Vigeant, a reporter who had once used the name Tracey Sacco, and her lover, Will Cody, who'd been known by many names. She was a petite blond woman with hazel eyes, and he was a rugged-looking, bearded rogue. His brown hair had been cut short only days before, and he still felt slightly naked. He was a shadow, and she decidedly human and determined to stay that way. They were lovers, and this rendezvous in one of Europe's most romantic cities was their first real vacation in nearly a year.

Five years earlier, Allison had been conducting a CNN undercover investigation into what at first appeared to be nothing more than a particularly vicious cult. But the Defiant Ones had turned out to be much more than that. They were vampires.

Not the vampires of myth, to be sure, but the Defiant Ones, now simply called shadows, were the basis for that myth. Like humans, however, they were not all of one nature. Some were vicious and cruel, others kind and helpful, and many, oh so many, in between. One and all they gathered each year, with humans who had volunteered to feed their red hunger, in New Orleans, Rio, a small village in Germany, a rotating slate of a dozen or more cities around the world. Five years ago it had been Venice, and it was there that the vampires' ancient enemy, the Roman church, had attacked them in force. The lives of the Venetian people were forfeit, as was the city itself.

The vampires, or shadows as the world called them afterward, had been victorious, and Allison, with her cameraman Sandro Ricci, got it all on film. Yes, Allison had been present for the Venice Jihad, and if it had not been for her chance meeting with Will Cody, things might have gone quite differently in the months that followed. But she had met him, and Cody had changed her thinking completely regarding his kind, regarding shadows. And she was not alone. It had been her interview with Cody and Peter Octavian, coupled with footage of the vicious and darkly magical attacks by the clergy, that solidified the world's opinion of shadows.

They were victims, scapegoats, imperfect creatures, so much more than human, and yet so similar; deadly exaggerations of human nature, human interaction, all too easy for people to understand when presented correctly. And Allison was sure to present them correctly. The Venice Jihad changed the world, for humans and shadows both. And it changed Allison's world, bringing her international fame.

And fortune, of course, let's not forget that. Between her CNN salary and the royalties coming from her book, *Jihad*, she had plenty of disposable income these days.

After serving as anchorwoman for CNN for sixteen months, she returned to the field, reporting from six continents on legal, political and social issues affecting the shadows. The travel was a huge perk, and Will met her whenever and wherever he could. She had always been gravely serious, but now she had matured enough to lighten up, to have a good time.

On the other hand, she was pretty certain that Will had regressed. Allison imagined that the Will Cody she saw now was the exuberant, childish and magnanimous Will of his heyday, more than a century before, when he was known as "Buffalo Bill." He rarely got tired, and when he did he still hardly ever slept. Which was fortunate, because Will had dedicated himself to three jobs simultaneously. For Alexandra Nueva and Meaghan Gallagher, his blood-sister and her lover, he was searching for the vampire named Lazarus, and an answer to the mystery of their origin. For the shadows he was an international media spokesman, and for himself, finally, there was the show!

As a master showman in the late nineteenth and early twentieth centuries, Will had acted in plays and written books. He had created the "Wild West Show," a world-traveling exhibition of riding, shooting and dramatization which, though exaggerated to near mythic proportions, still informed the world's perception of the American West. He had been a pioneer in the development of the motion picture, bankrolling and appearing in one of the first feature films.

Well, the Wild West Show was back—Allison had covered it for CNN—and now Will had made her book, *Jihad*, into a film, producing and directing it himself. They had spent a month-and-a-half shooting it, and then another six weeks in London editing the monster, and now they were, for real, on vacation. Time to just enjoy each other.

Allison truly loved Will, a good and decent man by any estimation, although most of the world would not admit he even was a man. No matter, though, they were happy. She had become a sort of financial advisor to him, because though he never had trouble making money, he had a terrible time hanging on to it. They talked about getting married someday, but there were no laws as yet to govern such a union, and with Will's involvement in the SJS, the Shadow Justice System . . . they'd decided to wait. And if that time never came, well, Allison was happy.

Now, hand in hand, they walked through the beautiful Mirabell Gardens, deep breaths drawing in the scent of the flowers and the unseasonably nippy air. They marveled at the design of the garden and its colors, the architecture of the palace, Schloss Mirabell, home to the city's mayor. They chuckled over the statuary, especially the gnome-like creatures carved from stone, and sat by the fountain. They talked and laughed, kissed and held each other close.

And yet their eyes, like the eyes of every other visitor to Salzburg, were always drawn back to the Festung Hohen-salzburg, the huge fortress overlooking the city from its southern edge, across the river.

"You're right, darlin'," Cody said finally, giving her a little squeeze. "The place is creepy. Still, it has a power and a . . . a majesty that is quite attractive."

"Okay, okay," she said, giving in. "Tomorrow morning, first thing, we'll go."

"Promise?"

"I promise. God, what a baby!"

"Why, madam," Cody said, lapsing into the cadence of the American West, "I do believe that was an insult."

"Believe whatever you want, Buffalo—"

"Don't say it!"

But she was off and running, with Cody in pursuit. As much as he was still trading off the nickname of his human life, with his books and the Wild West Show, that was for fun. In real life, he hated the name, and she knew it.

"You're in trouble now!" Will shouted after Allison as she headed for the gate and the road, Rainerstrasse, beyond.

Salzburg, Austria, European Union.
Monday, June 5, 2000, 7:26 P.M.:

Humanity had been surprised to find out how few shadows there actually were. When CNN had initially broken the news of their existence, most had an unrealistic reaction, honed from decades of first cold war, then terrorist paranoia—"*They're* among us, everywhere." In truth, Cody guessed that the shadows numbered in the mid-five figures somewhere. Not a lot of vampires to go around.

Still, most major cities had a few, and so it was not surprising that he and Allison ran into a shadow on the street outside their hotel that evening.

"Will Cody, right?" the shadow asked.

"That I am, sir. And you are?"

"John Courage, Mr. Cody, and pleased to meet you."

"John Courage?" Allison smiled. "As in, 'give me a pint of Courage'?"

"Yes, ma'am. That's right," Courage said, returning the smile with his own, self-deprecating version, then turning his attention back to Cody. "But that particular brew was named after *me*, not the other way around. And aren't I modest?"

They laughed politely, good-naturedly.

"I live here in Salzburg, now," Courage told them. "I'm a musician. Twice a week I play sax at the Urbanikeller, the jazz club."

Even though he shouldn't have been, Cody was surprised. They were really doing it, he thought. Shadows were actually merging with human society. Will smiled at the boy, who might well have been hundreds of years older than he was.

"What time's your show tonight?"

"Ten P.M."

"We'll be there," Allison said, reading Cody's intentions.

"I'm flattered, Ms. Vigeant," John Courage said sincerely.

"You know me?" she asked.

"Shouldn't I?" Courage replied, and raised an eyebrow. "Say, if you two are headed to dinner, I have a wonderful tip. Try the Peterskeller, off Kapitelplatz by St. Peter's Cemetery."

"It's that good?" Allison asked, knowing any meal was really for her rather than for Cody, and thinking how courteous it was for this shadow even to mention dining, since his kind needed such sustenance not at all.

"It's incredible!" Courage said. "I'm told the food is wonderful, but the atmosphere is . . . It's the oldest restaurant in the country, about twelve centuries old, and local legend says it's where Mephistopheles met up with Faust."

"Sounds great," Allison said, and meant it.

"Say, John," Cody began, "why don't you come to dinner with us?"

Courage looked surprised and pleased by the offer.

"Really I'd love to, but I've got a lot to do before tonight's set. Please do come by the club, though. It would be an honor, really."

Will looked at Allison, who nodded.

"We'll be there," he confirmed.

Courage continued on his way, and Allison and Will left their hotel, the Goldener Hirsch, behind. They walked along Getreidergasse, window-shopping the whole way, chattering about the wonders of the Old City, as that part of Salzburg was called. They had arrived late the night before, and that day had explored the right bank of the Salzach River, the Makartplatz, Mirabell Gardens and the shops along the winding cobblestones of Linzer Gasse. Tonight, though, they wanted to stroll, not explore. On their map, they found the location of Peterskeller, the restaurant John Courage had suggested, and now they turned their feet in that direction.

In Residenzplatz, they passed the archbishop's palace and the Salzburg Cathedral with little more than an appreciative glance. Music played somewhere in the background, Mozart, to be sure—the city was, after all, the composer's birthplace. The carillon bells of the Glockenspiel sounded out the harmony of 8 P.M. just as they reached Peterskeller but all of that was for tomorrow, for the day. Now that Cody could experience both, he set the daylight hours aside for the trivia of life. Nighttime was for actual living.

The restaurant was as wonderful as Courage had described it. Will and Allison had a chuckle over the shadow's name, and she threatened to call him "Bud Weiser" next time they met. Arm in arm, the couple passed through a courtyard with vaults cut right out of the mountainside, then ate in a brick cellar with extraordinary chandeliers. Allison was delighted with the flavor of the dumplings she had ordered, and she even convinced Will to try some of her cheese soup.

Later, as they made their way to the Urbanikeller to catch John Courage's ten o'clock set, Allison's eyes returned to the fortress, which towered still above their heads, above the city. She had been constantly aware of the huge castle, which could be seen from nearly any point in the city, ever present, ever vigilant.

"Even at night," she said to Will as they reached the club. "Even at night it watches."

"Maybe it's standing guard," Will suggested, grabbing her hand and squeezing as he opened the door to the place.

"Maybe," she answered.

But that's not how it feels.

Will and Allison sat down for a late breakfast in the hotel restaurant, though it was a lot closer to lunch. John Courage had played two sets the night before, and he was good enough that they stayed through the second. Between sets, Courage joined them for a drink, and they both found him refreshingly offbeat, even for a shadow. His self-deprecating humor was equally balanced by an often caustic wit, and he seemed to know everything there was to know about his adopted city. They returned quite late, and Allison slept in the next morning. Cody had found himself a bit tired as well.

After brunch, the couple wasted no time making their way to the base of the *festung*, the fortress of Hohen-salzburg. There was a small tram that carried visitors to the top, but after one too many pancakes, Allison insisted they walk. Halfway up, she regretted it, but there was no going back. Through the trees, as they made their way up the incredible incline, they could see the sides of the fortress. The sheer wall of the structure met almost precisely with the edge of the cliff; taken together, they formed a several-hundred-foot drop.

It was times like this when Allison felt her humanity most. Though she worked out regularly, she had to rest a couple of times on the walk up, and Will stood patiently by, understanding but not sharing her discomfort. As they finally approached the massive gates, they got their first real idea of the size of the place. Inside the fortress, yet still walking up an incline, they found alleys and paths that were almost streets, an open courtyard and a warren of hallways and rooms which must have housed the many soldiers stationed there over the centuries. Medieval art and arms were on display in several rooms, but Will and Allison found they had a common interest in the structure itself.

Battlements and watchtowers loomed above the city, offering clear views of the Alps. Cannon bastions peppered the walls, and the wind, even on a warm summer day, whickered through them with cold, grasping breath. The foundation of the fortress was begun in 1077, and the different areas of the castle completed over five centuries. It was this feat, this achievement, existing in the structure itself, that impressed them. Allison's creepy feelings about the fortress were gone, replaced with an emotion somewhat akin to awe. Even Will, who had been around much longer than she, was astonished by the immensity, the strength of the place.

"How much of this are we not getting to see?" Allison said, pulling on an iron grate which blocked their progress down a particular hall.

Will looked down at his feet, wondering whether there were rooms beneath them. Certainly the locked iron door kept them from exploring certain sections, maybe huge areas of the castle. It could be unsafe beyond that gate he thought. Then again, the people who arranged these things weren't used to shadow tourists.

"Let's find out," he said, and reached for the lock.

Salzburg, Austria, European Union.
Tuesday, June 6, 2000, 2:07 P.M.:

Matt and Tammy Monahan had left their baby son home for the first time. Even though he was with Tammy's mom, they were still worried. Nevertheless, they were determined to enjoy themselves. Along for the ride were Tammy's brother, George Esper, and Jack Rice, a family friend. The group split up soon after entering the fortress, Matt and Tammy wandering off to see the art on display and Jack and George finding their way up to a windswept watchtower.

"Watchtower," George said. "Like Dylan."

He started to hum the song and strum air guitar, but George wasn't your usual air guitarist. He actually played.

"The Hendrix version is better," Jack said with certainty. "Dylan sucks."

"Bullshit" was George's only reply. He'd grown used to such

statements from Jack, but he'd never been able to figure out if the guy was serious, or just busting his balls.

The two of them glanced furtively around and saw that they were alone, save for a decidedly non-American couple several feet away. George pulled out a joint and lit it, taking a long puff before passing it to Jack.

"It would really suck if we got bagged up here," Jack said. "I mean, what's the local law?"

"Don't know," George said. "Just be cool. Don't attract attention." They didn't.

"Hey, you know what I almost forgot?" Jack said. "Norm's got this rock collection thing going, pieces of stuff. The Berlin Wall, the Pyramids. He wanted me to get a piece of something, and this thing is fuckin' old."

George helped him look around, noticing that the stone walls and battlements, especially near the edge, were supplemented here and there with modern concrete. Chunks of the cement had fallen to the ground, and it was a simple task to find a big one.

"How 'bout this?" he asked.

"No, man," Jack said, as he continued his search. "It's gotta be somethin' from the oldest part, none of this cement shit."

Their search took them to an open doorway off to the left, and the floor within. Its surface was rough stone and dolomite chunks, and Jack knew they'd found what they were looking for. Now they just had to work a piece loose. He took a drag off the joint and handed it back to George, then kicked at several large pieces of rock that jutted slightly from the floor. After a few tries, he found a chunk a couple of inches wide that moved.

With his heel, Jack kicked the thing again and again, and it moved more and more. But it didn't come out. Apparently it was bigger than it looked. He had to stop for a couple of minutes as the couple on the watchtower came closer to them and then finally left. George tried kicking a bit, and then Jack took over again, going farther into the hall to lean against the wall and kick.

It happened on the fourth swing of his foot. One minute Jack's back was firmly against the wall, and the next, as George watched, he disappeared through it.

"Jack! What the hell . . .?" George moved toward the wall, but not too close. One of Jack's hands came back through, and George noticed for the first time that the wall had changed. Its color was almost silver, and its surface too flat, rippling like a pool of water where the hand broke through. George didn't want to have anything to do with this weird shit, but he and Jack went way back. George grabbed Jack's hand, scrabbling for a hold on the rough, stone floor. Bracing his feet, and holding that hand with both of his own, George pulled.

Jack moved forward, just barely, then stopped. To George it seemed as though the silver pool in the wall, whatever it was, *and I don't want to fucking think about that right now*, were jelly, or quicksand. Some kind of suction held Jack—wherever he was. And then, beyond that reflective surface, in which George could see his own face, beyond the quicksilver sand that held Jack in place, something tugged.

George was jerked roughly forward. He almost let go of his friend's hand as his boots slid over the stone, but instead his grip tightened. No way was he letting go. George slid farther, closer to the opening, and then noticed something that saved him from being pulled in right behind Jack. The opening in the wall was only so big, and on either side of it, the wall was still solid stone. Or at least it looked solid.

In an instant, George's feet were up, gripping Jack's hand and being pulled along, his ass cut and scraped by stone as he lifted his legs and planted his boots on either side of the opening. The muscles in his neck and back, in his arms and shoulders, strained for a few seconds, and then the opposing force, the one pulling Jack in, let up. It still wasn't easy, pulling him out of there, and George wasn't about to let go in case his tug-of-war opponent was giving him a false rest, but with a grunting effort, he did it. Slowly, once his head and upper torso had emerged, Jack crawled out of the wall, over the struggling form of his friend, and lay still on the stone by his side. They both rose, slowly, panting, moving away from the wall. George looked up.

"My God, Jack, what the hell—" And then George stopped. Because the man he'd pulled out of the wall wasn't Jack at all.

Sure, he looked like Jack. Same killer baby blues, dirty blond hair and beard. Same clothes, same smile. But this was an older Jack, a haggard, hard-looking man with something lurking in the shadows of his face that Jack had never had.

"What's wrong with you?" George asked him.

"Not a blessed thing," not-Jack said in a voice that George had never heard before, a voice that scared him.

"In fact," he said as he moved around to put George between himself and the wall, "I've never felt better in my life. I feel *perfect*."

Matt and Tammy came around the corner.

"What are you guys doing . . . ," Matt began, but he shut up when Jack turned to look at them.

Tammy saw it before any of them, even Jack, and she screamed. A huge hand shot out of the hole in the wall, clutching George like a child's doll, talons impaling his face, stomach and side. Tammy's was the only scream as her brother disappeared through the hole in an instant. Matt stared, mouth open wide, and Jack just smiled.

"Jack!" Matt finally said. "*Jack*! Do something!"

Matt ran to the wall, but by the time he reached it, it was only stone again, and he pounded his fists against it. When he turned, Jack was standing out on the watchtower with Tammy in his arms. She was sobbing loudly with her eyes closed. But Jack was staring directly at him, and as Matt started to move into the open, Tammy's crying began again. Jack lifted her, with incredible strength, and hurled her, wailing, out over the edge of the tower. From there, it was a straight drop to the trees five hundred feet below, and Tammy screamed all the way down.

Matt was on Jack in a moment, the two scrabbling on the stone floor of the tower. Matt was on top, and his hands locked around Jack's throat, choking him, but Jack stopped fighting back. Instead, he touched the bare skin of Matt's arm with one hand and the stone floor with the other hand and mumbled one word through his choking gasps.

Matt Monahan turned to stone, a statue, made from the same rock as the fortress itself, almost growing out of it. It was simple for not-Jack to pry himself loose from the statue's grip, breaking several stone fingers in the process. The statue looked quite alone. And somehow, too new.

"Well, this is an old castle," not-Jack said in his not-Jack voice. "And you, boy, have got to *look* old."

A hard roundhouse kick and the statue's head, a head which had once belonged to Matt Monahan, flew into the air and tumbled down the mountainside to join the corpse of his wife, broken and twisted at the bottom of the cliff, an offering to the fortress itself.

Above, the laughter began.

Salzburg, Austria, European Union.
Tuesday, June 6, 2000, 2:16 P.M.:

Just below the watchtower, in a crumbling hallway with large, open windows, an area off-limits for visitors to Festung Hohensalzburg, Allison Vigeant and Will Cody heard the screaming begin. As Cody searched for the fastest way out and up, Allison gasped and called for him to come back to the window. Only seconds had passed, but Tammy Monahan's body had already fallen too far for Will to rescue her, whatever form he took.

"Stay here," Will said to her, and Allison winced.

"I'll find my way up and meet you topside," she said.

Will bit his lip.

"Please," he asked. "Stay here?"

"Five minutes," she said, and looked at her watch.

In seconds, a large raven flapped out of that window and took to the sky, circling above the fortress, the only bird in the sky. As he dipped among the wind currents at that height, Will Cody watched as the man who had been Jack Rice turned Matt Monahan to stone, then smashed the head from the statue's neck and sent it flying over the edge.

Sorcery, Cody thought, and the very idea chilled him, ruffling his feathers. For as far as he knew, the one book that held the secrets to such magic, *The Gospel of Shadows*, was safe in Meaghan Gallagher's possession. But this was magic, just the same.

The sorcerer moved away from the watchtower, back toward the main section of the castle, where dozens of tourists milled about the courtyard, ducking into hallways and rooms. He raised his arms to begin a spell, and Cody dove toward him, determined to stop whatever the magician had in mind. But as he flew, straight toward the man in T-shirt and blue jeans, a ripple ran through reality, an illusion taking hold, and the man changed. His clothes became black, blond hair turned white-gray, and his words picked up in rhythm, a new spell.

He turned.

It was Liam Mulkerrin.

Cody turned toward the sky, veering up and away before Mulkerrin could notice him, his mind in temporary shock.

No! he thought. *He's dead. I saw him die, and Peter with him.*

But he knew that was untrue. He had not seen Mulkerrin die, but pass through into the realm of the real shadows, the demons that had done the sorcerer-priest's bidding. And Cody's friend, Peter Octavian, had carried him there, apparently sacrificing his life.

But if Mulkerrin was alive?

He did a slow circle, keeping behind the sorcerer, and when he looked again, Cody saw the spirits rising.

From out of the stone beneath the frightened tourists' feet, from the walls around them, ghostly apparitions oozed in wet clouds the color of parchment yellowed with age. They were dark things, yes, but not demons, not the shadows of hell. As they overtook men, women and children, each fell in turn, the apparitions disappearing within them. When the people rose again, seconds later, new intelligence burned in their eyes.

Will Cody looked closer, using other senses, senses born of all that was inhuman within him, to focus his vision. And he saw. The apparitions were just that—ghosts. The spirits of those soldiers, warriors who had served the prince-archbishops of Salzburg and had been stationed in the fortress whose souls must have returned there, to the place of their greatest duty, after their deaths. Regardless of everything he knew to be true, Will Cody had never believed in ghosts. And yet here they were; Mulkerrin had called them to his service, and with the humans in the fortress as physical hosts for the spirits, the sorcerer now had a small force of slave warriors.

The question, Cody realized, was how he had done it. Mulkerrin had not had this ability before, or he would certainly have used it. Now he worked such magic with no visible effort? Wherever he had been, Cody thought, as he glided on raven's wings, he'd been busy.

And what of Octavian? Where did that leave *him*?

Cody made one final circuit, soaring higher, away from the castle, and prepared to return to the time-worn window where he'd left Allison.

Allison! What if the spirits were all over the castle and not just around Mulkerrin? He dove now, hurtling down toward that window, but just before he passed out of sight of the courtyard, he saw something out of place, something not an attacking apparition or a fleeing human, something subtle—

It can't be!

But he knew it was. Allison had ventured upstairs not bothering to wait the five minutes, her reporter's instincts forcing her to break her word. She stood in the shadows of a doorway, and even now, as Cody crested the courtyard walls once again, she emerged into the light, to get a better look at what was happening.

Already, a dark and heavy cloud, the only true remains of a centuries-old soldier, drifted toward her as if it knew it had all the time in the world. After all, where could she run? And Allison, for all that she could see chaos had taken over, had not yet discovered the source of this anarchy. She had not yet seen Mulkerrin.

Where could she run? The question was moot; she wasn't running.

The raven, Will Cody, sped on, past the floating thing. He was larger than any raven the world had ever seen, and even now he changed, becoming something else, something completely new in the world. His talons grew larger, their sharp ends turning soft, strong. Before she truly knew what was happening, Cody had picked up Allison at the arms and carried her over the side, five hundred feet above the city.

Mulkerrin turned, hearing a woman scream, but did not see them disappearing over the side. Instead, he assumed some human had been so overwhelmed with the terrors he had raised, that she had thrown herself over the edge. He had taken over the mind and body of Jack Rice, who was, for all intents and purposes, dead. And yet, clad in illusion, it was Liam Mulkerrin's head that was thrown back, his mouth open wide, ringing with laughter. A maniacal gleam shone in the former priest's eyes as he surveyed his work, and he laughed again as he thought of the woman who had jumped to her death rather than serve him.

"Ah," he said and laughed, wiping tears from his eyes. "There's no place like home. There's no place like home."

He could barely catch his breath from laughing.

"No place like home."

*

2

Boston, Massachusetts, United States of America.
Tuesday, June 6, 2000, 7:45 A.M.:

The sun rose slowly over Boston, its heat marching inexorably forward, like the tide rolling in. It was the fifth day of the worst heat wave in a decade—over one hundred degrees by noon, and not less than eighty at night. Fortunately, there was air-conditioning in the Back Bay brownstone shared by Meaghan Gallagher and Alexandra Nueva. Though their shadow physiology was quite adaptable, and they certainly did not sweat much, or often, still the week had taken its toll. Even with the a/c on full blast, they were tired and slightly cranky.

"Come on, sweetheart, get your ass in gear," Alexandra said, and dragged Meaghan feet first out of bed.

"Noooo," Meaghan howled, pillow held over her head even as she slammed to the floor from the height of the mattress. "Ouch."

"Meaghan Rae Gallagher," Alex said, scolding, "we have got a video-conference with the shadow ambassador and the secretary-general of the United Nations in forty-five minutes. *You. Must. Get. Up*!"

Alex grabbed Meaghan under her armpits, pillow falling to the ground, and lifted her easily to her feet. At first Meaghan played dead, but then she whipped her face around to meet Alex's gaze, and spit her words like venom.

"Bitch! You couldn't let me sleep fifteen more minutes?"

"You don't have fifteen minutes," Alex snapped back, getting mad now. "And besides, you're dead. You don't need to sleep!"

A smile crept over Meaghan's face, as her feet finally took her own weight. She pulled Alex to her, pressing herself against the other woman. Meaghan's full breasts against her own reminded Alex that they were both naked. Meaghan's tongue snaked out, licking the ridge of Alexandra's chin, then her neck, and finally finding her lips. As their mouths met, Meaghan slipped a hand between Alex's thighs and began to stroke her there. Alexandra purred against her lover.

Meaghan turned her around, and began to lower her to the bed. Alex looked up into Meaghan's face, to share her pleasure, but was puzzled by the mischievous smile she saw there.

And then Meaghan dropped her, and Alex flopped onto the bed, already starting to laugh.

"Dead, am I?" Meaghan said, then she lifted an eyebrow, picked up her towel from a chair by the bed and headed for the shower.

"Well," Alex said, rising once again, her hand reaching down to rub where Meaghan's had been only moments before. "Maybe 'dead' was a poor word choice."

"Hey," Meaghan said, rushing to the bathroom as Alex followed, closing the distance between them, "I thought you said we didn't have fifteen minutes to spare."

"Not for sleep!" Alex said, kicking at the door Meaghan had locked behind her. It flew open, and Alex saw that rather than running the shower, Meaghan had begun to fill the big Jacuzzi tub they had installed. She was sitting on the edge of the tub, both hands on her left breast.

The hell with the office, Alex thought, *we'll take the vid-conference right here in the apartment.*

"Don't worry, sweetheart," Meaghan said. "I never start something I don't intend to finish."

Then there were no more words. Alex went to Meaghan, their kiss deep and full of truth and love, pushed her back into the tub and joined her there. They made love with purpose and without hurry.

Before the Jihad, before the world changed, their love would have seemed incredible. In the new world order, it was merely extraordinary. Meaghan: auburn hair and truly green eyes, her body subconsciously made near perfect by the shape-shifting ability all shadows shared. She had only become a shadow five years before, and yet she was one of the most powerful, both physically and politically. Before the Jihad, she had been a young, attractive professional woman, orphaned as a child and bored with her life.

Peter Octavian had taken her away from all that, made her a shadow and brought her into a war that changed everything, for her, for the world. And he died for it.

Alexandra: black hair and brown eyes, skin as dark and soft as sable. Tall and elegant, her heart made hard as diamonds by life in Karl Von Reinman's coven, she had also been a lover of Peter Octavian's. Later, she wanted to kill him. But the war had changed her as well; the loss of her lover, Shi-er Zhi Sheng, had threatened to shatter that diamond heart. Instead, Meaghan was there, and Alex felt alive again for the first time since Von Reinman had discovered her, a runaway slave not long off the trading ships, and brought her to the life of the vampire.

They were open about their relationship. They were lovers, plain and simple. They claimed neither homosexual nor heterosexual origin. Such terminology was useless to shadows, because of course if one of them had wanted a penis, they most assuredly could have managed such a minor change in form. Still, gay and lesbian groups around the world, still fighting against discrimination and injustice, claimed Meaghan and Alex as their own. While the discrimination went on, very few dared to be critical of the two vampire women. And if their status could help the plight of those fighting prejudice, the lovers would not deny them that. When Will Cody cast the film version of Allison Vigeant's book, *Jihad*, every woman in Hollywood vied for the roles of Meaghan Gallagher and Alexandra Nueva.

They were running late, but after their bath, Alex and Meaghan dried each other off, enjoying the afterglow of their lovemaking and the sensations of the soft cotton. The conference had been planned to discuss the hottest topic of the day: whether world government could, or should, put some controls on the passing of vampirism from one being to another. Within the boundaries of this subject fell many other, seemingly smaller topics such as marriage, integration, adoption, hiring practices . . . but what it boiled down to was, how much could the world really trust them?

Alex herded Meaghan into the bedroom, and they dressed hurriedly. If they were going to do this thing from home, the least they could do was look presentable. Meaghan was buttoning her shirt while Alex stepped into a floral-print summer dress.

"Button me up," she said, and turned her back to Meaghan.

As Meaghan reached out to do so, Alexandra went rigid, fell to her knees, then backward into Meaghan's arms. Her eyes were wide, dilated, and she twitched, a single tear rolling down her cheek.

"Alex!" Meaghan knelt by her. "What is it, honey? What's wrong?"

Alex's head was in her lap. Meaghan looked into her lover's eyes and saw no recognition there. Wherever Alex had gone, she was far away. Meaghan slapped her face, trying to bring her back. She knew what was happening. Alexandra's mind was linked to those of each of Karl Von Reinman's vampiric children. But as far as Meaghan knew, only two of Von Reinman's brood still lived: Rolf Sechs and . . .

"Cody!" Alex yelled from within her catatonia, confirming Meaghan's suspicions but frightening her as well. She had never guessed that anything could force Cody to communicate in this way. Years past, he had shut down the mind-link he shared with his blood-brothers and -sisters, as part of an ongoing feud. But now, his mind had opened again.

All vampires related by blood could converse, mentally, with words and pictures. In times of trauma, such linkages were overwhelming for the recipient as well as the sender. Whatever was happening to Cody, he obviously had no time for subtlety.

Meaghan could only hold Alexandra's head, stroke her hair and wait for the linking to end. As she waited, she wondered if she would ever experience such an intimate communication. Peter Octavian had been her blood-father, and had passed the gift to no one else. Now he was dead, or gone, and unless she passed the gift on, she would never be able to communicate the way Cody and Alex now did.

"Oh, shit," Alex said, choking and coming awake, and then Meaghan saw something she'd never expected to see.

Alexandra Nueva was crying. Tears streamed down her face as she gritted her teeth, babbling angrily to herself.

"How can we . . . got to kill that son of a . . . *Fuck!*"

"Cody," Meaghan said, bringing Alex truly around, "is he . . .?"

Alex looked up, her face ugly with rage but her eyes betraying a softness, a trace of fear that frightened Meaghan even as she kissed the tears from her lover's cheek. Meaghan smelled apples, their shampoo.

"Cody's fine," Alex growled, her upper lip drawn back in a scowl. "For now, Cody's fine. But we've got to act fast or we're all going to be dead."

Alexandra got to her feet, grabbed the blue jeans that lay on the bed and began to step into them.

"What the . . . ," Meaghan began, but Alex whirled on her, the warrior that she had become in Von Reinman's coven evident in her every move.

"I vowed that we wouldn't go through this again, Meg!" she snapped. "We've lost so much already, but I swear . . ."

Then she stopped, realizing that Meaghan did not know what she knew, had not been privy to the mental images, the message from Cody. Alex hated to have to tell her.

"He's back, Meaghan," Alexandra said, her teeth clenched. "Mulkerrin's back, and it looks like he's much more powerful than before."

"Back?" George Marcopoulos said, incredulous. "How could he be back? What does that mean, back?"

"What the hell do you think it means?" Alexandra shouted.

They had been fifteen minutes late calling in for the video-conference, and found that everyone else had been late as well. Things were just beginning.

"But he's dead," added Rafael Nieto, the UN secretary-general. "You both saw him die, along with Peter Octavian."

The thirty-five-inch screen on the wall of their apartment was split four ways, and each quarter of the screen held a face. Marcopoulos, the Boston doctor whom the shadows had chosen as their ambassador to the United Nations (Who better than a human, they'd thought, and though some member nations criticized his lack of political experience, he'd done an exceptional job thus far) was in the top left quarter, and Nieto in the top right. The bottom left corner held the face of Julie Graham, the United States secretary of state, and the bottom right showed the frowning countenance of Hannibal, once upon a time among the most feared of shadows.

Diplomacy and the will to survive had made Hannibal see the light, so to speak, and now Hannibal was the chief marshal of the SJS, the Shadow Justice System. Alexandra's blood-brother, the mute Rolf Sechs, was his deputy chief, and though the shadows had no true government, they all recognized Meaghan and Alex as the top of the hierarchy. The older ones, the elder vampires who would naturally have taken that spot, were less than interested.

At least for the moment.

"That is what you said," Secretary Graham chimed in. "The report is firm on this, that you saw Mulkerrin die."

"Actually," Hannibal finally spoke up, "that was mainly for the benefit of your, um, human sensibilities."

"Meaning what, exactly?" Graham asked. She was a hot-head, never mindful of her words, even when speaking to beings who could destroy her in an instant. Typical American politician.

"Meaning," Meaghan said, and all four faces on the screen came to attention, "quite simply, that we lied."

"You lied?" Now even Rafael Nieto was upset.

"Well, not lied exactly," Alex added, her natural belligerence making her placating tone sound more sarcastic than anything else. "Even though you'd been forced to accept our existence by the media and, of course, our physical presence, we didn't think you'd believe what really happened."

Of all the shadows, only Alexandra truly understood how much power they held in the world. The old doctor, Marcopoulos, who'd refused the gift of immortality more times than Alex could count, was probably the only human who understood. After all, acting together, the shadows would be virtually unstoppable.

"You've seen all the videotapes," Marcopoulos began, cutting off any further protest by the others. "Those portals Mulkerrin used to bring the other shadows, the demonic things, into our world? Well, that's where he and Octavian went. Peter carried the sorcerer through the largest of those portals, and into whatever was on the other side. We had to assume they were dead because of what we believe was on the other side of those portals."

"And what, Ambassador, is that?" Nieto said, calmer now.

They were all silent, until Meaghan finally spoke up.

"Hell, sir. We believe that Hell itself is beyond those portals."

The uproar was incredible, with the American secretary of state uttering several expletives ill befitting her station. When the furor died down, it was Hannibal who spoke, showing restraint that was, to Meaghan and Alex at least, nothing short of remarkable.

"Ms. Graham, Mr. Nieto, please understand that we do not wish to imply, even for a moment, that the 'Hell' of Christian teachings exists as it has been depicted in myth. Nor that the place to which we refer exists beneath the surface of the Earth. Rather, the 'Hell' we are discussing exists simultaneously in space with our own world, half a step to the right of what we would call reality. But make no mistake, it is very real in its way, and is the basis for all of the myths of that place of fire and suffering."

"But, is it supernatural?" Graham asked.

"Of course it is!" Alexandra barked. "Haven't you seen the monsters it has spawned? The magic which exists there? Anything science has yet to define is supernatural."

"Never mind this," George Marcopoulos cut in. "We're wasting time. What we've got is this: Mulkerrin is back, all communications to Salzburg are out. According to Secretary Graham, satellite recon is blacked out in that area. Obviously, wherever he's been, he's much more powerful than before. So, what are we going to do about it?"

"Thank you, George. Now, Rafe," Alexandra said and smiled, ruffling the UNSG's feathers with her familiarity and enjoying every moment of it, "what do you say we scramble a joint UN/SJS force and surround Salzburg, hum?"

"What about it, Julie?" Nieto asked the American secretary. "Will your boy jump in with the rest of us?"

"You know he will," Graham answered. "We're in, all right, but only under UN auspices."

"SJS will take command," Hannibal said curtly.

"I think not," Nieto snapped.

"Hannibal," Meaghan said softly, and they were quiet once more. "You *will* cooperate with the UN on this, but you'll only take orders from Rafael's appointed commander. Is that clear?"

"Quite."

"Good. Now let's stop fucking around and take this bastard down hard and for good."

Alexandra smiled to herself She was usually the one playing hardball, just naturally a bitch, but she loved to watch Meaghan take command. Mostly because, as smart as she was, Meaghan was almost never aware of it. She had yet to truly notice how much deference she was given, how much power she had, and she only shook her head whenever Alex pointed it out to her. Alex loved her for her innocence, but she knew that Meaghan's power would someday make her a target as well. International governments wouldn't touch her, for fear of shadow retribution, but the elders had already begun to question her right to lead. Eventually, it would become dangerous for Meaghan to retain even an ounce of her humanity.

They were preparing to disconnect the vid-conference when George spoke up. They all paid attention, for not only was he the shadows' ambassador, he had been Peter Octavian's best friend.

"Meaghan?" He paused, not sure how to continue. "If Mulkerrin made it back, what about Peter?"

"I don't know, George. I'm afraid to hope."

"Don't be," Alexandra said to her, to all of them, resolved to the battle ahead. "Hope is all we have."

Salzburg, Austria, European Union.
Tuesday, June 6, 2000, 2:33 P.M.:

When Cody put Allison down among the trees, and reverted to his true form, he saw that she was in a state of near shock.

"Allison," he snapped at her, and her eyes went wide in reply. "We've got to go!"

She paid little attention as Cody dragged her along, taking a short-cut behind buildings onto Hofstallgasse and then pounding the pavement toward their hotel. Only when they were almost there did she seem to come out of her daze, and even then she didn't speak. Rather, she picked up her pace so they were running full tilt toward the hotel. When they came bursting into the lobby, every head turned to take them in, arrogant scowls on so many faces. They realized then that the city was unaware of the danger, the evil, looming over them within the walls of the Festung Hohensalzburg.

Cody understood how foolish they must have appeared, but that was his last concern. Once again with Allison in tow, he bolted for their room, not bothering to wait for an elevator, bounding instead up three flights of stairs, then stopping to wait for Allison, who was quite out of breath. On the fifth floor, they walked briskly down the hallway to their room.

Allison picked up the phone immediately and began to dial an outside line.

"Shit!" she said, pounded the receiver down, then picked it up and dialed again.

"Come on," she growled, hanging up again and punching "0" for the hotel operator.

"Why can't I get an outside line?" she said, and as Will Cody watched, the color ran out of Allison's face.

"A coincidence, maybe?" she said, looking at Will.

"What is?"

"The phones are working in the city, but as of about ten minutes ago, nobody can get an outside line. Nobody! I'm sure you realize this, but we need a little goddamn help here."

"Don't worry," Cody said, sitting down next to her on the bed.

"Don't worry? Are you kidding me? The phones aren't out all by themselves, we both know that. This guy was supposed to be dead and instead he's back and stronger than before, and now we're all alone here, the two of us against him and whatever those things were in the fortress and of course, whatever other assistance he manages to raise. Don't worry? I'm terrified! And what about all these people? The nice people of this city? They're going to die."

She paused for a breath, a decision lighting her eyes.

"We've got to tell them," Allison said, and then she was up and headed for the door.

Cody caught her by the arm and spun her, effortlessly, to face him. His face was grave, his eyes frightened, but his voice was calm and pleasant as ever.

"Allison, sweetheart, wake up now and pay attention. First up, we *are* going to tell people, but the first person we'll tell is the mayor, and let him and his people worry about evacuating. We've got other concerns. Second, as far as help goes, you can believe it's on the way. I've already been in touch with Alexandra, and they'll be—"

"How? I was with you the—"

"In my head, remember. We're of the same blood-father. Everything we just lived through, she was there with me. She knows what's happening and I'm sure that she and Meaghan are already scrambling help for us. No, we can't take this bastard on alone, but we can start making preparations for when the cavalry does arrive."

Allison looked at the floor for a second, took a couple of deep breaths, then picked up the phone again.

"This is Allison Vigeant from CNN News," she told the hotel operator. "Get me the mayor, please, this is an emergency."

Cody smiled then. This was the woman he'd fallen in love with in Venice. She was back in action. And to think he'd been certain she and

Sandro Ricci, the cameraman who'd worked with her in Venice, would end up together. Will Cody thought he was pretty perceptive when it came to people, but he had to admit he'd called that one wrong. Though he'd seemed like a nice guy, and was certainly brave, Sandro had turned out to be an arrogant pipsqueak. When Cody saw her again, in Rome, three weeks after the Jihad, Allison, who'd been pointing a gun at Will's head the first time they met, had made her attraction to him no secret.

It was amazing, really. He'd spent his human life as two people, one man torn between two callings. One, William F. Cody, had been a buffalo hunter, an army scout, a scoundrel who gambled and drank and stole beer shipments with Wild Bill Hickok. The other, "Buffalo Bill," was an entertainer and the star of thousands of dime novels with barely an ounce of truth in them. One scalped Chief Yellow Hand in memory of an idiot named Custer, while the other was known around the world, even among the American tribes, as a kind, fair, generous man who was good with everyone's money but his own.

Two people, one man. When Karl Von Reinman had brought him to the life of shadows, as Cody October, Will had at once been excited and repulsed. He couldn't be changed. From the beginning, though he'd never really needed it, he continued to carry a gun. He rebelled against his coven, sought a life of adventure, and was reviled for it. Over time, his two natures merged, and by the time of the Venice Jihad, he had become nearly as much of a hero in his heart as he had been made by time and legend.

He remembered what it was like to be human, to be afraid. And his relationship with Allison helped to keep both things close to him, the fear and the heroism. She helped him be what he was without trying to fulfill the expectations of others, hard enough as a human, and harder still once the world found out he was alive, and a vampire. He was happy to license the revival of Buffalo Bill's Wild West Show, but he wouldn't perform. His serious commentary was in the film industry, and there he would be known as Will Cody.

Whatever shadows were, whatever William F. Cody had become, Allison reminded him, and he became a reminder to his own kind, that vampires had human hearts. *Never let it be said that we have no souls,* Meaghan Gallagher had said to him once. Words to live by, even if you lived forever.

"No!" Allison shouted at the mayor of Salzburg over the phone. "You don't understand . . . Yes, I am with Colonel Cody right now, and the threat is real. That is why your communications are malfunctioning. Believe me, troops are on the way, you must evacuate."

She was silent for a moment, and even across the room, Cody could hear every word the mayor said in reply. There was no way he was going to take any action based on her word alone, even if "Colonel" Cody backed her up. He just couldn't take such a risk.

"Can you afford the risk if you don't evacuate?" Allison said, getting angry now.

And then the earthquake began.

The hotel shook to its foundations, windows shattered and the floor beneath the bed began to buckle. Cody moved barely fast enough to knock Allison away from the bed and onto the marble bathroom threshold. Above them the ceiling was about to cave in, and Cody saw it just in time. He covered Allison with his own body as it gave way.

The quake lasted seventeen seconds. When it was over, Cody's back had been torn open by a falling beam, which even now he held up, away from Allison, with his body. As soon as the ground stopped shaking, he used his strength to turn slowly, sending the beam sliding into the hole that had opened in the center of the room. For the moment, their spot half-in, half-out of the bathroom seemed safe enough.

Even as he checked Allison for injuries, and found none, Cody's back was healing. By the time Allison had the presence of mind to look him over, the only evidence of any wound was his torn and bloody shirt. He looked around for a fresh one, and saw that most of their belongings had fallen down to the floors below. Aftershocks could come at any time, Cody knew, so he didn't waste a second worrying about clothing. He made do with an old Allman Brothers Band concert T-shirt that he'd worn to bed the night before. His tan-colored light cotton jacket was hung on the bathroom door, and he grabbed that as well.

The one other thing he was able to salvage, from behind a heating grate in the wall, was his holstered Beretta— nine-millimeter, semi-automatic, loaded with hollow points, fifteen in the clip and one in the chamber. He was a better rifle shot, but rifles were a tad conspicuous on most days. He slid into both holster and jacket, and turned to find Allison observing the entire transformation with raised eyebrows.

"I've never understood why you feel the need to carry that," she said.

"Call it a security blanket," he answered. "I'll never shoot as well as my old friend Annie Oakley, but then, I'm still around, aren't I?"

She looked as if she were going to say something, and then must have realized it was not the time.

"Well, I'm certain the mayor will get with the program now, so what's our next move?" Allison asked.

"You mean after we get out of here?"

"Yeah."

"Let's talk about it after we get out of here."

They smiled together, and then Cody walked to the edge of the hole, stepping gingerly. He wouldn't have any trouble getting back up if he fell, but it *would* be inconvenient.

What he saw when he looked down was unexpected. Where he had assumed that their bed and most of their furniture had collapsed into the room below, in truth a chain reaction had taken place, with the weight of each floor collapsing the next until they had all fallen in. And at the bottom . . . At the bottom there was only darkness. Cody struggled to concentrate, to focus his vision, and then realized what he was seeing. A huge fissure had opened up right beneath the hotel, tearing its foundation wide enough that much of its bulk had fallen into that hole. But then how deep was the hole if most of the debris had disappeared into it?

"Allison," he said, "look out the window and tell me what you see."

"Cracks," she answered. "A lot of cracks, why?"

They shared a look then, which was nearly as effective as telepathy. It had been obvious from the first tremor that Mulkerrin's power had caused the earthquake. They didn't know how, but they were certain it was him. Therefore, they could no longer put any limit on his abilities, not until they learned those limits for themselves. In the meantime they had to get out of the hotel, perhaps out of the city proper, before another quake hit. They had both realized that there would very likely be another.

The first problem to be surmounted was that between them and the door was approximately twelve feet of open space, its edges crumbling, and a fall of sixty or seventy feet, minimum, waiting below. The easiest way to go was out the window and onto the ledge which ran around the building on each of its three topmost floors. Once there, it was a simple task, as long as the next quake took its time to make their way along the ledge to the next room.

Cody smashed the remaining glass away from the shattered window frame and helped Allison through. The couple who'd been staying in the next room had either not been in the room or had already fled the hotel. The stairs, on the way down, were cracked and crumbling, and when they reached the lobby, they joined a large group trying to get a look into the hole without falling. As was true in any disaster, it would be some time before the police could clear the gawkers away.

Cody could see the bottom of the hole now, and all of the debris and furniture strewn there. In fact, he could see Allison's suitcase sticking out of the pile. The top of the junkheap was about thirty feet down. Cody thought of coming back for Allison's case later. But first . . .

"Okay, people," Allison said, in English, to the crowd. "We don't know when there will be another . . . an aftershock, and this is about the worst place to be if and when that comes. Why don't we all get into the street and wait for help to arrive?"

She received a dirty look from the hotel manager, who was now surrounded by people chattering at him about their losses. Several people were apparently injured, but it didn't seem as though anyone had been killed, at least not any guests of the hotel. In any case, people were beginning to file out now, and she and Cody turned to follow.

"*Ma che diavolo succede?*" a voice exclaimed behind them.

Neither Cody nor Allison understood more than a few words in

Italian, but they got the idea. Back at the hole, an older, white-haired man was peering into the depths, and as they watched, he backed off slightly, as if frightened.

Before they had reached the edge, Allison knew what they would find, and she was sure that Cody knew it too. But to see it was horror. The hole was now only ten feet deep, blocked after that point by a shimmering pool, a silver mirror that rippled with each stone that fell from the crumbling floor to touch its surface.

"*Out!*" Cody yelled. "All of you get out of here, now! Get out of the city, as far away as you can. Go!"

The manager approached, determined to put a stop to Cody's raving.

"Sir," he began, his English flawless, "I'm afraid if you do not lower your—"

Cody rounded on him, changing, his face growing fierce, feral, eyes burning red and canines lengthening to almost absurd proportions. His voice was a bass growl, from deep inside him.

"*Let me make something perfectly clear! Hell is breaking loose! If you want to live, leave. NOW!*"

The manager was gone. Cody whirled back toward the giant fissure, awaiting the emergence of whatever was beyond that portal, his blood boiling, hunger rising within him along with anger and frustration.

"No." A hand grabbed his arm, and he turned with a snarl only to see Allison looking at him sternly, no fear in her face.

But she should fear, he thought sadly, when the hunger comes on. Normally he was in complete control, but when his temper flared the hunger became nearly overwhelming. Bloodlust.

"I'm hungry," he growled.

"Come on, Will! We'll deal with hungry in a minute. For now, let's get out of here. We've got to figure out the extent of what's happening, otherwise the cavalry may be useless. Let's go."

Into the street they ran, only to find that the people from the hotel had simply gathered there.

"Away," Allison yelled at them. "You have no idea what's coming. Run, damn you! Have you forgotten Venice so quickly?"

That got to them. The whole world had seen the videotape of Venice, and now as they looked into fissures in the street, and saw the silver pools glistening there under the sun, they remembered where they had seen such things before, and terror took them. In the rush to escape whatever would drag itself through, several people were shoved, knocked or simply slipped into the pits. It was too late to help them, and Allison finally reached the harsh realization that the others would have to fend for themselves as well. Many of them would not make it. First priority, though, was Will.

Allison drew him close, amid the rising tide of panic that swept across the street and through the city, and forced him to take some of her blood. He argued that she would need all her strength, but she insisted he take a little, to tide him over until they could find a volunteer, or if necessary, an unknowing donor. She felt a sharp pain and a weird arousal which had become very familiar to her, and she smelled lilacs, as always. She never understood that, the lilacs, but the smell was there. When she had pushed his head away, she finally voiced her questions.

"This isn't a meeting place for shadows! Why is Mulkerrin doing this?"

"He wants to rule, that's my guess."

Cody and Allison turned to see John Courage standing quietly by. Allison noticed for the first time how handsome the shadow was, with his perfect smile, close-cropped brown hair and blue eyes.

"We'd better be getting out of here, don't you think?" Courage spoke again, and Allison let out a breath she hadn't realized she'd been holding.

"Leaving!" she said. "What a *good* idea!"

"Where to, John?" Cody asked him, deferring to the other shadow's knowledge of the area. "We'll talk about theories later."

"I think I know where we'll be safe for now," Courage said. "And I know where we might find some reinforcements as well. Unfortunately, it looks like we may have to fight our way out."

They turned to see soldiers coming toward them down the street, soldiers wearing armor at least four centuries old, swords drawn high above them. The screaming began as people were cut down in the street, and behind them something huge was rising from the fissure within the hotel. Cody realized that the soldiers were tourists from the fortress, possessed by the ghosts of dead warriors.

"Holy shit!" Allison gasped.

"Damnation!" Cody shouted.

"An excellent choice of words, both of you," Courage said with a smirk, already beginning to change into something else. "Obviously you share a certain eloquence . . ."

Allison reached inside Will's jacket and pulled his Beretta from its holster, aimed it at the oncoming soldiers and squeezed off a round. She addressed Courage without looking at him.

"Shut up and fight, wiseguy."

3

Washington, D.C., United States of America.
Tuesday, June 6, 2000, 9:36 A.M.:

The President of the United States spoke urgently into the videophone on his cherrywood desk while Julie Graham paced across the large Oriental rug. Julie liked the President, thought of him as a stand-up kind of guy, but she was worried about his temper.

Henry Russo had won the presidency primarily because of his stern view regarding the trade imbalance with Germany, but a large part of his popularity came from his wary, vigilant acceptance of the shadows. Russo was a serious man. In fact, he had little or no sense of humor about him. The President spent his days dealing harshly with corruption and slackers, trying to clean up Washington, so that even if he failed to visibly accomplish anything, his successor would have a much easier time changing the world. To some, Henry Russo was the best thing that had happened to Washington in a long time; to others, he was the Inquisition all over again. Either way he was a rarity, a President who, as he often said in private, didn't "give a flying fuck" about his image.

Julie Graham thought it was a miracle Russo had been elected at all.

They made a poor team, really, a gravely serious President with a temper and little patience, and his closest confidante, the first female secretary of state, whose own temper was notoriously short. Henry

Russo knew he'd never be reelected, and he had resolved to accomplish what he could in the time allotted.

Regarding the German trade imbalance, he and Julie were in almost constant contact with all of Europe's leaders, including Erich Strauss, the president of Austria. Henry didn't like the man, but liking him wasn't a part of the job.

"Erich, listen to me," Henry said. "The emergency resolution has passed. Britain, France, Germany, the U.S.—we *are* coming. Just cooperate with the UN on this, will you? You need our help!"

"*Ja*," Strauss said with a sneer. "I have seen the kind of help you offer, Henry. I don't want any. Even if this problem exists—"

"Communications are out, satellites are out and now you've had an earthquake!" Julie interrupted, stepping behind the President so Strauss could see them both on his own screen. "Is this all coincidence, Erich?"

Henry and Julie both watched the President's screen as Strauss fidgeted in his chair. Julie knew the man had seen footage of the Venice Jihad, and he couldn't accept that such tragedy might be occurring in his own country. But she also knew that quite soon, he wouldn't have a choice.

"What of the shadows?" Strauss asked. "I don't want them tearing my country apart, Julie. Henry. I think I'd better do this myself."

Henry Russo and Julie Graham exchanged doubtful glances, each silently questioning Strauss's grasp of reality.

"As far as the SJS is concerned," Julie said, "they've agreed to act as just another part of the UN security force on this one. There will be no raping and pillaging of your nation by shadows; that's what the SJS was set up to *prevent*."

Even while Julie was talking, she could see Henry's face reddening. Time was wasting, and the President could not bear to waste time.

"Erich," Henry snapped. "You are, of course, free to send all the troops you want into Salzburg, but our *suggestion* is that you attempt to evacuate what citizens you can and surround the city. Rafael Nieto has assured us that UN security forces will begin to arrive within the hour to assist you in that."

"I said I don't want—" Erich Strauss began.

"*Jeeezus Christ!*" Henry snapped, and Julie dug her fingers into his shoulder as soon as the words were out. Too late.

"Listen here, Erich: it doesn't matter worth a damn what you want. Rafael Nieto is secretary general of the UN, and the Security Council has passed an emergency resolution to go in there and pull that bastard out like a rotten tooth. Now, you can cooperate, or get your boys out of the way, but one way or another, you're not going to take on that crazy son of a bitch by yourself. Got it?"

"I really don't appreciate . . . ," Strauss began, but Julie wouldn't let him go on. She forcibly slid the President's chair from behind his desk and leaned over to look closely into the videophone, giving the Austrian president a clear view of her face.

"Erich, Henry's lost his temper, and we both apologize. But he does have a point. Don't be parochial about this; it isn't just an Austrian matter, it's a UN matter. As a member nation, you must respond to that. You have my word that the shadow troops will behave themselves, and that the rest of the security force will do its best to keep the damage at a minimum. But let's face it, you've already had an earthquake in Salzburg. The city is going to take some heavy hits."

Silence, uncomfortable enough on a phone, was made even worse by being able to see the person with whom you were speaking. As Henry Russo pulled his chair back up to his desk, appropriately ashamed of his behavior, he and Julie watched as the face of Erich Strauss finally registered the pain in his heart.

"You're right, of course, I just . . . I don't want Salzburg to become a war zone. I was born there, you know. My . . . my mother is there."

All the fire went out of Henry Russo. He didn't like Erich Strauss, but "like" had nothing to do with it.

"Erich, I'm sorry," Henry said. "I didn't mean to, well, I didn't know. Of course we'll all proceed with caution, and you should get in there as soon as possible, but you do realize . . ."

The President of the United States wished he'd kept his mouth shut, as his Austrian counterpart turned his face away from the videophone. Then the screen went dark as the video portion of the signal was turned off from the other end. Only the audio remained.

"Of course I do," Erich's voice said. "I've already said good-bye to the city in my heart. I only hope my mother fares better."

Then the connection was severed.

In the oval office of the White House, the President and secretary of state of the United States of America looked at each other with a terrible mixture of anger, fear and sadness. As homey as Henry Russo had tried to make the office when he was first elected, at that moment it felt colder and more heartless than ever.

Henry touched an intercom button on his phone and asked his aide to get George Marcopoulos on the line. Then he turned back to Julie, his only true "friend" in politics.

"This is going to be a nightmare," he said, remembering the tapes of Venice.

"Henry," Julie said, letting out a breath and shaking her head, "there'll be no waking up from this one."

London, England, European Union.
Tuesday, June 6, 2000, 3:01 P.M.:

His trench coat was not nearly enough to keep him dry, as Hannibal trudged along London's Baker Street in the pouring rain. He passed the address where a fictional detective had once made his home, and gave a broad, exaggerated smile to those humans he encountered. Its effect was exactly as he desired, clearing the sidewalk in front of him. A smile from Hannibal was sometimes more unsettling than a scowl.

Hannibal had discovered that, contrary to popular opinion, it didn't always rain in London. Just most of the time. Hannibal smiled again, and passersby gave him a wide berth. He was amused to find that the locals were more frightened than the tourists. Still, London had had more than its share of the weird and terrible over the centuries. The British had grown smart enough to fear, where Americans were still dumb with fascination.

The rain fell in a blanketing torrent which turned the already black-and-white streets of London into a misty gray wasteland, a classic film, but out of focus. It could be a truly enjoyable city, especially if one was familiar with the ins and outs of its nightlife, but the days were horrible. On the other hand, the gray rain meant no sun, and no sun meant Hannibal didn't have to think about it for once, about Venice and the change, and how his entire unlife was filled to bursting with lies and deception. He'd never had a problem with deception in the past, when he had been the engineer of such acts, but now that he *had* to lie, was forced to live a deception . . . He despised it.

A life of peace.

Hannibal had lived for centuries, first as a leader among men, then as a lonely, rebellious vampire, and finally, as time went on, as the leader of one of the most powerful covens of the Defiant Ones, helping to establish the traditions of his kind. He had been instrumental in building a corps of volunteers, humans who offered themselves once a year as blood sacrifices to Hannibal's kind. He had organized an international array of agents who answered only to him, who spied on whomever he wished them to, who kept him informed on every aspect of his people's evolution. He had been respected . . . feared . . .

Worshipped.

But no more. No, the actions of the clergyman, Mulkerrin, and the foolishness of Will Cody and Peter Octavian, had revealed the existence of vampires to the entire world—a world programmed by fictional representations of his kind as evil, vile, villainous creatures who must, at all costs, be destroyed. Humanity had been placated by soothing words, tales of the church's attempts at genocide, and the efforts by certain members of the shadow community to be accepted into human society.

Only Hannibal didn't want to be accepted.

Hannibal wanted to kill.

To feast, to drink the blood of *unwilling* human hosts—this was the destiny of his kind, the Defiant Ones. They were parasites who lived off the body of humanity, and Hannibal reveled in that knowledge. Evil, vile, villainous—this was an image he embraced, and a life he missed. But no, the children of his one-time adversary, the late Karl Von Reinman, now ascribed to a different philosophy, one which allowed a merging of two societies, shadow and human. But Hannibal knew such a merging was impossible.

Shadows and humans were natural enemies, predator and prey. They might toy with peace, but it could not last. The nature of shadows was to kill, to feed, to take without permission, without warning and without mercy, whatever was needed. And that way of life was not gone, only held in abeyance. For now, those shadows who, like Hannibal, lusted for the old ways, must hide themselves among the sheep, falsely advocating peace, or die. Hannibal himself had found the perfect hiding place, for in his position as chief marshal of the SJS, it was his job to hunt and often destroy those shadows who reverted to the old ways.

"Rebels" and "criminals" they were called. Hannibal called them brothers. While he was forced to destroy some, many others had been saved, organized, hidden away until the day Hannibal called them forward.

For the peace could not last. He would not allow it. Unified, the shadows would destroy their human counterparts. And if unity did not come naturally to them, especially to the children of Von Reinman, well then Hannibal would force it upon them.

Soon.

Now his plan had a new wrinkle. Mulkerrin had returned. Father Liam Mulkerrin, the last of a line of powerful sorcerers, a sect within the Roman Catholic Church, who had used magic to control all supernatural creatures, all shadows, except Hannibal's people. The church came to call the vampires "Defiant Ones," and sought to subjugate them for centuries, attempting genocide several times. The last attempt had been in Venice, the Jihad, when Mulkerrin had opened doors into hell from which emerged the true shadows, demon-things born of brimstone and death.

Though the Jihad revealed the existence of the shadows to the world, it also held a glimpse of the future for Hannibal. For the first time, he had seen the true potential in the unity of his people. Mulkerrin and his demons had been defeated, the sorcerer himself carried into Hell on the back of the shadows' self-appointed savior, the arrogant whelp Peter Octavian. And the Church had been brought to its knees.

Somehow, Mulkerrin had returned. Once again, Von Reinman's blood-children were at the center of things. And Hannibal had been ordered, *ordered*, by Meaghan Gallagher—herself not even the spawn of Von Reinman but of Octavian—to obey the United Nations commander, Jimenez. Well, that remained to be seen. Hannibal wanted Mulkerrin destroyed once and for all, a goal he shared with all other shadows, and humans as well.

But if Mulkerrin's presence could be used as the means to an end?

"Watch your step, ya bloody git!!" came the gruff voice of a burly Englishman, just as Hannibal collided with him knocking the big man back on his ass.

In seconds the man had regained his feet and pulled Hannibal up by the collar of his coat.

"Lissen 'ere, you fancy bast—"

No change had come upon Hannibal, he had not even bared fangs, but the man somehow sensed that something terrible was there and that he'd stepped in it. He smoothed the lapels on Hannibal's coat, then began to back away slowly at first, and then in a light jog. He was lost to the misty, rain-shrouded street in seconds, devoured.

The collision had done Hannibal some good, though. He had spent far too much time in the past five years brooding, lost in his thoughts. The big man had just jolted him from that reverie, and now he found himself just a block from his office, the headquarters of the SJS.

He took the steps two at a time, not to hurry, simply to get there.

A shorter stride was uncomfortable for him, unnatural. The door was closed, but a light shone through the opaque windows at either side of the entrance. Inside Hannibal quickly doffed his trench coat and shook the rain from his long white hair. The receptionist, a human named Marie, who was obsessed with vampires, nearly came to attention when he entered. She was as fascinated as she was frightened, and he smiled at her as she got up to make him a cup of tea. Thirsty for blood though he might be, he was never above a good cup of tea. And this Marie was attractive. Eventually, he would have her in all the ways they both imagined, and some she would never have dreamed.

Hannibal heard a file drawer sliding shut in the other room, and then the approach of his deputy chief, Rolf Sechs. The shadow was large, as burly as the man Hannibal had knocked down, and yet almost gentle, if such could be believed of any vampire. And silent. He had light brown hair and crystal blue eyes, and his kindly features belied his size and strength.

Mute, Rolf communicated with his face and hands, and when necessary with a voice-pad which vocalized his writing. Intelligent, loyal and a fierce warrior, he would have been the logical choice for deputy chief if he had wanted the job. Hannibal knew better. Rolf had no interest in the SJS. He had been asked to take his present position by Meaghan Gallagher, the de facto leader of the world's shadows. Rolf was also a blood-son of Karl Von Reinman, and Gallagher had given him the job to keep an eye on Hannibal.

"You have taken the appropriate measures, I presume," Hannibal said, but did not wait for a reply. "We leave for Salzburg in one hour. Be certain the entire unit is prepared."

Rolf simply nodded. Hannibal was comfortable with the knowledge that whatever happened, when he finally made his move, Rolf would have to be destroyed.

The mute German watched as Hannibal carried a cup of tea into his office and shut the door. When he was gone, Rolf flirted silently with Marie. Though he felt no special attachment to her, they had been lovers for more than a year, and she often told him about things she shouldn't have, things she'd heard Hannibal saying in the office. Rolf knew far more than Hannibal imagined, and was preparing for their eventual confrontation. Hannibal would have killed Marie if he'd known.

Rolf knew that thought thrilled her.

Boston, Massachusetts, United States of America.
Tuesday, June 6, 2000, 11:39 A.M.:

As far as Meaghan Gallagher was concerned, it was a stroke of luck that George Marcopoulos was still in Boston. He and his wife Valerie, who had been ill, did still live in town, but George spent so much of his time running back and forth to New York and Washington that it was unusual to find him at home. If Valerie's recovery were less than complete, George would most likely have to retire as shadow ambassador. The thought disturbed Meaghan, for she could think of no other acceptable human candidates.

Bitch, she thought to herself. *How can you be so selfish and cold?*

She ought to be thinking about Valerie, she knew, and about George's feelings. Though she was loathe to admit it, since her death Meaghan had become increasingly insensitive to the frailty of humankind. She imagined it was a trait of all shadows, and perhaps a natural one. As she became less and less human, her new chemistry distanced her more and more from her origins, so that she could hunt without feeling for her prey.

She would not allow it. Peter Octavian had overcome that same encroaching numbness, and he was her blood-father after all.

Now, as Alexandra made preparations for their departure and eventual rendezvous with Hannibal at the Austrian border, Meaghan stepped out of the "T" station at Government Center and began to walk toward Fanueil Hall. Though she could have flown and simply landed in the middle of Quincy Market, it had become etiquette for her kind not to do so. Such a display instilled fear and awe, and attracted a lot of unwanted attention. Though melodramatic by nature, she had determined that her people must refrain from such showboating, even if to do so made life more difficult.

The city block between Government Center and Boston Harbor was called Quincy Market, a group of buildings filled with shopping and food and, outdoors, merchants' carts filled with everything from Harvard University T-shirts to fresh-squeezed lemonade. Visitors and locals alike tended to refer to the marketplace as Fanueil Hall, the name of a colonial era meeting house at the front of Quincy Market. George Marcopoulos had never confused the two. Though they were going to have lunch inside Quincy Market, he met Meaghan where he always did, outside Faneuil Hall.

Meaghan loved George Marcopoulos like a father—her own had died when she was quite young—and he returned the affection.

"Hello, darling," he said, and bent slightly to kiss her cheek as she hugged him. George was an old man, or so he constantly told himself, and he knew that people began to shrink with age. But Meaghan had once been significantly shorter than him. He had not shrunk that much, he knew. She had grown. It was just one more in an endless series of fascinating discoveries he and the world were making about the shadows.

But as usual, he kept it to himself. Let the rest of them find out on their own, and not badger his loved ones.

"Mr. Ambassador," Meaghan answered, with a smile that reached her eyes. "How are you today?"

"Worried," he answered, his own smile disappearing. "But let's discuss it over lunch."

George offered Meaghan his arm and she took it. They walked, linked in that manner, across the cobblestones of Quincy Market, examining the wares of the merchant carts. The noonday sun beat down on them, though the ocean breeze made it bearable, and Meaghan squinted against the glare. They passed a vendor selling flowers, and their myriad scents joined into one, overpowering bouquet. Powerful smells also wafted out of other establishments, including the hypnotically sweet, commanding smell of chocolate chip cookies from the Boston Chipyard. Finally they reached

Cityside, a café which boasted the "best burger in Boston." Although red meat was definitely not in his diet, and Valerie would scream if she knew, George was dying for a cheeseburger . . . and damn the fat content!

"How's Alexandra?" he asked as they waited to be seated.

"Like the rest of us, scared. But the funny thing is that she's mainly scared for Will. It wasn't so many years ago that she wanted Will Cody dead, but now she's even more worried about him than I am. I never figured her for the mother hen type, but there it is."

"And how are things between you?" he asked, sincerely.

"Wonderful," Meaghan answered, and meant it. She was glad George was so comfortable when it came to her relationship with Alex. Most people his age wouldn't have been.

But then, the whole world had changed, and George had been through the changes firsthand. He had been forced to accept a lot of things in light of which her relationship with Alex appeared as normal as she and Alex knew it to be. Life went on, love went on, and George had a kind heart. They would miss him when he died. Meaghan, Alex and Cody had all offered him the gift of life, the Revenant Transformation, more than once, separately and together. He had always refused. They had offered to save Valerie's life, and she had reacted with fear and disgust, being not as open-minded as her husband. She would rather take her chances with the doctors. And George would join her when his time came.

But for now, he lived, and he was their greatest friend among humans.

When they had finally been seated and their orders taken, Meaghan asked him what, other than the obvious, he was worried about.

"We're clueless here," he began, quietly and calmly, so as not to draw the attention of the loud crowd seated around them. "We don't know where Mulkerrin's been or how he came back. We have no idea where his apparently new abilities come from, or what their limitations are. Peter's status is unknown. We don't know what's gone on inside Salzburg in the hours since the earthquake, or what's happened to Cody and Allison Vigeant."

"You can rest assured," she interrupted, "that if anything had happened to Cody, Alexandra would know of it."

"Well, that's something at least," George said, and was thoughtful for a moment before continuing. "The UN is afraid of you, all of you, I mean. But strangely enough, mostly of you. Because of the power you hold over your people, and because of the book."

"I won't . . . I can't give up the book."

"I know that." He looked at her sternly, a reminder of who he was. "I'm not suggesting that you do. The safest place for *The Gospel of Shadows* is with you and Alex, away from any government, especially America's, away from the less, shall we say civilized, of your kind, like Hannibal. In the wrong hands . . . Well, I don't have to tell you this, but they're also afraid because, while they know you're not really vampires, at least not the mythical kind, they don't have a clue as to what you really are."

"Neither do we!" She raised her voice, gaining her unwanted attention from the other diners, some of whom easily recognized her. She was a celebrity after all. "Neither do we," she said again, quietly.

"They didn't believe you before," George replied, "and now that they know we lied to them about the end of the Jihad, about Mulkerrin, they *really* don't believe you. They want to do research, to study—"

"Out of the question, unless they have shadow scientists," she said, stopping him. "We've been over this. I don't want them trying some synthetic replication of the process; you know where that could lead. I also don't want them developing weapons against us."

Meaghan reached across and held George's hand, tight. Their eyes met.

"The only thing keeping the world at peace right now is their fear of the unknown, their fear of us. The more they know about us, the less frightened they become. This new order is a tenuous thing."

"And Mulkerrin may be enough to bring it down," he said. "Listen, I'll continue to stall, and I think the truth of your words will hold them off a while, but we've got to find out everything there is to know about your people . . ."

His voice trailed off, but Meaghan heard the phrase he'd left unsaid. *Before they do.*

"Peace is a dangerous place," Meaghan said, her mind far away now.

"A mine field," George agreed.

International Airspace.
Tuesday, June 6, 2000, 12:15 P.M., EST:

High above the Atlantic, a military transport jet carried Roberto Jimenez toward Germany. He'd been visiting relatives in New York City when the call came through. There wasn't a person in the world he hated more than the UN secretary general, Rafael Nieto. His boss. He'd never met a more arrogant, aggravating man. And yet, Jimenez respected his boss. He knew the job, did it well, and earned the attention of the world.

At forty-four, hair white at the temples and streaked through the otherwise dark, close-cut fur of his head and mustache, Jimenez was still young to have been made commander of the UN Security Forces. Still, they didn't want him out there, fighting. But that was the condition upon which he'd taken the job. He'd trained with nearly every elite fighting force allied with his homeland, Spain. He was not going to give orders from safety. He couldn't, no matter how badly they wanted to protect him; the thought sickened him.

And they did want to protect him. The job had gotten that much more important in the three years since '97, when NATO and the UN had finally merged. The two organizations had been stepping all over each other's toes for years, but after the whole Bosnia debacle, there was no putting off the merger. NATO had begun to play diplomacy games, and the UN had moved more and more into the area of military intervention. Technology and time had made the Earth like a small town, and there wasn't room in town for both of them. The new balance of power made Roberto Jimenez one of the two or three most powerful military men in the world. Maybe *the* most powerful.

But he didn't let it go to his head.

Now the transport brought him at top speed toward a rendezvous in Munich with the UNSF troops gathering to take the hot spot. By dawn, they'd be invading Salzburg on his orders. For the moment, though, he was arguing with his boss on the phone. The duties of the UN secretary general had grown in the past five years, as more and more of the world's protection was heaped on his shoulders. The man was not one to mince words.

"I don't give a goddamn whether you like it or not," Nieto snapped, and the viewscreen was good enough that Jimenez could see a vein pulse on his superior's forehead.

"Listen, Rafe," Jimenez reasoned, "you know and I know that Hannibal has his own agenda. I don't know what the SJS is up to, or even if the whole group is under his control, but their presence will compromise this mission."

Nieto heaved a sigh, calming himself down.

"Berto," he said, "I know you don't trust him. I don't. Even the shadows don't. But chances are, you're going to need him. His people know a lot more about this shit than we do! He's agreed to follow your orders. Besides, Gallagher and Nueva will be there to keep him in line."

Roberto Jimenez listened, but wasn't buying any of it. He feared the shadows, and didn't trust any of them, even the "good" ones.

"Who's going to keep them in line?" he asked, sarcastically.

A cloud fell over UNSG Nieto's face.

"Just do your job."

The connection was broken, leaving Jimenez with the thrumming of the jet for company. He unzipped his jacket and reached inside to pull a sharp object from under his arm, where it had been hidden in a leather sheath. It was a crucifix, made of silver, whose base tapered down to a razor point. A dagger. A friend of his, a lieutenant in the Italian army, had found it in the ruins of Venice after the Jihad, and given it to Roberto as a gift.

And for protection.

Jimenez stroked the blade for a moment before replacing it inside his jacket, then zipping up. It made him feel a little better to have that weapon, and symbol, nestled against his body.

It bothered him that Nieto referred to the shadows as people. They weren't. They were exactly what they were called—shadows. Shadows of human beings.

And shadows were fickle things.

Roberto Jimenez didn't trust any of them.

4

Salzburg, Austria, European Union.
Tuesday, June 6, 2000, 3:14 P.M.:

It was amazingly quiet.

Everything human had fled this particular street except Allison Vigeant, and she stood between John Courage and Will Cody, Beretta in hand. They couldn't even hear screaming in the distance. No sirens, no vehicles. For a moment, the only sound was the chilly summer wind whipping down Getreidergasse.

In front of them, were humans whose souls had been torn out and replaced with the supernatural will of the ghosts of centuries-dead soldiers, their tourist clothing replaced by perfectly preserved, clanking armor, stolen from the museum at the Fortress Hohensalzburg. Behind them was a demon, eleven feet tall, with lobster-like pincers for hands and eyes all over its man-shaped body. Only the enormous, sharply glimmering horn on its forehead was without eyes. And certainly there were more demons where it had came from.

"We've got to get out of here," John Courage said aloud, and the silence was broken.

Noise came shrieking back into life: sirens started up in the distance, and the rumbling of trucks could be heard nearby. People were screaming as the demons emerged all over the city and the evacuation began in earnest. A large group of people ran screaming across the street several blocks behind them, and then something large and black charged after them.

In front of them, armor began clanking anew, as the dead soldiers rushed forward.

Behind them, a roar, as the demon lumbered ahead.

"Unless you want to leave Allison here, just how do you propose doing that?" Cody answered, acid in his voice.

"Only one way," Allison said, answering both their questions as she squared her feet the way Cody had taught her, aimed the Beretta, and shot the nearest soldier in the eye.

"Allison, they're tourists," Cody reminded her, right hand nervously tugging his beard.

"Get with it, Will. We've got no clue what's really happened to them. What Mulkerrin's done. Besides, it's them or us. That's a no-brainer."

She squeezed off another round, then pawed Cody's jacket for backup clips. There weren't any. And there were a lot of soldiers, moving in slowly, but inexorable as the tide.

"John," Cody said. "Can you burn?"

"Of course I can, but—" He wasn't allowed to finish.

"Take the demon." He flashed a look at Allison. "I'll take these guys; you cover me. We've got to get an escape route."

Behind the demon was a side street from which some civilians still appeared, screaming and shouting but afraid to turn back, fleeing instead to the east, away from them. That side street led to Franz-Joseph-Kai, and the Salzach River beyond. At least from there, Cody figured, they'd have space to figure out their next move. He transformed, in a heartbeat, from William F. Cody into a tiger, a form he'd first seen taken by Meaghan Gallagher. Then he sprang, launching himself into the armored, possessed creatures that hunted him. Shots rang out, as Allison fired her weapon. Bullets glanced off armor near him, one lodging in his flesh, stinging for a moment.

He tore into them, their armor no match for strength that could smash their ribs, tear the limbs from their bodies. Claws raked skulls and fangs bit deep. Allison would run out of bullets quickly, and then she'd be defenseless. Cody was not going to let anything happen to her. Swords bit deep into his flesh, and he knew he was lucky they were only steel. The sheer numbers of the soldiers, many with no protection—there were only so many suits of armor—began to overwhelm him, and he turned to mist to escape the press of their flesh.

John Courage lived up to his name, his flesh flowing like liquid, forming itself into the body of a huge hawk. His wings spread wide, and he dove to avoid the scrabbling arms of the many-eyed demon as it rushed toward them. Talons raked the thing's groin and thighs, eyes popped, spurting an acid ejaculate which soaked John's wings, and his scream was that of the bird. He changed fast, fire enveloping the demon, immolating it. Flames licked at the creature's body, and it let out another roar, using its hands to smash at the flames, slapping its burning, charring flesh in a feeble attempt to douse the flames. Eyes burst all over its form, the sound like popcorn popping, and the thing threw itself to the street, rolling around to kill the fire.

Allison watched as Cody fought the possessed ones off, then turned to mist as they overwhelmed him. One of the few armored attackers still intact rushed toward her, sword raised. She brought the Beretta up to meet him, trying her best to stay calm, her breathing steady. She fired, and the bullet struck the ghost-man in the shoulder, just under the armor plate. The soldier's arm spasmed, dropping the sword as he held the arm close to his body. Allison squeezed the trigger again, and nothing happened.

The gun was empty, useless. She dropped it.

With no time for hesitation, Allison ran toward the once human thing, rather than away. She had been trained to fight, to protect herself, in the years since the Venice Jihad. Now she used those newly honed skills. Four steps brought her left foot down on the sword before the possessed one could use his right hand to raise it. She grabbed his helmet as her knee came up and smashed, crunching bones, into his face. The spirit within this man obviously felt his pain, for it shrieked a hellish noise, then fell to its side on the street.

Allison picked up the sword. She kicked away an arm raised to protect the fallen man, and lifted the blade above her head. As it whickered through the air toward the man's bare neck, she saw in his upturned face, in his dark eyes, a trace of the humanity that had once resided there. Then the sword fell. It was not a clean cut, but it would do, for the neck had broken.

She knew it was an act of mercy.

Allison turned to face the mob again, but Cody had destroyed most of them. She could see the spirits leaving the corpses piled around him, and out of the corner of her eye for she did not want to look close, the ghostly form rising from the body of the man she had killed. She knew the soldiers themselves had not been evil, but what was left of them was easily manipulated by Mulkerrin's sorcery. The floating forms were gone from the street in an instant, and the way was nearly clear.

Behind her, in his own form, John Courage struggled with the charred and smoldering demon, who had only a handful of eyes left on his body. Courage was sinking his hand into the demon's flesh and tearing, searching for something vital. Allison turned to watch just in time to see him raise his hand to strike, but when the blow fell, it was not his hand at all. John Courage's entire arm had changed, but not in shape. It had changed its substance.

John's arm was made of stone.

Blows rained down on the demon, until it was almost whimpering in its defiance. It struggled and clawed at Courage, but could not shake him off. It had proven unusually resistant to fire, and now Courage raised his stone arm, and it changed again, to fresh wood, its bark slightly green. The wooden fist was lengthening, sharpening, until it resembled nothing so much as a newly carved stake.

"Cody," Courage heard Allison call behind him. He knew that he had their unwanted attention, but it could not be helped. He thrust his arm into the creature's belly, the sharp wood passing nearly through the thing, then wrenched around inside before pulling out and thrusting again. On the third thrust, he found something, his hand piercing it. The wood had the desired reaction, as the beast screamed.

The creature shuddered and expelled a fetid breath, and John

Courage looked up. From inside the hotel came another demon, this one snake-like of a kind he had seen only once before. It slithered in a lumbering fashion. It had no eyes but a sense of smell that led it slowly toward Allison, the human. Far down the street, other things moved and people ran in the streets. In the darkened corners, even smaller things scuttled, the size of human children. They were the scavengers, dark jackals, waiting for their larger counterparts to do the serious damage first. But in packs, they were just as dangerous.

It was getting worse; they had to get out. Courage turned toward Allison and Cody, and saw Cody finishing off the last of the soldiers as Allison stared at him. Cody, apparently, had not heard her shout, had not seen Courage's latest transformations. All the better for now.

John Courage walked toward her, and Allison turned to shout to Cody that it was time to go, while the getting was good. Then she saw them: more soldiers, former human beings who had been overcome by Mulkerrin's ghostly slaves, pushed from their bodies to make way for new tenants. Allison realized what had happened. For every human host Cody killed, the spirits simply found a new one.

They were fighting a losing battle, no matter what.

"Will, come on. We've got to get out of here." He ignored her, finishing off what he thought was the last of them. "Look behind you!"

Cody did, and they rushed him from all sides, all corners, and toward Allison as well. Courage was next to her, knocking several of her attackers away, one with enough force to snap its neck. She saw Cody buried beneath a mound of the creatures, who had jumped him all at once bringing him down. Then fire blossomed at the bottom of the pile, kindling under dry logs, and the whole group was in flames, their clothing burning out of control and their skin beginning to give off a greasy smell and a crackling noise.

"Allison, pay attention!" Courage said, then yanked her aside.

She looked up to see that the ghost had fled the body of the man whose neck he had broken, and was moving toward her. It would not approach Courage directly, and his arm burst into flame as he tried to wave it off.

"Why does it want me?" she asked.

"It doesn't care, it needs a host to stay alive, to stay here, in our world. You'll do as well as any human."

Finally, the thing apparently decided there would be easier targets, and fled the scene, even as Courage was lifting another of the soldiers and tossing him away.

In our world. Allison heard the words again. Not *on*, *in*. Not even on Earth, but *in our world*.

"What do you mean by . . . ?" she started, but there wasn't time.

"We've got to get you out of here, or you'll be one of them," he said, and then he was dragging her away, north toward the side street the demon had blocked.

She turned to see the huge snake-like thing, at least thirty feet long and three feet thick, sliding to block their way, and screamed.

"Will!"

She realized he was in trouble too. She looked at Courage out of the corner of her eye.

"What about Will?" she demanded.

"He'll have to fend for himself! He should be fine, but we've got to get you out of here! Once we're gone, he won't have to fight, he can run."

"I'm not going anywhere without him," Allison said, trying to stand her ground.

"I'm sorry, but you are," Courage answered, then threw her over his shoulder and shot into the side street just in time to escape the serpent, which even now coiled back to slither toward the overwhelmed Will Cody.

Will was fighting hard, but he was getting very tired. Changing from flame to mist to a tiger to himself and then back to flame again, the battle a constant, combined with the serpent he saw sliding toward him now, had begun to take a toll on his body, and his psyche. He was glad that Allison and Courage had gone. He knew of the danger to her, and he stood a better chance of getting out if he didn't have to worry about her. All he had to do now was change to something with wings, or to mist, and fly out of there.

A sword entered through his back and out his stomach, and he vomited blood, hunching over. He turned fast, his movement pulling the sword from its owner's grasp, then reached around behind him to pull the blade from his body.

"That . . . fucking . . . *hurt!*" he said, swinging the blade down into the shoulder of his attacker, a woman. The sword sank deep into the body, cracking through the collarbone and splintering ribs. He turned to face the rest, his wounds healing, but not as quickly as they should. Human hands driven by ghostly minds grabbed him from all around, and he felt a burning, searing pain that made him scream.

He clamped his mouth shut, willing the scream, the pain, away, even as he felt his arms yanked to his sides by the mob that surrounded him. He wanted to strike out, to burn them, to fly away, but he could not gather his thoughts, his concentration, enough for the change. The pain overwhelmed him, covering his entire body now, and despite his greatest efforts, he did scream again.

"Yeeaaarggghhhh!"

Then the hands were gone, the mob was gone, though the pain remained. His mind aflame, he fell to the pavement with a clank. Opening his eyes, he saw the chains. Silver chains, wrapped around his entire body. And then he heard the voice.

"*Well.*" The voice floated on the breeze. "*If it isn't our old friend, Buffalo Bill.*"

Cody recognized the voice.

It belonged to Liam Mulkerrin.

Boston, Massachusetts, United States of America.
Tuesday, June 6, 2000, 1:31 P.M.:

Meaghan was pretty ambivalent about being the boss. Here she was, one of the youngest shadows on Earth, certainly with less experience in their culture than the creatures she surrounded herself with. She didn't really rate, at a surface glance, the kind of attention she received. She was nervous and frightened sometimes, when Alex was sleeping and couldn't comfort her. She was insecure because not long ago she'd been human, a young woman with a so-so job and no steady relationship, who had no family and whose only real friend had been murdered. Not much of a résumé.

But other times, she knew all the reasons why she was the leader, and agreed with them. Other times she was confident in her strength and ability, and the rightness of her position. She had been strong enough as a human to walk among the walking dead, to befriend them, to take Peter Octavian as her lover. She had chosen to become one of them, to help them fight a centuries-old battle to the death. She had helped ease the pain of the reconciliation between Peter and his blood-brothers and -sisters. She had shown them the way out of their self-imposed limits, shown them that their shape-shifting abilities could be used for far more than even Peter had imagined, that they didn't have to limit themselves to bats, wolves and mist, forms imposed by Rome's brainwashing.

She was young, but she was strong. And good. And for those among them that had a difficult time remembering what it was like to believe in one's own, innate goodness, she was an example to be emulated. Her innocence was a beacon to them. To others, for the moment in the minority, that beacon became a target, and Meaghan knew she would be defending herself very soon. She also knew that chief among her detractors was Hannibal, and that keeping him in line would require more effort than she had believed.

That threat, she knew, would have to be eliminated. And if that required that Hannibal be eliminated, so be it.

Though voices screamed in the back of her mind at such a thought, Meaghan Gallagher resisted their input, their logic, which wondered if what she was doing were so much different from the culling of the herd practiced by the Church for centuries. She insisted to herself that it was different, that she was doing it, not for her own good, or any evil purpose, but for the good of her own kind, for humanity, and for the world, which could not stand a war between humans and shadows. The smoldering remains of Venice, the hundreds of bodies, proved that.

But still, Meaghan was a woman full of doubts and insecurities, and so she was glad to have the distraction of a common enemy. Though Mulkerrin's return frightened her almost more than anything else, it also gave her one problem upon which to concentrate her thoughts, and a time in which she did not have to concern herself with long-term questions. Only immediate solutions mattered. She was also glad to be returning home to Alexandra Nueva, whom she loved more than life, more than what little was left of her humanity, more than the goodness in that elusive thing she persisted in thinking of as her soul.

And Alexandra's kiss, her touch, her voice, served to soothe Meaghan's doubts, to quiet the storm in her soul. Alex gave her the first part of an answer to their forever question: the nature of their kind. Meaghan knew they had the capacity for atrocity, horror and great evil, but Alexandra, who had lived such terrible acts, been a hunter of humans and reveled in it, was now a constant reminder that the shadows also had the capacity for love, for kindness, for great good. Like humanity's, the shadow soul contained an extraordinary duality of spirit, but magnified a thousandfold.

But the question remained.

Meaghan shook such thoughts from her head as she rushed along the sidewalk toward her Back Bay home. Alex would be waiting, she knew, packed and ready to scramble off to Otis Air Force Base. They'd be in Germany in less than seven hours. By then it would be nearly 3 A.M. in Salzburg, and hell would be in full swing.

She rounded the corner by their brownstone, and there was Alexandra, sitting on the steps with their bags packed, like a child with whom no one will play. The image didn't last long, though, as she looked up at Meaghan and smiled that beautiful smile of hers. Whatever they faced, they would do it together. Always.

"Hello, sweetie," Meaghan called to her as she approached.

Alex stood up and handed Meaghan her bag, then gave her a firm kiss, nuzzling for a moment. When she pulled back, she sighed, knowing there was work to be done.

"Time to go, sugar," Alex said, and shouldered the strap of her own bag.

They locked hands, and Alexandra raised her free one to call over the inconspicuous government sedan that waited at the corner to rush them to Otis. The car was there in a moment, and the clean-cut, quiet type who stepped out of it was wearing sunglasses and did not smile. These two factors had always seemed to Meaghan a prerequisite for working in government security. CIA, FBI, OSP, NSA—the letters didn't matter. They all looked the same, as if they were all grown in the same laboratory somewhere.

Brrr. A chilling thought.

Their bags were in the trunk, and Alex had already climbed in. Meaghan had one foot in the door when a hand landed on her shoulder, strong enough to stop her.

"Wait," a cold, familiar voice said.

In the space between heartbeats, Meaghan turned, pulling the hand from her shoulder and toward her, prepared to strike its owner with a ferocity born when she died. Then she saw the face of the being who had accosted her, and could not have been more surprised. She knew she'd recognized that voice.

"Where the fuck have you been?" Alexandra spat the words as she got out of the car behind Meaghan, just as their driver finally freed his sidearm from its holster. For a distracted moment, Meaghan pitied humans their loss of superiority. They would never again be the strongest or the fastest, the best at anything. But the thought was passing. There were far more important issues at hand.

"Yes," Meaghan said with barely suppressed anger and frustration. "Where exactly *have* you been, Lazarus?"

The smile of greeting had left the ancient shadow's lined face as soon as Alex spoke. Only grim resolution remained.

"I would like to say I expected a more, shall we say, cordial reunion. But I did not, and so, shall not. Why don't we go inside?"

Meaghan and Alex looked at each other, both still quite angry. Meaghan spoke only because Alexandra had even less control of her temper.

"You may not realize this, but we have far more important things to worry about right now than you. If you'd wanted to talk to us, you should have shown up when we still wanted to talk to you."

With that, she turned and began to usher Alex back into the sedan. The driver still stood at attention, wary and stupidly unafraid, his ego denying his own uselessness.

But Lazarus was not through.

"Cody is Mulkerrin's prisoner," he said.

And now they were prepared to listen.

Meaghan and Alexandra had first met the vampire known only as Lazarus the night before the Venice Jihad. He had fought at their sides, in the sunlight. Octavian had just revealed Rome's treachery to them, revealed that they could exist in the sun without fear of death. But it was new to them, and painful, and many were afraid even to try. Lazarus, on the other hand, did not seem at all pained by daytime battle, or surprised by their newly expanded shapeshifting abilities. In fact, they were forced to surmise that he'd been aware of them from the start. Lazarus had participated in the battle only until the tide had turned irrevocably in their favor, and then he had departed.

Peter Octavian had known Lazarus was different, had suspected something of the truth, and Lazarus had hinted that he was on the right track. But then Peter was gone. Meaghan and Alexandra had made the same connections, but later, as Will Cody searched the world for Lazarus and found nothing.

Centuries upon centuries earlier, when the church realized it would be impossible to destroy all of the so-called Defiant Ones, the shadows who refused to bow to Roman Catholic rule, sorcerous clergymen trapped as many as they could. Using dark and hurtful magic, those sorcerers tampered with the minds of the vampires they captured, ingraining within them certain . . . weaknesses. These shadow creatures had complete control over their own molecules. With the church's influence, they now believed that they could not enter holy ground, could not bear the touch of silver or blessed water, could not change their shape into any but supposedly "unclean" animals or mist, and most importantly, could not bear the touch of the light of day. Of these all, only silver's poison had a grain of truth.

Lies all, but so effectively woven into the minds of these Defiant

Ones that they infected those others with whom they came in contact after their release, as well as each successive generation. Lies that would cause the vampires own minds, own powers, to destroy them.

Psychosomatic suicide.

The Church believed that these controls would enable them to control the shadows from afar. And for a time, it had worked. And then came Peter Octavian. He had overcome the pain of sunlight, though other such triumphs eluded him. Peter had abandoned the life of hunter, and instead spent his time in the service of humans, investigating their losses and broken hearts and crimes. It was a subject of great fascination for him. Eventually, this vocation led him in pursuit of a book, a book stolen from the bowels of the Vatican: *The Gospel of Shadows*. It detailed all of the atrocities perpetrated by the Church on their kind, as well as the many magical spells used to control other creatures of darkness, from beyond what they referred to as "the veil."

In the end, Peter had carried the church sorcerer, Liam Mulkerrin, to the other side of that veil, leaving The Gospel of Shadows behind in his people's safekeeping. Meaghan and Alexandra had kept it from the world's governments, even from the United Nations, and fear prevented any of those powers from attempting to take it.

And what of Lazarus?

Within the pages of *The Gospel of Shadows*, a tainted pope spoke of five Defiant Ones who had been captured but whose minds were impossible to tamper with. They were to be executed, but then in a terrible battle they escaped.

"You're one of the five," Meaghan said now, as they settled onto the sofa in the living room of the brownstone she shared with Alexandra. Alex took a chair.

"Pardon me?" Lazarus said, eyebrow arched.

"You are one of the five who were never brainwashed," she elaborated, knowing it was unnecessary. "Peter figured it out before he . . . died, and Alex and I did, not much later than that."

The room was silent, and the smile returned to Lazarus's lips. He looked at Meaghan, then to Alexandra, who stared at him in return with open hostility.

"Proceed," he said.

"Cody searched the world for you," Alex finally said. "We know you are one of the five. What we want to know is, who are the others? Where are they? Where were you in hiding? And how do you know about Mulkerrin's return?"

Alex paused, her tough exterior momentarily revealing the concern beneath. "And what makes you say Cody has been captured?" she asked.

Lazarus smiled now, wide and friendly, almost like an excited child.

"Well done!" he said, and for a half second, Meaghan thought he would applaud.

"Actually, there were four of us, not five. Mary was killed during the escape. Martha is in Salzburg now, preparing to help however she can. Who is the other? Good question. I tend to think of him as 'the Stranger,' and for now, that should be good enough for you. We were in Greece when Cody came looking, and we knew where he was all along. He could not have found me because I didn't want to be found. You three were doing quite all right on your own. As to how I know about Mulkerrin's return and Cody's capture, I cannot, or rather I will not, say. Know only that I wish to remedy both situations as expediently as do both of you. Which is why I am here, after all."

Lazarus could see the questions ready to erupt from the lovers, and so he continued.

"Cody is, as far as we know, all right. I expect he is captive in the Hohensalzburg fortress at the south end of the city."

"Well, what the hell are we waiting for?" Meaghan finally asked. All other questions could be put aside, but Mulkerrin must be destroyed and, if possible, Cody freed.

Lazarus stood, ran his hand through his shoulder-length brown hair and stepped away from the sofa. Meaghan watched him. His prominent nose gave his face an aquiline aspect, and the wrinkles of his olive-complexioned face and his brown eyes were quite expressive. She realized that he didn't look exactly the same as he had during their previous meeting. He was different in subtle ways: the shape of his nose, the point of his chin, even the color of his hair.

Was this by choice, or did great age such as Lazarus had endured wear away the memory of oneself? Did such ancient shadows become just that, shadows of their former selves? How different, then, did he look from his true countenance? How long must one live to forget his or her appearance? Disturbing questions all. She had asked what they had waited for, and yet she was aware that time, for Lazarus, would be different than it was even for them.

And yet, Alexandra was not quite so understanding.

"While we suffer your silence," she snarled at Lazarus, "my blood-brother awaits his death. Speak your mind, Lazarus, or we go, now."

Alexandra looked at Meaghan then, and although it was clear who was the leader among them, Meaghan knew that this time, her lover would accept no argument, no instruction, no suggestion. Once, Alexandra had wanted her blood-brother, Will Cody, dead. Now he and Rolf Sechs were her only family, and she would not lose them.

Lazarus walked toward the restored masonry fireplace, and rested a hand on the mantel as he examined the room. Art surrounded him: what appeared to be a genuine Monet next to a framed, toilet-paper sketch by Andy Warhol. And yet it was here, by his right hand, where lay the one piece of art that mattered. Lazarus knew that the two women, each once a lover to Peter Octavian, had taken it and perhaps these others, from his abandoned apartment after the Jihad. The sculpture was a perfect likeness, a bust of Octavian himself, ponytail and lopsided smile intact.

"This," Lazarus said sternly as he lifted the sculpture and turned it to them. "This is our weapon. Mulkerrin has returned from Hell, where Peter Octavian took him, far more powerful than before. He has achieved such a feat without even the so-called *Gospel of Shadows* to guide him. It makes one wonder, does it not? For if Mulkerrin has gathered such power to him, what might Octavian have accomplished beyond the veil? What powers has Hell given to him?"

Silence.

5

Salzburg, Austria, European Union.
Tuesday, June 6, 2000, 3:24 P.M.:

Allison Vigeant was being pulled, dragged really, across Makartsteg, a narrow bridge spanning the Salzach River. John Courage was trying not to be rough, but he would hear no argument. Not that he could have heard her over the screaming. Allison imagined that they must look like a swarm of insects from above, so many people clogged the bridge and the streets around it. Several times she had almost been separated from John, but he roughly shoved people out of the way if he had to.

Allison took an elbow in the chest then, and bent over to catch her breath while the rush of people flowed around and past her, as if she were a rock in the rapids. Then Courage was pulling insistently on her arm, and she was moving again, one hand clutched to her breasts. They reached the north side of the river, and headed east along its bank, but then she stopped again, even as the tide of panicked humanity started to thin out.

"Damn it, John," she said, her anger turning into a panic for her lover, "we can't just leave him back there!"

He wanted to ignore her, but could not.

"Look!" he said, sweeping his arm wide, forcing her to take in the hell that had sprung up around them. Back across the bridge, demons of all sizes roamed free, though she didn't see Mulkerrin's possessed soldiers anywhere. A splash made her look downriver, and Allison saw something impossibly huge, incredibly black, sliding up toward them. For the first time she noticed that the bridge they had crossed was the only one standing, that the other three in this part of town had been torn apart by the earthquake and that this thing was thrashing at their pilings, bringing even their remains down into the water. The bridge was still packed with people, and whatever was in the water would soon bring them all tumbling down.

"We've got to help them," Allison said quietly, but she knew the reality of their situation. The police and army were already coming in, starting to evacuate people. A small force of soldiers ran by them even now and stood at the river's edge, shooting at the black thing which splashed water up at them. No, Allison knew that she and Courage, and Will, of course, would have to find other ways to help. Mulkerrin had to be destroyed if any of these people were to survive.

Courage had a grip on her arm which never faltered, and he'd been pulling, hurrying her along. But now it was Allison who picked up the pace. They had not run into a single demon on the north side yet, among the frantic crowds, but she knew that was nothing more than luck.

"Where are we going?" she finally thought to ask.

"It's close," he said, "and I think we'll be safe there for a while."

Allison kept her mouth shut after that, concentrating on getting wherever this safe place was. They were rushing toward the plaza where Elisabethkai, the street they were on, met Linzer Gasse and several other narrow roads. The city which had seemed so vibrant to her before, smelling of chocolate and filled with the music of Mozart, was now a maze of danger. Blue skies which had reflected off cobblestones and golden domes had become black clouds hovering above shattered homes, churches and fountains. The stench of sulphur filled Allison's nostrils.

They heard screams ahead, and a woman ran into the plaza, floral dress torn down the back, blood smeared and running down her calves. Dozens of other maddened civilians scattered as she shrieked like a lunatic, stumbling into their midst. She tripped, nearly tumbling over crumbled masonry, and then stopped short at a huge fissure that separated her from the river side of the plaza. The woman was young and attractive, and terrified, her blond hair sweeping back as she spun to face her pursuers. Three small but ravenous-looking demons rushed toward her on all fours, the dark jackals stopping just short of her and snapping at her feet like wild dogs. More were behind them, and the scene became a near riot as people pushed one another aside in their attempts to get away.

Courage seemed about to move, to help, but it was too late. Even the jackals weren't fast enough, as an enormous head with skin like steel poked out of the crack in the ground, and a great length of tongue lashed out, wrapped around the woman and dragged her into the creature's gaping maw. Many of the city's people would survive this nightmare, but those with them in the square were doomed. Allison had never felt so helpless.

"Damned beast!" Courage said, sincerely, obviously stunned.

Then the jackals turned toward them, and there was no time for conversation. Even though the things could not leap across the ravine in the middle of the street, their shrieking bark caught the attention of the demon inside the fissure, and the thing was rising a bit farther from the hole, its eyes on Allison and John.

After Venice, Allison Vigeant thought she had seen it all, but today she was learning how arrogant that assumption had been. The creature began to slide out of its hole, dragging itself by three-clawed hands, a dragon seemingly made of metal. Allison had to tear her eyes away to look at John Courage, and her mouth hung open. Not long before, she had seen him use his vampiric shapeshifting abilities in ways Cody had never suggested, taking forms she had never imagined them able to assume. Now he was doing it again. John grimaced in pain as huge wings sprang from his back.

"Let's go," he said, then grabbed her around the waist with both his arms—and they were flying. The dragon gave a terrible hiss and shot its tongue after them, but they were already out of range.

It was a moment before Allison realized that rather than flying away, they were simply going up. Up and up and up. Hundreds of feet in the air they flew, compounding her terror, and she hugged John tight and closed her eyes. When she opened them, she was staring straight at the fortress, the spring from which Liam Mulkerrin's evil now over-ran the city. And she thought of Will.

"Oh, God. Will." And finally the tears came.

"He's alive," Courage said, and she looked up at him, not under-standing.

"How can you . . ."

"Trust me."

"Where are we going?"

"Actually, we're here," he said, and she looked away from the fortress and at the top of a cliff, so close at hand. In a moment, their feet touched ground and they were standing by a small, apparently ancient structure which looked as if a castle turret had sprouted from the hillside. Above them, forest stretched away as far as Allison could see, and below, the trees dropped off to nothing except the street far below and the river beyond.

"Let's go," John said, and started off a few paces before he realized Allison wasn't following.

"You bastard," she said, terrible knowledge dawning on her. Courage only tilted his head and raised an eyebrow in question.

"You asshole!" Allison said now, with more conviction. "You could have done that Icarus angel imitation back in front of my hotel, and Will Cody would be here, safe with us. What the hell's the matter with you, John? Why did you let that happen?"

Courage bit his lip, and for all the toughness of his appearance, the military-style hair, the square jaw, he looked vulnerable at that moment. His whole manner, his voice, his eyes were penitent.

"I don't have a good excuse," he said sadly. "You're right, I could have flown with you and we all could have escaped. But I wasn't thinking about escape then, Allison. It happened so fast, all I was thinking about was battle. Retreat is foreign to me. I'm not used to having humans around, not used to being . . ."

"Vulnerable," she finished for him, and it was not a question. John nodded.

"I'm sorry," he said, meeting her gaze finally.

"We're not done yet," she told him. "I was in Venice, my lover is a vampire, but I've never seen a vampire do some of the things I've seen you do today. And I have no idea how you could know whether Will is alive or dead. What's going on?"

The sadness disappeared from John Courage's face, replaced by a barrier of determination, a fierce secrecy.

"I've had a lot of practice," he said, but there was no sarcasm in his voice. "I've been around awhile. All shadows have the same abilities, but they must learn to utilize them. In fact, the vampires you know are much more powerful than even they are aware."

"So how old are you, and who are you really?" she asked.

"That," John said and let out a breath, "that you'll know soon enough. It's why I was in Salzburg in the first place, why I found you and Cody. But the answers to those questions must be found to be believed. If I simply told you, you'd never buy it."

Allison nodded, satisfied that, for the moment at least, that's all she was getting from him. They walked at a good clip, ducking low branches along their rough path. She scanned around them, expecting at any moment to see giant demonic things lumbering toward them through the trees, or those small, vicious jackals snapping toward them up the path. Nothing happened except that they continued to move uphill, and Allison began to believe that she could feel a difference up here. As if, for the moment, they had escaped.

"You knew there wouldn't be any demons up here," she said.

"Call it a hunch."

They slowed and Allison looked up the path. Ominous walls stood to the right, towering twenty-five or so feet above the path. As far as she could tell, there were no windows.

"What is it?" she asked.

"You didn't come up here with Will?" John smiled at her finally. "Shame on you. Bad tourists! It's a monastery. Capuchin monks, in cloister, as far as the locals know."

They drew up toward huge double doors of wood and iron, and as John went forward to ring a bell hung next to them, Allison watched him closely, frowning, thinking. He backed off to wait, and looked toward her again.

"Before you ask, it was a monastery once. The older brothers died over time, and the younger ones we shipped to other locations."

"We?"

"A couple of my friends and I. We own this place, now. Of course, not on paper."

A bolt slid noisily back on the other side of the doors, the left swung open slowly, and a short, portly but not unattractive woman stood there with a cross look on her face, like an angry mother.

"Next time, take your time, why don't you?" she said, then turned to Allison with a friendly smile, the crankiness gone from her face. "And you are?"

"Allison Vigeant," John said, "Martha. Martha, Allison."

They stepped into a great courtyard, around which the stone building stood, almost a fortress in itself In the center, an enormous fountain lay dormant. Two slender young men appeared in a doorway on their right, came quickly forward and bowed their heads to John Courage. They were twins, and quite handsome as far as Allison was concerned, but how many vampires weren't? Of course, Martha was a vampire as well, though certainly the least attractive Allison had seen. She had long since realized that with the control they could wield over their forms, the shadows honed their appearance, both consciously and unconsciously, throughout their existence. She wondered why Martha did not practice that particular art.

"Allison, these are the sons of Lazarus: Jared and Isaac," Martha said, and each man bowed as his name was said.

Lazarus! Her mind raced.

"You're full of surprises," she said, turning on Courage. He smiled at her, obviously enjoying the mystery.

"Come on, now. You're a reporter. You'll figure it out." Martha bolted the door behind them, then joined John and Allison as they went inside the monastery. Behind them, Isaac and Jared took up positions on either side of the great door. Once inside, they sat at a long wooden table in a completely bare room, and Allison wondered whether Courage had removed anything, or simply not added anything after the monks had gone. She shook her head and brought herself back to the business at hand.

"Why aren't there any demons up here?" she asked.

"Thin air?" Courage chuckled.

"Would you stop fucking around! The man I love may be dead, an incredibly powerful lunatic has apparently come back to life, demons are wrecking the city below us and ghosts are taking over the bodies of tourists. People are dying down there, John. Now what are you going to do about it?"

Courage wasn't smiling anymore.

"I'm sorry," he said. "You're right."

"He was trying to make you feel better by distracting you," Martha said, earning an angry glance from John.

"Distracted is the last thing I need to be," she hissed. "Now, can we please get on with it? What's going on?"

Courage sat up straight.

"There aren't any demons up here because we're protected," he said.

"By what?"

"Magic."

"Whose?"

Courage looked away.

"Mine," he said, and Allison forgot to be angry.

"Cody is fine," he continued. "I would know if he wasn't. We can only assume he is Mulkerrin's prisoner or he would have tracked us here by now. Here's what's going on. The UN and SJS have sent troops to Munich. They're amassing there now, and will begin to move on Salzburg tonight so that they can enter the city in the morning."

"Alex and Meaghan with them?" Allison asked, hopeful.

"No. They're otherwise occupied."

"How in hell do you know all this?"

"That's not important."

"So what do we do until they get here, just hang out while people are dying down below?" Allison shivered at the thought.

"Well, that depends on you," Courage said, smiling again.

He liked to smile, Allison thought, and realized that Cody shared that trait. It wasn't something she'd ever considered before.

"How's that?"

"We need reinforcements. With the power Mulkerrin has now—and I'm embarrassed to say I don't know his new limits—the humans won't be able to do a thing. The SJS doesn't have any shadows old enough to have the power, the ability, to destroy Mulkerrin. And that's if they can keep from killing each other, with the crazy politics involved. Ten miles south of here, there's a mountain called Untersberg. Inside that mountain are our reinforcements, old shadows. With them we'd have a chance. What we need to do is wake them up and bring them back."

"And how do we do that?"

"That's the catch," John said. "We need some blood from a willing, living human female."

"How much is 'some'?" Allison asked quietly.

"You'll live."

I don't want to die.

"How important is this?"

"Victory depends on it."

"Well, then, I think you know my answer," Allison nodded her head. "Just one thing. You won't tell me who you are or how you know all these things, but it's obvious to me that you know a lot of things without being told them. I think you knew Mulkerrin was coming back, or at least suspected. You know Cody's okay, right now.

"What I want to know is, will he get out of this alive?"

Courage looked sad for the first time, and suddenly Allison was terrified to hear his answer. She had to fight to avoid running from the room, hands over her ears.

"I wish I knew," John said, and though it was better than the answer she had expected, for some reason Allison was not relieved.

Boston, Massachusetts, United States of America.
Tuesday, June 6, 2000, 1:45 P.M.:

In their bedroom, Meaghan Gallagher and Alex Nueva held each other tight. Their embrace lasted minutes, as they inhaled the familiar smells of their life together: fresh cut flowers and light perfumes, Italian cooking and fresh-baked brownies. When their eyes opened, they pressed their foreheads together, eyes meeting, and smiled nervous smiles to hide their anxiety. They had changed into jeans and sneakers, Meaghan with a cotton dress shirt, and Alex with the Batman tank top Meg had given her the previous Christmas. They loved their place, their life together, and they didn't know if they would ever return.

In the next room, Lazarus began to weave the spell they would need to travel. Finally, Alexandra let her lover go and then held her at arm's length, searching her eyes.

"I hate this, Meaghan," she said quietly, almost whispering. "I hate being afraid. I thought fear was something I'd overcome. I've been afraid for others, in Venice, and now for Cody in Salzburg, but I forgot what it's like to fear for myself. I wasn't afraid to go to Salzburg, no matter what Mulkerrin has become, but this . . ."

She waved her hand toward the closed door, beyond which they could hear the voice of Lazarus rise and fall in an eerie cadence. The lights in the room began to dim, flickered for a moment, and then came back on full force, one of the bulbs exploding beneath its shade. Alex jumped.

"Alex, honey, listen," Meaghan said, holding her lover's hand tight. "You all fell for the myth of the vampire. We shadows are not creatures of myth, we're flesh and blood. Even if we're not really human anymore, we still have that humanity in us. Even if we're that much stronger, it's impossible to deny our fundamental nature. No matter how much we need the blood, at our core most of us know that it's wrong to kill humans. We do what we must to live, but we can't deny the humanity that's still part of us. At our core, we can still feel fear, and sorrow. And love. Sweetheart, these things are not our weakness, they are our strength, our tether to all the things we hope for the future."

Alex nodded; she knew Meaghan was right. That knowledge had been hard won, but now, in her heart, she did know.

From the other room, Lazarus called for them. It was time. They embraced again, their lips joining in a desperate kiss.

"Meg," Alex broke off, breathless, "what do you think we'll find?"

Meaghan was thoughtful a moment, then kissed Alex on the forehead and grabbed her leather jacket from the bed.

"I'm afraid to think about it," she said, taking Alex by the elbow and opening their bedroom door.

Meaghan and Alex had known Matt and Ellen Tillinger for three years. They were a fortysomething couple who lived in a brownstone diagonally across the street, and they were the only close, human friends the shadow women had made who were not already involved in vampire politics. They weren't blood cultists, they didn't worship vampires, they weren't mindless volunteers. They were friends.

The four neighbors exchanged nervous hugs and kisses, as Lazarus chanted silently above the open *Gospel of Shadows*. Alex hadn't told Matt what was going on over the phone, but the Tillingers had a good idea why they were there.

"What's going on?" Ellen asked, concern creasing her brow.

"We don't have time to beat around the bush, you guys," Meaghan said, her hands clasped together. "So you'll forgive us if we just sort of dump this on you. We're going away for a while; I don't know how long but probably not more than a few days. We don't know if we'll be able to get any sustenance where we're going . . ." She let her words trail off.

"You need blood?" Matt asked, and as Meaghan nodded, he shook his head nervously. "Look, we're friends, you know. I mean, we love you guys and we'll do anything you need us to do, but you don't want my blood."

Matt had HIV.

"It's okay, Matt," Alex said, soothing. "In fact, we had a doctor friend of ours confirm this last week, and we've been meaning to tell you. We can't be infected. Shadows can't get, carry or pass on HIV. We've always said it, but we've finally confirmed it, and since that's been the number one fear among potential donors, we've got to get a press release out about it as soon as we get back."

"I wish I had your blood," he quipped, and then fell silent.

"If that's so," Ellen said, "then of course we'll help. I know you wouldn't ask if you didn't have to. What should we do?"

"Just give me a hug," Meaghan said to her, and Ellen did.

Matt went to Alex in much the same way, then snickered and told them he felt awkward, "like we're playing strip poker or something." They all smiled, understanding. It was an intimacy friends rarely shared, and far more profound than simply seeing one another naked.

"Thanks for trusting us," Meaghan said when it was over, then looked at Matt. "You know about the Revenant Transformation. When we get back, Alex and I will tell you all about what it means to be one of us. I know you were being a wiseguy, but if you do want our blood, it's yours. Your life would never be the same, but you'd be alive.

"Think about it," she said, and then she and Alex walked them back to the door, kissed them good-bye, and shut it.

Lazarus looked up from the book, and Meaghan thought that, for a moment, even he looked afraid.

"They don't know you," Meaghan said. "I didn't feel I could ask . . ."

"Not to worry," he assured her. "I satisfied my, hm, cravings before I arrived. And now . . ." He slammed the book shut and stood up.

"The bus is leaving," Lazarus announced. "Shall we?"

As he stretched out his arm, bowing as if to say *After you*, that arm disappeared completely. Meaghan was startled, but Alexandra understood immediately. It was just what she'd expected. The closer they got to Lazarus, the more they could see of the portal, nearly invisible when looked at from the side. Its reflective surface made Meaghan shiver as she thought about Peter, and Lazarus seemed to read her mind.

"If I've read this right," he said, holding up *The Gospel of Shadows*, "this passage should be much less painful for us than it was for Peter and the sorcerer."

"Let's hope . . . Did you say 'us'?" Alex raised an eyebrow.

Lazarus nodded.

"The Stranger has said that if we can't find Octavian and bring him back, we have little chance of defeating Mulkerrin. In that light, I think I'll be more use to you than I will be in Salzburg. Not, of course, that I want to do this . . . but then I'm sure a little milk run to Hell wasn't on your agenda either."

Hell. He'd said it, and now Meaghan's own fear rose up to enfold her, whispering in her ear. She'd comforted Alex as well as she could, but that was what lovers were for. She could not let on how nervous she was, especially about finding Peter. Lazarus had told them that time passed much more quickly *there*. Peter had been gone five years, but what did that mean for him? If they could even find him, if he were still alive, what shape might he be in? What state of mind? Mulkerrin had been evil, and his time in Hell had obviously nurtured him, but Peter, shadow or no, had been the essence of good. A hero. Oh, shit, she didn't want to think about it.

"You're bringing the book, right?" Alexandra said, cutting off Meaghan's thoughts.

"Of course," Lazarus said. "How else will we get back?"

"Guard it with your life," Alex said, "or we won't get back."

Finally, the two of them looked at Meaghan. The youngest shadow in the room, and yet they both acknowledged her as the leader of this little expedition. She expected it from Alex; it had been that way since Venice. But Lazarus had seemed haughty, almost omniscient at times. Why would he . . . and then she realized that he must be just as frightened as they were, that he had no real, clear idea of what they might find through that portal, what it would feel like, look like, smell like. No matter what they'd faced before, the concept of Hell was buried so deep within them, the fear of it so pervasive . . .

"Fuck it," Meaghan snapped, slipping into her jacket. "We're outta here."

She stepped through the portal, and the others followed.

Salzburg, Austria, European Union.
Tuesday, June 6, 2000, 4:45 P.M.:

They were flying again, but there was no way that Allison was going to get used to it. Courage had spread his wings and, holding her tight, fallen off the side of the cliff For the count of three they had fallen toward the river, then leveled off, gliding, the wind whipping them in the face, the smell of fires, started by the earthquake, heavy in the damp air. John was trying to save his strength. There was no way he was going to be able to fly all the way to Mount Untersberg with her in his arms, but it would take far too long to try to fight their way out of the city. And so, for the moment at least, they flew.

They stayed, for the most part, above the river, where they had an excellent view of the surrounding area. At first, Allison had felt sick from the flying, and then from the sights below. Parts of the city and the countryside were in flames, and some of the demons were so huge they could be seen much more clearly than the houses and buildings. Twice, she saw things off in the distance, gliding on the air as they were, and her heart pounded in her chest as she imagined them being attacked in mid-flight, Courage forced to drop her or die himself. But mercifully, neither creature even noticed them floating above.

As they moved along the river, the number of shadows—no, scratch that, they don't deserve to be called anything but demons—diminished greatly. What she guessed was a couple of miles from the monastery, they finally made a rough landing beside a bridge marked "Hellbrunner," which was intact. There were cars everywhere, moving away from the city proper, and she was pleased to realize that word had finally gotten out. Action was being taken. Police and military vehicles screamed by, on their way to help evacuate those they could. To the southeast, there were homes and shops, but to the southwest nothing but countryside.

"Still a long way to go," she said, "what do we do now?"

"We do what we must," Courage answered. "We hitch-hike."

"Get out!"

"No kidding," he laughed, and stuck out his thumb.

Allison watched as the cars moved past them. Some of the drivers' faces were panic-stricken, others annoyed. It was easy to tell which of them knew why they were being evacuated and which did not. Allison figured nobody would stop, or if someone did, it would be one of those who had no clue as to what was going on. A few of the passersby actually noticed them, and a couple had enough perception to realize that John was a shadow. Those cars sped up as they moved away.

An old Volkswagen rumbled toward them, and Allison watched the driver's eyes take them in, narrow as if in disgust at their transience, and then open wide upon realizing Courage's nature. The car bumped onto the shoulder and shut off, and the driver stepped out looking angry, but motioning to his passenger to stay in the car.

"You!" the man barked in German, a language Allison understood fairly well but could not speak. "Why do you go away from the city, why do you not help the people there?"

Allison was stunned. The man was either very brave or very stupid. Not that John would hurt him, or at least she didn't think he would, but this man didn't know that. John Courage was a vampire, after all. But he just wrinkled his brows in a question, then tilted his head in further inquiry, and finally laughed his little laugh, that Allison had begun to appreciate. She trusted John. She hoped that was the right choice.

"Why do you not help your own people?" John asked the man. "Why do *you* go away from the city?"

The man's face burned red, with anger or embarrassment, Allison could not tell. He sputtered unintelligibly, then muttered under his breath, but before he could finally think of some response, John cut him off.

"We are heading away from the city to find reinforcements. We need more of my kind if we are to destroy the sorcerer, to save what we can of your city, your nation."

The man looked doubtful.

"And," John continued, "we need a ride."

The man looked completely bewildered, and Allison knew she had to step in.

"We need to reach Mount Untersberg," she said in English, hoping he would get at least part of it. "It's our only hope. Do you know it?"

"Of course I know it," the man said in flawless English his pride hurt by the question.

Allison shouldn't have been surprised. Many people in Austria and Germany who spoke English never let on that they do. She had always figured they thought Americans had it too easy as it was. Now she looked at the man, her face, she hoped, expressing all of the desperation that she felt.

"Fine," the man said. "I'll take you. My brother will be thrilled."

Just then the Volkswagen's passenger hopped out, beaming with pleasure, and rushed over to fall prostrate at John's feet. He started babbling something about honor and sacrifice, calling John his "blood-lord," and Courage finally hauled the man to his feet, his face the only question the car's driver needed.

"He's a cultist," the man said. "He thinks you're a god or something. If you need blood, he's your man. In the meantime, let's get out of here."

Very soon, they were creeping slowly along Alpenstrasse with hundreds of other evacuees. The driver's brother was not only a cultist, but a volunteer, and Allison began to realize how plentiful they'd become. John didn't take the blood the man offered, and Allison hoped that he'd made a wise choice, worried that before long he would need all the strength he could muster. The mountains rose up in the distance, and Allison wondered what might be left of the beautiful city when they returned.

And whether the man she loved would still be alive.

6

In the depths of the fortress, Will Cody began, quite painfully, to come around. He lay on the stone floor, and felt the cold of the hundreds of feet of solid stone that made up the foundation of the ancient structure. His eyelids fluttered halfway open as he glanced about the room, able to see well enough in the near-complete darkness. What surprised him most was that he still lived. Almost as surprising, however, was his pain.

Will had felt all kinds of pain, both in his human life and after. He'd suffered a broken heart, a broken spirit, broken limbs and broken promises. He'd been stabbed, shot, kicked and beaten, and eventually he'd died of old age and exhaustion, and that broken spirit as well. Karl Von Reinman's intervention had given him another life, but that first death had hurt him body and soul.

This pain was like that, only worse. It was despair over what might have happened to Allison, and it was the far-too-slow knitting of the gaping hole in his belly, where his innards had spilled out and were even now being replaced. The regrowth hurt even more than the wound. Still, he used his hands to sit up, and dragged himself backward until he found the support of a wall to lean against. He carefully avoided looking down at his gut, and concentrated on his other pain instead.

Allison.

Where was she? He'd seen Courage slipping down a side street with her, and fought that much harder to buy them time, expecting to follow. But then Mulkerrin had come . . . Still, he had to believe that Allison was okay or he'd go crazy in here. And somehow, it was not hard to have faith in Courage. There seemed more to that shadow than met the eye, and he certainly had mastered his abilities.

Yeah. Allison was okay.

Just keep telling yourself that, Will.

He held a hand across his stomach and was slightly disconcerted at the feeling. Under his palm, he could feel the wounds healing, the flesh growing back. Disembowelment was something he did not plan to experience again. And yet how could he protect himself when he was barely strong enough to move? Certainly he was too weak to make the change into mist, at least for the moment.

That was how vampires could be killed. If you were strong enough, fast enough, to stay alive, to batter away at a shadow over and over, to wound him and make him bleed, eventually, you could kill him, scattering the pieces far enough away that he'd never be able to draw them back together. Of course, if a vampire's mind were still clouded by the tampering of the Roman Church, it was even easier.

Will looked around for an escape, but found none. There were no windows, only a large iron door on the wall opposite him. Once he felt a bit stronger, he might be able to shapeshift, healing himself in the process. Then perhaps he could try the strength of that door. And if that didn't work, he would have to wait a bit longer, until he could make the change to mist. One way or another, he had to get out.

Cody was not used to being a captive. In fact, he had never been anyone's prisoner, unless he counted his business enslavement to that bastard Harry Tammen.

And at the thought of that, the memories flooded back.

Memories of Major North giving him his infamous nickname, of Ned Buntline making him a dime-novel hero, of his parents in Iowa and the death of his brother Sam, of his best boyhood friend, his dog Turk. He remembered herding cattle, scouting for Custer and the all-black tenth cavalry. He spoke the sign language of the Sioux (which he still could do), drank with Bill Hickok and fathered beautiful children. The death of his son Kit, his first standing ovation onstage in New York, scalping Yellow Hand, the murders of Wild Bill and Sitting Bull, the triumph of the Wild West Show, traveling around the world—a star. His affection for Annie Oakley, his love for his wife Lulu, and his mistress Katherine, and his daughter Irma and so many others.

All dead and gone, the way he often thought he should have gone, on to whatever there was past this plane. But he couldn't.

Harry Tammen had used Will's own irresponsibility against him, leveraging the Wild West Show until he owned the whole thing. Will was a prisoner. Even when Will "died," Tammen thought he owned Buffalo Bill, hook, line and corpse. Years later, when Tammen died, Cody was there. The look on Tammen's face made it all worthwhile. But at first, after Cody's supposed death, things only got worse. His wife, Louisa Cody, took Tammen's damned money and agreed to bury her husband, against his final wishes, where it would benefit Tammen's pocketbook. His country, which he had faithfully served, took back his Congressional Medal of Honor because he hadn't been a soldier when he performed the deeds for which he was given the award.

Betrayals abounded. And all those who refused to betray Cody, who truly loved him, died. If not before him, then later, while he was forced to continue the charade of his death, they all died. Since the truth of the shadows had come out, since the world had discovered he was still alive, supposed relatives had been attempting to contact him every day. For five years, he had refused to see them. He loved Allison, he had Meaghan and Alexandra, even Rolf and George Marcopoulos. He had gotten back into show business, made a movie, and gotten the rights to the Wild West Show back. He didn't need these long lost family members.

But now, with his guts lying in a pile in the middle of a cold, stone room, with a man who spelled almost certain death for him lurking somewhere about, with him captive once again and perhaps feeling a little sorry for himself, he realized that he'd made a terrible mistake. He should have embraced them all, poseurs or no. Possessions could be owned. In the modern world, even words could be owned. But emotions had to be freely given. He'd been afraid to really have a life again, to let those emotions free from the prison of his heart, because he could not forget the pain of the string of tragedies in his life as "Buffalo Bill."

How he hated that name. It signified every painful moment of his life. But now he knew that to truly live he had to risk tragedy again. Knowing his loved ones would die, he must still allow himself to care for them.

Perhaps being a prisoner again had, in a way, liberated him.

But enough of that—Will was getting out of there. He had to find Allison; they had to destroy Mulkerrin. He had a life out there, one that was just beginning, and he wouldn't let the evil bastard take that away from him the way Tammen took away the show, his old life.

Never again.

Colonel William F. Cody stood, clutching his stomach but already feeling much better. He coughed harshly, then spat several times, wads of blood and phlegm hitting the floor. He realized how much blood he had lost, and how hungry he was, and he felt badly for the tourists whose bodies had been possessed. They would have to sate his hunger.

But first he would have to get out of this room. He stumbled over to the door, propping himself against the wall with one arm. He pulled . . . and it opened.

But his moment of freedom was fleeting, for as he stumbled to his hands and knees in the next room, he knew he was not alone. All around him the ghost warriors rattled to attention. He could smell the demon-beasts in the room as well, and looked up to see two huge, snarling creatures chained to either side of a seat, hewn from the stone wall and positioned as if it were a throne. Upon it, he sat, looking just as he always had, and dressed all in black.

"Well, I was beginning to wonder if you'd actually died in there. More fool me. My Lord, Colonel, but you're a mess. And to think we're just getting started."

Cody tried to will himself to mist, to float out of this nightmare as if it were a fever dream. He felt the change coming, slowly, slowly.

Too slow.

Mulkerrin had stepped down from his throne, a strange green light playing about his open right palm. The armored creatures grabbed Cody and held him, their fingers digging into his flesh and destroying his concentration. He could not think straight enough to make the change, though his eyes were closed tight.

"Open them," Mulkerrin said.

And he did; he wanted the evil to see he was not afraid.

So he watched while the sorcerer's right hand was enveloped in green flame; he clenched his teeth when the once-priest touched that flame to his chest; he screamed as that hand plunged inside him and grabbed hold of his beating, blood-hungry heart and ripped it from his body; he fell to the ground, eyes open, staring, fading, as Mulkerrin knelt beside him and showed him his own heart, licked it, then opened his mouth and tore into it with his teeth.

Mulkerrin kissed Will Cody's forehead, lips smeared with the vampire's own blood.

"Delicious," he whispered, and then his laughter boomed, echoing through the fortress.

And somewhere, Cody's mind drifted, dreaming.

Of vengeance.

Munich, Germany, European Union.
Wednesday, June 7, 2000, 12:02 A.M.:

It was raining when Roberto Jimenez arrived in Munich, and his mood left him hard-pressed to remember a single sunny day spent in Germany. Castillians were a proud and emotional people, and though it had frequently jeopardized his career, Roberto had long since tired of hiding those emotions. Now, as he marched down the hallway of the air-base offices, his second, Gloria Rodriguez, at his side and his personal guard only two steps behind, he was one cranky son of a bitch.

Never one for ceremony, he opened the conference room door himself and stomped in. Immediately, the commanders of the six nations involved in this op stood in a gesture of respect. Toward the back of the room, a large, silent figure rose as well, yet next to him, sprawled on the room's one comfortable chair, another figure did not.

Roberto would not call him a man, and yet he was in such a mood as to allow himself to be annoyed by the creature's disrespect. He would have dearly loved to dismiss the SJS chief marshal, but even though he wasn't certain the shadows would be needed for this operation, he knew he didn't want them working against him. Not to mention, of course, that he had his orders. So, rather than reward his impudence, Roberto simply ignored Chief Marshal Hannibal completely.

"Commanders," he said, addressing the room, "please be seated."

They sat. Out of the corner of his eye, Roberto saw the SJS deputy marshal give his chief a disdainful glance. *Hmm*, Roberto thought, *dissension among the ranks*. Also interesting that the deputy marshal was the only subordinate, besides his own second, Rodriguez, attending the meeting.

"Commander Gruber, a report on our current status please."

Hans Gruber barked a single word in German, and the table upon which they leaned became an enormous video console. The picture that appeared there was a satellite view of Earth. In its center, a large portion of the picture was completely black.

"This is Land Salzburg," Gruber said in English. "The dark area is approximately three square miles, the focus of which is Fortress Hohensalzburg."

Gruber stood and began to walk around the table, pointing at various locations for emphasis.

"This would seem to coincide with reports from the shadow leader, Meaghan Gallagher—"

The SJS chief marshal coughed.

"We cannot confirm Mulkerrin's presence here," Gruber said. "However, Austrian authorities have reported sighting monstrous creatures as much as four miles from the fortress, especially in the river and air."

The room was buzzing.

"The evacuation is under way, with those troops and police within the city doing their best to get people out, and those outside surrounding the city upon your orders. Within, fires rage out of control and many buildings have collapsed due to the earlier earthquake."

"According to reports from Geneva," interrupted the French commander, Jeanette Surro, "that earthquake never happened."

"How's that?" Roberto said, raising a brow.

"Well," Gruber nodded, "though we have plenty of physical evidence that the quake indeed took place, it created no measurable seismic activity."

"How can that be?" Philip Locke, the British commander asked. "That's impossible."

"Apparently not," Jimenez said, then turned to the American commander, Elissa Thomas.

"Commander Thomas, you're awfully quiet today. What's on your mind?"

Thomas had been leaning back in her chair, eyes slitted, taking it all in with one finger tapping her lips and her chin in her hand. She continued that motion for a moment as she scanned the room, lingering on the SJS reps and finally resting on Jimenez.

"I'll tell you what's on my mind, Commander Jimenez," she said and sat up. "First, I want to know where the Austrian commander is, and why the German commander is speaking for them."

She nodded toward Gruber.

"Second, I want to know why Gallagher and Nueva are not here, since they know Mulkerrin's methods and alerted us as to his involvement in this. And finally, I want to know what we've heard about Colonel Cody."

Roberto was about to reply when a snicker from the back of the room distracted him. He was close to losing his cool, but Commander Thomas did it for him.

"Is there something you find amusing, Chief Marshal Hannibal?" Thomas snapped at the shadow who still looked quite comfortable in his corner. She had returned her attention to Jimenez, not really expecting an answer, when Hannibal stood and placed his open palms on the table in front of him, leaning forward.

"It's that whole 'Colonel' thing, if you must know," he said, unpleasantly. "Cody was never a colonel of anything, and I would think you military types would be insulted by his continued use of that title. Also your implication that Gallagher and Nueva are even needed is insulting to myself and my deputy, Rolf Sechs."

He motioned a hand to indicate Rolf.

"We had as much exposure to Mulkerrin and his methods as they, perhaps more. Not to mention the fact that I am far older than either of those upstarts, and far more skilled in matters of war. Surely you all know my record."

Hannibal smiled, and sat back down.

"You're not trying to imply—" Commander Locke began.

"I have never found a need for implication, Commander," Hannibal interrupted, dismissing the Brit.

"You have not answered Commander Thomas's question, Chief Marshal," Roberto said calmly, reasserting control of the room.

"No," Hannibal agreed. "I have not."

Rolf Sechs leaned forward, his size a distraction in itself and slammed his hand on the table. Even Hannibal jumped. The deputy marshal reached inside his jacket and withdrew a black plastic strip, in the shape of a small calculator but much thinner, and a pen. He scribbled on the black strip, and as he did so, a computer-generated voice rose from it. Technology had made his muteness less of a problem than ever.

"The chief . . . marshal's . . . evasiveness aside," Rolf wrote, "we are . . . unaware . . . of the reason for Gallagher and . . . Nueva's absence. They have . . . for the moment . . . disappeared. Colonel Cody . . . and I are blood . . . brothers. As such we share a . . . mental rapport. Several minutes . . . ago that . . . rapport was broken."

Roberto Jimenez was certain he was not the only person in the room to notice the way Hannibal's face lit up at this information, before being overcome by his usual mask once again. Clearly he considered it very good news. Jimenez did not.

"Does that mean he's dead?" Roberto asked, and Rolf scribbled in reply.

"I have felt the . . . death of a family . . . member before," the computer voice said. "This was quite . . . different. But, Commander . . . most certainly not a . . . good thing."

"Thank you, Deputy Marshal," Commander Thomas said, smiling at Rolf.

It was clear to Roberto that Elissa Thomas actually liked the big shadow. Though he hated the creatures, he had to admit to himself a grudging admiration for the mute, especially in light of his feelings toward Hannibal: disgust, mistrust, revulsion, hostility. Just to name a few. But Rolf Sechs seemed different, was different. Though he didn't want to, Roberto automatically trusted the man.

Not a man, he reminded himself, *a thing*.

"Yes," he finally said, no longer hiding his hostility toward Hannibal, "thank you for stepping up to fulfill your chief marshal's duties. Hopefully, it will not be a constant necessity."

"As for your other question, Commander Thomas," Commander Gruber began, "my speaking for Commander Friedrich was requested by the Austrian president, not forced upon them by my own country, if that was your implication."

"Curiosity only, Hans," Commander Thomas said, smoothing ruffled feathers.

"Friedrich is engaged in a relief and containment effort like nothing he has ever experienced. He is prepared to follow whatever plan we decide to implement," Gruber added.

"To the plan, then," Roberto said. "Deputy Commander Rodriguez will outline for you what we will refer to henceforth as 'Operation: Jericho.' Our job is to see that the walls come tumbling down."

Gloria Rodriguez had been silent until now. She stood and began to walk around the table, as Gruber had done, referring to the satellite image on the table.

"First let me say that during Operation: Jericho, using satellite and aerial recon, German and Austrian forces will be hunting and eliminating what we'll call 'strays.' These will be the so-called monsters who run free. According to records from Venice, this should be a relatively simple task, which will be performed gradually until we have destroyed or contained them all. Priority, however, is preventing any more of them from appearing, or, uh, coming through from wherever it is they come from."

Hannibal snickered again.

"Commander Thomas will join her forces with Austrian troops at the airport, here—that's about two miles west of the fortress—and then move east to Rainberg, half a mile from it. Commander Gruber's troops will rendezvous at Lehener Park, where the Ducks are being defended right now. This will enable—"

"Ducks?" Hannibal asked, and Rodriguez was surprised he showed any interest at all.

"Ducks, Chief Marshal, are what we call our land-and-water attack vehicles."

Hannibal grunted.

"The Ducks will proceed upriver, destroying whatever they find in the water, and come ashore on the southern bank at Mozart's Plaza, here. This will be the largest force and the most difficult section of the city. At that time, Austrian and German forces will move south from Itzling and Hallwang to take the old city north of the river. Eventually if possible, they will move to help the rest of us at the fortress.

"Commander Locke's forces will meet with the Austrians at Hellbrunn Castle here in the south, then proceed north to eventually take up position at the stadium, here just east of the fortress. Commander Surro's troops will meet up with Commander Locke there, after they have swept from the hospital in Heuberg, here, southwest to the river, and made the crossing. From there, both groups will take Nonnberg Abbey, on the mountainside, and will therefore be the closest to the fortress at that time.

"Chief Marshal Hannibal's SJS forces will be split evenly among six groups. Thirty-six each with Commanders Locke, Surro, Gruber and Thomas, thirty-six with my Spanish paratroopers, making the sky drop into the fortress, and thirty-six with a much smaller group, made up of soldiers hand-picked and led by Commander Jimenez. Chief

Marshal Hannibal and Deputy Marshall Sechs are also needed for this special force, which will, in effect, walk right up to this bastard's door and break it in."

Hannibal's face showed no surprise, only resolution.

"If you think I will give up command of the SJS—"

"Nobody is asking you to," Roberto interrupted. "You can maintain constant contact with them, but each force needs the knowledge and skills of your kind to—"

"My 'kind,'" Hannibal said and stopped him. "I don't believe I like the sound of that."

Roberto's eyes narrowed.

"I'm sorry," he said. "Your *people* are needed everywhere, to best assist with this operation. And I need both of you with me because our job is, quite simply, to take out the sorcerer himself, to kill Mulkerrin."

Rolf's voice-pad was still on the table, and now he picked up his pen again.

"Easier said than done," he wrote.

Munich, Germany, European Union.
Wednesday, June 7, 2000, 12:59 A.M.:

"I'm telling you, 'Berto, he's got something going, and whatever it is, it's going to be a danger to this operation!"

Roberto looked up from his desk, where he'd been keying in a coded message to UN Secretary General Nieto, and gave his second, Gloria Rodriquez, the once over. She was not angry, or afraid, only frustrated that she couldn't figure out what it was Hannibal had in mind. He could tell it was making her nuts by the way she was pacing, and the manner in which her eyes moved, never stopping to rest on anything long enough to focus, as if she were literally, visually, looking for the answer in that very room.

"He's dangerous," Roberto Jimenez agreed, "and he's certainly been scheming something, but we have no way of knowing it will interfere with this operation. Certainly it's in his best interests just as it is in ours to get rid of Mulkerrin once and for all."

Roberto could almost hear Gloria's mind racing. She was not a beautiful woman. Tough, yes, and in perfect shape. Those qualities, and her intelligence and personality, made her attractive. Her face was pretty enough, dark hair and eyes, but she would never be beautiful. Eye of the beholder, Roberto thought.

"You didn't see Sechs," Gloria said. She had already told him about the gesture Rolf Sechs, the deputy marshal of the Shadow Justice System, had made when she had made brief eye contact with him. Rolf had caught her attention, lifted a finger to his eye and bowed his head, almost imperceptibly, toward Hannibal. It was a clear message, an intentional warning: *watch him*.

"Look, Glory, I want you to understand something." Roberto keyed off his hand-held PC scrambler and slipped it inside his jacket pocket. "Whether our friend Rolf was signaling you or had an itch, we would still watch Hannibal more closely than we have ever watched anyone, even the enemy. I despise the creature, and would feel much safer, much more confident about the potential success of this op, if he were not around."

"But we have our orders," she said, finishing for him.

"Yes, we have our orders. But nobody said we shouldn't be careful."

Gloria looked at him, and Roberto felt her attention, like a physical thing, return to the reality of the room, to him. Her mind focused for the moment on him, and he liked that. He knew he shouldn't, but he did. Glory smiled at him, and Roberto couldn't help but return that smile.

"Don't worry, *bonita*," he said, "we'll keep him reined in."

She went to him, then, and he held her in his arms, giving her small kisses on her head and cheek and neck and rubbing her back. There was nothing sexual in it, for the moment, but Roberto knew that would come later. Their relationship had been building up to it for more than a year, and each day, as his feelings for her grew, so did his longing.

Gloria broke their embrace and looked up at Roberto, touching his face with her hand. She loved his eyes, the gray stripes in his cropped, silky hair. Part of her so wanted to just let go and rely on his plans for controlling Hannibal, but she couldn't. She was just as able as he, just as canny and intuitive, his equal in all but raw force and combat skill, and even with that she was catching up every day—thanks most especially to his personal training. No, she couldn't just leave the question of Hannibal to her superior officer. One mind might miss something that two would not, and they could not afford such an error.

"What do you have in mind?" she asked in a low voice, understanding his reluctance to discuss the matter. Still, when he looked at her, she knew he realized everything she'd just thought, and agreed with her.

"Well," he began, and his tone brought them both back to business, "in a sense we've already started. Hannibal will be with us during this op, and Rolf will be there. If anything happens, I'll dismiss Hannibal and hand Rolf his command. Beyond that, I've got a number of operatives on both of them at all times."

Gloria nodded slowly, but her mind was off again, a mile a minute, searching for extra precautions.

"His kind disgust me," Roberto said suddenly, the ferocity of the statement distracting Gloria from her thoughts. "I don't want to be anywhere near their kind, but we need them now, their abilities. And as long as we need them, I'm going to be as near to them as is necessary to see this operation through. You've read the file on this Mulkerrin."

Gloria nodded, then patted the holster at her hip, inside of which her H-K auto nestled snugly, heavier than usual, pregnant with the weight of sixty silver rounds. According to the file, the silver worked wonders on Mulkerrin's "creatures," the real shadows. But it also hurt, at least temporarily, the pseudo-shadows, the vampires. They couldn't supply that ammunition to their entire force—only she and Roberto carried it—but they'd see that the silver went to good use.

"I've read it," she said. "It seems we know more about Mulkerrin than we do about Hannibal. I would hate to think we're better prepared to take on this mad sorcerer than a soldier on our own side."

"He's no soldier!" Roberto snapped. "And you'd be hard-pressed to convince me that he's on our side, or that any of the shadows are for that matter. The SJS is looking more and more like a smoke screen, like a survival tactic, every day. I can't believe we're letting them become even more organized, more dangerous, than before, and we only have personal histories on a couple of dozen out of thousands. Hell, there could be thousands we don't even know about.

"Aw, shit," he said and shook his head. "I can't be worrying about this now. We've got to get rid of Mulkerrin first, before his blackness taints everything. Then we'll worry about Hannibal and his clan."

"Better the devil you know . . ." Gloria shook her head, sighing. "Takes on a whole new meaning, doesn't it?"

Munich, Germany, European Union.
Wednesday, June 7, 2000, 1:01 A.M.:

Rolf knew he'd taken a chance in gesturing to Rodriguez. If Hannibal had seen him . . . but he hadn't, and that was important. Hannibal had to continue thinking Rolf was no more than an inconvenience. It wouldn't do to tip his hand too early. Rolf had guaranteed Meaghan and Alexandra that he would be ready when Hannibal made his move, and that he would take the elder shadow down.

This way, the humans were also on the alert. Not that he'd needed to warn them. From what he could tell, they'd been plenty suspicious of Hannibal already, but he'd wanted to be certain. And there was no way Rodriguez had misunderstood his meaning; in fact, she had nodded in return and almost given him away. But Hannibal was too distracted by the smug game he was playing to notice anything.

Several shadows had been added to each platoon since Rolf had drawn up their duty rosters, yet each time he walked through the barracks, he did not see a single face he did not recognize. He knew that these extra bodies were the outlaws that Hannibal had enlisted rather than killed, rebellious shadows who wanted nothing more than to kill humans. He knew that they would make their move at some point during this operation, and to that end he had taken into his confidence a number of his own soldiers, those he could trust, to neutralize Hannibal's plans as soon as something unusual took place. If they tried anything, Rolf himself would kill Hannibal. It was the only way. And despite the elder's much greater age, Rolf felt that his own evolution had become so rapid that he was at least a match for the old hunter.

And yet, he hoped that Hannibal had enough sense to wait until Mulkerrin was dead, to assist in the extermination of one threat before presenting another. Unfortunately, Rolf didn't have much faith in that scenario. More likely, Hannibal intended to use Mulkerrin's atrocities as a springboard for his own, and come back to take the sorcerer on later. Rolf knew such a strategy would not work in the long run, and he wondered how Hannibal could believe in it. For one brief moment, Rolf had believed that shadows could live in peace among humans, could become a society of their own and merge with the world, in the light of day.

His faith had been fleeting.

Now he steeled himself for battle again, fighting the poisons that threatened to destroy his kind from outside, and in.

And what if I'm alone now? he asked himself, then shook it off, not daring to address such questions. He had not felt his brother Will Cody, die, but he did know what it was he *had* felt: pain; extraordinary pain for one of their kind, and then nothing at all. Cody's mind had been shut to him before, a trick few of the shadows could perform, but Rolf didn't think this was a trick. Whatever had happened to sever Cody's psychic bonds with his family, it had not been by the old showman's own choice. Rolf had once shared his family's hatred of Cody for reasons he had never been too clear on, though he knew his brothers and sisters had been completely certain of their motives. But in Venice, he and Cody had stood side by side, fought together for their people, for their lives, and Rolf had been proud to stand with him.

Heaven help Mulkerrin if Will Cody were dead. Meaghan and Alex were closer to him as friends, but Rolf shared a warrior's bond with Cody, a thing of pride and honor.

And what of Alexandra and Meaghan, his sister and her lover, both his friends? What had become of them? They had been planning to reach Munich today, and yet George Marcopoulos and Julie Graham had sent a joint communiqué saying that they had disappeared from their home just before they were to leave for the airport, apparently intercepted by another shadow. Rolf could not begin to guess who this shadow was, or what business could take Alexandra and Meaghan away from something as dire as Mulkerrin's return.

But of course, that's not what had happened. Rolf knew that they had not simply gone off on some other adventure because when he reached out with his mind, to attempt to locate Alexandra, she too was gone. Not dead, for he would have felt such a tragedy, but simply gone.

All of this confusion wore away at his confidence, at his resolution, but he pushed it back. There was Mulkerrin to deal with, more powerful now than when Peter Octavian had been victorious over him in Venice, and this time they didn't have Peter to rely on. And Hannibal . . .

Rolf rose from where he'd been sitting, staring out the window at the gray dusk falling over Munich. Very shortly it would be time to muster the forces of Operation: Jericho. Before then, he would see if he couldn't learn a bit more of what Hannibal had in mind.

Before he was halfway to the door, someone knocked. He opened it to find the American commander, Elissa Thomas, alone in the hall.

He stood for a moment, unsure how to respond to her visit.

"May I come in?" she finally said, and he gestured for her to enter.

"I think we need to talk," she said as she passed him, and the lilt in her voice, the pride in her step and the sweet, sweet smell of her convinced Rolf that Hannibal could wait a few minutes. He didn't bother to remind her that he was unable, really, to talk. She knew that, of course. And there were, after all, other forms of communication.

Rolf closed the door and turned to find Commander Thomas leaning against the bare desk. His eyes flitted involuntarily to the single bed in the corner of the Spartan quarters he'd been given, then back to her. The commander had not missed the glance, and her lips turned up at the edges. Without the power of speech, Rolf had learned early how to interpret facial expressions, and there could be no mistaking the woman's intent.

He was surprised, even a little suspicious, but he was also excited. He had been attracted to Elissa Thomas the moment he laid eyes on her, and he respected her strength of will, her boldness and the courage in evidence within the personal records the SJS had on all UNSF commanders. He wondered if there were an ulterior motive, hoped there were not, and walked to her across the room.

Rolf motioned with his large hands, shrugging his shoulders, asking why she had come. Commander Thomas tossed her hair to one side like a schoolgirl, and Rolf felt his erection growing. An intelligent woman confident enough to allow her sexuality through. Yes, he wanted this woman.

"Rolf," she began, and he liked to hear her say his name, "let me lay it on the line here. I have no reason to trust you, but I do. I see in you a courage and cunning that I can respect and admire. And, of course, other things."

She reached up and put a hand on his neck, and the warmth of it made him even harder.

"Later, I'd like to talk to you about, shall we say, a strategic alliance. But for now . . ."

And her other hand moved forward and rested on the enormous bulge that had grown under his pants. Rolf closed his eyes a moment, a light breath escaping his mouth, warm on her cheek as she went to kiss him. Their lips met, and now Rolf's hands came up and held her face, enveloped it, and he pulled her to him and kissed her deep. Their tongues intertwined and then he broke off, leaving her breathless. His tongue flicked out and traced her lips, engraving a promise there of what he would do when he reached lower.

Rolf picked her up and carried her to the small bed, where he undressed her slowly, kissing, nibbling and licking at each newly bared region of her body. He caressed her so softly, gently, that she could hardly believe it was this great, powerful man who touched her. He rolled her nipples between his fingers as he lay her back and spread her legs with one strong hand. She didn't feel the urge to speak, because he, simply, could not. It wasn't just his tongue, but his lips and teeth, the stubble of his chin—he took control of her in a way no one had before.

As she approached her orgasm, building to something she knew would wrack her body with convulsions, just as she took that final breath . . . he stopped. He looked up at her in that moment that she thought she would suffocate, that she would never be released from the frozen muscles of her body, and he grinned at her, a naughty child, knowing what he'd done.

He had barely entered her when Elissa bucked up against him, pulling him deep into her. Then her legs were around his back, her fingernails raking his shoulders as she urged him on, her orgasm rocking her entire body with convulsions. She bit her lip and it bled, and somewhere in the back of her brain she wondered why he had not bitten her, but she couldn't hold any thought for long.

After he shuddered into an orgasm of his own, she wondered again why he hadn't taken her blood, but found she didn't care. She became suddenly aware of the muscles in her face, as he lay his head on her breast and snuggled close to her, and realized that she shared that grin of his.

And they slept.

7

Somewhere Between.
Thirty-Seven Seconds After Departure:

Lazarus had said that passing through the portal would hurt them less than it had Peter. As the three of them emerged on hands and knees, all retching and shivering, or perhaps convulsing, Meaghan and Alexandra were unaware that they shared a thought. If it had been this bad for them, exactly how bad *had* it been for Peter?

"Lions and tigers and bears, oh my," Alexandra said, weakly, and Meaghan attempted a soft chuckle to reward the effort, but couldn't manage it.

Lazarus didn't even try; he only moaned as he slowly worked himself, trial and error, to his feet. Meaghan was standing first, if only because her muscles ached more lying down. She thought that they might have experienced a weird sort of birth, and she wondered if babies experienced that kind of trauma. She reached out and pulled Alex to her feet, letting Lazarus take care of himself. He was, after all, supposedly older and stronger than either of them.

They had emerged in a dark alleyway, which was nothing like what they had expected, though if they had discussed it aloud they would both have realized that they had not really expected anything. Alex and Meaghan walked in silence to where the alley opened onto the main street, and Lazarus was right behind them.

"Lazarus," Meaghan said. "Where are we?"

It was, of course, Hell. But not the Hell they had expected. The street upon which they now stood was lined with old stone buildings, a crumbling inner city that resembled so many they had known, and yet was none of them. There was something about the architecture that was at once familiar, and yet accented with so many unfamiliar details and almost nonsensical geometry as to make them completely certain they were no longer "home." And it seemed that everything—buildings, street and sky—was gray.

Indeed, they had passed through to somewhere else, but not necessarily to the elsewhere they'd intended. And as Lazarus took his time responding to Meaghan's question, she realized what his answer would be before he could voice it.

"You don't know, do you? You don't know. Oh, well, that's just fucking wonderful."

"What now?" Alexandra asked.

Meaghan thought her lover sounded quite courageous, but she herself was nearing a panic. If Lazarus didn't know . . . Uh-uh. She wasn't going to let that happen.

"Lazarus," she said, back in command, "look through the book and try to find out where we went wrong, and how to get us out of here and on our way again. Alex and I will head opposite ways up the street, only a block, to get our bearings and perhaps a clue as to what this place is."

There was no discussion. Alexandra began to drift off down the street in one direction, and Meaghan in the other. The one thing that struck Meaghan as most chilling, the fact that threatened to undermine her new resolve, was the complete and unrelenting silence. This was a city, though not one they were familiar with, and yet it had no loud vehicles, no construction, no people. It was deserted. Up ahead in the distance, above the row of buildings that were like brownstones but not, the city's skyline shot up into towering glass-and-metal structures. Meaghan thought, not for the first time, that the word "skyscrapers" was incredibly appropriate.

But these were like no skyscrapers she had ever seen and their weird geometry—harsh, cutting angles—confirmed for her that they were nowhere on Earth. There were lights in those distant towers, the same way there were streetlights burning just above her now, and yet Meaghan was suddenly sure that those signs of life were false. She knew, intuitively, that those buildings were as empty as the streets around them.

"Meaghan!" Alexandra called from behind.

Meaghan turned to see Alex waving for her to come back. Obviously she'd found something, and Meaghan hoped it was an answer, rather than more questions. She walked back past Lazarus, and as she got closer to Alex she began to notice the destruction. She had to step around a huge crevice which had torn open the ground. To her left, charred embers were all that remained of two adjacent homes. To her right, all of the windows in one building were shattered, the lack of glass in the street suggesting an external force as the cause. Several others had their heavy wooden doors torn out, frames shattered, brick and stone smashed, steps crushed under incredible weight.

Fifty feet from Alexandra, with no wind at all, Meaghan could smell it. Filling her nose and activating an all too human gag reflex— it wasn't the smell of death, but of what comes after, the rotting. She came to a halt two yards away from her lover, but Meaghan didn't need Alex to point the way. Her nose brought her around to the sight of the crumbled remains of an entire building, most of which had collapsed into a huge crevice much like the one in the street. Other than the remains of the foundation wall and what had fallen outside that wall, the building was gone, into the crevice. But the crevice was apparently not a bottomless pit, because it wasn't empty now.

The bodies were not piled, they were packed, tight, with no discernible relationship or continuity. The dead, many burned, maimed and disemboweled, were all ages and races and both sexes. Some clothed, some naked, their stink was the only thing they shared besides death. Intertwined like dozens of lovers locked frozen in the midst of an orgy, the dead were, without question, human. And yet Meaghan could again detect an essential difference. Perhaps it was the heightened senses she had as a shadow, or mere logic in the face of their alien surroundings.

"My blood!" Alexandra said finally, and Meaghan realized they had both been holding their breath.

"We don't know where we are," Meaghan said and shook her head, "and now we have no idea how this happened. What did this?"

"More importantly," Alex said, grabbing Meaghan's hand, "is it coming back?"

"Let's get back and see if Lazarus has some answers."

They turned to go, but Meaghan caught sudden movement out of the corner of her eye, and as she turned, she noticed that the street was no longer silent. Staring out over the sea of dead once again, she was prepared to think she had imagined the movement, though the new sound, a sort of distant chuffing, like a powerful pump, remained. And then the movement came again, a ripple, a wave sending arms and legs flailing and blood spattering, as something huge moved under the dead. With the drying scab ripped from the top of the mass grave, a new, more powerful wave of odor rolled over them, and this time Meaghan did gag.

And then the cesspool erupted in a fountain of gore and decaying flesh, spraying sixty feet into the air. Meaghan and Alex were spattered by the initial burst and then showered in gobs of humanity, body parts raining down and slapping the ground around them. In front of them, rising up through the falling dead, was a behemoth unlike anything either of them had seen, even during the Venice Jihad.

At the same time, however, both Meaghan and Alexandra knew immediately that this creature was a sibling to those from Venice, a shadow-demon from the Hell Mulkerrin had dredged once too often. Its long snout was huge, the eyes on either side a dozen feet apart. Its hundreds of bared teeth were long and sharp as sabers, covered with gore, flesh hanging in strings from its black lips. The nostrils of the snout were flaring, blood spraying in a fine mist, and it occurred to Meaghan that the things were like the blowholes of a whale, and that the remains of the dead the creature had consumed had been blasted out of those nostrils with explosive power.

And thinking of that power, she had to wonder how much of the creature was still underground, to supply the energy for such a burst.

Its green-scaled flesh was still coming and they had yet to see limbs. Its head seemed snake-like, or more accurately, sharklike, as it continued to rise from the hole. Then, heavy under its own weight, it flopped forward, its jaws clacking together only yards from where they stood. At the edges of the hole, they now saw relatively small, lizardlike talons appear and begin to claw at the remains of the building's stone foundation, pulling forward.

Watching in fascination, Meaghan's attention was finally brought back to their safety as Alex grabbed her arm.

"Meaghan!" she said, obviously not for the first time. "Do we fight, or get out of here?"

Meaghan looked at her lover, saw the concern in her eyes, the questions there, held for later. She knew them for they were the same questions in her own mind. She looked at the huge shadow, then back to Alex.

"Screw that," she said, "we're out of here. If it catches us, then we fight."

Lazarus was running up behind them now, the *Gospel* clutched in his hands. As they turned to flee from the creature, they nearly ran him down.

"Run!" Meaghan shouted at him.

"What?" Lazarus looked as if he'd been goosed, his eyebrows lifting as his mouth fell open.

"Run!" Meaghan said again, and this time Lazarus did turn his steps back the way he'd come, but not without a frown of great displeasure. Meaghan knew it was difficult for him, who had probably not run from anything since his human death.

But, she thought, *wisdom being the better part of valor, he can go to . . .*

"So," she said as they ran, "where are we anyway?"

"Well," Lazarus said, slowing down now and looking over his shoulder, "we're not in Hell if that's what you're wondering.

"It's stopped," he added, coming to a complete halt and turning back the way they'd come.

Meaghan and Alex also stopped, and now they watched from several blocks away as the huge creature settled itself back into the mass grave that had become its home. As far away from it as they were, they could still hear the chuffing noise, which meant the monster was sucking the flesh and bones of the dead into its mouth, but this time there was no explosion from its nostrils. Soon, the thing was out of sight and the hole itself was merely a gap in the block of buildings.

"So if we're not in Hell . . . ?" Alexandra said, making a conscious choice for all of them to put off discussion of the demon until they were gone from this place.

"Where are we?" Lazarus mused aloud, holding up *The Gospel of Shadows* to emphasize his words. "A good question, but the answer isn't in here . . . Or maybe it is."

"How do you mean?" Meaghan asked, but she could see in Lazarus's eyes that his mind was drifting someplace else. She repeated the question, and finally he faced her.

"I have a theory," he said, spreading his arms to encompass everything around them. "The Stranger has told me many times that there are worlds other than our own, but I thought he meant this 'Hell,' and whatever passes for Heaven, if anything does. We know that Hell exists because that's where these creatures come from, and it's discussed in the book. But what if there are other planes as well, planes not mentioned in the *Gospel*?"

Alex and Meaghan exchanged glances, and Meaghan was amused to see the way her lover's brows arched in obvious doubt.

"Just a minute," Alexandra interrupted. "Are you trying to say that we're in some kind of alternate world, like a parallel dimension or some such thing? I mean, give me a fucking—"

"Don't jump to conclusions, Alex," Meaghan broke in. "Lazarus may be on to something here."

Lazarus was surprised at her defense, but appreciated it.

"Don't forget, Miss Nueva," he said, "you are, after all, a vampire."

Meaghan's mind was racing, and she paced in time to its rhythm, chewing on her right index knuckle in a way that Alex had always found endearing.

"Okay," she said and stopped pacing. "Are either of you familiar with the theories of Stephen Hawking?"

Both nodded then began to speak, but Meaghan cut them off.

"No, just listen. Hawking postulated that the existence of black holes, which he has proven, themselves prove the existence of parallel universes because some matter which passes into the hole does not emerge. It has to go somewhere. Now, if Hell is one of these parallels, then the portal that we used to travel here, and those Mulkerrin was able to create, have got to be . . . what? Gray holes? Somehow they allow matter to pass in both directions but do not have the vacuum effect of a black hole."

"Do you know how crazy this sounds?!" Alex yelled, frustrated and already tired.

Meaghan flinched.

"Honey," she said. "There's no need to yell like that."

"No need to . . .?" Alex was dumbfounded. "This is not like a domestic squabble or something, Meg. How can you be so calm?"

"You're not," Meaghan smiled. "I have to be."

Alex was sorry, and the two embraced a moment as Lazarus spoke.

"The only problem," he said, "is that if all of this is true, we still don't know exactly where we are, what happened here, or how to get out."

They were all quiet then, and in the silence finally heard the noises in the buildings all around them. Lazarus spun quickly and saw a thin, bony face disappear from behind a window. He started for the house, thinking there were people there after all, but Meaghan stopped him.

"I saw some too," she said. "In fact, I think they're all around us now, but they're not what you think."

"How can you know what I think?"

"'Cause it's exactly what I would have thought, if I hadn't seen that." She pointed down the street toward the city skyline, and in the shadows of buildings, small, bony wolflike creatures scampered, with faces like those from the windows around them. A pair of huge, fat, hairy bipeds, one with tusks pushing out from its face, emerged from the distant darkness.

"He's been here," Meaghan whispered, and then louder: "Mulkerrin had to have been here!"

"We were waylaid here en route to our destination," Lazarus started in, "and so was he. Now it becomes clear. Mulkerrin isn't just after vampires now, he just wants to conquer, to destroy."

"So this is a sneak preview of what happens if we don't stop him?" Alexandra asked. "So what are you waiting for, Lazarus? Get us out of here."

Though he still didn't like to flee any more than he wanted to let these females fight for him, Lazarus knew what their responsibilities were. As the skeletal demon-wolves moved in for the attack, their gargantuan brothers slowly falling in behind, he opened the book to the spell that had gotten them where they were. He hoped the same spell would allow them to complete their trip. He didn't bother to tell them he had no idea if it would.

Unlike most younger shadows, Lazarus prayed. The Stranger had assured him that someone was listening. And at that moment, Lazarus made a conscious decision to believe him.

The first of the demon-wolves reached Alex and Meaghan, but they didn't have a chance. The vampire women were much more powerful, and shattered the creatures' bony frames with ease. But the huge, brown, ape-like shadows approached now, so slowly, and the tusked one in the lead became uglier as it moved closer. Its black lips pulled back from blacker gums in a roar through strong, sharp, clenching teeth. Alex clamped her hands over her ears.

"Come on, Laz," Meaghan shouted, "how 'bout it?"

And then the portal was there.

"Go," he shouted, standing with the book in his hand, and in seconds Meaghan and Alexandra were through the passage, magical or scientific, and the two great beasts roared their displeasure.

Lazarus turned to go, clutching the *Gospel* to his chest and leaping for the portal. In midair, his legs were snagged crunching painfully in the huge hands of the tusked creature, whose anger had added speed to its attack. Lazarus fell face-first toward the ground, his hands flying out to break his fall and *The Gospel of Shadows* tumbling into the air . . . through the portal.

Furious, Lazarus turned on the creature, its mate not three steps behind, and ignoring the pain in his crushed legs, forced them to burst into flame in the creature's hands. Matted with disgusting hair as it was, the creature's body caught the fire, and it spread rapidly over its form. The creature howled in distress and began to beat at its burning arms and chest, only succeeding in spreading the flames. As it crawled to the portal, the last sight Lazarus had was of the demon's mate arriving to help, and having the flames leap from one to the other instead.

As the cold womb of pain presented by passage through the worlds enveloped him, Lazarus had to wonder about those creatures. Other than vampires, he'd never seen shadows with mates before, never seen them care for one another. Had they, then, been an example of the native life forms of that universe that became demonic half-breeds the way Lazarus and his kindred had been?

As he was belched out onto hot, hard stone, at the feet of Meaghan Gallagher and Alexandra Nueva, Lazarus felt momentarily sorry for the creatures and wished he could take back the flames. And then his companions were at his side, helping him up even as his legs finished their self-healing. He breathed a sigh of relief as he scanned the cavern in which they now stood.

They were on a rocky shelf, which was slashed out of the wall behind them. Though apparently made of stone, the wall and shelf were black, charred by terrible flames, and their feet kicked up a fine powderlike soot while flakes and bubbles crunched under them. Flames burned from cracks in the walls, and burning ash fell in a light shower from somewhere high above, whirled into eddies by wind currents that buffeted them with heat as well. The wall behind them curved around, and in the distance they could barely make out the shimmering flames from the opposite wall. They could see hundreds of feet above, and no ceiling, so that all three assumed they were in a hole of some kind. And far, far below, the fire burned.

"It's a wonder our portal didn't open above that," he said, looking down at the red glow of the pit beneath them. "It reminds me of a stovepipe. Though strangely it does look somewhat like what I'd expected."

"We were just talking about that," Meaghan said. "Maybe part of the spell controls the point of egress?"

Lazarus thought about that, the spell. *The spell*! What the hell happened to . . .

"The book!" he snapped at them, noticing that neither held it. "What happened to the book?"

Meaghan and Alex looked quite alarmed.

"What do you mean?" Alex hissed. "You had the damn book!"

"I was attacked," he mumbled. "It flew from my hands and through the portal. I thought it would . . ."

They all looked down, around their feet, realizing the futility of the act even as they performed it, and then out over the abyss.

"Do you think?" Alexandra said, but Meaghan shook her head as they looked down into nothing.

"No. I think we would have seen it come through and go over."

"So then what?"

Meaghan didn't have an answer, but Lazarus turned to face the black wall where the portal had been.

"Lost," he said. "Lost somewhere between that devastated world and this place."

"Great!" Alex snapped.

"Now how do we get back?" Meaghan said to no one.

"We find Peter, of course," Alexandra said, stepping to the edge. "If he's still alive, maybe he can get us out. If not, we'll die here with his bones."

Meaghan looked at Lazarus, and he shook his head.

"We have little choice," he said, then turned to Alex. "But we have no idea how to find him. For starters, do we go up or down?"

Alexandra laughed then, a sick, angry, frustrated, frightened laugh that scared Meaghan in a way.

"Don't be stupid," she said. "This place even looks like the Hell of myth, at least for me. If there's anything to be found here, we *won't* find it by going up."

"I don't know if we ought to fly through that," Lazarus said, pointing at the cinder and ash tumbling down the center of the pit.

"We don't have to," Meaghan broke in, standing at the edge of the shelf, pointing along the wall. "There's a kind of ledge over here that seems to wind down and around."

Hell.
One Hour, Four Minutes, Twenty Seconds
After Departure:

Meaghan estimated that they'd been descending for at least half an hour when she fell. It was getting hotter, and Lazarus had left his light jacket behind. They knew that it must be far hotter even than it felt, for temperatures that would force humans unconscious were just enough to make shadows break a sweat. It was very uncomfortable. Not to mention how filthy they were, covered in the black soot that seemed to blanket everything.

They had yet to see a single of Hell's shadows, but agreed that it would only be a matter of time. Still, they found themselves alone. They had given up conversation and conjecture almost completely, setting their minds to the task at hand, when Meaghan stepped forward, over stone that Alexandra had just crossed, and fell away into nothing. The ledge did not crumble beneath her feet; rather, it simply fell, in one block section, away from the wall and hurtled down toward the inferno she imagined waited below.

She heard both Alexandra and Lazarus cry her name, but Meaghan was not terribly concerned. Though the heat made it slightly more difficult, it was a simple task to shift her shape into that of a bat, and rise on the hot breeze she now realized was flowing up from the huge hole in the ground that they had been circling. Soaring back up to where the others stood, looking down after her, Meaghan knew that the ledge went all the way around, spiraling down to lead them eventually to the point she would have found faster if she'd simply kept falling.

They could fly. How stupid of them to be moving so carefully, so delicately. Lazarus was concerned about the embers falling in the center of the stovepipe, but they didn't have a lot of time, and this was time wasted. They could survive a flaming shower if they had to. Certainly there were risks, as they never knew when they were going to run into the demon-creatures who called that plane home, but—

And then she knew she'd jumped the gun. Winged monsters appeared above and below her, as if she were a diver who'd fallen into a pool of sharks. They circled, leather wings barely moving, long, pterodactyl-like beaks snapping in the air, making a terrible noise, like doors slamming over and over again. And there were at least a dozen of the flying creatures.

"Meaghan!" She heard Alexandra calling her name even over the snapping of the creatures' beaks and the high-pitched, roaring call that now went out, like nails on a blackboard.

Meaghan feinted in one direction, then turned toward Alex's voice and dove. One of the creatures was right behind her, its snapping beak ready to swallow her nearly whole. Ahead, she saw sanctuary! Alex and Lazarus had somehow found a cave or tunnel leading off the ledge they'd been following, hopefully leading far away from the stovepipe. Now that these guardians, or whatever they were, had discovered them, they would not be safe in the open.

But she wasn't going to make it, was she? She thought she could feel the heat from the thing's nostrils on her back, and knew that at any moment that beak would clamp down on her, destroying her bat form . . . unless she wasn't in bat form! And what was that Lazarus was screaming at her from the hole in the wall? Yes!

"Mist!" he screamed.

And Meaghan angled away from the hole in which her friends hid, the flying demon right behind her, and others on its tail. She flew straight at the soot-covered walls, and then she changed. The demon's beak snapped down on the spot she had occupied a second before, and the moment of confusion, in which it realized it held nothing in its throat, was enough. It was too late for the thing to turn away, and the flying demon slammed into the wall, sending a puff of charcoal smoke into the air, bones splintering, black blood spurting. And then it tumbled down into the pit, and as Meaghan floated over to the cave mouth, Alexandra and Lazarus watched the thing fall. It took so long that

Meaghan was with them, watching, when the thing was finally out of sight.

And then the demons were flying, up and away, shrieking as they went . . . and the flames came. Fire rocketed up through the center of the stovepipe, scorching everything in its path, the walls charred even further as the furnace blasted for several seconds. Meaghan felt her face blistering and heard Alexandra crying out, and then it was over and the flames subsided.

"That sucked," Alex said with a sniffle, but as Meaghan looked at her lover, her burnt flesh was already healing itself. In fact, she could feel her own flesh healing as well. Lazarus, who'd been farther back, was barely singed.

"A good thing we weren't on that ledge just now," Lazarus said. "I don't want to guess whether we'd survive something like that."

Meaghan slumped against the wall of the tunnel, which is what it was after all. Her mind raced and she frowned, looking at Lazarus.

"What is it?" he asked.

"Well," Meaghan began, "does it seem to either of you that we're not really thinking very clearly? I mean, since we got here? We could have flown from the beginning, especially with time of the essence, but we were deterred by that flaming . . . avalanche or whatever it was in the center there. And I ought to have turned to mist immediately when I saw those creatures, but it took much longer than normal for me to think of it."

"You're right," Alex said, wincing as the last of her blisters cracked and healed. "But what can we do about it? We can't exactly leave here."

"The only thing we can do," Lazarus said, "is watch each other very carefully for signs of muddled thinking. Otherwise, none of us will ever get out of here."

"So, I guess we're going down this tunnel," Alex said. "'Course we have no idea what we'll meet down there."

"We've been lucky so far," Meaghan said grimly. "But look at it this way, we can't stay in the stovepipe, and anything we meet in here has to be a lot smaller than those pterodactyl things."

They looked at each other, and then all three of them were smiling, chuckling, and shaking off the dangers they'd just avoided. Alex gave Meaghan a kiss, then helped her up, and they turned to join Lazarus as he started into the tunnel.

"I hope this thing isn't just a smaller chimney," Lazarus said, and they stopped smiling.

And that's when the screaming started.

All three of them turned around to face the tunnel mouth, and outside, in the stovepipe, they could see the screamers, falling, arms and legs flailing, trailing fire from their burnt and broken flesh. The chorus of wails came from dozens of beings, some apparently human, men, women and children, and countless other sentient but alien races, tumbling through the air down into the pit of flame far below.

When Alexandra could not stand to look anymore and turned away, she saw Meaghan with her back against the wall, eyes closed, hands covering her ears. Bloody tears were wet on her cheeks, and Alex went to her and held her tight, kissing the tears away.

"We're really here," Meaghan whispered. "This is really it, isn't it, Alex?"

"Yes, honey, we're really here." Alex hugged her even harder. "But once we find Peter, we get to leave. Don't worry, we'll get out of here."

"Well," Meaghan said, breaking off their embrace, "what are we waiting for? Lazarus, you watch our backs; I'll take point."

"No," Alex said. "If you can mind-link, you may be our only chance of finding Peter and getting out of here. You're in the middle; I'll take point."

And without another word, they proceeded into the tunnel that way, Alexandra first, then Meaghan and, finally, Lazarus. Meaghan was pleased. She'd thought they would have to rely on their vampiric senses to "see" in the darkness, but there were open flames burning through cracks in the tunnel's stone walls. The tunnel itself was warm, but not nearly as warm as she'd imagined it would be, considering. In fact, it was cooler than the cavern they'd come from. Still, though it was barely perceptible, the tunnel sloped down and to the right.

Several times they came to a fork or intersection where other tunnels ran into theirs, and each time Meaghan made the decision, led by an unidentifiable feeling, a sense of "right."

They heard no sound but that of their own rustling movement, their snippets of murmured conversation and the slap of Lazarus's shoes on the stone. Meaghan and Alex both wore sneakers, and their footfalls sounded much quieter in the flickering dark, but in that silence, they too were audible.

Alexandra stopped suddenly, leaning against the wall and bringing one hand up to stroke through her black hair. Meaghan thought how funny they all looked, covered in grime, but she wasn't laughing.

"What is it, honey?" she asked Alex.

"Haven't you guys noticed it yet?" Alexandra said, surprised. "The tunnel has gotten smaller."

Lazarus looked around, eyes narrowed, and realized that Alexandra was right. The tunnel had been shrinking gradually as they moved. In fact, he had even begun to stoop slightly because of the encroaching ceiling, and had barely noticed it. Meaghan leaned against the wall next to Alex, holding her lover's hand to her lips and kissing it in that way that meant nothing and everything, requiring a complete response, and none at all. She felt Alex's fingers tighten in her own, that squeeze the only affirmation her heart needed.

"There's something else we missed, or at least I did," Meaghan said. "The incline is getting steeper."

"So we started in a tunnel," Lazarus said, "but we may end up in a well."

"I don't like the sound of that," Meaghan said, then pushed off from the wall. "Let's go."

They began walking again, and Meaghan took the lead over Alex's protests. Immediately, they realized it had gotten darker. With their senses, it was not an issue, but it was strange. Also, the size and slope of the tunnel was changing more rapidly now, so that they all had to bend to avoid hitting their heads, and shift their weight to avoid falling forward.

"You know what's strange?" Alex said after they'd been moving along that way for several minutes. "The only demons we've seen were those prehistoric-looking things, and nothing like the creatures Mulkerrin brought through during the Venice Jihad. I mean, if there are any intelligent demons, anybody running the place, don't you think they'd know we were here by now? Isn't anybody in charge? It's just too quiet. Doesn't it seem the least bit—"

A cry of pain, or rage, perhaps of both, but definitely human, called to them from the depths of the tunnel. The time for talk was over then, and they hunched over even further and headed down the tunnel as quickly as they could.

And then something had hold of Meaghan's ankle, and she was falling forward, arms stretched out, face slamming hard into the sharply angled stone floor, cheekbone cracking, breath knocked out of her. It happened fast, as she instinctively pulled hard on her foot, the momentum of her fall helping to free her ankle. She heard a surprised gasp from Alexandra behind her, and attempted to turn and look, but halfway around she was pummeled by the weight of Lazarus landing atop her in the small, confined space of the tunnel. They struggled, tangled together by their limbs and momentary panic. Freed, finally, they managed to turn themselves around.

"Oh, shit! What the fuck is—" Meaghan crawled forward and grabbed Alexandra's arms, pulling, just as her lover began to scream.

"Get'emoffme! Meg! Get'emoffme!"

Alex was up to her neck in a hole lined with human bodies, corpses in a living death, whose arms and legs trapped her there, tore at her pants and the already bare flesh of her upper body, whose heads leaned out and fastened lips and teeth to her. Meaghan had nearly stepped right over the hole, a single hand snagging her, but she pulled free. Alex had not been so lucky, had stepped right in the narrow pit of writhing bodies just as Meaghan fell forward. Finally, Lazarus had stumbled over Alex, kicking her in the back even as she was pulled down and he plowed into Meaghan's fallen form.

Now Meaghan stared in horror, and Lazarus said nothing but moved up next to her in the cramped space to grab Alex's left hand with both of his own so that Meaghan could pull on the right.

"It's okay, honey," Meaghan started, "we're getting you out! We're getting them off."

Meaghan closed her eyes as they pulled, hard, and she thought the popping she heard might have been one of Alex's shoulders coming out of the socket. When her eyes opened again, Alex was still screaming but her head had sunk deeper into the hole.

"No!" Meaghan snarled. "*Alex!*"

But Alex wasn't listening.

"*Alex!*" she screamed again, and this time Alex looked up, away from what was happening below, as claws tore chunks of skin from her immortal flesh, as jaws gobbled down bloody scraps of her flesh.

Meaghan saw that it was a throat, the gullet of Hell, pulling her lover down for digestion.

"Change!" she yelled. "Alex, change to mist, you've got to do it now!"

"I . . . uff . . . I caann't," Alexandra sobbed, then giggled, the madness of the pain creeping over her.

"*Do it!*" Meaghan screamed. "Change!"

And Alex began to transform, mist swirling in the throat cut out of stone. But the dead creatures there would not stop, and their mouths and nostrils opened, heads craning as far out from their woven mingling as possible as they *inhaled* Alexandra, breathed in as much of the mist as they could.

Meaghan was nearly sick, about to scream to Alex again, and then one of the faces in the hole caught her eye. It was looking at her as it sucked in the essence of her lover. Its eyes locked on hers and its grin widened. Meaghan looked around at the other faces and saw that many of them, some not human-looking at all, also stared at her, also grinned. And then she knew Alexandra had been right. Their presence in Hell had been no secret, and whatever knew they were there was truly evil, and intelligent.

And before she could try to help any further, Alex changed again, to fire this time, and Meaghan wanted to cheer but could only watch and hope. She and Lazarus had to back away slightly, as the throat seemed to widen and hands reached out and groped around its stone edges for them. She wished for *The Gospel of Shadows*, for any power it might have held, but knew that wishes were only that.

A twinge of triumph swept through Meaghan as the flesh of the throat, the arms and bellies, breasts and legs, penises and buttocks, faces and eyes, especially eyes, began to blacken and blister under the fire that was Alexandra Nueva. The eyes that had been staring at Meaghan burst, spurting some black, malodorous liquid, but the faces kept on grinning. With a scream of fury, Meaghan began to crawl forward, but Lazarus held her back.

The dead mouths were sucking in the flame as easily as they had the mist. Even as lips charred to the teeth, the flames disappeared through the open mouths of the damned creatures. Meaghan broke Lazarus's hold and rushed forward, upward on her knees. She lay on the stone and reached down into the burning gullet and began smashing faces, breaking skulls, shattering bones.

And then they had her, and were pulling her down, headfirst, into the throat of Hell. She could feel Lazarus pulling from behind, and she thought she felt the bones in her left ankle break in his grip. Claws tore at her face and throat; teeth took a bite from her cheek. She opened her eyes even as a burnt, skeletal hand reached out to pluck them from her skull—and then Alex was there, face-to-face with her, blocking the attack of that hand. Her face was covered in blood, her beautiful chocolate skin shredded to the bone from the lips down. Hanging upside down as she was, Meaghan could see that Alex's left breast had been torn away with her left arm. Below that, she was just gone.

Gone.

Hanging gore was all that remained there, but still, Alexandra thrashed her upper body, her right arm broken but flailing at the voracious damned around her. Her efforts were a distraction to the creatures of the throat, and their hold on Meaghan loosened, only for a moment, but long enough for Lazarus's pulling on the other end to make a difference. Meaghan's head, shoulders and arms, all that had been pulled into the hole, popped out, and then she was being dragged on the stone. She had one, final glimpse of Alexandra, love and pain in her eyes, and tears on her cheeks, and then nothing.

Meaghan sat up, backing away, and she could feel her broken ankle, the tears in the flesh of her face, neck and arms, all healing, even as she heard the sounds of what remained of her lover being consumed. She backed into Lazarus, who had saved her, but neither had been able to save Alex. Their strength was meaningless, she thought. How could they have thought to survive such a journey? Mulkerrin's creatures had been mindless, but here, in Hell, it was different. She had seen those eyes, the cruelty there.

Hell was aware, and it knew them.

Meaghan turned her head from the sight of the burnt hands grasping at the air around the open throat, scratching at the stone for the food that had escaped. She fell into Lazarus's arms, and he held her uncomfortably, as she wept in a manner all too human. She knew he could not find words to comfort her, and she was glad. She did not want to be comforted.

"Alex," she sobbed. "Oh, my God."

Meaghan had purposely not addressed God since becoming a vampire during the Jihad five years before. She'd been confused, uncertain, no matter what she told her own kind. But now she knew.

She'd seen it up close, and now Meaghan Gallagher knew that, no matter what she was, she was not evil.

"Dear God," she sobbed, her heart crying, her chest exploding, "We need you . . . We all need you."

Lazarus held her hand tight as he led her farther down into the tunnel, and soon the only sounds were of her weeping. First her parents, then her lover and best friend, Janet Harris, then Peter Octavian, and now Alexandra—everyone Meaghan Gallagher loved, died. She could not help but think that she was just one more tortured soul, suffering, in Hell.

＊

8

"Where the fuck did they go, George?"

Henry Russo was not fooling around. George Marcopoulos sat in the study of his Washington, D.C., home and argued with the President of the United States. In addition to the two men, both U.S. Secretary of State Julie Graham and United Nations Secretary General Rafael Nieto were attending the video conference.

George wasn't in the mood.

"Listen, Henry, you can play hardball all you want, but I'm in the dark just as much as you. The difference is, I care what happened to them, not just why they aren't on their way to Austria. Give me a break, will you? These are my friends!"

"That's what has me worried, George," Julie Graham said grimly.

"And just what the hell is that supposed to mean?" George snapped.

"What it means," the President resumed, "is that we think you know what happened to Nueva and Gallagher, and we want to know if it poses a threat to us and to Operation: Jericho!"

"If it poses . . . Are you out of your fucking mind?" George lost it completely. "Don't you know who you're talking about here? These two women—"

"Vampires," Graham said, stabbing.

"Vampires, yes!" George roared. "Women first, human beings

whether you believe it or not. They are your greatest allies among their kind. Without them, the entire world might have suffered in the wake of the Venice Jihad. They are almost solely responsible for the peace you have today, and you dare imply—"

"What peace?" Rafael Nieto finally spoke up, and the mere fact of his calm was enough to defuse George's rage for a moment.

"Yes, yes, Austria," George said and nodded, understanding Nieto's implication. "But the shadows have nothing to do with that. Mulkerrin is their sworn enemy. They have vowed to destroy him, with or without your help."

George gave a *hmph* to let them know exactly what he thought of their insane suspicions. Why, the very idea! And did they think he was stupid? A man of his age and reputation, his closeness to the shadows—well, he ought to know oughtn't he?

But of course, he ought to know where Meaghan and Alex had gotten to as well. And now this news of Cody's capture.

"And where does Rome fit into all this?" George asked. "Is anybody actually listening to the Vatican these days? If the Pope has got you guys all introspective, it's because he wants you to forget that Mulkerrin was a priest once, not to mention all the Vatican busboys who ended up corpses in Venice."

"The Pope," Rafael Nieto said patiently, "has not contacted anyone. In fact, I'd guess right about now he's hiding under his desk. Now, if we could get back to our subject, a moment ago you referred to the Shadow Justice System. That, dear Doctor, is exactly where all of this sudden mistrust is rooted. My Field Commander, Roberto Jimenez, is on record regarding his feelings toward shadows in general, and now his suspicions relating to the SJS chief marshal."

Hannibal, George thought. *So that's what this is about.*

"Now I understand," he said and nodded. "You suspect Hannibal is up to no good, and you fear that Nueva and Gallagher's disappearance bodes ill, perhaps indicates some conspiracy?"

He chuckled, and watched all three faces on his viewscreen frown at the act. *The hell with them*, he thought. *They could indulge an old man.*

"If Meaghan and Alex's disappearance is cause for alarm, it is because of some harm which may have befallen them," George said sharply, nostrils flared. "Not, certainly, because they have planned some insane insurrection at a time when their worst enemy walks the earth again. Talk about stupid! I'll let you in on a little secret."

Ah, he had their attention. Did he ever!

"Hannibal is a liar, a killer, and an incredibly intelligent creature with a network of operatives all his own. He is as vicious as the legends portray his kind to be, the antithesis of everything Meaghan and her team stand for."

"But," the President sputtered, "what were you thinking when—"

"We know Hannibal too well," George said, though he was really speaking for the shadows, for he'd never actually met Hannibal. "The creature wanted the SJS job so that he would be above suspicion, and therefore, above punishment for his own misdeeds. He has pretended to be above reproach so that humanity will not demand his destruction. The position was intended to be, in a way, a prison for him. A way for us to keep an eye on him."

"But how can you—" Julie Graham began.

"Rolf Sechs, the deputy chief?" George continued. "He and Cody and Nueva shared the same blood-father, as they say. He is one of them, and he is also Hannibal's watchdog. Don't worry, my friends. If Hannibal gets out of hand, Rolf will simply kill him, or die trying, and then you've got the rest of the SJS to keep the beast in check. Now, can we discuss what's truly important here, like destroying Mulkerrin before his madness spreads any further, and perhaps what's being done to find Meaghan and Alexandra?"

George Marcopoulos looked at his viewscreen and saw three of the most powerful individuals in the world looking back at him like cowed schoolchildren. *Good*! he thought. They were acting like fools, and here he was, nothing but an old sawbones, telling them what to do. A sudden memory nearly forced a smile onto his face, but he stifled the urge before they could see it. Still, the memory came, of younger days, laughing with his kids in front of the television set.

Damnit, Jim, he thought, *I'm a doctor not a diplomat.*
Who would have guessed?

St. Leonhard, Austria, European Union.
Tuesday, June 6, 2000, 6.23 .P.M:

They had ridden in near complete silence as the miles ticked away on the odometer. The only thing Allison Vigeant and John Courage had learned about their driver was his name: Kurt Wagner. Beyond that, the man was silent. He seemed both frightened and fascinated by being in the same car as Courage, and it occurred to Allison that humans had become quite adept at picking the shadows out of the herd, which was ironic because the vampires had hidden among them for so many years. On the other hand, much to Wagner's chagrin, his brother, the volunteer, had babbled continuously, until Courage finally ordered him to be silent, which he was.

Now, though, they had pulled to a stop in Saint Leonhard, at the foot of Mount Untersberg, with the Alps rising all around them and a cable car hanging in the air on the mountainside. This, apparently, was their destination, though Allison had held off asking the many questions sprinting across her mind. She was not comfortable with the Wagner brothers there.

As they got out of the car, with barely a few syllables to spare for the men, Courage set off toward the cable car at a brisk pace. Wagner's tires turned up stones pulling away. Allison looked up toward the mountain.

Shit!

The cable car was not moving. Assuming they needed the car to get where they were going, and John's direction certainly hinted that they did, they had finally run into a major obstacle. She followed him quickly and arrived at the car's enclosed terminal several paces behind him. The door had shut, but even as she opened it, Allison could hear Courage yelling.

". . . you're dealing with!" he roared. "Do you have any idea what's going on in Salzburg? If you don't get this thing up and going, a lot more people will die!"

Two men, obviously the operators of the car, were on the receiving end of this tirade, and they looked completely overwhelmed, but not necessarily cooperative. Courage leaned forward, his eyes narrowing, and bared his fangs, hissing at them. His nose elongated slightly and his ears began to point.

The cable car was operational in seconds, and on its way down to them.

"What happened?" Allison whispered to him as the hum of the descending car filled the terminal.

"They've been shut down since the quake," John whispered back, "expecting aftershocks."

"You could have gone on without me," she said.

"No," he answered, a hand on her shoulder. "I need you for this, remember? And I have to conserve my strength for the battle; it would have been a huge drain to try to fly you up there."

She nodded, and the car arrived. As they got in, John turned to snarl at the operators again.

"When we're out, shut her down again," he said. "We won't be back this way."

Then the doors were closing, they were moving up the mountainside, and reporter that she was, Allison couldn't hold the questions back any longer.

"Why won't we be back this way?" she asked.

But Courage took it the wrong way. His face fell, disappointed, and it was a moment before Allison understood. Her question had been motivated by innocent curiosity, but in it he had heard suspicion, and now that she thought of it, she had reason to be suspicious. After all, if she needed the cable car to ascend, she couldn't conceive of a form of descent that would not require the car . . . unless she weren't coming back. It was an awkward moment between them, but John seemed finally to decide to ignore the less palatable implications of her question.

"There is only one way in, but there are many ways out," he said.

"In where?"

"Inside the mountain."

Allison raised an eyebrow, then looked out the window of the rising cable car, at the peak high above. When she turned back to John, he read the question in her eyes.

"You wouldn't believe me if I told you," he said, and she laughed.

"Give me a break, John! My boyfriend is Buffalo Bill! Man, get a grip, would you?"

Courage smiled and shook his head, but Allison felt a tightening in her chest as she thought of Will, trapped in that fortress. She shook it off, for the moment. They'd get him out. For now, her curiosity was getting the better of her.

"Well?" she asked.

John Courage joined her at the front of the cable car, looked up at the peak and put a hand on the glass.

"Inside that mountain," he said softly, "is a king."

It was only seven or eight minutes before they reached the top, and the view all around them was breathtaking. They were in high Alpine terrain, but the cold was not what Allison had imagined it would be. Still, it was early summer, and she didn't want to think about being up on that mountain in January. From the cable car terminal, they hiked up the mountain to the top of a steep, dangerous-looking trail. To Allison's surprise, there were still tourists on the mountain, as well as two employees who seemed quietly annoyed at having to baby-sit them. The employees didn't bat an eye as she and Courage crested the hill.

"Their friends at the bottom must have radioed up not to bother us," John said. "That's good. Still, now that the car's running again, it's going to be almost impossible for them to keep these people up here."

"I'm sure they'll be happy to be rid of them," Allison said, noting that the squabbling of the tourists was already getting results.

They started down the path, Allison stumbling from time to time, and came across a number of dead birds along their way.

"Ravens," Courage told her. "According to the legend, the king sleeps in the heart of the mountain with one hundred of his most loyal soldiers, and when Europe needs him most and the ravens no longer fly at the summit he will return. Magic works strangely at times," he said sadly, "but I didn't expect it to kill the poor guys."

Allison thought about the implications of those words, the suggestion that Courage at least knew a heck of a lot about magic and how this king had come to be under the mountain in the first place, and perhaps Courage had even been the one to put him there, to cast the spell about the ravens, whose death he now regretted.

Agh! There was so much she didn't know, but she was certain he wasn't about to tell her. They made their way along the face of the mountain, and their path grew more rough and narrow as they went, until finally it petered out altogether. Still, they went on, picking their way along a windblown ledge for a few minutes, with John holding Allison's elbow to keep her confidence up, until they came upon a crevice in the mountainside. The ledge they were on continued on the other side, but they weren't going that far.

"Fifth floor," Courage joked, "cosmetics, lingerie, young miss. Going down!"

Allison wasn't laughing.

"You're kidding, right? You've got me climbing along a mountainside and now you want me to crawl into a crack in the ground?"

"What did you expect?" Courage asked sincerely. "An escalator?"

"Well, maybe a ladder at least," she said weakly, looking upon the fissure with dread.

"For vampires?" he laughed. "Well, I'll go you one better."

John's hands slid under her arms and lifted her from the ground. Allison shrieked and struggled until she saw that the ground was no longer under her. She berated him as he lowered her into the hole in the ground, afraid he would drop her, certain he would drop her. And when he was kneeling at the edge of the crack, his arms extended as far inside as possible, and while Allison was yelling "Don't let go! Don't let go," that's just what he did.

"Now, don't move a muscle," he ordered as she dropped mere inches, her feet landing on a rocky shelf in the darkness of the hole.

"You son of a bitch," she snapped, angry and embarrassed. "You scared the daylights out of me."

When John had lowered himself down, they began to work their way along a stone path that sloped gently into the mountain. In minutes, Allison felt blind, and the darkness had become total.

"I can't see a blessed thing," she said, scared though his hand held hers tightly.

"Are you sure you want to?" he asked, and Allison nodded.

John's hand suddenly burst into flames, a torch of flesh, throwing flickering illumination around the cavern they'd found themselves in, and down into the blackness to their right. It looked like a nasty drop, and Allison realized why Courage had wanted her in the dark. Luckily heights were one thing she'd never had a problem with, and she did have him there to watch out for her should anything go wrong.

She noticed that up ahead a pile of huge stones lay in their path, effectively putting an end to the shelf they were walking on. She wondered what John would do about that, but he didn't even seem to slow down as he neared the rocks.

Even with the light from John's flaming hand, it was dark. Ghostly shapes flickered on the stone walls inside the crevice, and the world fell away into nothing only feet away.

Allison was afraid.

It was a difficult realization for her. After everything she'd been through in her life, she'd promised herself over and over that she'd never be afraid again. It was a promise she never kept. As a child, her parents had beaten her badly, for punishment rather than recreation, but it was still terrible abuse. Her mother had once broken her nose; blood had shot from her nostrils, and the old woman had actually hit her harder, as if that would stop the bleeding. She only thanked God that they hadn't been pedophiles, or she might have killed herself one of the many times she considered it.

The authorities had taken her away from them. She was an only child, and then she'd been set adrift in the foster care system, some of whose chosen parental replacements were no better than her originals. But finally she had found a home with Rory and Carole

Vigeant. When she'd gone undercover for CNN, in an elaborate ruse that included the very public termination of her job, she had used names from her past. Terry and Shaughnessy had been the last names of two foster families that she had particularly liked, so she became Terri Shaughnessy. Later, when she was working her way into the circle of volunteers, people who willingly gave up their blood and their lives to the Defiant Ones, she had been Tracey Sacco—her birth name, which she hated.

The Defiant Ones—what a joke. She had originally thought they were some kind of death cult, and they turned out to be vampires. Some were as evil as legend claimed. Others, unfortunate victims of an ancient, insane church conspiracy. She had watched a woman she knew be ravaged by Hannibal, who had raped her, held her captive, and was now a "respected" member of the shadow community. Then, later, she had met Will Cody, Peter Octavian and the rest, watched them fight for their lives, and fallen in love with Will.

And now she was following another vampire, one she barely knew, into the bowels of the Alps, where supposedly a hundred powerful vampires slept, and she would have to give her blood willingly to one of them in order to wake them up, to loose them upon an unsuspecting world. In order to do that, she had to put all of her faith in a man who wouldn't even tell her his real name . . . but then, she'd never been terribly forthcoming with her own. But what frightened her the most was that not far away, her lover's life, and thousands, perhaps millions, more, depended on their success.

Trust me, he says. As if she had a choice.

"There are two ways to do this," John said as they stopped short at the stone blockade across their path. "Hard and fast, or easy but slow. And we can't be wasting time. Step back a few yards, Allison, and lean against the wall. I'm afraid it's going to be dark in here for a minute or so. Whatever you do, don't move."

She didn't argue as John's flaming hand returned to normal. He took a deep breath, and she thought for the first time about the strain such a sustained combination of forms might cause . . . and then she couldn't hear him breathing anymore. In fact, though she wasn't about to move forward in the dark to test her theory, she didn't think he was even there, in front of her, anymore.

"John?" she called, and sure enough, there was no answer. It didn't occur to her that there were many forms he could take in which he couldn't answer. What did occur to her was that she did not hear rocks being moved, thrown over the side, stones grinding out of the way. The nothingness, which stretched out, away from the wall for several yards and then fell away into nothing, began to coalesce into something tangible. The lack of substance, the knowledge that there was nothing in front of her, and so much mountain above her, began to make Allison feel claustrophobic. And worse, she became disoriented, her center of gravity moving forward, her equilibrium unbalanced as if she actually wanted to go to the edge of the ledge, and past it, as if that were, somehow, right.

Once before she'd felt something like it, standing on one of the observation decks of the Empire State Building in New York City. But it had been a beautiful sunny day then, and she'd been with the Vigeants, her adoptive parents. Her body had felt strange, "funny," she'd said, but she hadn't been afraid then, hadn't been alone in the dark.

"John? John!" she yelled, slamming her back against the wall, bending over slightly to counter the magnetic draw the edge, the danger of it, held for her body. Could he possibly have brought her down here only to leave her?

No. That's idiotic. What purpose would it serve? And besides, she knew he was good, could sense it in him.

But then where was he?

Her eyes searched around her, frantically trying to pierce the darkness, trying to force her brain to access some hidden reserve, to *see* . . .

And then there came a roar, loud but muffled, as if it were beyond the stone barricade, and a terrible crashing, scraping, plowing sound as something shattered that barricade, tearing it down, sending stones ricocheting off the opposite wall, over the cavern, only to knock and skitter their way down into . . . whatever was down there. Allison automatically flung her arms up to protect herself and was glad she did when several small stone shards hit her and a good-size chunk of rock slammed into her shoulder, throwing her to the ground.

At first she sucked on her right hand, which was bleeding, but then she gave up and rubbed vigorously at her left shoulder where she'd been hit. She sensed it, sensed him, for she knew it was John, standing over her. But it wasn't him really, at that moment. Whatever stood there, it was huge, and its breath was heaving, panting, and it wasn't at all comfortable on two feet. A gorilla? she wondered. No, more likely a bear. But when his left hand burst into flame finally illuminating their path once again, he was just John Courage again, and she understood what he'd done.

The path they wanted was not along the ledge, beyond the barricade, but behind it, where the rocks had been piled up against the wall. He must have turned to mist and found his way through the rocks, only to transform again inside, taking a shape with the size and strength to drive through the barrier. A whole lot faster than trying to dig from outside. She wondered for a minute why there was such a good-size opening at all. Why take the chance, she wondered, when only vampires were inside? But then she remembered why she was there. Blood from a willing, human female. They needed to be sure their sacrificial lamb could get inside.

John was quiet now, and he looked exhausted, which didn't really surprise Allison. They made their way into this new tunnel, which went forward half a dozen feet, then turned a corner and down a crumbling, rocky slope for another dozen, after which it came to an end at a huge wooden door. The door was strapped together with iron, but it had no handle or knocker as far as Allison could tell. Somewhere, she heard a trickling sound, like a brook running, and she thought of melting snow from high up on the mountain.

John pounded on the door, but there was no response. Once again, he held up a fist and slammed it against the door, again and again, but still they heard nothing but their own mutterings and the echo of his "knock." Courage kept it up, knocking every minute or so, louder each time, though it seemed impossible.

And then they heard it, a rustling of movement behind the door, light footfalls on stone and then, finally, a voice, low and ominous, in a language Allison didn't think she'd ever heard before. Even so, she knew what its question must have been. John Courage replied in that same language, though it didn't seem to her that his reply included his own name, and certainly not hers.

And then another sound joined the others: that of a bolt being drawn back, large and rusted. The wood of the door seemed to have swollen tight with moisture, though Allison thought it quite dry at that moment, and though it scraped both floor and ceiling, the figure behind drew it open without any trouble.

And the tip of a long sword rested on John Courage's throat.

The holder of the sword was dressed all in a sort of linen, with a scabbard hung from his leather belt. On his feet he had leather shoes, which Allison immediately recognized as having been handmade, and probably not in this century, or the last. Over the linen pants he had wound some cloth around his legs, for what reason she could not guess.

He was not an attractive man. Though obviously clean, he had a scraggly beard and wild hair which, when combined with his thin lips and wide, flat nose gave him a bestial appearance.

Not to mention that sword.

John Courage spoke again in that language, which sounded familiar to her, fluid like Italian or Spanish, yet guttural as well. He spoke in calming, friendly tones, but the holder of the sword barked something in return, and Allison was discouraged.

"Can't you disarm him?" she hissed, and the warrior's eyes flicked to her for the first time, examining her as if he were window-shopping at the butcher's.

"Unnecessary" was Courage's only reply.

If you say so, she thought, but didn't speak again, because she didn't like the way the man with the sword looked at her. He barked something else and shook his head, and John continued to speak in that soothing voice. And then the voice changed suddenly, became deeper, older. Though she couldn't see him clearly from behind, Allison could tell that John was changing. His head seemed longer, his body thinner; his hair hung, now, long down his back, and she could see even from behind that he had a light edge of beard. His skin had darkened significantly, to almost an olive color. In short, though she couldn't see his face, she knew that John Courage looked nothing like the shadow she had come to know.

The sword fell clanging to the stone floor inside that door, and a moment later, its wielder was also there, prostrate on his knees, eyes downcast, hands together as if pleading for forgiveness, which was obviously what he *was* doing. When John leaned forward to urge the man to stand, Allison caught a good glimpse of his face in the fire-light he himself generated, but his features had returned to those she knew.

Clearly, John had been here before, and had worn a different face, one the guard, for she was sure that was what he was, had not only seen before, but respected, even feared.

Allison wasn't sure she liked that idea.

The warrior turned now, and led them through a stone tunnel and to a set of stairs, which eventually opened into a large cavern. The stairs went down and down, with John's fire lighting the way, and before long Allison realized that there were two more of the warriors behind her, following them.

"What language was that?" she asked John.

"Frankish."

"Uh-hmm," she said and nodded. "They seem to know you."

"Oh, they don't know me much better than you do," he said.

"Which is not at all," she said archly. "Never mind that I haven't yet prostrated myself before you."

John was quiet for a while, so Allison voiced the question currently on her mind.

"Why won't you tell me your real name?"

John stopped, turned and looked at her, studying her a moment. Allison was defiant, unintimidated, but not petulant. She needed to know what the hell was going on. The guards around them stood still, waiting for John to continue. He smiled at her kindly, without any trace of menace, and she felt somewhat more comfortable.

"You thought you had a story with Venice," he said. "Wait till you get to the bottom of this one."

Then he chuckled and turned away, and they continued down the stairs for a good five minutes more. Finally, the stairs ended at the floor of the cavern, stretched out far before them. Allison thought she could see still forms on the ground around them, but her eyes would not focus much past the circle of light thrown by John's flaming fist.

"Here we are," he said to her.

"Here?" she asked. "How 'bout some light?"

Courage said something quickly to their companions, and the one who had confronted them pointed ahead to the right. John walked forward, leaving Allison in the dark, but she was nervous about doing anything that might set off their guards, so she waited for him to give the word. He didn't. But she could still see him as he moved to the wall of the cavern. As he moved farther from her, but closer to the wall, she saw a huge iron chain hitched by a single link to an iron spike that had been hammered into the wall. John said something, and the two who had been following Allison rushed to him and, pulling the chain from the spike, played out two dozen rusty feet of slack that had been coiled on the stone floor.

Above them, Allison heard a creaking and rattling as a huge weight descended. It drew her attention but also made her suddenly aware again of the sound of running water, which had disappeared for a while but now was back, and louder than before. Courage, with his light, came closer to her, and they both craned their necks to see whatever was rattling its way down to them. As it came lower Allison began to make out a huge circle of iron, more than twenty feet in diameter, and through its center the elaborate network of chains that held it aloft. In seconds it hung six feet above the floor, and John walked over and stood under it.

And Allison finally realized what it was: a chandelier.

John turned in a circle, his fiery touch reaching out to the huge candles melted onto the iron. Allison wondered how long it had been since those candles had been lit, but she didn't need to worry about whether they would still burn. Moments later, the two guards were hoisting the chandelier once again toward the ceiling of the cavern, and Allison looked around, nearly overwhelmed by what the light had revealed.

She thought back to what John had told her, to his vague words: *The king sleeps in the heart of the mountain with one hundred of his most loyal soldiers, and when Europe needs him most, and the ravens no longer fly at the summit, he will return.*

She had been able to pass off the dead ravens; after all, they might have been some sign of Mulkerrin's return, his influence. But now, in the heart of the mountain, Allison Vigeant was looking at one hundred sleeping soldiers in linen and leather, covered in furs, with swords at their sides. Far to her left, an underground stream ran through the cavern, above her the candles burned on, and across the huge room, opposite the stairs they had walked down, was what might have been an altar. On top of it was a bed carved of stone, and upon that bed lay the creature of legend. Even in that repose, he looked like a king.

"Come," John said, taking her by the hand and leading her across the room. They moved carefully around the dead-looking forms of the soldiers, and the three who had escorted them followed behind and kneeled at the base of the stone upon which their leader lay. But she and John continued up those steps, and in a moment, she was looking down upon his face.

His eyes were closed, but there were bags under them and his face was deeply lined. His long hair and equally long beard and bushy mustache were a reddish brown, streaked with gray. His nose was aquiline, his cheekbones high and proud, and his skin was the white of ivory, as had been the skin of the sleeping men behind Allison. He was dressed very much like his soldiers, save for the blue cloak that was wrapped about him, the silk edges of his tunic, and the pure gold belt and scabbard he wore. His crown sat next to his head on the stone bed. It was gold, encrusted with jewels, and had a cross on top. Only when John Courage touched her arm was Allison able to tear her gaze away. The man was fascinating to look at.

"Are you sure you want to do this?" John asked, and she thought that was a pretty stupid question. She'd come all this way, and the life of the man she loved, not to mention so many others, hung in the balance.

She raised a sarcastic eyebrow, a comment he'd become used to in the short time they'd known each other, and no other reply was necessary. The blood of a willing human female was needed. As far as she could tell, she was the only female at the party, not to mention the only human!

John reached behind him, and one of the soldiers kneeling there stood to hand up his sword. He took Allison's hand and lay the sword in her palm, and then before she had time to think about it, he drew the blade across her flesh. She flinched, wanting to pull her hand away, but his strength held her there as her eyes began to water.

"*Mother of God!*" she hissed, but that was all, as she bit her lip. John curled her hand into a fist and kissed her knuckles before handing the sword back to its owner. He nodded his approval of her strength, of her determination, and yet Allison could see the sympathy he felt for her pain.

"Let it drip on his lips," John said, and she turned, held her hand above the old king's face and bled.

His lips parted slightly, and Courage told her it was enough. Allison stepped back as the king's eyes opened and he smiled. His tongue slid out and cleaned his mouth of her blood, and she couldn't help but shiver. She watched as John Courage helped him sit up, and then stand. They exchanged greetings in a language she recognized—Latin—but again she could not understand. The old king had known John immediately, not needing the shapechange that his soldier had, and to Allison's incredible surprise, attempted to kneel before him. But Courage wouldn't have it, looking around at Allison with an almost annoyed glance, muttering something to the king.

Finally, the old warrior's eyes rested on her, and then he smiled benevolently and took the few steps toward her. One hand on the pommel of the sword hanging at his side, he made a deep, regal bow and then looked at John Courage for assistance.

"Your Majesty," John said in English, "it is my pleasure to present Allison Vigeant."

"Allison," he said, finally turning his attention back to her. "I'd like you to meet Carolus Magnus, whom some have called the father of Europe. Better known to you, of course, as Charlemagne."

And behind them, an army began to rise.

9

Hannibal was many things, but foolish was not among them. He was perfectly aware that every ranking officer, and probably most of their subordinates, involved with Operation: Jericho suspected him of duplicity. When they separated, he had earned several suspicious and even fearful glances, and certainly every member of Commander Jimenez's strike team had been prepped for his possible betrayal.

No, Hannibal was no fool, but he suspected those around him, human and vampire alike, were fools indeed. Did they actually believe he would side with Mulkerrin? Such a concept was ridiculous. However, Mulkerrin's presence did provide Hannibal's own plans with a perfect diversion. If the sorcerer managed to defeat the forces arrayed against him, *then* Hannibal would step in and finish the job. In the meantime, he would use the opportunity to set his plans in motion. Hannibal was crafting a new future for the world, and though some might disagree with him, he vowed to become the savior of his people. One day, they would revere his name.

For the moment, Hannibal sat calmly in the back of a troop carrier, along with his deputy, Rolf Sechs, six other shadows, and a crowd of human soldiers including UNSF Commander Roberto Jimenez. Jimenez was making inquiries and delivering orders over a complicated communications system that each member of the United Nations security force carried in the collar of his or her uniform. Even the agents and marshals of the Shadow Justice System had been given uniforms with these collarcomms for Operation: Jericho. Though unadorned, the uniforms of each unit were different colors, all dark variants on green, blue and brown. The shadows wore gray, and the rest of Jimenez's strike team wore black.

The collarcomms interested Hannibal only in that he was privy to every conversation among the UN commanders. Each unit's leader, in this case each commander had two channels, one on either side of the head. The left side was for general communication within the commander's own unit, the right for communication with the other commanders and with Jimenez himself. Some of the seconds, including Rolf, had both channels as well, but Hannibal was not concerned. Rolf could listen, but not speak. And Hannibal had a third channel, which he could switch to whenever he wished by depressing a button on his collar, and which cut off communication to all SJS agents who were not on his handpicked team.

"All units have reported arriving at preliminary rendezvous, Chief Marshal," Roberto Jimenez said. "We are the last to reach our position. Everything proceeds on schedule."

These were the first words the UNSF commander had spoken to him, or any of the shadows, since they had departed Munich. He had not even spoken to Rolf, whom Hannibal thought Jimenez might actually trust.

"I have ears, Commander," Hannibal said, having indeed listened quite closely as the other commanders made their reports to Jimenez. "We are not *that* different."

Hannibal turned to Rolf then.

"And so thus far, Commander Thomas is safe and sound. An admirable woman, don't you think?" he asked his subordinate.

Rolf glared at Hannibal, but did not bother pulling the voice-pad from his belt. Roberto Jimenez raised his eyebrows but said nothing, and the other soldiers on the strike team, shadows included, were intelligent enough to look only at their feet.

Hannibal chuckled to himself as Rolf looked away. Did the fool really think he was not spied upon? Did he truly expect Hannibal to miss something as monumental as the coupling of the American commander and the deputy marshal of the Shadow Justice System? Ah, well, sex will do that, Hannibal thought. He mourned once again Rolf's unflagging loyalty to his dead mentor's clan, to Gallagher, Nueva and Cody. The mute would have been an asset, no question, to Hannibal's plans, especially considering his new involvement with Commander Thomas.

The lingering smirk on Hannibal's face finally drove Rolf to reply. He took out his voice-pad and wrote: "None of us is safe while Mulkerrin lives."

Hannibal only nodded, with a slight shrug and an innocent look on his face. Oh, Rolf certainly knew something was up. In fact, Hannibal took a particular pleasure in confusing his deputy. For instance, he had allowed Rolf to handpick the six shadows who would accompany Jimenez's strike team. Rolf could then be certain Hannibal's accomplices would not be among them, or so he thought. Hannibal had enjoyed the surprise on Rolf's face when he had not argued the choices, and in his frustration, Rolf had changed the lineup several times, finally giving up when Hannibal still did not respond.

The truck rolled along the *bundestrasse*, Route 155 according to the signs, and out the back they were able to see the traffic leaving the city, the broken-down vehicles, and . . . *Ah, there we are*, Hannibal thought, *a stray*! As the truck carrying the strike team passed, Austrian soldiers emptied automatic weapons into the still moving body of a demon-creature who had strayed too far from the city. There would be many who wandered away from Salzburg without being killed, Hannibal knew, and he made a mental note to try and round those up when all of this was over. It was likely they could be put to good use.

The strike team did not stop to help the Austrian troops, who may or may not have succeeded. Hannibal looked over at Jimenez, but his face was a mask of meditation, as were those of the rest of the soldiers. Only Hannibal seemed above the grave atmosphere in the truck, and he knew his levity was unappreciated. He glanced at Rolf and saw that, though also serious, the mute was concentrating on something other than Operation: Jericho. He was staring at Hannibal with open suspicion and dislike, even hate.

Excellent. Hannibal hated phonies.

The truck slowed down and took a right turn. Hannibal saw the sign for Rudolf-Biebl-Strasse, and snickered at the street name.

"All units," Jimenez touched his right collarbone, "move to secondary positions immediately. Rodriguez, lock in holding pattern above Jericho. Austrian emergency personnel will be behind you so, do not, I repeat, do not stop to assist civilians. Sweep the streets, flamethrowers up front. Destroy all hostiles. Move out."

Hannibal closed his eyes, knowing that Rolf would be certain to notice and not caring if he did. He listened carefully as each commander detailed his or her unit's move from preliminary to secondary position.

Commander Thomas's unit had encountered fourteen demons of varying sizes on her short trek to Rainberg. There had been no concentrated resistance whatsoever, as the demons seemed to be roaming about with no direction. Commander Gruber's troops had met with an extraordinarily large water-based shadow in the river, and two of the Ducks had been capsized, several men killed. Still, they made it to Mozart's Plaza with nearly their entire complement, thanks in large part to the efforts of the SJS soldiers with them.

Commander Locke's unit had met almost no resistance on their march from Hellbrun Castle to the stadium. In fact, there had been little by way of destruction, either from demons or from the earthquake, and the area had been the fastest and easiest to evacuate. Commander Surro's troops had had slightly more trouble, but were lucky to find the bridge intact when it came time for them to cross the Salzach. The two units had combined and scaled the mountainside, encountering a huge number of shadows and setting fire to a large portion of the woods below Nonnberg Abbey, where Maria Von Trapp was said to have been a novice. When Locke brought this up, Surro merely scowled at him over her collarcomm. Nevertheless, and again with the help of the shadows, their secondary position was attained.

In all, though the total number of troops including the paratroopers had been nearly twenty-five hundred, only thirty-seven soldiers had been lost, twelve of them Austrians who had been killed during earlier evacuations. It had been much too easy.

"It's a mousetrap," Hannibal suddenly said aloud, and this time the strike force did look at him, some with open hostility. Rolf looked ready to pounce if he made a move.

"What?" Jimenez snapped.

"It's a mousetrap, Commander." And now Hannibal smiled, for though this was not a part of his plan, it would certainly be a joy to watch.

"Mulkerrin is the cheese, you see," he said seriously, lecturing. "He's there, all right, waiting for you. The real thing. But the closer you get, the greater your danger of having your back broken."

"There are thousands of us!" Jimenez said.

"Ah, true," Hannibal said, "but his reinforcements are endless. He can demolish your troops even if you're a million miles away, in safety, but to stem the tide of his creatures, you've got to kill *him*."

"We've destroyed all the creatures we've found."

"Ah, yes, but now reverse the analogy," Hannibal said. "For every rodent you kill, there are usually a dozen more lurking about, in their holes, waiting for you to turn your back."

Jimenez just looked at Hannibal for a minute, and the vampire knew that the commander was trying to decide what to believe. Hannibal watched as he looked over at Rolf, obviously seeking a second opinion. When the mute simply nodded, Jimenez swore loudly, even as he thumbed his collarcomm.

"Do it!" he ordered. "Move in, fry anything that gets in your way, and watch your asses. It's possible we've been flanked. Rodriguez, when the front door goes down, your people hit the silk."

There was one thing Hannibal admired about Jimenez, though he was loath to admit it. The human had a no-bullshit attitude and didn't rely on moronic military jargon, code words and the like. He was all soldier, and showed not a trace of the officer he'd become. He played by his own rules. It was a shame the commander hated shadows so much, or Hannibal might have made him one.

On the other hand, Hannibal realized, that could still be amusing.

As the huge attack force began to converge on the fortress and the strike force abandoned their vehicle to walk the last half mile—knowing that being inside the truck would be a liability—around them, before them and especially behind them, portals that had been opened during the earthquake now spewed forth hundreds of demonic creatures. New portals began to open in the side of the fortress wall itself, demon-creatures leaping from within to tumble down the slopes out of control, savaging whatever soldiers were in their way when they finally regained their footing.

And while Jimenez barked orders into his collarcomm, Hannibal began to change. By the time Jimenez turned to seek his help, all he saw was Rolf Sechs diving through a cloud of mist, trying to grab at it as it drifted away.

Hell.
Twenty-Four Days, One Hour, Sixteen Seconds
After Departure:

Meaghan Gallagher knew very little about her current situation, but there were two things of which she was certain. She and Lazarus were in Hell, which for the first time in her life she really thought of with a capital H, and her one, true love, Alexandra Nueva, was dead.

It was not a simple bit of knowledge, but rather one she had come to understand over days, weeks. Her first love, Janet Harris, had been killed by the sorcerer Liam Mulkerrin. They were now in search of her second, Peter Octavian, whom, though she had never been certain of his death, she had never expected to see again. She felt nothing regarding a possible reunion with Peter, except a slight glimmer of hope that they would somehow escape this place in time to prevent Mulkerrin from turning Earth into a world overrun by monsters, a world like that darkened plane they had passed through on their way to Hell.

First Janet, then Peter, and now Alex, whom she'd loved most, and best. Alexandra had been an angry woman at first, and a vicious one, but their initial coupling had led quickly to Alex remembering her humanity, regretting many of her actions, and allowing love and kindness back into her world. Meaghan had fallen in love with her easily after that. It had been Alex who'd engineered Meaghan's leadership of the shadows, not anything of her own doing. It had been Alex who had brainstormed the Shadow Justice System. It had been Alex who pushed Cody back into the limelight, forced him to become everything he was capable of.

Alexandra Nueva had been the rhyme and reason behind so much of the new existence for their people, and behind Meaghan Gallagher's entire existence. And now she was dead. Of course, at first Meaghan had argued with Lazarus. She knew that there were very few things from which shadows would not recover. But Lazarus brought her again and again back to the moment when she had seen the horrible, burning faces in that hole sucking Alex's flames in through their mouths and nostrils, flames that were Alex herself, body and soul. She had been consumed by dozens of different creatures, split apart and digested in so many pieces. Only now, after countless days, could Meaghan really admit the truth.

Her lover was dead. The hours of begging Lazarus to return to that spot, to attempt to revive Alex—that was all over. After it had happened, they had continued down the ever-steeper, ever-narrower tunnel, until it had indeed become a hole. As mist, then, they had floated down that well, finding nothing for hours, perhaps more than a day. Once in a while, tired of keeping the one form, or perhaps too comfortable in it, they would shapeshift into bats so that they could rest, tiny claws stuck to the rock walls of the hole.

Twice they had floated on past "throats" similar to that which had consumed Alexandra—killed her—but they were mist and passed so quickly the hands and mouths could not touch them. In the end, the hole began to widen, and turn so that eventually it became a tunnel again, and when it did, they changed into their human forms and took turns sleeping, something neither had *had* to do in a long time. Lazarus's patience grew ever shorter in dealing with her outbursts concerning Alex, and he became more and more concerned with the barrenness they'd found thus far in Hell. Their prospects of finding Peter and escaping with him seemed to grow more dim with each passing hour.

As the days had passed, Meaghan lost her faith in Lazarus. Once he had seemed so powerful to her, so filled with knowledge. She had respected that, feared him in a way. No more. Though she was certain there were many things about their plight that he kept from her, she knew there was also much he had been unprepared for, unaware of, and she didn't look to him for answers anymore.

Now, as they made their way through the tunnel, after weeks of traveling, Meaghan found it quite strange that she had no need of sustenance, and apparently neither did her companion. Had she gone so long without blood in her own world, she would have been a ravenous lunatic by now. Perhaps, she considered, though they felt each moment pass, though their bodies told them when another day had ended, perhaps the bloodthirst was still governed, through some tenuous connection, by the far slower passage of time in their own world.

Suddenly Meaghan was sure this was the truth. Which would mean that, though weeks had gone by in Hell, less than a day had passed on the other side. Why, the battle had barely begun! Though she knew her certainty might be somewhat premature, Meaghan was excited. She and Lazarus would now be able to tell time in their own world based upon the bloodthirst. Their suffering would be their clock.

She was about to tell him when the tunnel began to widen drastically, and she saw that they were coming into a cavern ahead. Unlike the stovepipe where they had first arrived, and the tunnel in which Alex had met her end, the solid rock path they had been following had very little light. There had been few of the fiery cracks in its walls, but luckily there had been enough for their vampiric vision.

The cavern they entered now had plenty of light. Flames licked the walls of the enormous, empty space. At the opposite end, the cavern opened onto the edge of a flaming pit at the bottom of a stovepipe. It might have been the pit they'd appeared in originally, or it might not— Meaghan could not say. At the edge of the pit stood a naked man, or something like a man. They approached with caution, yet before they had taken half a dozen steps in his direction the man turned and motioned for them to come closer.

"Take a look," he said, motioning to the pit. "It's really quite fascinating."

And they did. In the pit, atop huge stones red with fire, bodies writhed in ecstasy and torment. Like those they had seen tumbling through the stovepipe so long ago, some looked human while others were not even vaguely humanoid. It was impossible to tell how many different beings were in the pit. Meaghan refused to consider the implications, to wonder how these creatures had gotten to Hell and what their crimes had been. She would not bow to the Judeo-Christian myths she had been taught as a girl.

"That would be wise," the man said, and she flinched.

He had read her mind! This could not be one of the damned, whatever they were, she thought. This was a true demon, not like the shadows they had battled before, not like those creatures who had been enslaved by Mulkerrin's magic.

"Everything you see is real, tangible," the demon went on, apparently ignoring her thoughts now. "But the logic behind the Suffering, which is what we prefer to call them, the reasons for their presence, their purpose, is nothing you could ever hope to understand."

Out of the corner of her eye, Meaghan noticed movement, and far across the pit she saw a shadow-demon, apparently slave to the true demon, the size of an elephant. It plowed through the damned, the Suffering as the demon called them, with its huge snout. Every so often, it hung its head back, chewing—its jaws munching the bodies—and swallowing, not for a moment distracted by the shrieking and moaning all around it. The thing digested the sufferers and, as the three of them looked on, shat them out whole, covered with some kind of waste. The thing moved on, and the shit-covered sufferers shrieked insanely, knowing that it would be back for them again.

Meaghan was finally able to turn away, and she felt quite sick in her stomach. Even though she would have found an open artery quite attractive at the moment, the shit and blood that swirled in this enormous pigpen disgusted her beyond words.

"It's a dirty job, but someone's got to do it," the demon said, and giggled, reading her mind again.

"Lazarus?" she asked when she realized he'd not spoken a word since they'd emerged from the tunnel. She turned to find him with his back to the pit, though keeping the demon in his peripheral vision. Standing there, erect and proud, his face more sad than repulsed, he gave Meaghan a sense for the first time of an innate goodness in this vampire. Though many others, herself included, tried hard, there was something in Lazarus she had not ever sensed in their kind. At that moment, he looked almost—*No*. Meaghan stopped that line of thought. No matter what good could be found in her people, no matter what words could be used to describe them, she found it impossible to think of any of her kind as "holy."

Lazarus smiled at her then, dispelling the image. He looked as if he were about to speak, finally, but his mouth snapped shut, and they both turned their full attention back to the demon at the pit's edge. It was changing.

"Really," the creature said, "this was just for you two. I didn't want to scare you off, you know."

The demon grew then, its true form bursting through the skin facade it wore. A ripple of horns like daggers stood along its spine, and its talons hung nearly to the ground. The thing's hair burned, and the face fell down around its neck like a scarf. Its true head was cloven halfway to the snout and flames leapt from inside the beast's skull.

It lifted its hands, and fire sprang up from the pit, singeing their faces and shooting up through the stovepipe in a terrible torrent. It lasted for several seconds, and when it ended, a shower of bodies began to fall, their flesh slapping into the pile and onto the rocks with the sound of raw meat dropped into a sizzling pan. When the demon finally turned its three eyes back on them, all the humor had fled its demeanor, and only a cruel cynicism remained. Meaghan thought it strange that she had never worried about the creature's attacking them, but Hell had been affecting their thought processes from the beginning. She promised herself that they would be more careful.

"Lord Alhazred," Lazarus said, bowing, and the demon's eyes narrowed.

"How do you know my name?" the demon-lord demanded, but Lazarus ignored the question.

"I bear the greetings of the Stranger," he said, and the demon blinked several times, surprised, and then sneered.

"Do you, now?" it said, with a voice like an echo in an empty room. "It has been a long time since we have seen the Stranger, down here," the demon said to Lazarus though it continued to look at Meaghan.

"He is well," Lazarus said. "However, he needs your assistance."

"Does he?" Lord Alhazred said, and Meaghan noticed the demon's penchant for responding with questions.

"You are surprised?" Meaghan asked, quickly, earning a sharp look from Lazarus and a noticeable twitch in the huge horn that now protruded from between the demon's legs.

"Should I be?"

"You don't know?"

"You don't think so?"

"Should we think so?"

The demon-lord stopped then, staring at her, tired of its own game. "What do you seek?" it asked.

"One like ourselves, Peter Octavian by name," she said "also known as Nicephorus Dragases."

"He's a prisoner?"

"We don't know," Lazarus said, trying to regain control. "He came here a long time ago, with another named Mulkerrin. Mulkerrin has escaped, and the Stranger wishes to send him back to you, but to do so we need this Octavian."

"I remember the arrival, I admit," Alhazred said and nodded, finally giving up its game of questions. "But they weren't my responsibility."

"Can you help us?" Meaghan pushed. "Will you?"

"A request from the Stranger?" The demon-lord laughed shrilly, cynically. "Of course I'll help."

It gestured toward the tunnel from which they'd emerged, and then it disappeared. A portal appeared in its place, burning red with flame rather than silver like those they had seen before. Meaghan was immediately concerned. This demon-lord seemed malicious enough, and she suspected malevolent was closer to the truth. Could this portal be a trap?

"Oh, it's safe, foolish vampire," the mind reader said and laughed. "It would be in bad form to destroy agents of the Stranger. This is the fastest way for me to help you. Through there you'll find many more of the Suffering, but if you ask the other lords, you may find your friends' point of arrival. From there, well, you never know."

The creature turned back to its work, raising its hands so the flames leapt up again, bodies raining down in their wake.

"How do they come to be here?" Meaghan forced herself to ask.

Lord Alhazred turned around, shaking its head.

"Silly thing," it said. "The Suffering are always here, no matter where else they may be."

Lazarus grabbed her hand and pulled her toward the portal. The passage was not as painful as she had expected. And of course, nothing compared to what the Suffering endured.

Salzburg, Austria, European Union.
Wednesday, June 7, 2000, 7:11 A.M.:

Knowing.

That was the strangest thing about it. The knowing. He knew, for instance, that dozens of feet above the chamber in which he lay, the sorcerer Liam Mulkerrin worked his magic, marshaled his forces. The fortress was like a small village surrounded by stone walls, and it was nearly filled with his soldiers, living, breathing human beings whose bodies had been invaded, possessed, by the spirits of those who had once been posted to that place. The spirits themselves were not evil, but the semblance of life Mulkerrin offered them in exchange for their service was irresistible.

He knew.

Soldiers manned the open windows, though many were hundreds of feet atop sheer walls. Huge, mindless slave demons patrolled the battlements of the fortress and prowled the many halls of the lower levels even as hundreds of their kindred poured out of new passages onto the Earth plane, tearing into those who would lay siege to Mulkerrin's base.

He knew.

The battle raged all around the monolithic structure and though the humans held their own, in the end, the battle was destined to be quite one-sided. Mulkerrin's resources were almost limitless, and yet he could feel that the once-priest did not know his own abilities well enough to use them, and what he did use took a toll on him, his grip on the magic being tenuous. The sorcerer stood in the middle of the open courtyard in the center of the fortress, his concentration complete. He was surrounded by a black, swirling mist through which he was nearly invisible, though the sun shone down on the courtyard.

And that was beginning to change. Thunderclouds pregnant with a monstrous storm, glowing with a sickly, reddish radiance which the human soldiers below deemed wholly unnatural, moved slowly in from the south, as if answering a call Mulkerrin had sent.

He knew, but it wasn't knowledge that came from experience— not from seeing, or hearing, or touching. It was a transcendant awareness which reached out from that cold, dark chamber and encircled the fortress, not yet able to envelop completely the battle, the attacking forces, but spreading. He knew Mulkerrin, then, completely and totally, the sorcerer not believing such an intrusion possible and therefore not registering the subtle penetration of his soul. Of his magic. The knowledge, the awareness, met the magic, and danced with it in the ether, becoming intertwined with the magic, intrinsic to it. Whatever Mulkerrin commanded, that joining gave him knowledge of, awareness of. And that awareness sent tendrils of anger, hatred, disgust, into the magic, not tugging or pulling, not screaming, but insinuating, tainting, whispering to it, so that it changed.

And in the glory that was his evil, Mulkerrin barely noticed.

Down in that cold, dark chamber, at the center of the awareness that enveloped the fortress, that joined with and unsettled the magic, he lay. And below the awareness, the knowing, the magic, was pain. Pain both simple in its totality and incredibly complex in its persistence.

His blood had been spreading in a large pool for many hours and was beginning to cake into many of the grooves between the stones of the floor. The gaping hole in his chest, where the bones stuck sharply out at all angles, had long since stopped sucking at the air. His eyes were open, but he did not see. He did not blink, or breathe, did not smell, or hear.

His hair was long and white, the beard and mustache the same color, and his skin was mottled, wrinkled and pale. His body was tiny, shriveled, the hands like claws, the limbs truncated. Rot had appeared in several places, especially around the ragged chest wound.

Thum-tum.

A trill went out, into the awareness and the magic, and Mulkerrin felt it, through yards of stone, like a pre-orgasmic shiver. The sorcerer merely laughed, thinking it nothing more than the rush of the magic.

Thum-tum.

This time, the awareness suppressed the trill, confined the tickle of it to a more subtle level. He reached out, with his own awareness, and smoothed out the lines of what he felt. Above the pain, within it, enveloping it and giving it birth, he knew.

Thum-tum, thum-tum, thum-tum.

He knew.

Thum-tum, thum-tum, thum-tum, thum-tum, thum-tum thum-tum, thum-tum, thum-tum, thum-tum, thum-tum, thum-tum.

The newly formed, tiny, infant heart rattled along like a freight train, speeding out of control to do a job it was never meant for. It screamed at the trauma of the pain, but kept drumming as a thin film of muscle stretched across the open wound. Around the body, blood that had dried, scabbing the stone floor, was wet again, warm again. And just as it had slowly seeped from him, pooling on the floor, so now it was absorbed by his skin, through his pores, flowing back into his body like the tide rolling in. And high tide wouldn't be long.

Cody knew.

10

The American media had become far too powerful over the past few decades, and as Henry Russo, the President of the United States, prepared for his midnight address, he silently vowed to himself to research new ways to stifle their nagging, insistent voices, at least to quiet them long enough for a man to think! *Call it censorship*, he thought. *Call it whatever the hell you like!* Nevertheless, he would not be bullied by a bunch of reporters.

Or so he told himself. In reality, that was exactly what had happened in the past, and what had happened today. Doubtless, despite his best efforts, it would continue long into the future. Though there was not yet news from inside Salzburg, word from Austrian media had been pouring in all day. First about the earthquake, felt by a very few, and then about the military evacuation taking place. In addition, several people had been picked up on the outskirts of the city, apparently refugees, spinning tales of monsters rising from the earth. Of course, it didn't help that Doris Toumarkine from *The Hollywood Reporter* had called to confirm a story that Will Cody and Allison Vigeant had been in Salzburg at the time. Heaven forbid somebody not know where celebrities were vacationing!

Just fucking dandy!

Henry had held off as long as he could, but with Operation: Jericho already under way, it would do no harm to present the news of that op to the world. Certainly, it was his duty as President to be sure his own press conference was held before that of the UN secretary general. And he knew Rafael Nieto would be up at first light with a report of the battle. No matter that they fought the war together—the political skirmishing must go on. And maybe then he could get these reporters out of his hair, just for a little while.

"Henry?" Julie Graham stepped into the Oval Office and he smiled at her, despite his mental grumbling.

"Come on in."

"Bill was a little worried about you, wanted me to check in," she said, her raised eyebrow enough to make him certain of the joke.

Ah, the joke. William Galin, the vice president, hated him more than anything else in the world. In fact, it wouldn't have surprised Henry to learn that Bill Galin wanted him dead. He had, after all, chosen Bill as his running mate essentially to keep an eye on him. Bill was an excellent politician, but to those who knew him, he was also a bigoted, classist, sexist, petty egotist who might have given Henry a terrible time down the road.

With Bill as his running mate, Henry had been assured of a certain number of ultraconservative votes, as well as almost the entire middle-of-the-road constituency. Once in office, he had put Galin under his thumb, had, in effect, banned him from the White House. The man had become more invisible than any public official since Dan Quayle. In fact, the only time the public really saw him was behind the President at the podium. But it just went back to something Henry's parents had taught him growing up: children—especially petulant children—should be seen and not heard.

"Henry, you okay?" Julie's concern wiped away the scowl Bill Galin always brought to the President's face.

"Yeah, Jules. Sit down."

"Look, I know you've got this thing scheduled for midnight," she said, taking the leather chair in front of Henry's desk she had long thought of as "hers," "but the media is going crazy. Maybe we should bump this thing up, startle them for once?"

Henry shook his head.

"What do you mean? Why are they any crazier than they were?"

"Nobody tells you anything, do they?" Julie said, eyebrows creased and without a trace of humor. "Somebody leaked word of Gallagher and Nueva's disappearance, for starters. And to top it off, the name 'Mulkerrin' is already on the wire."

"Shit."

Henry was up and out of his chair in no time. He didn't even bother to grab his jacket.

"Is Marcopoulos here?" he said as he swung the door open.

"I don't know," Julie answered, following swiftly, even as Henry's personal contingent of Secret Service jumped to attention and swarmed around them, muttering into their collarcomms as they went. Gary Williams, the agent-in-charge at the moment, flanked the President on one side, and Julie was on the other.

"Get the VP," Julie said to Williams as they hustled, the fed-up look never leaving the President's face. Williams merely lifted a finger, and two agents ran on ahead.

As they approached the conference room, George Marcopoulos stepped out of a side corridor, followed immediately by Vice President Galin and the agents Williams had dispatched.

"Henry?" Galin frowned, obviously flustered. "What's the rush?"

The agent in the lead banged open the conference room doors, throwing the press into a whirl of activity, for once taking them completely by surprise. Henry almost smiled at that, as he turned to look at Galin, who fell into step just behind him.

"I'm through playing games," he snapped, and then he was mounting the dais amid a hundred voices asking questions, camera lights popping on. Galin, Marcopoulos and Julie Graham stood behind him, as their chairs had not yet been set up. Henry tapped the mike to see if it was on, and when he discovered it was not, he simply shouted.

"Quiet!"

The room was suddenly silent, and behind him Julie Graham tried not to laugh, wondering how this would all play out in the press. She knew that was the last thing on Henry's mind, and she was glad. But beside her, Bill Galin cringed.

"Now, ladies and gentlemen of the press, a brief statement and then I'll be happy to answer any questions," the President began, rising up to his full height behind the podium and lowering his voice when the microphone suddenly snapped on. Behind him, chairs were put in place and the others sat down.

"Please be aware that what I'm about to do is almost unheard of in politics: I'm going to give you the facts. I'm tired of rumor, hearsay and outright falsehood. So here goes.

"Early this morning, Liam Mulkerrin took over the Fortress Hohensalzburg in Salzburg, Austria. Not long afterward, an earthquake reportedly took place in Salzburg. I say reportedly, because this quake did not register on the Richter scale at all. William Cody is apparently Mulkerrin's prisoner at this time. A UN Security Force operation is under way to assist Austrian troops in the evacuation of the area and the capture of Mulkerrin.

"Questions?"

The Warner Network correspondent was the first with her hand up.

"Yes?"

"Mulkerrin was reported dead after the Venice Jihad. Why? And what involvement do Meaghan Gallagher and Alexandra Nueva have in this operation?"

The President scowled, openly, on international television. Anyone watching could easily have seen the smile that spread across Julie Graham's face then.

"Mulkerrin was *believed* dead, Marinna," the President said. "As far as Nueva and Gallagher are concerned, as you may have heard, their whereabouts are unknown."

The room exploded with new questions, but Henry pointed to Pamela Martin from CNN.

"Mr. President," she said grimly, "we've all seen the video from Venice. What of the reports of similar creatures in Salzburg, and do you know whether Allison Vigeant was taken captive with Mr. Cody?"

"I've seen the video too," Henry answered. "I hope there's no truth to that, and no, we've no word about Ms. Vigeant."

Before he could even choose another hand, the Fox correspondent spoke up.

"In light of their suspicious disappearance, could the shadows be involved with Mulkerrin's return?"

Even from behind, Julie Graham could see that the President was about to blow his stack. Barely thinking, she elbowed George Marcopoulos, who was on the same wavelength and already standing up. Marcopoulos cleared his throat, and the President turned around even as he began a stern warning to the media never to jump to such conclusions.

"Ah, it appears that Ambassador Marcopoulos has a response to your question," Henry said, and stepped from the podium to allow George to approach.

"You may be sorry," he whispered to the President as he stepped up next to him and leaned into the mike.

"I am appalled that such questions may be asked at a time like this. Human and shadow are united against a common enemy. The SJS fights side by side with the UN Security Force. Will Cody is captive, perhaps dead. If two prominent shadows have disappeared, we should be concerned for their safety, not accusing them of betrayal. As you say, you've seen the video, you know how many of their people were murdered by this madman. And you suggest they are in league with him? Like all minorities before them, like all humans in fact, there is evil to be found among the shadows. But we cannot turn on our allies because they frighten us!"

Bravo . . . A voice floated out, over the audience, seemingly soft but loud enough for everyone to hear clearly . . . *Well said, dear George, but you see, your services are no longer required.*

And then they were there, six of them, in the room where they hadn't been before. Nobody, not even the Secret Service, had seen the mist creeping along the floor, so fine as to be almost invisible. Now, for some, it was too late. Four of the creatures were in the audience, tearing the cameras from the grasp of frightened, soon-to-be-dead media personnel. The two others, a tall black male and a slick, deadly-looking Asian, were on the stage.

"Mr. President!" Agent Williams shouted, up the steps with other agents in tow. But the Asian vampire, apparently the leader, already had him.

Knocking George Marcopoulos into the vice president and the secretary of state behind him, the creature clutched the President's neck with one hand, lifting him from the ground, and grabbed the microphone with the other. Before it could speak, it was buried, along with the President, in a pile of Secret Service agents. A dozen more brought their weapons to bear on the other creature, even as agents in the audience moved in on the shadows there.

It was over quickly. The leader, buried in flesh with the President, burst into flame under the pile, sending agents screaming, rolling off the stage and into the stunned media. Two agents tried to drag the singed President away, even as the others emptied their weapons, to no avail, into the tall one. Knowing that the President was as good as dead, Gary Williams made a decision. Ignoring his orders, he grabbed the two nearest VIPs—Vice President Galin and Ambassador Marcopoulos—and shoved them through the escape panel behind the curtain, pressing the button that sealed the corridor behind them. They ought to have been safe back there, but already Williams could hear a terrible pounding on that panel. He wished he could have saved the secretary of state, but she'd been moving toward the President instead of away.

Julie Graham grabbed Henry Russo's charred hand and began to pull him toward her, ignoring the dead and dying agents surrounding her. The screaming continued from the press, and she couldn't hear a thing, but even as she made eye contact with Henry, a heavy, booted foot came down on her forearm, shattering the bones. Wailing in her agony, she looked up into the face of the once-human thing that reached down and took the President's hand from her own. It leered at her, then ground that boot back and forth on her broken bones, and mercifully, she blacked out.

The once-Asian thing, the leader of the band of assassins, stepped back to the podium. It hoisted the President by the neck once again, and those in the audience who did not turn away saw that Henry Russo was quite awake, though barely able to whimper with his throat so tightly clutched.

"Good evening," the shadow said into the microphone. "I have a message from Lord Hannibal. Humans take warning, vampires take heed."

Henry Russo, the President of the United States, screamed one last time as the creature leaned its face in and tore out a chunk of his throat with its teeth. It sank those fangs back into the wound, drinking deeply and moving its face around, purposely wetting its cheeks with the President's blood. Finally, it turned back toward the press, toward the cameras now operated by its fellow shadows.

"*This!*" it cried, blood dripping from its face onto the podium. "This is our destiny!"

Then the creature lifted the President's body above its head with both hands and brought it down across one knee. Henry Russo's corpse broke in half and was flung into the pack of media hounds he'd once considered his greatest burden. The shadow-assassin turned back to Julie Graham, who was just coming around, and smiled.

It took its time with the rape and murder of the secretary of state, and though the other vampires controlled the cameras, the broadcasters could easily have stopped the feed, chosen not to show the atrocity live on the air. None of them did. The rules changed during war, and there were, after all, ratings to consider.

"*Go! Go! Go!*" Agent Williams shouted, even as he shoved at the vice president's back. Williams was nearly dragging Ambassador Marcopoulos, slowed by age, down the narrow, "safe" corridor that led from the room where the press conference had been held—and where carnage now reigned—to the Oval Office, which had its own defenses. Still, the office had only so much protection, and its parameters did not really include safety from vampire attacks.

Williams had been studying the creatures since their existence had been revealed, and as far as he could tell, their abilities and weaknesses were spread across a broad spectrum. He knew from books and articles, as well as from rumors along the national security grapevine, that only a very few were still unable to bear sunlight or the presence of religious symbols. Nearly all of them had recovered from the mental programming that had been spread among them like a virus by the Catholic Church. While silver was not fatal to them, most still had a reaction to it, and science reports indicated that they did weaken in its presence, as if it were some kind of poison.

According to numerous accounts, the shapeshifting abilities of the creatures varied widely, but government studies postulated that eventually the things could learn to become almost anything. Though no one wanted to discuss it very loudly, there seemed only one sure way to destroy the creatures. They had to be dismembered, and the parts of their bodies separated, kept apart. Of course, in light of their capacity to become mist or fire, and depending on the individual vampire in question, such an act could be quite difficult, almost impossible.

And here he was, Gary Williams, with the lives of the vice president and the shadow ambassador in his hands, one big motherfucking vampire on their backs and a bunch of hypothetical bullshit as his only weapon.

They were halfway down the corridor, and not nearly far enough away, when the steel door they had used flew off its hinges and clanged fifteen feet down the hall. Williams noted that the shadow had chosen to use brute force rather than attempt to mist through the door frame, and filed that thought away. He hoped he'd get a chance to use it.

"*Run!*" he roared, and shoved the ambassador forward, hoping he was fast enough, knowing the vice president was a scumbag and wouldn't bother to help the poor old guy.

Williams had reached the first control junction, just after the halfway point, and with the speed that was the shadow's legacy, the black male one, who looked as if it'd grown even larger with its anger, rushed down the hall toward him. It would be only seconds before the vampire had him, and then the other two men as well. Agent Williams's handprint was enough to activate the safety program's voice control, and it ticked away three seconds as the inhuman thing bore down on him, its mouth open to reveal fangs, lengthening even as it came. A loud pinging indicated that the program was on-line, and Williams responded.

"Blast door twenty-one," he yelled, noting the number on the wall, "*down!*"

And another steel door, much stronger than the first, its seals airtight, slid into place. As the pounding began, Williams flipped on the comm at his control junction, to hear the sounds on the other side of the door more clearly, and even then, he began to run again, toward the Oval Office and his duty there.

"Garth!" a voice shouted, far away, and Williams knew it was addressing the creature who was after him.

"What?" Garth shouted back, its voice almost a howl as it continued to pound on the door.

"Mission accomplished," the first voice, obviously one of the other vampires, back in the conference room, shouted again, barely audible. "We're pulling out!"

"Not until I kill the other two," Garth wailed.

And now Williams slowed, stopped in the steel corridor, almost to the next control junction, almost to the door leading into the Oval Office. The outcome of this conversation could save lives.

"They're not a priority!" the other voice yelled down the hall. "We're leaving, but suit yourself. You can find us later."

And that was it—no more conversation, just more pounding, and though Garth couldn't have misted through, it didn't even bother to try, just continued to rely on its strength. Williams turned around and sprinted to the next control junction, the Oval Office only ten feet behind him. He thought he caught a glimpse out of the corner of his eye of the shadow ambassador lying on the floor in the office, but his priority was stopping the vampire.

The pounding continued, and Williams began to wonder whether the thing would be strong enough to break this door down. And if not, what then? Whom did it kill on its way out? Or would it leave at all? Would it try to find another route to the office? Williams couldn't let that happen.

At the control junction, he primed the voice comm, then hit the release that would open the door. It slid up, revealing a somewhat stunned vampire. The creature's eyes narrowed as it looked at Williams down the hall. Williams wondered if the vampire was at all concerned that it might be walking into a trap, but he doubted it. Vampires were nothing if not arrogant.

"Shadow containment door twenty-one," Williams said softly, "down."

The door slammed shut behind the vampire, and it spun around to look, then back to Williams, its grin widening. The creature did not notice that this door was somewhat different from the one it had been attacking moments before.

"Don't worry," the thing known as Garth said to Williams. "I won't run away from you, my friend."

"Shadow containment door twenty-two," Williams said loudly, "down."

And a foot in front of Agent Gary Williams, another door fell into place, in which there was a small window two inches by four inches, made of glass a foot thick, just like the door.

"Shadow containment measure one," Williams said, and watched through the hole as the ceiling between the doors dropped slightly, the floor rose, and the vampire, Garth, looked entirely off balance.

A second later, the vampire looked up at the tiny window and rushed, roaring, at the door to begin pounding anew. But as soon as the first blow fell, the vampire shrieked and fell back, cradling its right hand. The walls, ceiling and floor were made of silver in this part of the corridor, installed five years ago but never expected to be used. Now, Williams knew, some shadows could escape just about any containment. But most would not be able to free themselves from this one.

All surfaces were of silver, and even the glass of the window was sealed, airtight, and covered with a fine silver mesh. Had Garth been barefoot, it would have known much sooner that it was chasing its prey into a trap, and yet Williams was fairly certain now that the vampire would not have stopped. Even now, as he watched, Garth stepped forward again and, painful though it must have been, began to pound against the silver door, its rage growing with each touch.

Still, though its rage grew, its strength began to leave it. Surrounded by that much silver, it was only a matter of time before it would be incapacitated, though all evidence showed that such an effect was temporary at best.

Williams watched through the window as Garth struggled, falling to his knees. In moments it would be too late for the vampire to shapeshift, and though it had shown an aversion to it, Garth did so now. Turning to mist, it floated toward the upper edge of the door, and Williams knew that the vampire had given up its former targets and narrowed the field down to one bothersome Secret Service agent.

In the Oval Office, George Marcopoulos felt as if he were having a heart attack. He'd run all the way down that long corridor, and as soon as he'd stepped through the steel door, the pain had hit, momentarily paralyzing him with pain and fear, the agony in his chest and arms driving him to the ground, where he hit his head. He'd been unconscious for only a moment or two, but when he came around, he saw Bill Galin, the vice president, sitting behind the President's desk.

"Ah," Galin said as George began to move. "You're alive after all, what a shame."

The man looked terrified still, his eyes wild, but his mouth was split by a gleeful, maniacal grin.

"If that thing doesn't get in here," he went on, "and I'm willing to bet that it won't, that makes me the President . . . President Galin. I rather like the sound of that."

"You didn't call for help," George mumbled, his voice sounding somehow off as he tried to sit up, hand still clutching his chest.

"Too bad, so sad," Galin said in a singsong voice.

And then he was up, stepping up onto the President's desk and then dropping down from it to crouch by George on the rug. The vice president, more than likely about to become President just as he claimed, leaned in to whisper to George.

"Mr. Ambassador, your Hannibal doesn't know what he's done—"

"He's not my . . .," George began, but Galin put a finger to his lips.

"Ah, ah, ah," he scolded, "it isn't polite to interrupt. Anyway, as I was saying, you and I know that Hannibal doesn't represent all of those monsters, but he *is* chief marshal of the SJS. With this attack attributed to him, the world will believe that the shadows have declared war on humans. It's open season on those . . . things you have befriended, and I'm now the chief hunter."

Galin smiled, and his hands slipped around George's neck and began to squeeze.

"You, Mr. Ambassador, are out of a job."

Heart pounding in his ears, George could not breathe, and Galin's hands continued to tighten.

I'm dead, George thought.

"I think not," a polite voice said, and then the hands were gone and George heard a crash.

Looking up, he saw that Galin had been thrown backward, across the desk, knocking videophone, lamp, everything, from the desk and landing in the President's chair hard enough to knock it over. Galin sprawled on the ground, and George Marcopoulos knew he hadn't gotten there by himself. Out of the corner of his eye, he saw movement, and he looked back toward the open emergency door where the Secret Service agent was still trying to destroy the vampire that had followed them.

Standing in front of it was a man he had never seen before, all in black as though he meant to be inconspicuous, but more conspicuous because of it. He was a slight man, and George couldn't imagine he had thrown Galin across the room. And then he turned around, and though George had never seen him before, he recognized the man. As a vampire.

He knew immediately that this shadow was not with the others, but he still flinched when the creature kneeled at his side.

"Dr. Marcopoulos," he said, in a respectful, almost feminine voice, "my name is Joe Boudreau. My uncle was Henri Guiscard. Meaghan Gallagher asked me to watch out for you, and I really think we ought to go now."

Guiscard! Henri Guiscard! The mind boggled. George nodded even as the shadow delicately lifted him and carried him to the window. Henri Guiscard had been the start of it all, in a sense, a Roman Catholic cardinal who had discovered *The Gospel of Shadows* accidentally, then abandoned the Church, fleeing to Boston, where he hoped to reveal the book's contents to the world. Liam Mulkerrin had followed Guiscard and killed everyone the old cardinal came into contact with, dragging Peter Octavian into the web of that mystery, a mistake that led to Mulkerrin's defeat in Venice.

Yes, George thought he remembered Peter saying something about Guiscard's nephew. He'd run the bookstore where the cardinal had hidden the *Gospel*. But he'd never heard anything of the boy becoming a shadow himself! Still, those questions were for later. They had enough to worry about just getting off the White House grounds where the new President had become homicidal and the shadows' tenuous relationship with the world had been shattered.

"Let's go," Boudreau said, dumping Bill Galin's unmoving form off the broken chair, then lifting that chair and hurling it through the bay window behind the President's desk, all with one hand while the other cradled George Marcopoulos as if he were a baby.

"Yes," George agreed. *But go where*?

The shadow known as Garth was in mist form and drifting quickly toward the door frame. Williams knew the thing could kill him in seconds, but he wasn't about to let it get that far.

"Air lock," he said, and with a double bang and the sound of hydraulics, the room was sealed.

Even as mist, the vampire couldn't find any way out of the silver-lined room, and it turned back to human form after floating around nearly every corner of the room. The ceiling was blocked off into circular tubes, and Williams experienced a moment's worry when the mist disappeared up inside them. But several seconds later, the mist emerged again, its attempts fruitless. Finally, Garth returned to human form and curled up on the floor, eyes burning into Williams's own, where he stood behind that foot-thick glass.

Eventually, there would be no more air in the room, and that on top of the silver should make Garth weaker and weaker. Williams didn't know whether vampires needed to breathe at all, or if their bodies just kept breathing out of habit. Regardless, the silver was doing its job. Garth wasn't going anywhere.

Agent Gary Williams knew what he should do. He knew what his government required him to do. He knew he ought to simply stand guard until somebody came along to help, preserve this insanely powerful creature for study by the Pentagon. He knew he should do that.

"Fuck it," he said. "Canisters."

And inside that silver room, the last phase of the never-before-used special anti-shadow security precautions activated. As Williams watched through the tiny window, the ceiling fell, hundreds of silver-plated steel cylinders with razor-sharp edges slamming into the ground with a thousand pounds of weight behind them. Garth didn't have time to move as its body was dissected into more than a hundred pieces, each trapped within a cylinder.

Almost as quickly, the floor began to slide out, into the wall, and as it fell away, the cylinders snapped down, rotating, sealing themselves so that in moments silver-lined canisters filled with the flesh of a shadow filled the inside of that room in neat rows. They could still study it, Williams figured, but now he wouldn't have to fight it anymore.

He turned, rotating his head, neck and shoulders to relieve the tension, and walked into the Oval Office. In the middle of the confrontation he'd just ended, and over the shouting and screaming of the vampire, he thought he'd heard banging and the shattering of glass from this room but he didn't have a moment to spare. Now that he was there, in the office, he couldn't believe what had happened.

The bay window was smashed, the President's chair was gone, his desk was a wreck and the vice president, his face bruised and bloody, sat propped against one wall, cradling his left arm.

"They're in it together," he said as Williams entered the room. They were joined a moment later by a group of agents who burst through the main door of the Oval Office.

"Who is, sir?" Williams asked, wondering how badly the man was hurt.

"Marcopoulos, Hannibal, all of them. The ambassador tried to kill me!" Bill Galin snapped. "They're all in it together. This whole Mulkerrin thing is part of it too."

"Sir," Williams started, reaching to help the man up as the other agents went out the window after Marcopoulos and whoever else had gone out that way. "Mr. Vice President, do you think that's likely?"

Galin leaned against the big desk, then looked up, glaring at Williams.

"Don't ever question me again, Agent," Galin snapped. "And that's Mr. President to you."

※

11

More than two months had passed since they had met Lord Alhazred, and there had been other demon-lords since. These lords were nothing like the shadows which they had battled in Venice and which were plentiful in the deep caverns of Hell. Those others were work beasts, slave demons, and Meaghan thought that perhaps they were made from the flesh of the Suffering, the damned. They had seen many such damned beings, displayed in abject humiliation, abused in every way imaginable, tortured and physically, literally torn apart, only to re-form so that it could begin again. The demon-lords they had met, including Erim, Yezidis and Azag-Thoth, were polite when Lazarus mentioned the Stranger, though he refused to tell her why. Some, a cowardly few, looked frightened; others were hostile but still cooperative.

Through it all, Meaghan could not forget the words of Lord Alhazred: *The Suffering are always here, no matter where else they may be.* She didn't truly understand it, and though she no longer trusted him, Lazarus claimed he did not know what it meant. Eventually, Meaghan decided it might be better if she remained ignorant.

Since Alex had died, they had not been attacked at all. Not by demon-lords, or their hellish slaves. They had been completely unmolested, and the more Meaghan thought about it, the more she wondered if they weren't being manipulated the entire time. Days, weeks and months had passed as they moved from one pit of Hell to the next, without a trace of Peter. All of the demons—and it seemed to her they had become progressively uglier—knew exactly what they were talking about, but couldn't tell them where they might find Octavian.

Meaghan had to think, eventually, that they were being led on a wild goose chase. She also became very concerned about the time they had been gone. Lazarus had told her that time would move much more quickly here, but how much? They had been in Hell for months. Was the battle all over in their world? Had Mulkerrin been victorious? Had their dimension become nothing more than a playground for Hell's work-beasts, freed from their masters?

On this day, which seemed like every other, she was at her wit's end. They were standing in the center of a cavern in which jackal-like creatures raped the Suffering over and over in every orifice, splashing some kind of sulphuric ejaculate all over the damned things, all over the stone floor, its acid eating through flesh and bone and stone.

"I wish I could do more for you," the demon-lord said, sitting back in its stone chair and overseeing the terrors visited upon the damned in its care. This latest lord was almost blue and seemed made of chalk. Its belly was bloated and for the most part hid the bony phallus between its legs, though the thing's testicles were the size of melons and hung low enough in their sack to rest comfortably on the ground. On its head was a crown of penises, woven with flesh ropes unmistakably made of women's labia. Its jaws were long and filled with suckers like those of an octopus. Apparently, it had no eyes.

"So do we," Lazarus said, obviously wanting to leave as much as Meaghan did.

"I can send you on to—" the thing began. but Meaghan couldn't take it anymore. Alex was dead; she wouldn't let her world die too.

"What's your name?" she asked the thing, and it turned its head toward her, mouth open. She wondered if it would try to attack her, but then realized the thing didn't have a nose, that the suckers in its mouth were for breathing, for smelling, among other things.

"My . . . name?" it asked.

"Yes, your name. What is your name? I wouldn't have thought this a difficult question."

Lazarus whipped his head around to stare at her, jaw agape, thinking she had lost her mind. And perhaps she had.

Then, what looked like fleshy folds of skin on the demon's huge testicles parted, revealing, finally, the thing's eyes. Meaghan wanted to vomit, but she wouldn't show her disgust, or fear.

"So you *can* see," she snapped. "What I want to know is if you can hear."

Her words had the desired effect. The demon had expected her to be silenced by the opening of its eyes, and was sorely disappointed and quite angry. It rose to its feet and took a step toward them, and Meaghan thought she saw the suckers inside its mouth elongate just slightly, and when it spoke now, in anger, it had something of a lisp.

"I am Pa-Bil-Ssssag!" it yelled. "How dare you ssspeak to me in sssuch a manner?"

Before it could continue, Meaghan interrupted again.

"How dare I?" she shouted back. "Simple. I dare because I am an agent of the Stranger. We come here on the Stranger's mission, not our own, and we have been played for fools for far too long!

"Now, Pa-Bil-Sag, if your name is as you claim, then I know you, I know your power, I know your name and I know the spell of binding, taught to me by the Stranger," she lied. "I can think of several places to relocate you that you would not enjoy!"

Pa-Bil-Sag merely stared at her then, and Meaghan found it disconcerting to be looking down at its testicles when the danger of its gaping jaws was much higher and doser to her. But she would not be the first to look away. This was a staring contest, like the ones she had had with her childhood friends, but this one was for much higher stakes.

Pa-Bil-Sag's eyes closed, and it sat down. Meaghan heard an audible sigh from Lazarus behind her, but she resisted an urge to step back, to uncross her arms, to look away.

"You are strong, female," it said. "Though perhaps not as strong as you would like me to believe. We owe the Stranger no allegiance, only courtesy, and my courtesy is hard-pressed with you. Still, I have no wish to confront your master again, and this charade was purely for the amusement of my brother, not myself. As such, I see no reason to perpetuate it."

Meaghan saw Lazarus move closer, stunned to realize that they were about to receive answers, but she listened carefully, searching for the deception she had found in all demon-lords' speech.

"This Mulkerrin and the one you seek are and have been the play-things of my brother, who found them when they first arrived here," he said. "I am certain they have endured extraordinary suffering. I am also certain that my brother will be very pleased to add to his collection."

"What is your brother's name?" Lazarus asked.

"Not that it will help you any," Pa-Bil-Sag said and grinned, tentacles reaching out from inside its mouth, sucking at air, latching on to each other and to the demon's face. "My brother isss Beelzebub, but he will not be concerned with your sssmall magicksss. Beelzebub is sssecond in power only to the First Fallen and will never allow an alleviation of sssuffering for one of his toysss."

"And where is the lair of this brother of yours?" Meaghan asked, still arrogant on the surface, but filled with sadness and dread.

"Outsssside."

"And how do we get there?"

And now the demon laughed, a huge, bellowing roar. On its crown, though apparently not connected to it in any way, the penises seemed to grow erect, and Meaghan finally had to look away. A mistake, she knew, but it couldn't be helped.

"A bargain," the demon-lord said, stifling its laughter. "I will transsssport you there, to the outsssside, and you mussst only walk toward the fire to find my brother'sss land. For this ssservice, you will do one thing for me."

"And what might that be?" Lazarus asked, waiting for the catch.

"Tell him I sssent you," Pa-Bil-Sag said and chuckled down in some phlegm-filled throat. "Tell him I sssent you . . . as a gift."

Salzburg, Austria, European Union.
Wednesday, June 7, 2000, 7:19 A.M.:

It was madness.

Gloria Rodriguez floated out of the sky, H-K blazing. As they approached, her paratroopers unhitched, dropping the last fifteen or twenty feet to the ground, rolling over and blasting Mulkerrin's possessed "warriors" into as many pieces as they could. It was clear to them that the sorcerer was somehow controlling these people, but they would have to be listed as "casualties" in the destruction of the city. The repercussions of those civilian deaths couldn't be taken into consideration here. A war was on.

Many of the paratroopers didn't make it to the ground alive, savaged in the air by flying things, chutes destroyed, bellies torn open. But most of them did make it, and some of those who did had flamethrowers. Fire was their most effective weapon, and getting it inside the fortress was key. As demons and weird, mind-controlled soldiers burned, the intensity of the green glow surrounding the sorcerer at the center of the fortress's courtyard seemed to dim just for a moment. One of Gloria's men fired on Mulkerrin, but the bullets seemed to pass right through, appearing on the other side to scatter among the others, wounding one shadow, who shook it off and kept going.

"Shadows!" she shouted. "The door! Let's go!"

And then they were around her, in arrow formation, as they headed for the huge door to the fortress. Here she was, in the middle of the battle, surrounded by vampires, and all Gloria could think of was the giant gate in the original *King Kong*. She forced the thought back and spun to fire at a figure rushing her from behind. A torrent of bullets cut across the body, but even before it hit the ground she knew she'd made a mistake.

Gloria Rodriguez had killed one of her own men.

"Carlos!" she shouted, but even as she considered kneeling at his side, she sensed something different about the battle in the courtyard.

Looking up, Gloria was stunned to see that, even though most of Mulkerrin's civilian warriors had been destroyed, and the main portal in the courtyard was being continuously blanketed with fire, torching everything that came through, they were not winning. In fact, they were losing.

Losing, because her troops were killing one another. She watched as Maria Santos turned and blasted her blowtorch in the faces of two of her fellow soldiers, her friends. Gloria's unit began firing at one another, bodies falling rapidly.

"What the hell?" she began to say, and then saw the movement out of the corner of her eye, where the body of Carlos, the man she'd killed, lay. From his still form, a sickly yellow cloud rose and floated toward her. A quick glance showed her that others of these clouds flitted among the soldiers in the courtyard, and she watched one disappear into one of her paratroopers, who pulled out a knife and leapt on his nearest comrade.

"God, no," she whispered to herself, and then heard a ghastly, sickening chuckle.

Mulkerrin, whose eyes had been closed as he wove his spells, protected from the fighting around him, had finally opened them, and was looking right at her. Rodriguez turned to run, and then realized she couldn't. Mulkerrin had to be stopped or all human troops would be useless.

"Go!" she shouted at the contingent of shadows around her. "Help your people get those doors open, now!"

Gloria turned back toward the sorcerer, and the ghost, or whatever it was, had come much nearer. She moved as fast as she could, and faster, obviously, than that yellow, evil mist. She dodged right past the thing, firing at Maria as she went. Thirty-five feet separated her from Mulkerrin, and she closed that gap in seconds. Gloria slung her H-K over her shoulder, knowing bullets would do no good, and pulled her knife from its hip sheath. Steel flashed in sunlight even as she passed through, into the green glow surrounding the former priest.

Reflexively she had taken a breath, and without reason she held it, though it tasted of death, the burning of stinking monsters and a bitter poison she imagined came from those tainted, ghostly things. None of that worried Gloria, but something inside her warned against inhaling whatever was causing the glow around the sorcerer. And Mulkerrin just stood there, arms wide, head hanging as if in supplication. He looked up at her, his eyelids drooping, his stare either tired or seductive. The smile remained on his lips as he spoke to her.

"Welcome, little girl," he said, and even as Gloria thrust the knife toward his belly . . .

. . . she stopped. Or something stopped her, still, paralyzed where she stood. The mad being who had once been Liam Mulkerrin reached out and passed a hand through her black hair, and Gloria opened her mouth and breathed in. The smell was awful, rotten, dying, and she wanted to throw up but could not command the muscles in her stomach to do so.

"Kneel before me," Mulkerrin said, his smile turning into a leer even as the weight of his words forced her to her knees, "and I will give you your communion."

All around the fortress, the United Nations security force was fighting on two fronts. While they tried to get over the walls of the fortress, past the demons that continued to emerge from the portals, only to be destroyed but often at the cost of lives, they also had to guard their own backs against those demons that had come up into the city and were now rampaging there, hunting down the many humans still left cowering in basements and hiding under beds. Many of the demons also attacked the troops from behind and prevented a good portion of the forces from reaching the fortress at all.

Commander Gruber's unit, having come down the river and into Mozartplatz, had been almost completely slaughtered, and even the commander himself had been killed. The majority of the shadows with Gruber had also died, though several had disappeared at the same time that Hannibal had abandoned Commander Jimenez's strike team, a couple hours earlier. In fact, each unit lost a handful of shadows at that time, and there was no trace of Hannibal or the other AWOL shadows. They were, simply, gone.

The other commanders—Locke, Surro and Thomas—all continued their attacks, and the more than one hundred fifty shadows still in action had finally been moved close enough to diminish the danger from the portals, so that the troops could concentrate on the walls themselves.

Finally, it seemed to UNSF Commander Roberto Jimenez, they were getting somewhere.

Roberto and his team were outside the gate. Including Rolf, there were thirty-five shadows with Jimenez, and though they could easily have flown over, they had to open the gate if the rest of the forces were to enter. Jimenez had attempted to blow the gate to splinters using a pair of CAMELs, easy-launch, hand-held missiles with computer-aided targeting to find the weakest structural point. They exploded before ever reaching the door. In fact, any artillery used on the gate was rebuffed, and even the strength of as many shadows as could line up in front of the gate couldn't budge it.

Though nervous, even frightened at first, Jimenez's men had warmed to the shadows immediately. Handpicked by Rolf Sechs, for the most part they were top-notch soldiers and engendered an easy camaraderie with their human counterparts. All of them, that is, except for Jimenez himself. Though he had a grudging respect for Sechs, he was glad to have the cold, sharp silver of his dagger hidden safely away in his clothing.

"Rodriguez," he snapped into his collarcomm, "what's taking your guys? We need extra strength on the gate, I said. Get those shadows out here."

Rodriguez didn't reply, but a sudden squealing shrieked from Jimenez's comm, forcing him to cover his ears, and the commander couldn't be certain his message had been received. Satellite communications were out, so they'd had to rely on primitive broadcast methods in the field. Still, they seemed to be working for the moment.

"They're here, Commander," came the computer-generated voice of Rolf Sechs behind him, and Jimenez looked up to see a bat flying above the gate, signaling the arrival of Rodriguez's shadow unit. Sechs put away his voice-pad then, and the assault on the gate began anew, joined by pulling from the other side. As Jimenez's strike force, of which forty-six men still lived, stood and watched, roughly sixty gray-clad vampires tore and dug at both sides of a magically protected gate. On the hill to their left, soldiers shot grapples into the sheer stone wall and began to scale it. Shadows with no immediate chore changed form and flew to the top of the wall with ropes, anchored them, and let them down for the human soldiers to climb.

By God, Jimenez thought, they were going to do it.

And then the gate opened and swung wide, crushing a number of shadows behind it. It was clear that it had not been their diligence that opened the door, for even now it pushed tight against the wall, attempting to destroy the vampires it had trapped. Jimenez let out a breath he hadn't been aware of holding as he saw the mist float from behind that door, signifying that the shadows were all right. He had no love for the creatures, but he needed them. And now the gate was open, though apparently by choice.

What to make of that?

"Move!" he shouted, though he needn't have. The team had passed the point of waiting for his order. Under normal circumstances, he would have felt bound to reprimand them. But now . . .

"Get the son of a bitch!" he yelled as he led the pack, screaming, up the curving path toward the courtyard, the air around him turning suddenly cold, and the sky darker than ever. Rolf Sechs ran beside him, and Roberto was pleased to see that the shadow did not shapeshift, but remained in human form. Also, though his speed was greater, Sechs stayed with him, and Roberto had to wonder whether the creature thought he was *protecting* him.

"Rolf," Roberto thought he heard somebody whisper, and then the vampire fell to the ground, writhing in pain, with his hands on his head. But Roberto Jimenez was commander and could not stop for one soldier.

He rounded the corner and came into the courtyard just behind several of his men and half a dozen shadows. The tableau that unfolded before him was grotesque. His forces had begun to come over the walls, firing into Mulkerrin's soldiers and demons and at the sorcerer himself, though none of the bullets were able to reach him. Several dozen shadows had already come over the wall, and they engaged warriors and demons alike, shrugging off the friendly fire as Jimenez had known they would. And in the center of it all, sheathed in a greenish glow, was Mulkerrin.

Kneeling before him with her head buried in his crotch was Gloria Rodriguez.

"*No!*" Jimenez screamed, and started toward them.

Rolf lay on the cold ground, feeling every stone and pebble that pressed into his flesh, hands holding his head as the voice boomed his name again.

Rolf, it said, but softer this time, as if it knew it had hurt him.

And then it wasn't an "it" anymore, for Rolf recognized the voice.

Cody, Rolf thought, sitting up and shaking his head.

Yes, it's me.

You're all right?

Strong enough to mind-link at least; otherwise I don't know. But never mind that. They've got to go—the humans. They've all got to go.

And then the words stopped, and the rapport that they'd always shared, the mind-link which had allowed them, as children of Karl Von Reinman, to experience events as one, to know things the other knew, to hold actual, mental conversations, told Rolf the story, everything he needed to know. In seconds, he knew Cody's pain, knew he was not yet healed, but knew that he had somehow joined his spirit to the magic flowing around the castle. And Rolf also knew why the humans had to go.

He moved more swiftly than ever before, knowing that Cody would be safe for now, knowing what he must do. In two heartbeats he had come in sight of the sorcerer, and Commander Jimenez racing toward him. Rolf had to prevent that meeting, for hovering about Mulkerrin, just outside of that vile green glow, was a spirit cloud, the ghost of a dead soldier, and it began to drift toward Jimenez.

Rolf caught up to the commander just as the ghostly mist started to waft around his head. Rather than simply knocking him out of the way, the mute shadow bent and threw the commander over his shoulder on his way to the other side of the courtyard, where there seemed to be relatively little going on.

"What the fuck are you doing?" Jimenez yelled as Rolf put him down, then turned to look back at Mulkerrin. "Gloria!"

He went to run back there, but Rolf grabbed him by the arm, shaking his head in a firm *no*. But Jimenez's eyes were wild; he wasn't paying attention. He reached inside his shirt, and in a second he brandished a silver dagger-crucifix in front of Rolf's eyes, something Rolf had seen before. In Venice. He didn't have time to wonder where the man might have got something like that. Jimenez lunged for Rolf, stabbing forward toward his belly, but when his knife and hand got there, they passed only through flame.

Jimenez cried out, briefly, in pain, then switched the knife to the other hand and, holding the burnt one gingerly away from his body, made to go after Rolf again.

"Damned thing!" he shouted, but Rolf grabbed his wrist, holding it nearly tight enough to crush it, then shoved him to the ground, the dagger clattering to the stone. By the time Jimenez had regained his feet, Rolf was searching frantically inside his jacket for his voice-pad.

Jimenez came after him again before he could pull the pad out of his jacket, but Rolf stopped the commander, with one hand this time, and then slapped him, hard, across the face. Their eyes locked, Jimenez's burning with hatred and Rolf's imploring, trying to send a message. He held up a hand and with incredible speed whipped out his voicepad and scrawled upon it with a suddenly elongated fingernail.

"Soldier spirits possess you. Humans must leave," the electronic voice said, translating Rolf's stunted scribble.

A woman screamed, and they turned. The two warriors, shadow and human, saw it at once. Mulkerrin had thrown Rodriguez out of his sphere of influence, onto the stone floor of the courtyard, and the vile cloud was hovering over her . . . and then it disappeared inside her.

In seconds she was on her feet, H-K in her hands, and firing up at the soldiers, her own troops, coming over the wall of the fortress. Rolf glanced at Jimenez, and knew that the commander understood, that he had seen the look on his lover's face, in her eyes, and that it wasn't her anymore.

"Dear God," Jimenez said, then looked back at him. "But they can't possess *you*?"

Rolf shook his head, pocketed his voice-pad, bent down and retrieved the commander's dagger and returned it to him. Jimenez barely looked at the thing as he sheathed it. Rolf shooed him away, using both hands.

"Dear God," the commander said again, then spoke into his collarcomm. "Withdraw! Immediately! All human troops withdraw from the fortress immediately. SJS troops assist in the evacuation and keep Mulkerrin's human soldiers away from our people at all costs! Do it now, people, or we're done for! All units converge at the Nonnberg Abbey. SJS forces keep Mulkerrin contained within the fortress."

And then the comm was off, and Jimenez turned to Rolf.

"Now what the hell do we do?" he asked, knowing an answer would have to wait.

The exodus began, the shadows acting as guards, protecting the humans from their former comrades, trying not to kill those possessed, for the ghosts within them would only find new hosts. But as Rolf and Jimenez followed the outside wall, passing Mulkerrin on their left, the sorcerer laughed louder and louder, and several of the possessed soldiers turned their guns on one of their own, on Gloria Rodriguez. They kept firing until each had an empty clip, and only then could Jimenez look away, look up at the man, the thing, responsible. Rolf dragged the commander away even as Mulkerrin looked straight at them, clearly aware of his actions, enjoying himself immensely.

Outside the gate, and over the roar of gunfire, Rolf heard the cawing of birds above him. He looked up to see three eagles fly overhead, then swoop down to land, transforming into shadows he'd never seen before: a short, stout female and two young males, twins.

"Rolf Sechs," the woman said and nodded, and next to him Commander Jimenez turned toward the newcomers obviously wondering if this were another threat. Rolf wondered as well.

"I am Martha, and these are Isaac and Jared, the sons of Lazarus," the woman went on. "We are here to assist you with the sorcerer, and you should know that reinforcements are on the way. Also, I am saddened to inform you that the disgusting Hannibal has returned."

"Hannibal!" Jimenez snapped. "Now? He's on Mulkerrin's team after all then."

"Actually, Commander Jimenez," Martha said calmly as they jogged down the path that would lead to the abbey "he will not attack your forces, because he wants you to destroy Mulkerrin, so that he does not have to. In fact, he and his coven have eliminated a great many of the demons left behind in the city."

Rolf could sense Martha's hesitancy, and though he guessed what was coming, he was not prepared for it.

"Then what's the problem?" Jimenez asked.

"They are murdering those of the townspeople they are able to find, feeding off them."

A scream built in Roberto Jimenez's throat, but whether it was the name of his murdered lover or a damning curse he would never know. For he swallowed it, and as the scream dropped down into his belly, it burned.

Oh, how it burned.

Salzburg, Austria, European Union.
Wednesday, June 7, 2000, 7:32 A.M.:

Liam Mulkerrin was a madman, and he knew it. More to the point, he reveled in it. Once upon a time, so long ago to him, he had been a Roman Catholic priest. But more than that, he had been a sorcerer, the most powerful in centuries, whose power led him to engineer what should have been the destruction of all "Defiant Ones," and the seed of his own eventual control over the world's most powerful church.

Indeed, it would have been so, if not for Peter Octavian and the other children of Karl Von Reinman. Octavian had become the savior of his people. Mulkerrin had been stopped, his followers killed or dispersed, his power gone, and he had been taken, body and soul, into the very Hell from which he had been calling his servants for nearly a century. Once the demons had discovered he was there, within the confines of their world, they were . . . less than charitable. He and Octavian had been there together, for what seemed like forever, among the Suffering, amid the politics of Hell.

And though they'd suffered, so had their strength grown. With pain came power, and Mulkerrin began to see his previous goals as foolishness, locked into parameters created by his human experiences. As years flew by, as Hell worked changes upon his body, and his soul, Mulkerrin grew to be something more than human, with the taint of the demonic upon him. His desires followed suit, informed by the demonic infection in his soul. Though the minds of the Suffering were easily invaded by Hell's masters, the demon-lords, Mulkerrin used his agony to blind them. Even as his body suffered, and his mind registered every excruciating moment, so did a part of it, the part he would call "soul," become more aware. He spread his spirit, his aura, as far out from his physical form as he could, searching for a sign, any sign, of a weak spot in the barrier between worlds.

And eventually, when he found that spot, the sorcerer made his escape, leaving his demon-masters in a terrible fury, for they could not come to this plane unless individually, and specifically, called.

In the forever he had spent in Hell, Mulkerrin's faith in Heaven had only grown. And while his body and mind had been tainted by his time there, and his power, his magic fed upon the fires of the place, he knew his soul was pure. For he had talked to God. While in Hell, the voice had come to him, and Liam Mulkerrin had experienced revelations that had humbled even him.

"Let's make a deal," God had said to him, though not in so many words. And Liam was in ecstasy. God wanted him to escape back to his birth-world to begin a new, and final crusade. Liam was to cleanse the world of the taint of Hell of the vampires that now lived among God's children and of all other impure souls. The world was to be subjugated to the will of a new church, with Mulkerrin as the rock upon which it would be built. He alone would judge the guilty, he would mete out their justice. The world would become purgatory for its inhabitants, and when they were judged ready by Mulkerrin himself, he would send them to their God.

And any who attempted to prevent God's word from becoming reality would be cut down by his right hand Liam Mulkerrin, and sent to Hell. When Mulkerrin was done, when he had achieved all God had set out for him then the Lord had promised to wipe the taint of evil from him and take the judge, the once-priest, to His bosom. And God helped Liam to rise above his suffering, to escape. God promised that if Hell sent its vile issue after him, or one of its foot soldiers, like the fiend Peter Octavian, then Liam would be given the power he needed to prevail. God told his former priest that he'd been right all along, that there was glory in pain—his own and that of others. It was this skill that made Liam the perfect tool, God told him: the ecstasy such work brought to him.

Liam Mulkerrin, madman, believed it all.

And now he stood amid the bloody warfare, his magic reaching out from the fortress he'd made his own, surveying the landscape around it, aware of the soldiers fleeing his influence, of the Defiant Ones working with them. That alone was proof that these humans must be purified, cleansed or sent to Hell if purification were impossible. As for the Defiant Ones, Mulkerrin sensed that he'd known some of these, even just one or two, before, but could not locate them just yet. But his power, his magic, still grew.

Mulkerrin was past simple spells, though they were still sometimes useful. No, now he controlled true magic, could manipulate the flow, the essence, of the world around him. But such magic was difficult. His primary concentration must go to his own protection, self-preservation. His hold on the other magics he controlled—the portals, the ghosts of dead soldiers, the weather—was much more tenuous.

Mulkerrin would rest now, though his influence would continue to grow and spread further out from the fortress. For the moment, he was content to replenish his supply of demon-slaves from the portals, and to wait for the humans to attack him again. That was their test and one he knew they would fail miserably. They could not face their own evil, and so they would fight his—God's—judgment. Fight it, yes, but not escape it.

As a priest, Liam Mulkerrin had been fond of saying that God's work was never done. But now that God had set him this task of judgment, the day would soon come when the Lord's work would finally be complete.

Judgment Day had arrived.

---------------------------------- ✳ ----------------------------------

12

Inside Mount Untersberg, Austria, European Union.
Wednesday, June 7, 2000, 2:03 A.M.:

"Are you blushing?" John Courage asked with a smile. Allison Vigeant turned away, furious at having been discovered and blushing even more. Behind them, Charlemagne and his men bathed in the underwater stream that ran through the cavern. The emperor had ordered all of his men into the water, but there was only room for perhaps a dozen at a time, so they crowded at the stream's edge awaiting their turn. For his part, the emperor swam as best he could in the shallow stream, up and down its length, not bothered at all when one of his men would block his path. In truth, he seemed to be enjoying himself.

When they had disrobed, Allison had been more interested in their vampiric nature than in their nakedness. These shadows were different from all those she had known, even Cody and Peter Octavian. Though they were naked in her presence, not one of the men turned to leer at her. There was no bickering among them, no shoving, no posturing, only a deference to their emperor (and to Courage) and pride in themselves. And then Allison realized that there was one shadow who seemed somewhat like these soldiers, and that was Courage himself.

Pushing her thoughts aside for later examination, when she would confront John with her many questions, Allison realized that while she had been staring into nothing, not focusing, her eyes had been on the naked men at the stream's edge. Now she noticed that some of them, at least, had noticed her looking their way and seemed uncomfortable themselves. And that was what had caused her to blush, and then to look away as John made a joke of it.

Allison's eyes came to rest on the bed carved of stone where she had given her blood to the sleeping emperor, and the strangeness of what had happened since came back to her. She didn't know what she had expected, but the surprises grew by the moment, and not the kind of surprises she had been prepared for. First, Charlemagne had seemed ready to kneel before John Courage, but John had stopped him. No matter what else it might indicate, it certainly proved that Courage was far older than he let on, as he had admitted to her that Charlemagne had not been out of the cavern in nearly twelve hundred years!

If that were not enough to think about, the emperor had then knelt, along with Courage, and led one hundred vampire soldiers in what was apparently a prayer, at the end of which all present made the sign of the cross! And that she didn't understand at all. The vampires greatest enemy had been the Church, and here they were using its symbols, praying to its God. After the prayer, Courage had looked at her and smiled, and Allison had wanted to slap him. He knew what was going through her mind, the confusion she felt, and he was enjoying it!

Charlemagne had then taken John aside, and Courage had suggested Allison get some rest while he explained all that had happened and tried to prepare the emperor for what was ahead, not only in battle, but in the world outside as a whole. They had spoken quietly in Latin as they sat together on Charlemagne's stone bed, and the soldiers had become silently industrious, sharpening and cleaning their weapons and repairing worn clothing. It amused Allison quite a bit to see these ancient warriors performing such quiet duties. And so, though she had assumed she could not possibly do so, Allison had fallen asleep on the cold, stone steps leading up and out of the mountain.

She had come awake a short time ago, only to be confronted by the sight of one hundred naked men. And now she sat with John Courage as Charlemagne pulled himself out of the stream, dried himself and dressed.

"Do you speak Latin?" Courage asked her, even as the former emperor approached.

"No, sorry."

"Italian?"

"Just a little bit, a few words," Allison said apologetically.

"Greek?" John suggested, but Allison only raised an eyebrow, which was answer enough.

"I do speak some Spanish, if that helps," she said, finally, as Charlemagne joined them, and Courage's face lit up.

"Spanish!" he said. "Excellent. Charles spent years fighting in Spain."

Charles?

Allison had the urge to giggle, but suppressed it as Courage turned to the other shadow and began speaking rapidly in Spanish. It was a dialect she was unfamiliar with, and she hadn't studied the language for years, but concentrating hard, she picked up enough to know that John was simply asking "Charles" to speak in Spanish when he could, as well as asking if he minded the two of them referring to him as Charles. Apparently, he did not like the name "Charlemagne" very much. In any case, he didn't seem to care, and so Charles it was.

The more he spoke, the easier it became for Allison to understand him, and once he got going, Charles spoke quite a bit. He was fascinated by her, and yet she sensed it was not because she was a woman, but rather because of her newness, her youth, her familiarity with a world nearly alien to him. Eventually, as the soldiers finished their bathing and set about drying and dressing, John Courage wandered off to leave her alone with Charles, and Allison barely realized it. She liked this old king, who smiled at her in a grandfatherly way and patted her hand when she said something that amused or concerned him. His eyes had crow's feet around them, which became quite pronounced with either emotion.

"I'm proud to know you," he said, or at least that was how she understood his Spanish. "I gave my daughters the same education as my sons and, so many centuries later, see what the world has moved on to."

"Thank you," she said, beaming herself, for his energy was infectious.

Allison knew that Cody had gotten younger after he became a vampire, and though she thought Charlemagne—Charles, rather, had been older when he died, she wondered aloud why he hadn't reverted to a more youthful appearance. She complimented him on his looks, admired his beard and mustache to soften the question, but he waved her words away.

"I am satisfied with my appearance," he told her. "It is appropriate that an emperor look somewhat older, more . . ."

And then she couldn't understand him, but she knew that he meant many things: distinguished, regal, noble, venerable. And he had all that. Yet still, he was far friendlier than she had ever imagined such a ruler could be. In school, she had always imagined historical figures to be either vicious madmen, or wise, grave, slightly curmudgeonly old men. Charles was a pleasant surprise.

And a vampire. It was so strange to think of one of the most pious of historical figures becoming such a great enemy of the Church, and yet she seemed to recall vaguely that Charlemagne had dealt harshly with those who had executed people believed to be witches. And her mother had told her she'd never do anything with a history major!

They were laughing about something, and for Allison it was not important what that something was, only that they were, indeed, laughing. And then the vampire's face grew dark, and serious, and he looked at that moment precisely as she might have pictured him.

"We must go," he said. "You are a beautiful girl, who does not belong in this thing. But I understand that women are no longer made to stay safe at home. Your lover is captive, and we will free him, so let us go, and pray to God for his assistance. With the Lord's help, we will destroy this Mulkerrin. The Irish were my subjects once, and it seems that this one needs to be reminded.

"Come," he said, and stood, offering Allison his hand and helping her to her feet.

When she looked around, she was surprised to see his soldiers, one hundred of them, prepared to depart and awaiting only his command.

John Courage stood with them, but apart, and those nearest him would not even look in his direction.

Allison realized that once again she had not been able really to question John, but promised herself that she would make the time on the march. For that was what was ahead of them: a march across miles of Austrian countryside. They could have flown, sharing the burden of carrying the token human in the bunch, but Courage had said they wanted to conserve all of their energy. Certainly it would not be easy for her to keep up with the shadows, who would walk the entire way without tiring a bit, but she would make it.

For Will.

Morzg, Austria, European Union.
Wednesday, June 7, 2000, 7:17 A.M.:

A dozen ravens flew in arrow formation a mile or so to the north, and to anyone else looking up, they would have appeared to be nothing more than birds. But Allison knew that they were far more. There had been so many other things to wonder about that she'd barely considered the strange deaths of those ravens that had flown at the top of Mount Untersberg, but she thought of them now. She watched the progress of the birds, scouting ahead as they'd been ordered, and not for the first time, she wondered what it would be like to fly, to be one of them.

Not a raven, of course. A vampire. For that is what those birds were, soldiers of Charlemagne, surveying their path, mentally communicating the images of the land around them to their emperor. And Allison had to wonder what it would be like to have wings, to glide on the wind. It wouldn't be the last time she would wonder such things, but she knew that she would always push such thoughts aside. For the pain, the sadness, the little tragedies of immortal life seemed far too terrible to her. Though her friends, even her lover (if they got through this), would live on while she grew old and died, she could never accept the "gift" that the so-called Revenant Transformation offered. She saw it as a double-edged sword at best.

She walked between John Courage and Charles, and though the two tried to engage her from time to time, they invariably lapsed into Latin, apparently discussing both the battle to come and the status of the world. She noticed more and more that Charles deferred to John, but decided to wait until they were alone to ask Courage about it.

Their exit from the mountain, or at least Allison's, had been less than graceful. A return to the cavern ledge by which she and Courage had entered led to a slope disappearing down inside the mountain. They had gone down that slope, many shifting to forms better suited for the descent, and eventually, she had ridden on the back of a bear that was actually John Courage himself. Regardless of everything else she had seen, that ride, holding so tightly to this thing that had become her friend, had unsettled her. Then she had realized that they were out of the mountain, and on the march.

Now, with the ravens at the point, they trooped along Morzgerstrasse, a wide highway, already cleared of cars in the evacuation. Twice they had been confronted by Austrian and German military roadblocks, and both times Allison had been called upon to speak for them. Though they obviously did not trust the shadows, and the German soldiers wanted to hold them back, or try at least, the Austrians wanted their nation saved, and so waved the shadows on. Allison didn't know whether to be more surprised that they had been confronted, or that they had been allowed to move forward.

"Demons," Charles said, finally, and Courage barely noted the word. Apparently the ravens had alerted their blood-father—for Allison was fairly certain that that was what Charles was to his soldiers—of the presence of Hellish creatures ahead.

Quickly, the vampires moved around Allison and John Courage, and Allison realized they were protecting her the way a herd would protect its young from predators. Courage was with her as extra insurance, but Charles was at the front of the group, preparing to confront the few demons they had come upon.

"It's a good thing we're here," John said to her. "This area is being ravaged. It looks as though most of the military is concentrating on the fortress, but these people need some help."

"And that's us, huh?" Allison asked, and her tone was such that John looked at her strangely.

"Something?" he wanted to know.

"Lots of things."

"Ah, your questions again," he said and smiled. "Well, let's hear what you've got so far, my journalist friend."

Allison just didn't know what to make of Courage. Though he seemed unwilling to speak of his origins, he was perfectly happy to have her discover them; he seemed, in fact, to want her to do so. *So be it*, she thought.

"Okay," she said, eyes narrowing. "You're at least twelve-and-a-half centuries old, and capable of metamorphosis that is beyond any other shadow I've known. Wood, metals, things the others haven't even considered. Your current appearance is not your true appearance—"

"Why do you say that?" he interrupted.

"Let me finish. You receive a deference from those familiar with you that is unlike anything I have ever seen among your kind. You pray to God, are aware of events before they take place and know things about other shadows that you should not know. And you seem to be in the right place at the right time. Also, you know a lot more about the origins of your kind than any other shadow I've known, yet you refuse to discuss them. Finally, call it a hunch, but I'd say you're blood-father to both Lazarus and Martha, as well as to our friend Charles here, and I can't even begin to imagine where that train of thought will take me."

They kept walking, Courage looking down at the road. When he raised his head and spoke, he was looking around.

"I can tell you're exhausted," he said. "Why don't we find you something with wheels on it?"

"Fine by me," she said, and meant it—she was exhausted. "But first let's finish our little chat here."

"You mean you aren't finished?" he said, a false innocence coming over his face.

"Don't even . . . ," she began, warning him, but she didn't need to. He was prepared to talk to her. As for how much he would tell her, that was another question.

"First, tell me a couple more things," he said. "Like why you don't think this is my true appearance, and what makes you think I'm blood-father to those you mentioned."

"When you introduced me to Martha," she began, "you told me she was Lazarus's sister, and Jared and Isaac his sons. If she was your sister as well, you would have said so. The way the three of them treated you, I got the feeling that you were in charge, and that Martha didn't need to speak to communicate with you.

"As far as Charles is concerned, that was even more of a hunch, but it also ties in with your age and appearance. The soldiers who first met us did not recognize you immediately. You had to perform some change which you purposely—no, don't argue—purposely did not allow me to see. Only then did they know you. But even though Charles had been down there just as long as they had, and therefore had not seen you for at least twelve centuries, he knew you immediately. I guessed that this was through your mind rather than appearance. And of course, for such an emperor to defer to you, who would seem so young in the scheme of things, there could only be one answer as far as I was concerned.

"You're the boss," Allison said, and watched him for a reaction.

John Courage smiled then and gave a small clap.

"Bravo," he said, even as the noise of the slaughter of demons continued to the north. "But as you can tell, there really isn't a 'boss' per se."

"Not in general, but certainly you have a coven of your own, though its size is still a mystery to me." Allison nodded, satisfied with what she'd determined thus far, but Courage seemed deep in thought and did not reply.

So she punched him, hard, in the shoulder, the way a child might punch her younger sibling to get even for some imagined transgression. John looked at her, eyes wide, simply stunned at the action, and Allison gave an exasperated sigh and frowned. And then the corners of John's mouth began to turn up, and they couldn't stop themselves from laughing at what Allison had done. John gave her a little shove, to let her know he understood her game, and she punched him again.

"Don't mess with me," she said, in a boxing stance. "Now, give with some answers."

As John's laughter subsided, Allison wondered what she was doing, playing around with a being as old and powerful as Courage obviously was. She'd never really thought about it, but put to the question, she realized she would have expected shadows as old as John and Charles to be crinkly old wise men. And that couldn't have been further from the truth, though Charles looked the part.

"You're right on track," John said. "I've got to hand it to you, Allison, your instincts are very, very good."

"What about the praying?" she asked. "What's the story with that?"

"Charles is a pious man, as am I in my way," he answered, quite serious.

"But, the others, the younger ones . . ."

"A product of their long persecution by the Church, which you helped to end, by the way." He put a hand on her shoulder. "Thank you."

"John," she said, exasperated, *needing* to know, "what's the truth? What aren't you telling me? Will and the others are tortured because they don't know what they really are, what their origins are. If you know, you've got to tell them."

Courage said nothing.

"Do you know?" Allison pleaded. "If you're praying, does that mean vampires aren't evil by nature? But then what of Hannibal, and the others like him?"

Courage nodded, as if deciding something for himself.

"I do know," he admitted. "But it is in searching for the answers to those questions that our friends, and the rest of my kind, will create them. To you I say that we are not natural, we do have a taint of evil, but we also have a trace of the divine. Like man, we have free will with which to determine our individual destiny. I will tell some of them, to ease the burden the question lays on their souls, but only those who have already chosen which side to follow, the demonic or divine.

"And I will tell you," John said, sincerely, "but not now."

Allison's mind was spinning, hungering for the answer to a mystery the depth of which she was only just beginning to understand. She realized something else, something the existence of Hell should have tipped her off to. No matter what she'd believed in the past, here was a creature telling her that God did exist—not that he had faith that God existed, but that, in no uncertain terms, there was some kind of . . . of being that exerted an influence on Allison's world, something "divine." Something to be prayed to. And as much as she believed it, more than ever now, she didn't *know* it, the way John did.

But she wanted to. Still, he had said he would tell her the whole story, the true nature of the shadows, and she knew that there were revelations to be had in that story. And if he wasn't prepared to tell her now, it was worth waiting for.

"Just one thing," she asked. "At least tell me who you really are, your name, where you're from, how old you are."

John's smile returned, even as they started to move ahead once again. The demons had been dealt with, and she and John were shuffling forward to join Charlemagne in front of the soldiers.

"Ah," he said to Allison, almost in a whisper, "but that would give it all away."

And now she was really confused. But at least it kept her mind off Will Cody.

Just then they were passing a convoy of evacuees and were once again questioned by Austrian troops. Allison was relieved to hear that the military believed that all or nearly all civilians had been evacuated from the area, and as John and Charles spoke to the officer, a bizarre thing happened. From the backs of several troop carriers, now filled with frightened people driven from their homes, several figures rose and jumped.

A total of eleven men and women came toward them, ignoring the shouts of the soldiers, and Courage translated for her as they spoke to Charlemagne. They were offering their blood. Some were blood-cultists, others volunteers and worshippers, but at least half were merely people who wanted to see that their homes were returned to them, that their city was saved from further destruction, and Charlemagne's soldiers were the only ones they had seen heading into the city rather than away from it. Once the soldiers had given up attempting to stop the people, several of them also offered their blood.

Charlemagne accepted, and the convoy waited as each vampire in turn took only a taste of life, to bolster his strength. It was a bizarre tableau; vampire warriors lining up to share in the blood of those people whose lives they were attempting to save, but it gave Allison infinite hope for the future, and pride in humanity. Maybe they could win this thing, and share the world after all. Maybe.

Above them, the sky was blue and the sun warmed their faces, but up ahead death hung over the city of Salzburg in a terrible curtain of unnatural clouds. Allison had enjoyed smelling the early summer air, but now the wind shifted, and her nose wrinkled at the scent of something rotten that was carried south to them on the breeze.

Salzburg, Austria, European Union.
Wednesday, June 7, 2000, 7:58 A.M.:

Hannibal was no fool. He was very concerned with the apparent retreat of Roberto Jimenez's troops from Hohensalzburg Fortress. After all, if the foolish humans and their traitorous vampire allies could not be counted upon to destroy the sorcerer Mulkerrin, then Hannibal would have to sway from his plans and join the battle as well.

For the moment, however, he continued upon his original course, secure in the knowledge that his new coven could act without fear of any serious opposition.

The President of the United States was dead, and that bitch Julie Graham as well. Hannibal was upset that his blood-son, Garth, had been destroyed during the assassination, and that the vice president, and the old Greek, Marcopoulos, had escaped. He had learned as much through his psychic rapport with his blood-son Sitoshi, who had led the attack, and torn out the President's throat with his own teeth. However, in retrospect, Hannibal thought that leaving Vice President Galin, a rabid xenophobe, alive might only serve to speed his plan to fruition.

In the days before the Venice Jihad, Hannibal had set up a world-wide coven, a network consisting of more than one hundred of his own blood-sons and -daughters and their offspring. He had an international stable of human spies as well, inside nearly every nation's government, which pulled strings in human politics and carefully monitored those of shadows. Hannibal had been one of the architects behind the volunteer program, through which humans enamored with the vampiric mystery of the Defiant Ones offered their own blood, often their own lives, for a chance just to be in the presence of an immortal. He had been a power.

And then Venice, and Von Reinman's coven proved themselves to be far stronger than he had ever realized. They averted one disaster, gaining a huge following among their people, and caused, in Hannibal's eyes, another. Many of his coven had died during that final battle with the Church, and Hannibal had been confused, unsure of his support in the community. He had had no choice but to seemingly conform to the new world order that was quickly established.

But only with words.

For in action, Hannibal never changed. He rebuilt his power base, reenergized his coven, used his status as chief marshall of the SJS to draw other shadows, not his bloodsons but powerful and like-minded vampires in their own right, to his cause.

Blood.

Hannibal took pride in his savagery, his bloodlust, his skill as a hunter of men, and his coven. His people had always been the scourge of humankind, and would be again. It was their nature, their destiny, to take the blood and the lives of humans. They were predators, and humans their only prey. And now that their existence had been revealed to the world, all the better, for rather than stalking one human, Hannibal would now prey on the fears and the political weaknesses of an entire world.

The first step, of course, was to shatter the peaceful co-existence of vampires and humans, one which had been tenuous at best. It was not proving terribly difficult. Though Hannibal's plans had not been fully conceived, Mulkerrin's return had presented the perfect opportunity to execute them. There would be so many shadows in one place, at one time . . . and so many humans. His assassins had killed the President, and now he was certain that the United Nations secretary general, Rafael Nieto, was trembling in a well-guarded room somewhere. Well, let him tremble. Hannibal would get to him eventually.

And now, with the world's attention focused not only on the battle with Mulkerrin, but on the state of the UN's alliance with the shadows, he had upped the ante yet again. While his softhearted brothers and sisters fought alongside the humans above, Hannibal had gathered more than fifty of his coven to him in the north of the city, out of range of the communications-inhibiting magic of Mulkerrin. While at the fortress the UN commanders could not be told of the President's assassination, the actions of Hannibal and his men were easily recorded and transmitted around the world by media cameramen. Through that bitch Allison Vigeant, whom Octavian's clan had rescued from his cellars, the world's media had discovered the Defiant Ones. And Hannibal would use those same tactics to his own ends.

He let the cameramen live. Otherwise, it was a slaughter.

It had begun when his followers gathered and dispatched the stray demons that rampaged through that portion of the city. And yet, the vampires destroyed the demons only because they, themselves, were threatened. But once the demons were destroyed, they had gone after the police and military in the area. And once the people had no more protection, Hannibal and his coven went hunting through the streets and alleys, through crumbling homes and still intact blocks. Hunting for blood.

And now, Hannibal knew, he had drawn the attention of the combined human and vampire forces at the fortress. They had withdrawn from that battle, but he knew it was only a matter of time before they made another attack. He was right, and wrong, as it turned out. They would, of course, mount another attack, but Hannibal's assumption that they would not be able to spare troops to come after him was obviously wrong.

Even now, as he watched his blood-daughter, Pamela, feast on an adolescent boy she had dragged into the street, even as he received mental reports that at least a dozen of those SJS members he had not recruited had defected to his cause, Hannibal's first son, Hector, flew to him as a bat, changed to his true form and growled a warning.

"They approach!"

"What?!?" Hannibal was incredulous, for he had heard Jimenez issue no such orders over his collarcomm . . . but of course the commander would be smart enough to change frequencies if possible! Damn!

"A large force comes down from the fortress, and it is made up almost entirely of humans!" Hector said, obviously stunned himself that an event Hannibal had been certain would not happen was now happening.

Hannibal was confident that his coven could destroy the humans if necessary, but he was also confused. Why would they abandon their attack on Mulkerrin, a more immediate threat at least in their perception, to launch an assault on him?

"How many of the human soldiers come after us, and how many remain to battle the sorcerer?" he asked.

"They are all coming after us," Hector said, shaking his head in wonder. "It seems only shadows remain to launch another attack on the fortress."

Astonishing, Hannibal thought. *They're sure to lose*. It was outrageous in his mind. First, Hannibal would be forced to slaughter the human armies (which he had intended to do only after they had destroyed Mulkerrin), losing many of his own in the fight, and then he would have no choice but to use his remaining forces to help his traitorous kindred destroy Mulkerrin.

Jimenez must be insane!

As much as it hurt him to do so, Hannibal had to create an alternative possibility, a new course of events.

Stop, he commanded them mentally, no more killing.

And how he hated those words. As he sent his psychic orders to his blood-children, so they passed them on to members of the coven not of Hannibal's family.

Take as many of the humans as you can, he told them. *We will use*

*them as shields in order that I may speak with the human commander.
I must know why they turn away from the fortress. None of you will
attack, none of you will draw the blood of the captives you now
take . . . until my order. This is a minor delay, nothing more.*

Hannibal vowed to enforce that guarantee. He was furious with the
unforeseen change in plans and wanted nothing better than to tear
Roberto Jimenez's head from his body. And he promised himself that
he would indulge that urge, as soon as Mulkerrin was out of the way.

13

Salzburg, Austria, European Union.
Wednesday, June 7, 2000, 7.49 a.m.:

"Commanders!" Jimenez barked into his collarcomm. "Set up perimeter guard and get a head count. Locke, take command of whatever's
left of Gruber's troops. Anyone left from Rodriguez's paratroopers,
converge on me. All shadows . . ."

Roberto shot a look at Rolf Sechs, in effect the new chief marshal
of the Shadow Justice System, and got a nod in response.

". . . converge on myself and Marshal Rolf Sechs. Yesterday! All
commanders report immediately after these orders are carried out."

Jimenez turned to look at Rolf again, and the mute vampire realized
that, no matter what, the two of them had become partners in the outcome of this thing. They had to prevail, and therefore they had to rely
on one another.

Rolf's human family had been murdered ages ago, and he had
never had any other children. He had never created a blood-child,
made another vampire, and he didn't think he ever would. Therefore,
though it would have eased the burden of his muteness, he shared his
mental rapport only with his blood-brothers and -sisters, of whom only
Cody and Alexandra Nueva still lived. He knew sign language and,
when necessary, his second, Stefan, could translate it for him. But the
voice-pad was an adequate substitute.

Just in case, Rolf motioned for Stefan to come forward, effectively promoting him to deputy marshal the way Rolf had taken Hannibal's post. The group around Jimenez was growing, and as they awaited word of their next move, Rolf turned to the newcomers: Martha, the woman had called herself, and the men were Isaac and Jared, supposedly the sons of Lazarus. Martha had been the one to tell them of Hannibal's actions in the city, and now she cleared her throat to get Commander Jimenez's attention. The man whirled, ready for trouble, and then relaxed, realizing how high-strung the battle had made him. The female shadow looked at Rolf then, deferring to his command, and he nodded for her to go on.

"Chief Marshal Sechs, Commander Jimenez, on behalf of my brother Lazarus, who apologizes for his being unavailable, we," and at that she noted Jared and Isaac, "offer our services to you. Also, it will please you to know that reinforcements are on the way."

"What?" Jimenez asked, and Rolf knew that the commander's whole attention was on Martha now. She had his own as well.

Rolf motioned for her to explain, and Martha went on.

"Well, it seems obvious," she said, "that the human soldiers cannot return to the fortress. In fact, so that the ghostly beings up there cannot find new hosts when they are killed again, it would be best if all humans got as far away as possible from the fortress. Therefore, it seems only logical that the human troops move to prevent Hannibal and his coven from committing any more murders. We shadows must return and confront Mulkerrin on our own. A corps of one hundred powerful vampires is on the march here as we speak, to assist in just such an attack."

"How do you know this?" Jimenez asked, shaking his head. "Who sent you? And who's bringing these so-called reinforcements?"

Martha opened her mouth to speak, but Rolf held up a finger, indicating she should wait, and then pointed to Jared, lifting his hands in a sign that he should continue in her stead. Rolf thought that Martha sounded too practiced, and he wanted to hear this from the boy's perspective. Rolf knew what Jimenez was thinking—that perhaps Martha was working with Hannibal—and he couldn't help but consider the same thing.

"Me?" Jared asked.

Rolf nodded, brow furrowed in expectation.

"We are here to help," Jared said. "What's so difficult to understand? Who sent us and who's bringing the reinforcements are one and the same being, but his name will mean nothing to you."

He was lying. Rolf knew he was lying, but strangely, he didn't sense any menace or ill intent in the lie. He cocked his head slightly, allowing his doubt to show through, prompting Jared to continue.

"His name is John Courage," Jared said.

Courage! Will Cody's voice boomed in Rolf's mind.

Turn down the volume, Rolf shot back. *I didn't even know you were still with me.*

Sorry, Cody sent, from his prison within the fortress.

You know this John Courage?

Oh, yes, Cody thought, and in those thoughts, Rolf could sense the weight of not just knowledge, but secrets that Cody wanted to share.

I know him, Cody sent, *and somehow, now, I know the truth of him. Work with this Martha, Rolf, and I'll tell you the rest when I see you.*

You've recovered from your wounds? Rolf asked.

Not quite, but I will be in time to help when my help is needed. Do me one favor. Ask Martha if Allison is all right.

Rolf realized he was the center of attention. Martha had apparently continued to speak, but with Cody's voice booming in his mind, Rolf had not heard. Now she, Jared, Isaac and the commander all waited for his response.

"What's your recommendation, Marshal?" Jimenez asked, and Rolf noted that the gray at his temples seemed to have spread a bit farther since dawn.

Rolf didn't think twice. Cody was his brother, and his word was the only assurance Rolf needed. He motioned for his deputy, Stefan, to come forward, then pulled out his voice-pad and began to scrawl with a fingernail.

"Stefan, here," the electronic voice said as Rolf pointed at the vampire, "will take orders from Martha, as will the rest of the SJS agents.

I will pick a dozen shadows and accompany Commander Jimenez to confront Hannibal. It is the only path open to us."

Martha nodded in approval, and Stefan stood at attention, accepting his orders, but Jimenez shook his head as he looked at Rolf.

"What are you talking about?" Roberto asked. "Sechs, we know nothing about this . . . woman. How can you . . . ?"

"I know you'll have a hard time with this request," Rolf scratched onto his voice-pad, "but you're going to have to trust me."

Jimenez was speechless, even as Rolf turned his words to Martha.

"Martha, Will Cody asks if you know the whereabouts of his lover, Allison Vigeant, last seen with John Courage?"

"Will Cody?" Jimenez snapped. "Where the hell is he?"

Rolf waved for the commander to be quiet.

"Tell Mr. Cody," Martha answered, aware of the true origin of the inquiry, "that Ms. Vigeant is safe for the moment, that she is with John and on her way here, now.

"Also," she said, smiling at Rolf, "tell him he's a lucky man."

"How can you tell him anything?" Jimenez said, exasperated, stepping closer to Rolf to get his attention, even as Jared and Isaac moved forward to block his way.

Rolf held up a hand, and the vampires stopped.

"You all misunderstand," he wrote. "The commander is not a threat to me, or to you. He does not trust us but we stand together."

Rolf turned to Jimenez now, writing faster.

"Vampires made by the same father can communicate mentally. I was out of communication with Cody for a time but now, this close to the fortress, where he is a prisoner, we are in contact again."

"It couldn't be a ruse, a trick to throw us off course?" Jimenez asked, needing to understand, to be sure.

Rolf shook his head, and then Jimenez was equally silent. The man was not a fool; he was aware of the stakes. Commander Thomas appeared then, responding with the other commanders to Jimenez's earlier orders. Immediately, she and Rolf exchanged glances that communicated their mutual concern, for each other and for the situation but professionalism and discretion allowed no greeting. Rather, Rolf nodded to all of the newly arrived commanders, even as Jimenez opened his mouth to voice his decisions.

"Commanders," he said to acknowledge them. "I admit that I have a difficult time putting any faith in shadows, but it seems we don't have much of a choice. If we attack the fortress again, all we're going to end up doing is killing each other."

Rolf nodded as Jimenez issued the only orders he could. The commanders' faces were grim.

So that's it? Cody's voice came to him again, much quieter this time. *We'll just have to wait for Courage and his "reinforcements," I suppose.*

Any ideas on that? Rolf asked. *You seem to know a lot more than you're letting on.*

The only thing I can say, Cody answered, *is trust John Courage. Even if you think he's crazy, trust him. He may be the only one we can trust.*

You "heard" about Allison? Rolf asked.

Yeah, thanks. I just wish she wasn't coming back with them. But then, I guess I wouldn't love her if she was the kind of woman who turned tail and ran home to Momma. Still . . .

There was silence a moment, around Rolf and in his head, and then he had to ask . . . *What about you, brother? There are so few of us now; what are you waiting for? If you need help to escape, let me come, let me help.*

Rolf could sense Cody's laugh, even if he didn't "hear" it.

Amazing, isn't it? Cody thought. *A few years ago you wanted me dead, and now you want to save me. It means a lot, Rolf, but no. I'll explain it all, or as much as I can, later. But I think I can be of more use to you if you leave me right here.*

As you say, Rolf sent, and then Cody was gone from his mind.

Turning his back on the gathered humans, though not without catching Elissa's eye again, he signaled for Stefan and Martha to give orders to the dozens of Shadow Justice System agents who had gathered there.

"Martha will lead the assault on the fortress," Stefan said.

"However, when Will Cody finally makes his escape, he will assume command of all shadow forces there. Try not to kill the humans if possible, for their possessors will only search out new hosts. The object is Mulkerrin's death, as quickly as possible."

Rolf had put away his voice-pad, and now he scanned the vampires gathered around him. He would take twelve of them with him to help the humans against Hannibal, a paltry number, but Mulkerrin was the priority. The three newcomers, this Martha and Lazarus's two sons, certainly knew more than they were letting on, and Rolf wondered whether that might not come in handy later.

He pointed to Jared, who looked at Stefan for instruction.

"He wants you on his team," Stefan said, not needing any communication from Rolf to understand.

Rolf had expected the apparently young man, who might have been far older than he, to look to Martha for approval of this choice, but he was pleasantly surprised when Jared only nodded and stepped forward to stand beside him.

When he had chosen eleven others, Rolf turned to face the humans again, and Commander Jimenez had just finished giving the details of the plan for their attack on Hannibal. With demons running loose down there, buildings burning and locals in the line of fire, it was not going to be easy.

This time, when Jimenez turned to meet Rolf's stare, that was all the communication which was necessary.

"Let's hit it," Jimenez said quietly. "And God bless us all."

Hell.
One Hundred Three Days, Two Hours
and Twelve Minutes After Departure.

Lord Pa-Bil-Sag had been as good as his word. He had indeed, transported them to the surface . . . a surface they had never expected to exist. And yet they'd found themselves there and so had to incorporate that into their view of this world. Hell was apparently a planet. They had discussed, at first, whether they were in a different dimension or an uncharted part of their own universe, but neither could come up with any real evidence or logic to support either question. And what was important was that they were there.

They had walked through a fiery portal conjured by Lord Pa-Bil-Sag and found themselves stepping out onto a broad, dusty plain. The darkness of the sky was cut by the light of fires shooting from the earth like geysers all around them, cinders floating away on the hot breeze that whipped past, roasting the planet. Rock formations went from familiar to incredible, and some looked as if they'd been built rather than occurring naturally. Despite the fires around them, they'd had no trouble determining which way their destination lay. Pa-Bil-Sag had referred to "the fires," and far off in the distance, flames engulfed a mountain ridge shooting high into the air, lighting the entire horizon line as if it were dawn at that end of the world. But no sun ever rose; the dawn was perpetual, a promise, a cruel tease.

After two weeks of walking, after they had spent three months in Hell, both Meaghan and Lazarus had finally started to feel a little hungry. Though they would be able to function completely for quite some time, hunger would eventually unhinge them. They had known then that slowed time or not, they would need to find blood eventually.

Two more weeks had passed. They had alternated between walking and flying, though Meaghan had been a bit nervous about flying when she thought about the winged creatures that had attacked her in the stovepipe. Finally, their trek had led them to a huge gate in the middle of what could only be described as a desert. In some places. the sand had been blasted with such high heat that it had turned to glass. Beyond the gate, glass spires stood tall at the foot of flaming mountains, and it was hot enough that Lazarus wondered aloud how the spires kept from melting.

"A better question is how we've kept from melting," Meaghan said, only partly joking. After all, though they could have turned to flame and ashes themselves, their human shapes would not have been able to withstand the kind of heat necessary to create glass from sand.

"It does seem," Lazarus admitted, echoing Meaghan's thoughts, "that those mountains aren't giving off as much heat as you would expect."

They stood for a moment in silent reflection. They'd been quiet through much of the month it had taken them to get here, Meaghan mostly thinking of Alex, and of what she might say to Peter if they found him. She had no idea what Lazarus was thinking, but guessed part of it was the other thing on her own mind: time. If they'd barely begun to hunger after three-and-a-half months, that meant barely more than a day had passed in their own world. How much time had passed for Peter in Hell while five years had gone by on Earth?

All of those things were on Meaghan's mind now, and she assumed on Lazarus's too. Not to mention the new questions as to Lord Pa-Bil-Sag's "brother," the glass spires beyond the gate, and the most obvious question of all.

"What now?" Lazarus asked, and Meaghan snickered then smiled to show she meant no offense.

"No idea," she admitted. "Though I don't think the denizens of Hell take kindly to uninvited guests. I'd like to vote against flying over this thing. On the other hand . . ."

She looked at him, and knew he understood.

"We could just knock," Lazarus said, and they nodded together.

And so Meaghan stepped forward and pounded on the gate, its ringing sound making them both realize that what they had imagined was some kind of metal was actually a dark black glass. The gate, then, was hollow glass, offering no protection at all.

Meaghan shot a look at Lazarus, who merely shrugged.

"Then again," he said, "who would come here uninvited?"

They waited a long while, and each pounded on the glass several times more, but there was no answer.

"It's not as if we can come back later," Meaghan said finally. "And then again, if the place truly is empty, what better time to try to get Peter out of here?"

"If he's actually in there," Lazarus said.

"Oh, he's in there," Meaghan said, "I can feel him."

Which was true. Throughout their entire journey, she had sensed that they were going in the right direction, and as they got closer, she had known that he was there, at the fires that were their destination. She had called out to him with her mind several times each day, but what bothered Meaghan was not that she received no answer. What bothered her was that when she tried to reach out and make contact, force the connection, she was shunted aside. It disturbed her that she was forced to consider that Peter might be consciously blocking her out, shielding himself from her the way that he and Cody had shut out the rest of Von Reinman's coven for many years.

And if Peter was intentionally blocking her out, Meaghan couldn't begin to guess why. Or perhaps she could, but the path down which those thoughts led was one, at least for the moment, better left untraveled.

"That's it," she said, breaking the silence and startling Lazarus, who'd grown used to it. "We're going in."

Meaghan became a cloud of mist, spreading herself thin to be as inconspicuous as possible, and Lazarus followed suit. Floating above the black glass of the gate, their minds, ephemeral things in that state, were able to feel the place, the sprawling city of glass, the fires that burned within, and its emptiness. As they floated through the city, Meaghan reaching out her mind for Peter, they did not see anything living—not a demon, not a human, not a thousand suffering souls. Still, Meaghan focused on the mind of her bloodfather, Peter Octavian, and though he tried to block her out, those efforts were almost a beacon, leading them toward him.

The city was vast, its glass buildings of widely varied styles, some imitating those of their own world, with turrets, terraces, eaves and steeples, and many of boring, square design. Others were foreign, alien, and at first glance seemed ugly because of it, though as they became more familiar, Meaghan found many of them to be strangely beautiful. And above it all, at various heights, were the spires. As if they were a trap laid for some beast that might fall from the sky, the spires stretched up throughout the city, sharp as spikes. Nearly every other building rose from its foundation, many of which were mediocre, to become, at its apex, a towering knife of glass. Other spires simply sprang from the ground, no building for a base, no purpose other than themselves.

Meaghan thought of icicles hanging up rather than down, and was pleased with the image, or as pleased as she could be, considering how unsettling the overall picture of the city was. They neared its far border, where the black cinder mountain stood blazing in the sky, and the closer they got, the hotter it became and the more she could sense Peter.

Why are you blocking me? she asked in her mind, nearly frantic. *Can you have been here long enough to forget? To forget your people? To forget me?* And though her love for Alexandra had superseded everything that had come before, she could not suppress the sadness that that thought instilled. How long would she have to live to forget those she had loved? It was a question Meaghan never wanted to answer. And unbidden came the memory of the loss of *The Gospel of Shadows*, the fear that they might never escape from here. That they might join Peter here forever, rather than returning him to his own world.

They were close now, and she floated to the ground and returned to her human form. Lazarus followed close behind and questioned her as soon as he had changed.

"Have you found him?" he asked.

In truth, she could not say yes. She knew that Peter was very close, but so close that she was finding it difficult to choose one direction over another.

"He's near," she told Lazarus. "But we'll have to search."

Meaghan realized that the elder vampire was no longer paying attention to her. He stared past her shoulder, then turned away from her and looked around them, disgust and disbelief etched in his features.

"God, no," he muttered, and Meaghan barely caught it as she whirled . . . and understood.

Though she had sensed the buildings while in mist form this was the first good look she'd gotten with her true eyes. And she shared her companion's horror. The glass was not perfectly clear, but rather tinted red. There were no doors, no windows. In fact, it was easy now to see that the structures were solid glass, without any rooms or interior at all. Almost.

Lazarus walked to the nearest building, a huge thing that looked for all the world like a medieval castle, battlements and all. Meaghan watched as Lazarus stared into the glass, and reached out a hand as he bent to peer into its pinkish red depths. He laid his palm on its surface . . .

. . . and screamed in pain. Pulling back his hand, Lazarus left the first layer of skin behind, and Meaghan looked at that flesh as it blackened, charring down to nothing and sliding down the glass.

"It's impossibly hot," Lazarus snarled, and Meaghan turned to look at him just as his hand began to heal up.

She knew what he meant. If the glass all around them was that hot, why wasn't the air itself hotter, never mind the fire burning on the mountain nearby? Still, those questions paled in comparison with the others racing through her mind. Meaghan walked to Lazarus and put her hand on his shoulder, and he lifted his head to again peer into the glass. Neither spoke.

Trapped inside the glass, faces frozen in horror and pain, bodies locked into place like flies encased in amber, were this region's Suffering. They could not move, and breathing did not seem to matter. The heat of the glass seared their naked skin red, but nothing more, as if they were constantly being healed enough to withstand continued torture. They looked at one particular woman, limbs contorted wildly, legs up and out as if she'd been frozen in the midst of a terrible rape, and Meaghan had to wonder if the glass was inside her, inside all of them, as well.

"Her eyes moved," Lazarus said, almost in a whisper, and Meaghan shivered.

She had to turn away, and Lazarus turned as well, eyes closed as he walked with her, as if to deny what they'd seen. It dawned on her then that the reddish tint to the glass had to be the blood of the Suffering, and she was glad she had looked away. Beside her, Lazarus opened his eyes and they both realized that they could not avoid seeing the Suffering here. The entire city was a Hell of glass, with no relief for the damned, or their witnesses.

"Peter's here," she said, but almost couldn't believe it. "This way, toward the mountain."

Lazarus nodded and they moved on, the fire so huge that even at this distance its roar was incredibly loud, the crackle nearly deafening. As they approached, ash fell from the sky like fine snow, and soon they realized they were walking on, and in, layers of it that had fallen over time. They had not noticed before, but now they could see that the blaze did not start at the base, but more than one hundred feet up the mountainside. There, even over the roar of the flames, they could hear another sound. That of suffering. The damned burned there, on the mountain, cried out for deliverance that never came. Yet Meaghan wondered whether they were not fortunate in comparison with those within the glass. For at least the flames varied, died down at times. For the others . . .

And Peter was probably one of them. She refused to think about it any longer.

"*Where are you?!?*" she screamed finally, the thought bursting from her aloud. "We need you, you son of a bitch."

"Meaghan," Lazarus said softly, and she turned to her right to see him pointing along the outskirts of the glass city, along the mountain range, to a structure they hadn't seen before. This one was closer to the mountain than any of the others. It was tinted red, or appeared to be in the flickering flame from above. Its spire climbed higher than her eyes could see.

And she knew. Lazarus had sensed it as well, the difference in this one. Its red was darker, and yet where every other structure had clearly held dozens of sufferers, their dark forms visible even from a great distance, they could see only one form in this spire. Lazarus had pointed it out because of that difference, and because it was set so close to the mountain, but as soon as she looked at it, Meaghan's focus grew sharper, into certainty.

It was Peter.

Salzburg, Austria, European Union.
Wednesday, June 7, 2000, 8:12 A.M.:

Hannibal's coven had been moving through Salzburg when his blood-son Hector brought the news that the UN security force was moving down into the city proper. He'd known immediately that they were after him, but he'd also been stunned. How could they abandon their attack on the sorcerer, a much greater and more immediate threat? And yet they *were* coming.

He had instructed his vampiric troops to take human prisoners, not to harm them, and then he had moved to find more open ground in which to face the humans. Residenzplatz, with the Salzburg Cathedral filling the south end, was large and open, offering ample space, and even as the coven moved into position around the fountain in its center, the plaza was suddenly filled with soldiers, streaming in from Mozartplatz and Kapitelplatz. They hadn't even bothered to surround him, and in a strange way, Hannibal admired them for that.

Several shots rang out, and then the warm June morning was silent. Even the birds were quiet, unless they'd been driven out by Mulkerrin. The French Commander, Surro, and the American, Elissa Thomas, brought their people in from the north, while the Brit, Locke, moved in from the south. There were several alleys and side streets leading into the plaza from the east, and hundreds more came through that way, with Commander Jimenez in the lead. Hannibal saw that his former deputy, Rolf Sechs, was with them.

Traitor, he thought, but there was little venom in it. How could they have abandoned their attack on Mulkerrin?

"Hello," he shouted, breaking the silence in the plaza, which had previously been broken only by the working of gun mechanisms and the shuffling of feet, perhaps a whimper or two from his captives.

So many hostages, so many vampires, all those guns—it was a messy picture that could get even messier, and very ugly, very fast. Hannibal could see that Commander Jimenez understood that. The human had hundreds awaiting his command, Hannibal as many, but the vampire knew the outcome. But, he chided himself, he'd also *known* that there was no chance Jimenez would break off the attack on the fortress. So perhaps the outcome was not as inevitable as he wanted to believe.

"What can we do for you, Commander?" Hannibal asked softly into his collarcomm, assuming Jimenez would be back on that channel. "What brings you down from the mountain today? I would have thought you had better things to do."

Hannibal had worldwide information networks and centuries of experience gathering such material. He hated ignorance, in himself more than anyone else. It pained him to admit he didn't know something, and it was agony to do so in front of so many enemies.

"Release your captives, vampire!" Jimenez snarled in response, loud enough for Hannibal to hear on his comm and across the plaza. "Release them now, unharmed, and surrender."

"Oh," Hannibal said and laughed, mocking him, "I think not, sir. Now you will draw back and leave us alone or these people will die."

Even from across the plaza, Hannibal could see the scowl that crossed the face of Roberto Jimenez, the look that was exchanged between Jimenez and Rolf Sechs, the way Jimenez patted his hand over his breast, as if calming his heart, or searching his pocket.

"You had planned to kill them before we arrived," Jimenez said finally. "Give them up and you will be treated accordingly. You will not escape justice for your actions, though you seek to use the sorcerer's presence to mask them!"

Silence again, as Hannibal thought.

"Why did you abandon your attack? Mulkerrin must be destroyed before either of our futures can commence," he said, his voice dropped lower, insinuating. "I had counted on you handling that end of things for me."

"For you!?!" Jimenez sputtered into the frozen battle in the plaza, which awaited only a thaw. "The only thing I'll do for you, demon, is end your godforsaken, misbegotten life. Your kind are dangerous, and you the worst of the lot."

Hannibal smiled then, as he watched the look Rolf gave Jimenez. The big mute was unhappy with this exchange of words, but Hannibal could see that he would let it slide.

"Oh, I do hope so," Hannibal said. "For after today, my kind will be more dangerous than ever, out of necessity. I'm sure that your communications have yet to be reestablished, so I'll share the good news with you myself. A couple of hours ago, operatives of mine assassinated the President of the United States, and when I feel like it, whenever I feel like it, I'll have other heads of state murdered. I have that power. Your boss, Rafe Nieto, is tops on my list."

"Thomas," Jimenez said into his comm, obviously no longer speaking to Hannibal, "can you verify any of that?"

"It doesn't matter whether she can or not," Hannibal said and laughed. "It's all true. What you fail to understand, all of you, including my treacherous shadow brothers who are obviously launching a private attack on the fortress, is that this is war. War! After Venice there was a new world order, but that was just a stepping stone. My kind, the real vampires, the hunters and bloodsuckers, have been driven from hiding. That will be our freedom. The order of the world will change yet again, return to days eons past, hunter and hunted in a final war, one without end.

"And it starts . . . now!"

At Hannibal's signal, the vampires' human captives were broken, bled and gutted in three heartbeats, and seconds later, the gunfire began again and the tide of soldiers swept in to close the ranks, a small number of shadows and flamethrowers in the front line. Hannibal consoled himself with the knowledge that he had tried, albeit halfheartedly, to prevent this massacre. But now that it had started, the very thing he'd fought so hard for, the savage hunter, the predator in him, took control.

In a far corner of his mind, he wondered who would be left to battle the sorcerer, to lay siege to the fortress, when they were done. And then all such thoughts were gone, and the scent of the blood spilled all around him, the violence that slashed the air, formed a sensual symphony, to which the vampire, Hannibal, now moved in primitive sync.

14

The remnants of the Shadow Justice System, those vampires who had not been killed or betrayed their new lives in favor of Hannibal's return to savagery, were fifty-nine males and thirty-six females. With the addition of Martha, Isaac and Jared, the total number reached ninety-eight. Twelve had accompanied the human forces down into the city to attack Hannibal, which left eighty-six shadows to attack the Fortress Hohensalzburg in a second attempt to destroy Liam Mulkerrin.

Stefan bit his lip. He was worried that it wouldn't be enough. Though he would never have questioned his orders aloud, he could not help but doubt the wisdom of such an attack. Certainly the humans could not join the siege, but the shadow forces attacking Mulkerrin had no leadership. Hannibal had turned against them, Rolf was trying to protect the citizens from him, Will Cody was a prisoner, and the rest had simply disappeared.

Now Rolf had put this newcomer, Martha, in charge, though none of them knew anything about her. Sechs was lucky more of his people hadn't followed Hannibal, and Stefan knew that if not for their respect for the new chief marshal, and the overwhelming threat of Mulkerrin, many of them would have done just that. Especially since a lot of them were beginning to get *hungry*!

"Now!" Martha said next to him, and Stefan gave the order to attack.

Where before they had had to worry about getting the human troops in, this time they had no such concerns. The shadows moved as one, in many different forms, flying or floating over the walls of the fortress and engaging Mulkerrin's demons immediately. The plan was to destroy them as fast as possible, without attacking Mulkerrin directly unless he acted first. In the initial skirmish, he had seemed preoccupied enough with controlling everything around them. As horrid, and as dangerous, as the demons appeared, Rolf had schooled the shadows on the easy destruction of such creatures. And without responsibility for the human troops, they could force a much more direct and sweeping attack.

"My hope," Martha had told them only minutes ago, "is that we can clear out the current wave of Hell-creatures, and then by putting all of our pressure on Mulkerrin, force him to let the portals throughout the city close in order to protect himself. If we can get him off balance, that will be the first step."

Stefan only hoped that it worked. They were also supposed to try not to kill the human soldiers, as the warriors possessing them would only find new hosts. Martha suggested they attempt only to knock these soldiers unconscious, thinking that perhaps the ghosts would be trapped within their hosts' minds . . . Stefan had almost laughed at that. It might be a legitimate plan, but she couldn't possibly expect dozens of starving vampires in the frenetic madness of battle to treat their enemies with such tenderness. Oh, they might try, even succeed for a short time . . . but not for long.

They were on the ground now, in the courtyard of the fortress once again. Stefan reverted to human form from the hawk shape he favored while flying, and signaled for the flamethrowers to start burning the demons down. They could have transformed into fire and swept through the yard, and probably would have to eventually, but for now the throwers were less painful. Demons howled as fire leapt into the air.

Mulkerrin was safe within his protective shield of magic, and he barely looked up as the assault began. Then he called out to them in a strange voice—not loud, but somehow loud enough for all of them to hear.

"Yes, come," Mulkerrin said. "Come and be purified."

Stefan frowned. The sorcerer didn't think of them as a threat, for the moment. Stefan vowed that would change.

"Stefan!" someone shouted in warning, and he kicked one of Mulkerrin's soldiers in the chest, knocking him down and out of the way, even as he turned to respond . . . too late. Stefan was lifted from the ground by a huge crablike pincer, one of the largest demons having shambled, burning, through the firewall. His chest was being crushed, and he cried out in pain even as he transformed himself into burning cinders. Escape would be simple, but it was not the order of the day. Instead, Stefan's flames engulfed the huge, gray thing, and withdrew only when its howling form was writhing its last on the cold stone floor of the fortress.

"Stupid beast," Stefan said, and finally looked to see who had warned him. It was Isaac, allegedly the son of Lazarus, several feet away and doing his best to battle half a dozen of Mulkerrin's ghost-inhabited soldiers without killing them. It was a noble struggle, but Stefan could see that Isaac was suffering unnecessarily.

In seconds, he was by Isaac's side, his fist caving in the skull of the closest soldier. He sank his teeth into the dead man's neck, drinking deeply.

"What are you doing?" Isaac asked, annoyed, even as he threw another soldier away from him, the possessed woman's ancient armor clattering to the ground.

"Getting my strength up, and helping you, fool," Stefan snapped, throttling the man closest to him, then twisting his head around fast enough to break his neck. "What does it look like?"

"It looks like you are killing innocents," Isaac said, huffing as he ducked out of the way of a thrusting sword, only to be slashed across the back for his trouble. "Killing them for no reason other than expediency."

"Expediency," Stefan said grimly, "is its own reward."

They met then, face to face and eye to eye, over the thrashing body of the swordsman who'd slashed Isaac's back. Isaac held him by the arms while Stefan's hands were around his neck. Isaac looked angry, and sad, and Stefan realized that the other shadow truly felt for these unfortunate humans. But it did not stop his hands from tightening around the soldier's throat.

"No!" Isaac yelled.

"By the time the warrior spirit finds a new host, and makes its way back here on foot," Stefan growled, as he twisted and they both heard the grinding snap of bone, "this battle could be over!"

Stefan wiped his hands on his pants, tossed the corpse toward several of his SJS agents who'd complained of hunger, then turned to defend himself as another soldier rushed toward him, weapon raised high. He was not in the mood, so he swiftly sidestepped the attack, grabbed the soldier and propelled him, with incredible strength, into the stone wall of the fortress. The man fell, and did not stir again. All around Stefan, an oily yellow mist was floating up from where dead men lay. Isaac was at his side, berating him still, and then Martha was there, between them, and she held up a hand to stop his protest.

"I saw it all, and heard it, nephew," Martha said to Isaac. "But Stefan is right, I'm afraid. Right now, expediency may, in fact, be mercy, but in any case is far more important in this battle. Not to mention that if our brother and sister shadows don't get their strength back, these few lives will be nothing in comparison to what Mulkerrin will do. The needs of the many, Isaac—though God help me, I never thought I'd say it—take precedence.

"Kill them," she said, and her face showed the pain of those words.

Stefan moved off, away from them, and closer to Mulkerrin, where the shadows were beginning to converge. He was almost set upon by a dark jackal, which had escaped the others, but it was intercepted by Lisa, one of his most powerful operatives. She was lithe, pale, beautiful, with long sable hair, and he was fascinated as he watched her dispatch the thing in seconds. Still, he thought of Martha's words, and the ease with which she had uttered them.

God help me, she'd said. Stefan had thought for an eternity that his people were beyond God's help, but now, for the first time, he wondered.

Cody was nearly healed.

He sat up against the wall of the room in which Mulkerrin had ripped out his heart, and held his hand against the pink, new tissue that covered that wound. It was tender, it hurt, and he was, for the moment, still too weak to move very far. His shirt had gone somewhere, and it had taken him a while to remember that Allison had used and lost his gun during their battle outside the hotel. How long ago was that? He didn't know. He was just happy that he still had his blue jeans and his boots on. The boots were made of very soft calves' leather, and he would have hated to part with them.

He smiled to himself; already his priorities were back on track.

Cody leaned on his hands and tried to get his legs under him to stand up. It wasn't working. Thinking again, he arched his back, bracing it against the wall, and pushed with his legs, which seemed a little stronger. Slowly, he slid up the wall until he was standing, leaning against it. He couldn't support himself yet, but he was getting there.

The only problem was that as he was regaining his strength, healing, he was losing whatever it was he had gained when he'd been . . . dead. Or whatever. His mind or soul if you wanted to believe in that kind of thing, had obviously been elsewhere, wandering around out there. He wondered if the sorcery, the power of the magic Mulkerrin was generating, had helped to heal him. He knew for certain it had enabled his spirit to . . . What had it done?

It had traveled, it had spread. It had merged with the magic somehow, and he had been aware of all the goings-on around the fortress, of many of Mulkerrin's twisted thoughts. But that wasn't all. He had become, suddenly and completely, aware of many things, including the loyalties and the hostilities of any combatant inside or outside the fortress upon whom he wished to focus his thoughts. He heard the screams of those living hosts whose bodies had been commandeered by the ghosts of dead warriors, had, in fact, nearly been drawn himself into a human host before all the humans had been forced out of the fortress. If his spirit had not been so intertwined with the magic surrounding the place, he might not have been so lucky.

And was that part of it? Mulkerrin's spell to raise the spirits of the dead warriors—had that kept his own ghost around long enough to reinhabit his naturally healing body?

It was too much. Cody took a deep breath and pushed himself away from the wall. His legs were wobbly, but he could walk now. He searched for something, a shirt or jacket, to wear, but found nothing. The healing wound felt vulnerable.

He knew that above, the shadows had returned, and that they were even now surrounding Mulkerrin, battering against the sorcerer's protective field, trying to break his concentration, wear him down at least enough to close the portals so no more demons could come through.

Cody still had some of the knowledge and awareness he'd gained when his body had been so traumatically wounded, but it was fading fast. He remembered certain things, or was aware that he *had* known specific things, but with his healing, and the growing consciousness of his brain, his body, that other awareness had slowly slipped away.

He could barely feel the connection he'd had to the rhythm, the life of the magic pulsing within the fortress, but it was still there. He could barely sense Mulkerrin now, but knew that the siege was indeed wearing on him. He still didn't know how Mulkerrin could have not sensed his presence, his awareness lurking there in the bowels of the fortress, but he was grateful that the sorcerer had not noticed him.

And as for the knowledge, as he steadied himself with a hand on the wall, moving toward the steps that would take him up, there was one thing he concentrated on, one thing that he had learned which he struggled not to lose. In his awareness he had examined his handful of meetings with John Courage, the words they'd exchanged, the battle they'd fought side by side. He'd searched the shadows out there for knowledge of Courage, and when he'd been in mental contact with Rolf, and the woman Martha had brought up Courage's name, he'd been able somehow to read her as well.

At least a little. He didn't know, really know, what Courage was. But he had a fairly wild guess. It frightened and thrilled him all at once.

But enough of that, he had to help his brothers and sisters. He had to help them be rid of Liam Mulkerrin once and for all. And he thought he might know how to set the sorcerer off balance just enough for his people to accomplish their first goal.

MULKERRIN! his mind shrieked, sending the angry, savage, attacking thought out along the thin strand of awareness that still connected him to the magic, a magic he had been able to sway just a little when he was a part of it. The final bit of influence he had retained over the magic was used up now, as his mind slammed into Mulkerrin's brain like a bullhorn screaming into his ear.

The sorcerer recoiled as if struck with a physical blow, shook his head, and Cody felt his surprise, his shock, and his immediate awareness of what had happened, of who his attacker was. Every one of the portals to Hell Mulkerrin had opened, throughout the city, had disappeared in that moment, and with his concentration gone, the barrage of physical force, the attack by dozens of vampires on the barrier around Mulkerrin, continued. The sorcerer was off balance, and before he could attempt to retaliate, Cody cut his own connection to the magic, which was like letting go of the string on a balloon and watching it drift away, sad to see it go, but fascinated by the beauty of the thing. The last thing he felt was Mulkerrin's rage.

Cody felt better with each step he climbed. First things first, he thought. There had to be someone topside who would give him a shirt.

Salzburg, Austria, European Union.
Wednesday, June 7, 2000, 8:56 A.M.:

Hannibal wasn't winning. Unfortunately, as far as Commander Elissa Thomas was concerned anyway, he wasn't losing either. She knew from the files she'd read that some shadows had developed to the point where they were almost impossible to kill. The majority, however, had not become completely used to their abilities, or to walking around during the day, even though five years had passed. Hannibal's coven was no exception.

A constant attack might be enough to throw some of the less experienced of them off balance so that they lost control, or confidence, and began to fear the sun. If they ran, tried to find cover, they'd never make it. Likewise, concentrated gunfire, hand-held rockets, even an overwhelming hand-to-hand attack might be enough to literally tear apart one of the creatures. If the pieces of the thing could be kept from coming back together, it would be truly dead.

The problem was that the casualties among the UN security forces were as completely disproportionate to those among the vampires as their original numbers were. For every shadow they were able to destroy, dozens of human lives were lost. As far as Elissa was concerned, that was far from a fair trade, but she didn't know any other way to stop the evil bastard. She knew now, after all the moments of curiosity, of wonder, how the myths and legends of vampires got started.

And then there was Rolf. Commander Thomas did not love Rolf Sechs. She barely knew him, after all. But even in so short a time, she'd come to care about him. She knew that he was not the evil creature Hannibal was, and yet he had the same savage heart, the same talents, and that fascinated her. She had already decided she would stand by him when the shit hit the fan. And it certainly would do that. Even now Roberto Jimenez was beginning to doubt Rolf; Elissa could see it in her commanding officer's eyes.

But could she blame him? After all, it was the President of her own country who had been murdered. Life would never be the same for any of them, human or vampire, and Hannibal had changed it all, thrown it all away. And for what? Ego? Bloodlust? Power? Or was he simply lonely in his cruelty, needing others to share in his perversity?

She didn't know, and though she was curious, Elissa realized that the answers wouldn't make a bit of difference.

We're dying out here, she thought, lifting a CAMEL tube to her shoulder. She was well back from the real hand-to-hand stuff, knowing that her troops would be hard to rein in without her guidance, but she wasn't out of it. She leapt to the hood of a nearby Mercedes, the light plastic of the CAMEL no burden, then sighted down the tube. The computer-aimed system zeroed in on a number of targets, and she searched the sight for Hannibal.

She found him, cut off from his pack, surrounded by a large group which included Rolf Sechs and Roberto Jimenez. Roberto held in his hand a dagger, obviously silver, which she realized suddenly was actually a weapon made from a crucifix. With the CAMEL, Elissa might have had a shot at destroying Hannibal, but Rolf and Jimenez were in the way. They'd have to do it themselves.

We planned this very poorly, she thought, and then reminded herself that they hadn't actually planned it at all. It had just sort of happened. In the battles to come, and she was sure there would be many such conflicts as the world frightened by the U.S. President's assassination, began hunting the vampires, there would have to be more planning ahead. If they'd had only one-third the men and twenty times the CAMEL tubes, they would have destroyed all the shadows already, and a lot of lives would have been saved.

She sighted the CAMEL at another shadow, a female she had seen close to Hannibal and who she assumed was one of his elite. The sighting locked on target, Elissa pulled the trigger as easily as she might a pistol's, and the missile launched. She'd counted to one when the vampire erupted in a great splash of body parts. It was a messy death, Elissa decided, closing her eyes to the carnage, but it was the fastest way to kill them, merciful really.

Hannibal was surrounded. The human soldiers had slung back their firearms so as not to kill one another, and pulled out sharp knives instead. Jimenez brandished the crucifix dagger that Rolf had seen him use at the fortress, a dagger exactly like those Mulkerrin's followers had used in Venice five years ago. Rolf and Jared and two other shadows were there, closing in on the renegade.

Renegade. A strange word for a vampire, Rolf thought. There was a time, not long ago, he knew, when only kind-hearted creatures like Octavian and Cody were considered renegades. Rolf had done his share of hunting, along with all the others. In the ignorance that comes from arrogance, he had believed that humanity were little better than cattle. He had never been the vicious killer that Hannibal was, enjoying murder for its own sake. Rather he'd been like a human, kind to his creatures until it was time for the slaughter, and even then, sometimes sad for them.

What a pompous fool he'd been! They did not have to kill. There was another way to live, a better way. They'd had to be forced into it, by being thrust into the public eye, but it was a good life. And now Hannibal was going to ruin everything. The American President had been killed, and if Rolf knew his former boss, the murder would have been quite a spectacle. It might already be too late to prevent the changes Hannibal intended, Rolf knew, but that did not mean he could go unpunished.

It was a silent vow: he would see Hannibal dead.

But what was Hannibal up to now? They had the renegade surrounded, but he wasn't running. He could simply transform and fly away, but instead he stood his ground against the mob around him. Certainly Hannibal knew that if he fled, Rolf and the humans would follow, but he had to know he would have a better chance of survival if he did run.

Rolf looked at the elder vampire, saw that his eyes were desperate, white hair flying wildly as he whipped his head from side to side, looking at his attackers, looking over them where he could to gauge the rest of the battle. And then Rolf understood. Hannibal was overwhelmed, trying to run the battle from where he fought, cornered. He sent orders and received information through the mind-link he shared with those of his followers who were his blood-children, and with the battle not going as well as he'd hoped, he must have been confused about his next move.

Next to Rolf, Jimenez lunged for Hannibal.

No! Rolf thought, reaching out to snag the back of the commander's jacket, even as Roberto's arm swept out, dagger slashing through the arm Hannibal held up in protection. Even as Hannibal hissed at the pain of the silver passing through his flesh, Rolf pulled Commander Jimenez back just in time to save him from retaliation, a swipe of Hannibal's talons that was meant to tear Jimenez's face off. Hannibal went after the commander, and Rolf stepped in the way.

The battle was joined.

Rolf growled, motioning to those around him to stay back, and they did.

This must be it, Rolf realized. Hannibal had not fled because he knew any clash must come to this, a one-on-one, tooth-and-claw battle with his former deputy. While working together for the SJS, the two had woven a pretense of mutual sufferance, no more. Five years of unspoken hatred, mistrust, hostility, now seethed within them both. Rolf was elated that the day of reckoning between them had finally come.

Renegade, he thought. *Killer*!

And perhaps his hatred was enough to carry the essence of his thoughts to Hannibal's mind, because the savage seemed to respond.

"Traitor!" Hannibal yelled into Rolf's face. "Coward!"

Rolf lost all sense of self, and of time. He and Hannibal were now inseparable, their transformations, metamorphoses, almost one with each other. In their hatred, their explosive bloodlust, their minds forgot the patterns of the deadly creatures they had shifted their shapes to in the past. Instead, the flesh flowed, picking and choosing among the deadliest attributes of those forms, claws lengthening, fur sprouting, snouts stretching to accommodate razor teeth. Hannibal twisted his head and tore a chunk from Rolf's face with a horn that had appeared on his head.

Blood and flesh flew around them. The gore-spattered faces of his comrades gravely looked on, but Rolf was blind to it all as he found an unguarded spot, an unprotected moment, and shoved his right hand into Hannibal's now hard and scaly belly. His claws were sharp, and his strength was enough to slide the hand in, grab a fistful of the vampire's guts and pull. Even as he struggled to eviscerate Hannibal, Rolf had left much of himself unprotected, and the other's terrible jaws clenched on what had become his own snout. His body reacted, changing shape again, his flesh trying desperately to escape the many teeth of his enemy.

Part of his face tore away even as Hannibal's intestines spilled out, flopping on the cobblestones at their feet. In his pain, Rolf's awareness of his surroundings returned. Some of his comrades were moving to assist, but Commander Jimenez motioned for them to stay where they were. Silently, Rolf thanked him. He would kill this creature, and perhaps the disaster Hannibal had planned could still be avoided, perhaps peace was still possible for the weary shadows.

They held each other, like lovers, like weary boxers, though their claws were deep in each other's back, head, neck, scoring to the bone. Hannibal's grip relaxed a bit, and Rolf tried to look him in the eye.

But Hannibal wasn't looking at Rolf. He was looking over Commander Jimenez's head. Rolf followed his line of sight and saw what had drawn his attention. Commander Elissa Thomas, Rolf's lover, stood atop a vehicle, behind many of her troops, with a CAMEL rocket tube on her shoulder, waiting for a clear shot.

Rolf had been winning; it was only a matter of time, and Hannibal had to know it. Rolf was faster, stronger; Hannibal was badly wounded, weakening. But that moment of distraction, seeing Elissa above the terrible battle that raged around them, was an error. Hannibal used all the strength he had within his undead frame to heave Rolf up and away from him. Rolf slammed into a group of soldiers, taking them down, and the vampire Jared as well.

He looked up, his face throbbing, and Hannibal was gone. And then Rolf saw that he had changed. Weakened by his torn belly, the vampire had not the strength to become mist, but he apparently had enough concentration left to transform into a huge bat. In seconds, he was darting across the plaza toward Elissa's perch. Rolf swore, and gunfire spat into the air, and a number of bullets tore right through Hannibal's black form. They slowed him down some, but didn't stop him.

Rolf and Jared changed then, almost simultaneously, and they flew after Hannibal as a wounded eagle and a raven. Around them, several bats rose into the air, but whether they were Hannibal's followers or his own, Rolf could not tell. And neither could the soldiers, as they were all fired upon. Rolf was hit twice, but ignored the small pain, the momentary lack of balance. Commander Thomas was a soldier, that was true, and as such she faced death constantly. But Rolf cared for her, and he would not be responsible for her death.

Elissa brought the CAMEL around to aim it at Hannibal, but the fiend was almost there. She didn't have the two or three seconds it took for the computer to aim, and she didn't wait. The CAMEL's missile blasted from its tube . . . and missed. The target, Hannibal, was too small and too fast, and the computer had not had enough time. Behind him, Rolf heard an explosion as the dome of the Salzburg Cathedral exploded, the missile finding a target after all.

And then it was too late. Before the debris of the dome had begun to fall, before Elissa could even drop the tube and long before Rolf could come to her aid, Elissa was in Hannibal's arms. He spun her to face his pursuers, and she flailed behind her, striking him uselessly with her elbows and feet. But her head and upper body did not move, because Hannibal's left arm was around her neck, the crook of his elbow powerful enough to snap it at any time. His right hand was at her face, and the long talons rested on her right cheek.

Hannibal didn't have to tell Rolf to stop. Changing back into human form, the mute vampire stood twenty feet from the car atop which Hannibal prepared to kill a woman he had so recently made love to, caressed. Rolf didn't know what to do. He felt his loyal shadow warriors step up, behind him, and knew that Jimenez and his soldiers were back there too, every weapon aimed at Hannibal. It also occurred to him that Hannibal's forces must be nearly destroyed for the battle to come to such a sudden halt.

"Ah," Hannibal said, a guttural laugh showing he was still in pain. "This woman will be the death of you, mute."

One long claw etched a red line across Elissa's right cheek, and though she did not scream, Rolf could feel her pain, see her teeth clenched against the cry that lodged in her throat. She stood rigid, but no longer struggled, resigned to whatever might come. Rolf was proud of her, and knew that he cared about her more than he ought to care about someone he'd known for so brief a time. He considered the possibility that he might love her, and couldn't deny it.

A new rage began to build in him, fueled by the futility he recognized in it. For the moment, Hannibal held all the cards. He could only watch as his enemy let the same hand that had scarred her move down Elissa's body to cup her breast through the cloth of her uniform.

"Yes," Hannibal said softly, and only then did Rolf realize the silence that truly had fallen on the plaza. "I can understand your attraction, mute. I'll enjoy this woman quite a bit."

Why didn't they fire? Rolf wondered. Why did the soldiers do nothing? She was just another human to them, surely. So many others of their kind had died there that day. But he knew why they did not, could not, fire. It was the way it had happened, the spectacle, the confrontation. And now, in the midst of a very impersonal, faceless battle, where death was a means to an end, a moment had arrived that made things very personal, made death a thing to be feared, made them all feel as vulnerable and helpless as Elissa was.

He felt it too, and his rage burned higher, and darker.

When Hannibal's jaws opened wide, and his fangs sank tenderly into Elissa's neck, Rolf could not move. But as he looked away, wanting to see anything but the atrocity Hannibal was committing, he saw that Elissa's eyes were closed. He knew that she had wanted him to bite her the night before. She had not said it, but it had been clear just the same. Just as now, she said nothing, but Rolf could see what this meant to her, this violation, rape of a sort. She was a proud soldier, the commander of the American division of the UN security force, and a single tear ran down her cheek until it was stopped by the slash Hannibal had made there, disappearing in the bloody streaks that dripped to her chin.

Before he was aware of it, Rolf was in motion.

15

George Marcopoulos couldn't sleep. How had everything gone so wrong, so fast? The question was unanswerable, but its truth was evident in his every thought, every movement. Joe Boudreau had saved him from death at the hands of a man whom tragedy had just made the President of the United States of America. They had fled across the White House lawn, Joe not advanced enough to fly George out, and his vampiric savior had been forced to injure seriously several Secret Service agents to make that escape possible.

George had been amazed, and relieved, to discover that Boudreau had a car parked nearby. A quick drive to his D.C. apartment, so that George could retrieve those few things that mattered, and they were off, cross-country, driving for the temporary safety of Virginia highways. It wasn't long before they were headed south on Route 81, toward Tennessee.

They had spoken little during all of this, for George had a lot on his mind. Valerie, for one. His wife and family in Boston would more than likely never see him again. He didn't think he had to worry that they'd believe whatever charges Bill Galin (George had a hard time thinking of him as "the President") lodged against him. But Valerie was very sick, and their humiliation by people who wouldn't know better was a terrible thing to consider. George worried, but knew he was powerless.

He was, after all, the worldwide symbol of human cooperation with the shadows. And the whole world had just seen shadows murder the President as a declaration of war. Their ambassador, once a mild-mannered medical examiner from Boston, had disappeared, and could only be considered to be in collusion with their efforts. George had considered trying to change his appearance somehow, but hadn't come up with a plan so far.

The world was at war, and it didn't even know it yet.

In the meantime, there was Salzburg.

As they drove through Virginia, George watched with dread as events unfolded on the dash-screen cellular TV in Joe's car. Armed guards had surrounded the United Nations building, and Rafael Nieto was under 24/7 protection. In Washington, Bill Galin was sworn in as President, and immediately ordered all agencies to investigate the disappearances of Meaghan Gallagher, Alexandra Nueva and George Marcopoulos! CNN reported that its own Allison Vigeant was under investigation, though her status in Salzburg was unknown.

And an international manhunt was declared for Hannibal, the chief marshal of the Shadow Justice System. Of course, that order, made jointly by Galin and Nieto, was essentially an indictment of the SJS in its entirety, and a clear message that it was open season on all vampires.

"What do you think is going to happen?" Joe asked, finally breaking a long silence, and in his voice George heard a tremor of vulnerable, childlike fear. He knew the answer, knew it was not what the young shadow wanted to hear, but its truth was inescapable.

"Armageddon," he said.

Joe only nodded, and they were quiet again as the news anchor switched to a reporter flying above Salzburg in a helicopter. The aerial view was bizarre, to say the least. Where the ground rose up on one side of the river, in the spot where the reporter insisted the Hohensalzburg Fortress was, and where he noted that half of the battle was going on, the picture was completely out of focus, showing only a kaleidoscope of colors.

The reporter claimed that the helicopter had been prohibited from taking off until it appeared that all of the "so-called" demons capable of flight had been destroyed, but also noted that it wouldn't have done them any good previously, because until mere minutes earlier, none of the cameras within the main city had been able to get any picture at all. With that problem solved, the reporter said, a ground team was working its way through Salzburg, broadcasting the carnage it found, the destruction left by the earthquake, the fires and other, less natural disasters. The ground team was attempting to get closer to the fighting now taking place not at the fortress, which still proved impossible to film, but at a place called Residence Plaza. where human and shadow forces were clashing. It was a clear, bright, sunny morning in Austria, and the helicopter offered a fairly good view of the battle.

It looked, to the world and to George Marcopoulos, as though the shadows were attempting to prevent the human troops from reaching the fortress. The reporter repeated several times that the blacked-out area, at the fortress, was where the shadows were battling the sorcerer Liam Mulkerrin. But the audience couldn't see that. All they saw was shadows and humans killing one another. And after the President's assassination, it was exactly what they expected to see.

Joe looked at George out of the corner of his eye, the same way he'd been watching the TV while driving.

"Meaghan knew this would happen eventually, but not so soon," he said to George.

She never talked about it with me, he thought, but didn't open his mouth.

"Is Meaghan the one who made you a—"

"She gave me the gift, yes," Joe said. "I asked her, begged her really. I told her I was dedicated to helping any way I could, and she said the best way I could help was by hiding out. She knew Hannibal had his agents, and I suppose I was meant to be the first of her own.

"She never expected it to happen so soon," he said again.

"Is there a plan?" George asked.

"Not really," Joe admitted. "But there is a meeting place."

George raised an eyebrow. "Are we headed there now?"

"Yeah," he said and smiled a bit. "New Orleans."

"That's a long drive."

"You sleep," Joe said kindly. "I don't need to, remember."

George thought a bit, especially about Meaghan's disappearance. He asked Joe about it, about why Meaghan disappeared.

"She contacted me, in my mind, you understand?" He looked at George, and when he saw that the old man did actually understand, he went on. "She and Alexandra and Lazarus—"

"Lazarus?"

"Yeah." Joe nodded. "They went after Peter Octavian."

Now George was thoroughly confused.

"But Octavian's in . . . ," George began, but he couldn't get the word out.

And all Joe said was "Yeah."

"God help us all," George said softly. Perhaps too softly, because Joe Boudreau didn't say a word in reply.

Salzburg, Austria, European Union.
Wednesday, June 7, 2000, 9:03 A.M.:

Mulkerrin had power enough to destroy them all, despite the confusion he'd begun to experience as the shadows infiltrated the fortress and slowly overwhelmed his hellish forces, his ghostly soldiers. He'd been preparing to do just that, drawing close much of his power, weaving his magic around him as a stronger protection, as well as a battering force with which to strike. This was all new to him, a new kind of power, and he was still growing comfortable with its uses, testing its limits. It seemed only to be limited by his own ability to concentrate on several things at once.

He'd been preparing to destroy the Defiant Ones when the magic itself contracted around him, a familiar voice screaming his own name, in his head, tearing at his brain from inside like something struggling to be born. And then he'd known. Will Cody was alive and had access to the magic! His magic, the power God had given him to purify the world! It was impossible, not only that Cody was capable of such a feat, but that he was alive at all. Mulkerrin had torn his heart out!

The former priest looked up, the action itself his first signal that things had gone drastically wrong. Rather than standing triumphant as his power swept over the vampires, he was on his knees, hands clamped vise-like to the sides of his head. In a moment, along the tendrils of sensation he felt through his magical influence, he knew that all of the portals were closed. The sky above was free from his control, communications would have returned, and the sun was shining down.

And his own protective aura was rapidly deteriorating as vampires slashed and raked at it, coming ever nearer to him in their many forms.

No! He had the power!

"*Away*!" Mulkerrin shouted, and the aura surrounding him nearly exploded with the force of his magic, obliterating several of the vampires that had come nearest to him and throwing others across the courtyard, to slam into the stone walls around them.

Even as he reached out with his mind to find Cody, to retaliate, he was on the attack once again, more ferocious than before. And yet he was startled once again, for now he could not find Will Cody anywhere. Only moments before the vampire had been as attuned to the flow of magic around the fortress as Mulkerrin himself, and now he was nowhere to be found.

What then? Had the death of the vampire's spirit created some backlash which struck while Mulkerrin was vulnerable? No, he could not accept it; Cody was truly still alive and yet Liam was blind to him. He felt very strongly that Cody lived, yet he could not sense his location. *But enough foolishness*, he thought. It was a mystery, but if Cody no longer had access to the magic, he could not truly harm Mulkerrin no matter where he was, and the battle was far from over. He was toying with them now, really. He could destroy them all, though he might have to drop his shields to do so, to summon the concentration. That would be foolish, when taking his time was so much more . . . gratifying.

The time for play was finished. No more portals were necessary, for the moment. Later, demons would be useful to frighten the human race, to make them see exactly what their rotting lives had wrought upon the eternal scales of justice. But for now, Mulkerrin was concerned only with this shadow race of beings without any true place. Their insolence and interference, their *defiance*, was at an end.

"Attack!" shouted the shadow he knew was called Martha. "Kill him now! He is weakening!"

And the fool led the new charge against him. The scene had changed, but it was still familiar. Mulkerrin, all in black, white hair disheveled as the air around him, tinged green by magic, protected him from harm. But it was more that the reality around him was altered by the magic, than it was that the air itself had changed. The portals were gone, the demons all dead. Many of the spirits of dead soldiers he had raised had already found new human hosts and were making their way back to the fortress even now. But once they were killed again, they would return to their rest. He had given up sustaining them.

It was now just Mulkerrin and the vampires, and his magic could protect him as long as he desired it to. But protection was not what he wished.

"Fool," Mulkerrin snarled at Martha as she rushed toward him, and she changed the course of her attack slightly as he held his hand out to her, palm up, as if he meant to hold hands with her, to walk, quietly, joined in that way like lovers. Even as Martha's hands became talons, with which she planned to tear at Mulkerrin's weird force shield, she watched a tiny cloud of smoky darkness whirl into life above the palm of his outstretched hand. The darkness sprang into being; half a second later it was as large, or larger, than she. Dozens of red embers burned within, and Martha knew they were the eyes of a sentient being, a creature from Hell, yes, but another Hell than the one from which Mulkerrin drew most of his slaves.

There was the world, the universe, and then there was Hell, but her brother Lazarus had taught her that there was much in between those poles, many other worlds, other dimensions, and many races darker and more evil than the denizens of Hell. This thing of the burning eyes and the countless mouths filled with infinite gleaming ebony teeth, this was one of those things, a *Nachzehrer*, or at least fitting the description of one.

And it was upon her even as she exploded in flame, attempting to use her natural shapeshifting ability to drive it off. But it was no more corporeal than she, and though it could not surround and douse the flames that Martha had become, it could unfortunately consume her, a bit at a time.

"*No!*" Martha heard Isaac shout, even as the thing's attack gave her some kind of psychic pain, and then he screamed as the thing fell upon him in her place.

Martha changed back to her true form, lashing out immediately at the thing of darkness. Her talons passed through it, as did the hands and arms of those who had come to her aid. Even as dozens of vampires rushed past them to attack Mulkerrin's shield, she could hear the sorcerer's laughter as her nephew, Isaac, the son of Lazarus continued to scream. His shouts of agony, coupled with the slurping, bone-crunching sounds of the thing consuming him, emanated from within it, but he was not there. Martha could reach right through and touch Stefan, the SJS deputy, on the other side of the *Nachzehrer*.

And then the screams stopped, but the gnawing sounds, and Mulkerrin's laughter, continued.

Cody had pulled a light sweatshirt off the first corpse that looked to be about his size, a tourist who'd been possessed by one of Mulkerrin's soldiers. And now he was making his way up a long walkway toward the courtyard. The bestial sounds of attacking vampires echoed back to him, but no gunfire, no traditional sounds of war.

When the screams began, he ran toward them. At the top of the walkway, he found himself above the yard, a short stone staircase leading down into the thick of things. From up there, he saw it all; the thing of darkness, not a shadow or anything he'd ever seen before, and the vampires swarming around Mulkerrin, who laughed and laughed. And he'd seen quite enough.

"Mulkerrin!" Cody shouted, and he could almost *feel* it as the sorcerer turned his attention away from his attackers and toward the new threat.

Not almost, he realized. Cody could feel it, the magic around Mulkerrin, pouring through the castle, surrounding them all, really, ready to be bent to the sorcerer's will if he had the strength to do it. Unlike before, when Cody's spirit was in it, was a part of the magic, he could not sense anything through it, but he could feel its presence. He knew that it was there, and that Mulkerrin wielded it with violence and hatred.

Even from forty yards away, as he descended the stairs, Cody could feel Mulkerrin's power find its focus on him, could feel the anger seething, boiling into action. Cody knew an instant before that a tentacle of magic, formed from the greenish aura that surrounded Mulkerrin, would lash out at him, slamming like a battering ram into the stairs where he'd stood but a moment earlier. He knew when another of those fearsome night things was born in Mulkerrin's hand and sent rocketing toward him.

Cody went to defend himself, but in a moment, he found he did not need to. He could feel the thing's confusion and, in a flash of his own, realized that it couldn't see him. He was somehow invisible to it.

"You will die, Cody," Mulkerrin screamed as Will came closer, though the former priest did not attempt any new attack, perhaps sensing the disturbance Cody created in the magic. The aura around the sorcerer blossomed suddenly, growing in a flash from a ball surrounding his body to a dome which stretched ten feet above him and twenty feet all around. Vampires were thrown backward and to the ground. Others were borne aloft by the growth of the thing, and changed to flying creatures so they did not have to slide down the side of the shield, so they didn't have to touch it more than necessary.

Cody reached the outer edge of the dome and helped Martha to her feet.

"You know me?" she asked, seeking confirmation.

"From Rolf's mind," he answered.

"It's impossible to estimate Mulkerrin's power," she said even as the other vampires struggled around them. "Every time we think we've got it pinned down, it changes and grows a little more."

"I don't think even he knows how much power he has," Cody muttered, turning to lock eyes with the madman, twenty feet away. "But I would like to know where he got it."

Cody had known Mulkerrin was a madman, and he had not been disappointed.

"Where did my power come from?" Liam Mulkerrin asked, stunned that any should question such a thing. "From God, you vile, evil thing. The Lord Himself endowed me with these abilities so that I could purge the Earth, beginning with you and your kind!"

Cody shook his head, still tired from everything he had been through, but energized by the situation, knowing that many others of his people would die if he were to fail.

"You tried that once already, didn't you?" he asked, mocking, feeling Mulkerrin's hatred of his kind, but more, of him personally. "That's the only shot you get."

And then suddenly he knew he could do it, and just as quickly he *was* doing it. With Martha and the rest looking on in astonishment, Cody began to wade right through Mulkerrin's protective field, the greenish aura surrounding him, welcoming him.

"I'm coming for you, Liam," he said with a low growl.

"No!" Mulkerrin snapped. "You cannot. My magic protects me."

"Not from me, apparently," Cody said grimly.

And he could feel it, the strain Mulkerrin put behind his efforts, the magic that stretched out, searching for Cody, hoping to hurt him, or at least to reject him. But it couldn't find him, and therefore could not affect him. Mulkerrin was vulnerable, and Cody had been taught the lesson early in life that in a true war, you must exploit the vulnerable. He was wading through Mulkerrin's shield when he saw the resolve appear in his old, mad eyes.

And then those eyes closed. Mulkerrin raised his hands, muscles straining in his neck, and the ground shook, buckled, cracked beneath Cody's feet. The stone floor of the fortress, which had withstood the siege of many centuries opened wide and swallowed Will Cody and several others ... Then, with a terrible shout from Mulkerrin, it slammed together again, tearing new cracks in the foundation of the fortress.

But Cody was no fool, and neither were his comrades. All but one of the vampires who had fallen transformed to escape—into mist, into fire, one into a sharp-clawed owl. Cody knew now that even if Mulkerrin could not attack him directly with magic, it did not mean the madman was powerless against him. On the contrary, as the fortress continued to shake, its battlements crumbling and the stairs Cody had only just descended disappearing into a crevice, he realized that the sorcerer was creating another earthquake for the entire city, not merely the fortress.

It must stop. Cody made his way toward Mulkerrin again, the sorcerer apparently ignoring his approach. But only apparently. For as Cody neared, once again at the edge of the greenish aura that surrounded the sorcerer, the entire floor beneath both of them collapsed. A hole forty feet in diameter opened up in the center of the courtyard falling into the rooms below, and thinking to confront Mulkerrin there, Cody allowed himself to fall, did not change shape. Only when he lay there, bruised and bleeding but not feeling the quickly closing wounds, did he realize that, in fact, Mulkerrin had not fallen at all.

Above him, Mulkerrin hung suspended at the center of the glow that was his strength, his access to magic. Dozens of vampires, in flying or floating forms, hovered around that bubble-like shield, attacking it, testing its strength, but Mulkerrin ignored them. Instead, he stared down at Cody, who lay in the rubble, and his grin was a combination of hate, insanity and fear. Fear, yes, for Cody was a threat to him, an unexpected one.

"The strength of Hell is inside you!" Mulkerrin shouted, or Cody thought that was what he heard over the noise of the subsiding quake. Then, more clearly: "Your purification will set an example, the Lord Himself demands it."

And Cody wondered yet again where Mulkerrin had gotten the power to control the flow of magic, of the ether, the way he now did. Certainly it was not from "the Lord." But the maniac believed it was, and perhaps Cody could use that against him. In any case, Cody was apparently now immune to direct attack by magic, invisible to demons and other such creatures. He recognized then that he might be their only hope to destroy the sorcerer once and for all.

A new rumbling pulled Cody's attention from Mulkerrin, and even as he stood among the rubble, he turned to look in the direction the sorcerer now pointed. Cody looked up, and the wall was coming down on top of him.

Salzburg, Austria, European Union.
Wednesday, June 7, 2000, 9:11 A.M.:

Residence Plaza was a shambles, the Salzburg Cathedral destroyed and dead civilians and soldiers strewn on the cobblestones with their throats slashed or bellies torn open, their blood painting the ground in a terrible montage. Hannibal stood on the hood of a shiny Mercedes and sucked blood from the neck of Elissa Thomas as hundreds of UN soldiers and a handful of shadows looked on.

And Rolf Sechs, her lover, was in motion.

But so was the ground.

As Rolf took to the air, flashing past his own shadow troops and the UN forces led by Roberto Jimenez, the earthquake began with a gentle tremble, like a frightened shiver down the back of every being in the plaza. But by the time Rolf was closing in on Hannibal, only feet away from those green eyes that locked with his own even as the fiend licked several stray drops of blood from Elissa's neck . . . by then the plaza itself had begun to crack, nearly in half in a direct line from the shattered cathedral, through the gathered army and to the street directly in front of the car upon which the renegade Hannibal stood triumphant, his white hair flashing in the sunlight.

Everything happened at once. The ground opened up beneath the Mercedes, tilting the car forward at a drastic angle, dumping Hannibal and Commander Elissa Thomas from its hood, toward the huge crack yawning open before them. Before Hannibal could fall, Rolf slammed into him, sending both of them flying over and behind the car. Commander Thomas landed just at the edge of the crack, and only managed to scramble away from the crumbling street with the help of two of her soldiers. The Mercedes slid into the gaping hole, and the ground continued to shake, making it impossible for many of the soldiers to stay on their feet.

Behind the jutting tail end of the Mercedes, Rolf and Hannibal faced each other once again. Finally free of the disorientation and confusion of battle that had surrounded them up to now, they knew the time had come. Elissa was weak, though Hannibal had not really taken much blood from her, and as the earthquake subsided, she signaled for her troops to ready themselves for the outcome. She wanted to take Hannibal down and keep him down, negating this duel, but Rolf was in the way. Her lover and his enemy would have their final battle, it seemed.

She wanted to shout, wanted to stop it. But she also wanted Hannibal dead, and knew that Rolf had the best chance of achieving that feat. Her interest in him paled by comparison to his strategic importance. She resigned herself to that. Elissa Thomas was a practical woman.

And then she heard two words coming through her collarcomm, words spoken by Roberto Jimenez, commander of the United Nations Security Forces: "Open fire."

"No!" she said sharply, preparing to countermand that order among her own troops. But it would not make a difference, and she was too slow.

The rapid bursts of gunfire that filled the plaza joined together in one terrible rumble, as if the earthquake had come again, and Elissa could only watch as a swarm of bullets pulverized both Hannibal and Rolf. Their bodies danced with each wound, pushed back farther and farther along the Alter Markt as the soldiers advanced. Elissa heard screaming among the soldiers, as shadows, both friend and enemy, turned on the humans as one.

"Stop this!" she screamed into her comm. "Jimenez, he is our ally!"

And Commander Jimenez surprised her by bothering to reply at all.

"He is a vampire! Nothing more!"

And then Hannibal turned to mist, a pinkish cloud stained with the blood he'd shed only a single breath earlier, and the bullets merely passed through him. Rolf continued to dance under the barrage of metal, but the cloud that was Hannibal moved forward, toward the army toward Elissa. Even as she began to back up, to stumble through the soldiers at her sides, she knew what was happening, knew it was too late to stop.

"Commander," a whisper said in her ear, "I am Hector. I'm pleased to make your acquaintance."

And her arms were seized, each by a pair of hands, and then she was rising above the broken earth, above the soldiers and Jimenez's shout of "Hold your fire!" She was surrounded by at least a dozen shadows in forms both familiar and strange. One seemed almost reptilian though it had wings, almost like a small dragon. And the bloody mist of their master floated along with her, too close. She could feel Hannibal's fury.

In the plaza, the vampiric SJS agents continued to battle the humans who had turned on them when the bullets began to fly at Hannibal and Rolf. There were only five of them left, and Commander Jimenez didn't really want to kill them, but he didn't want them alive either. The older and smarter they became, the harder they were to kill. The American President was dead, and the world would be hunting vampires. He realized that this had to be the first move in that hunt.

"Traitor," a voice called out, over the brief bursts of gunfire and the sounds of struggle, and Jimenez turned to follow it. Six, he realized as he spotted the vampire named Jared, the son of Lazarus, or so he'd been told. He was about to order his troops to fire on the creature, but then Jared disappeared. One moment he was there, on open ground just waiting to be taken out, and the next he was gone.

"Jimenez, you are a traitor! A betrayer! Without honor!" the voice came again, and Roberto looked up along the Alter Mark, where Hannibal and Rolf had battled, where they'd been concentrating all their fire only a moment ago . . . and Jared was there. In his arms, the youthful-looking vampire held the bloody corpse of Rolf Sechs, lifting it with ease and walking back toward the troops.

Automatic weapons swung to bear on Jared, and in the moment before the shooting began, Roberto felt an emotion unfamiliar to him: confusion.

"Hold your fire!" he shouted again, and even those who hadn't listened the first time acknowledged the order now. In seconds, the other shadows had flown to Jared's side, and now the five vampires stood facing down hundreds of armed humans whose mistrust and fear had turned to hatred and disgust.

It was an insane picture, those few creatures against so many soldiers, and Jimenez could not prevent the possibility of merciless slaughter, of genocide, from entering his mind. Just what the Church had attempted. And suddenly he was certain that the world would complete the genocide that Liam Mulkerrin had begun, even if the priest were defeated once again. Though for those five short years, it had seemed to work, humans and vampires were not meant to live together, he knew now. Each group reminded the other too much of itself. Roberto knew that if he let these vampires live, he would only have to hunt them again later. And though he hated them, he thought, *Dear God, how much the world has changed, been redefined, in the span of mere hours*.

"What is wrong with you?" Jared snapped, glaring at Jimenez. "We were your allies. I could feel your hate from the start, but we have goals in common, at least. Are you stupid?"

It was silent in the plaza, as if the whole scene were being played out underwater, and when Jimenez spoke, he did so quietly, knowing the vampire could hear him.

"Not stupid," he said sadly. "Efficient."

And he was somewhat sad, which told him his actions had been correct. He had begun to respect Rolf Sechs, even to like him. That was dangerous in the new, new world. Dangerous for all. It was fortunate that the mute had died.

Died? Even now, as Roberto looked on, Rolf was stirring in Jared's arms. Jimenez looked closer, saw the sadness in Jared's eyes, the set of his mouth. Jimenez nearly dropped his weapon to his side when Jared shifted and the commander could see that Rolf's mouth was locked onto Jared's bicep, drinking his blood. Even as Roberto watched, Rolf's wounds were healing.

Then Rolf's head lolled back, his eyes opened, and he looked directly at Jimenez. He motioned for Jared to put him down and began limping toward the soldiers. Weapons clicked and ratcheted as they were brought to bear on the still staggering but quickly healing German, but Jimenez shouted for them not to fire, to allow him to approach.

Rolf's gait improved as he crossed the last ten feet, until he stood immediately in front of Jimenez, who finally lowered his weapon, giving up on preventing retribution, if that's what Sechs wanted. He owed the creature that much at least. He felt rage, but no violence.

Silence reigned once again, and Rolf Sechs, a mute, ruled that world. He had apparently lost his voice-pad, for he reached out a hand, pointed a finger and tapped Commander Jimenez on the chest. The other hand pointed to the sky, in the direction Commander Thomas had been taken, then dropped to his pocket, from which the vampire drew a single British coin, which he turned so Jimenez could see each face.

And Roberto Jimenez dropped his head, for he understood the pantomime, at least its fundamental meaning.

You're no better than Hannibal, Sechs was telling him. *Two sides of the same coin.*

And then the silence was broken once again, by a new voice.

"I would translate for you," the voice said in Spanish, from across the plaza, "but I have a feeling you understood quite well."

The troops scrambled once again, running to find new cover, new positions from which to attack, as a formidable force of strangely dressed warriors, armed only with swords, lined the open street where Residenzplatz and Mozartplatz met. Jimenez fired orders into his collarcomm advising caution, as the man who had spoken, looking ancient and regal, stepped forward into the plaza.

"Your name?" the man said, once again in Spanish, and before Roberto knew it, he was answering, as if to a superior officer.

"Commander Roberto Jimenez . . . ," he started to say, and then he was angry at his compliance. "Who the hell are you?"

The man smirked in a way that was not obnoxious in someone his age, turned to a companion who was dressed in modern clothes and then looked back at Jimenez.

"I've been away too long," he said. "But many still remember the name of Charlemagne. You will accept our assistance, or surrender your weapons."

Roberto wanted to laugh, but knew that nothing here was funny.

✳
16

Time. They'd had none of it, confronted with yet another potential enemy, another potential battle, chipping away, life by life, at the soldiers, the men and women, that Roberto Jimenez had led into Austria. It had started out ugly, but simple. It had gotten progressively uglier, and quickly became total chaos. Rather than storming one fortress, getting past hundreds of unholy monsters to sanction one, very powerful man who had already nearly destroyed the city of Salzburg and intended to continue on that path they had been forced by Hannibal to begin a bloody confrontation on a second front. Some of the shadows fought at their sides, others tore out their throats, and every human soldier in Salzburg stood on a razor edge of suspicion and fear, of not knowing if any vampire were trustworthy.

It was an impossible situation, one in which Roberto could only lead by his gut, and where the hand of destiny pushed him. They hadn't had a choice in leaving the siege on Mulkerrin at the fortress to the vampires' forces; human soldiers would have been killed or possessed by the dead. They hadn't had a choice in descending into the city to save whatever remained of the civilian populace from Hannibal and his renegade vampires. They had failed in that effort. Roberto felt that he had failed. The civilians had died, Hannibal had been defeated but escaped, and Roberto had nearly killed the leader of his vampiric allies in his efforts to win. To win.

But winning was a hope long since past, and he knew that now. Instead, he could only hope to accomplish his goal, to complete his mission, to destroy Liam Mulkerrin. His noble wish to save lives had disappeared. And now this newcomer, who claimed to be one of Europe's greatest leaders, and who led a shadow force of about one hundred warriors who dressed the part, had offered to help Commander Jimenez's soldiers, or destroy them.

Roberto had perhaps five hundred men and women left, and with the number of corpses littering the plaza, he couldn't be certain there were even that many. Five humans to one vampire: automatic weapons and missile launchers notwithstanding, those were terrible odds. Even if he managed to defeat the newcomers, Roberto would not have enough soldiers left to make any kind of attack on the fortress, and that was assuming the shadow force currently battling Mulkerrin had been able to destroy the ghosts, to make it safe for the human soldiers to return there at all.

He had little choice, really.

"We would welcome your assistance, sir," Jimenez said in English, then in Spanish when he realized it was possible that none of this newly arrived army spoke English.

"A wise choice," the leader said, in Spanish still, and Roberto was consciously aware for the first time that the darkness that had hung in the distance over Hohensalzburg Fortress had lifted, and now the whole city shone with the brightness of the June morning. The air smelled fresh and clean, the wind having carried away the stench of the demons they had killed, and the sky was blue and bright. But no birds sang. The morning, the beauty of the day, was a lie.

You must go after Hannibal now, Rolf.

The voice in Rolf's head surprised him so much he nearly fell down. He was recovering relatively quickly from the terrible wounds he'd received, thanks mainly to Jared's offering of blood, but for a moment he had to wonder whether he was hallucinating. The only blood-relatives he was aware of who still lived were Will Cody and perhaps Alexandra Nueva, wherever she was. But then . . .

You might consider me an ancestor, came the voice again and Rolf shook off Jared's assistance, standing tall once again to scan the army brought by the creature who called himself Charlemagne.

Oh, but he is Charlemagne, said the voice.

Then who are you? Rolf thought, and he saw a figure separate itself from the crowd of soldiers blocking Mozartplatz. While the entire army seemed dressed from another time, with cloaks and tunics, and cloth straps wound up their legs from their shoes, this vampire wore blue jeans, brown bootlike shoes and a fashionable pullover jersey.

My name is John Courage, and Rolf knew he was looking right at the shadow who used that name, whose voice was in his head.

Then Rolf threw a glance at Jared, who gave him a small smile in return. Martha, Jared and Isaac had been sent by this man, and Cody had known of him . . . Cody. Rolf looked up at the fortress and could see from where he stood that many of the walls had crumbled, several parapets collapsing down the side of the hill.

Isaac, unfortunately, is dead, Courage told him.

Rolf began to walk forward, across the plaza, winding his way through the bodies of fallen soldiers, trying not to smell their blood as he realized that he was still in need of sustenance. The other five surviving members of his team—Sebastiano, Carlo, Annelise, young Erika and Jared—followed behind, and Jimenez motioned for all of his people to clear a path, to allow the six vampires to pass. By the time they emerged from the pack of humans, Rolf saw that there was a single female with them as well. She too was dressed in modern fashion.

And Rolf knew her.

"Rolf!" Allison Vigeant yelled, and with John Courage walking casually behind her, she rushed toward him, arms outstretched for a hug.

And he gave her one, happy as he was to see her alive. He wanted to balk at getting his blood all over her clothes, but she didn't seem to care. She began to introduce him to Courage, but Rolf waved such niceties away. He already knew the man. In the meantime, she wanted to know what had happened to her lover, Will Cody, and Rolf was happy to have Courage there to relate his thoughts to her. Through him, Rolf explained what had happened with Hannibal, and why the human troops could not approach the fortress. Through him, Rolf was able to tell Allison that Will Cody had nearly died, but that as far as he knew, he had recovered and was even now fighting Mulkerrin at the fortress.

"Well, we've got to help him," Allison declared, her matter-of-factness distracting Rolf from his obsession with Hannibal and the confrontation of only moments before with Roberto Jimenez.

"And we will," Courage said, "though first we've got to deal with these humans . . . No offense, Allison."

"None taken, John."

Who are you, really? Rolf thought suddenly, and Courage's eyes met his again. *My ancestor, from how far back*?

But this time, Courage didn't answer with his mind.

"We'll get to that, Rolf," the man said, sounding as if he meant it. "First things first, though. You've got to go after Hannibal and his new coven. Stop him now or he may become even more dangerous to us in the future."

Oh, I'm going all all right, Rolf thought, *even if it takes me forever to find him. I mean either to save Elissa or avenge her.*

"Vengeance is the work of the Lord," Courage said, startling him. "Hannibal must be destroyed to protect our race. And it won't take you forever to find him, for I suspect I know where he is headed.

"Jared," Courage said and turned to the other shadow, "go with Rolf Help them track Hannibal, and destroy him. At any cost."

"And fast, Jared," Allison added, and Rolf felt her pain as a terrible memory clouded her eyes.

"Rolf," she said, "I was Hannibal's prisoner once. He did terrible things to me, but you freed me before the worst could happen. You've got to do the same for this woman. I know what Hannibal does to his female prey, and I've seen what he does when he's through with them.

"Hurry."

"And what of them?" Jared asked Courage, and they all turned to face the humans, who stood alert, vigilant in the morning sun. The wind carried the mutterings of Roberto Jimenez and the French commander, a woman named Surro, across the plaza, but he could not make out their words. The whole scene seemed like a Western showdown to him, but on a much larger scale, and for much higher stakes.

It was still fairly early in the morning, but already it was beginning to get unseasonably warm for June in Austria. Blood was beginning to dry, corpses to stink of death. Rolf had to wonder how long it had been since Charlemagne's troops had eaten, and what it would take to push them over the edge. They had to be quick about things, no matter which way it went.

Then, without word or thought, Charlemagne came forward to join them, and he, Courage, Rolf and Allison began to walk toward the human army. Weapons were leveled at them, but they kept walking, stopping midway between the two forces. Jimenez had said he would accept Charlemagne's assistance, but not that he would enjoy it.

"Please keep in mind," Courage said loudly, "that the woman you see here is as human as any of you. Should you fire, we vampires would survive but she would most assuredly die!"

"What a comforting thought," she mumbled to him, and Rolf couldn't hold back a smile.

Moments later, Jimenez and Surro stepped out to meet them, accompanied by several other, junior officers. Introductions were cold, and Jimenez glared at Allison as though she were a traitor.

"The American President is dead, I understand," Courage said, and Allison's mouth dropped open. Rolf put a hand on her shoulder and nodded, though he was surprised by Courage's knowledge of the fact.

"Assassinated by Hannibal's agents," Jimenez agreed.

"I'm glad you chose to phrase it that way," Courage nodded. "Still, we are at war, are we not? Vampires and humans? As of that event, have we not become the prey of human armies around the world?"

Rolf had understood, somewhat, but now the implications of what Courage was saying truly sunk in. There would be no recovery for the shadows. There would be some people, certainly, who would stand up for the idea that just as there were good and bad people, the same was true of vampires, but most of the world would be too frightened to see it. Most of the world had been, in fact, waiting for such an ugly incident, for their fears to be confirmed, their secret nightmares to take a tangible form, so that they could strike out. The dream was over. Vampires would have to hide in shadows once again.

And now he needed to leave, to be off, after Hannibal. For vengeance, no matter what Courage said, but also for the future of his people. They might survive if they disappeared into the night for a decade or two, perhaps tried again in another era, but if Hannibal were allowed to live, none of that would be possible. Hannibal wanted war and death and destruction.

"You are savages," Jimenez said bluntly, and Rolf could see that he was uncomfortable revealing these feelings. "You are predators born to kill, and humanity must protect itself. Look at Hannibal."

"You fool!" Allison snapped at him. "Their race created Hannibal, yes, but ours created Liam Mulkerrin! I have been Hannibal's prisoner, and I would rather be that again than be in Mulkerrin's hands. Human beings are no less monsters than shadows are."

She turned to Rolf.

"Go, Rolf. Go now. Kill that bastard.

"And you," she turned back to Jimenez, "you can do whatever you want after today, hunt them if you must. But they are going to take care of their own monster, and it's your responsibility to help us take care of yours, to defend the human race against whatever Mulkerrin's become."

For a moment, nobody spoke a word, then Jimenez nodded. Charlemagne stepped forward then and said something in Spanish, which Rolf did not understand. From the look on his face, it seemed that Jimenez didn't get it either but Allison apparently did, and she was looking at Charlemagne with eyebrows raised.

"Your silver," Courage translated, though they all knew Jimenez spoke Spanish. "You have silver on you, most likely a weapon. We will likely have a better opportunity to use it than you will."

Jimenez was obviously stunned, but so was Rolf. He had seen the dagger Roberto Jimenez carried; it had come from the ruins of the Venice Jihad, had been used by Mulkerrin's troops there, but . . .

"How did you—" Commander Jimenez began, but Courage interrupted.

"We can smell it," he said, even as he held out his hand.

Incredibly, Rolf watched. Jimenez reached inside his shirt, withdrew the knife and handed it over to John Courage. Even more incredibly, Courage did not even flinch, but rather lifted the dagger and admired it, sunlight glinting off its surface, then kissed its crucifix handle.

I don't understand, Rolf thought.

You will, my son, Courage said in Rolf's mind. *When you return, all will be explained to you.*

Then Jared was at Rolf's side again, and he saw the four other survivors of his team standing ready.

"Let's go," Jared said. "John has shown me where we must seek out Hannibal. He must be destroyed."

And moments later, they had left the plaza, the corpses and the armies behind and begun their hunt.

Allison was afraid, anxious and angry. Angry at humanity, anxious about the battle with Liam Mulkerrin, the second that she would witness in her life, and afraid of the outcome. Afraid for Will Cody, the man she loved. She thought of Will's tenderness, the sensitivity within his showman's exterior, the kindness of his heart and the way his words changed in the quiet moments they had shared over the past five years. He had, in many ways, become her life. Her professional life had become defined by his shadow race, and her private life had become one with his own.

They might as well have been husband and wife, though they'd been waiting for the world to change enough so they could be legally married. Now it looked as though that would never happen. It made no difference to Allison. In her mind and heart, Will Cody was her husband.

She didn't know what she would do without him. And she vowed she would never have to discover that. From what she could gather, Cody and the other vampires seemed to be holding their own against Mulkerrin. But Charlemagne and his warriors were different—older, stronger, more confident and much more in control of their vampiric abilities. Their arrival would make the difference: it had to. They were devoted to God, did not fear silver, though it did have a debilitating effect on them, and believed in themselves, in their goodness, in a way that none of the shadows she had known ever had.

And that only reaffirmed what she had believed all along. She knew that the shadows were basically good, the way humans were, maybe even more so. But they could be twisted, made into something terrible, as Hannibal had been. Again, as the humans they once were.

And then there was Courage. He was the reason, she knew, that Charlemagne's men, and the vampires she had met at the monastery, Lazarus's family, were different. He was the reason—his leadership, his charisma, his words. She was not certain yet who he was, but she suspected . . . Oh, what she suspected! She might have guessed much of it earlier, but her mind wouldn't let her conceive of it. The more he told her, the more she realized how different he was, what he could do. When he told her that he could communicate with Rolf, and why . . . she could barely stand to be near him without screaming at him to be truthful, to reveal everything to her.

She needed to talk to Will, to reason it out with him. Even though she knew he would laugh at her, tell her she was out of her mind, she needed to hear him say it. And then she would convince him, some-how, and in doing so convince herself.

For Allison Vigeant truly believed that John Courage was the first vampire. The very first.

Courage smiled at her then, as if reading her mind though she knew—was fairly sure—that he couldn't. Charlemagne and Commander Jimenez were speaking Spanish so fast she could barely understand a word here and there and the more Jimenez apparently learned, the paler his face became.

Allison saw movement from the corner of her eye and turned back to see John holding both hands to his head bent ever so slightly. His face showed terrible pain.

"John," she said and went to him, held his arm, "what is it?"

"Martha, Isaac, so many others gone . . .," Courage said quietly, almost to himself. Then he met her eyes, and was suddenly terrified for herself, for Will, for the future. She was only human, after all, and they were so much more.

Allison looked around wildly, her mind seeking some respite, perhaps somewhere to hide from the events unfolding around her. Charlemagne and Jimenez had stopped speaking, were staring at John Courage, and Courage stood up straight, the pain in his face turning to fierce determination.

"It's over up there, gentlemen," Courage said. "Mulkerrin's won."

"Is Will . . ." Allison was finally able to get the words out, but John shook his head slowly, as if he couldn't believe it himself.

"I don't know," he said.

"Let's move!" Jimenez said, and turned to signal his troops, but a gesture from John Courage stopped him.

"Don't bother," Courage said, almost cynically. "He's coming to us."

Hell.
One Hundred Sixty-Seven Days,
One Minute After Departure:

It seemed as if they had been chipping away at Peter Octavian's crystal prison forever. Meaghan knew it hadn't *been* forever, but it had been weeks. Just when they might have stopped, after more than three weeks had gone by and they were prepared to give up hope, Peter had opened his eyes, looked at them, recognized them, pleaded with them, all with those eyes. Meaghan wondered why he did not communicate through the mind-link they once shared, the natural rapport she had with him as her blood-father. She told herself the only answer was that he could not, though she had no idea why.

And there was another reason she and Lazarus kept at the glass, kept working to free Peter Octavian, but one the two vampires refused to discuss: their other options. What other alternative did they have, wandering around Hell without the spells necessary to return to their own world? They had come to find Peter because the world needed him in its battle against Mulkerrin's madness. But now they needed him as well, if they were ever to escape.

The other question that had haunted them was why they had been allowed to continue to hack away at Peter's prison without any demonic interference. Meaghan and Lazarus had both been at Venice, been a part of the events for which the demon Beelzebub now punished Peter Octavian. Surely the demon-lord would enjoy their suffering as well.And yet, though the Suffering continued to wail in agony on the mountain above them, where they were burnt to cinders again and again, and though a new, bloody crystal prison would sprout every day from the glass beneath their feet, filled with damned souls, they never saw a demon-slave, much less a lord. Nothing.

They had first used their hands, formed into razor-sharp claws that were less easily burned by the heat of the glass, to shatter the edges of Peter's prison. They pounded at it but it wouldn't crack, and Meaghan and Lazarus realized that they would be forced to chip away at the thing until they reached its occupant. Meaghan had been astounded when Lazarus transformed his fingers into solid but completely functional steel. She had caused the same reaction among the shadows in Venice when she had shapeshifted into a hawk and then a tiger, but most of them had adapted quickly to those hidden abilities.

It had taken Meaghan a week of Lazarus's explanations before she could duplicate the trick. And during their times of rest, he helped her with other forms, like wood, stone and water. It was all the same, he had insisted, and was right. But she was still surprised by that development.

After that, the work had gotten easier, and they had continued their efforts unmolested by the denizens of this Hellish world. As they worked, Meaghan had become convinced that the theory she had developed on their walk across the surface of Hell was correct—it was a planet—somewhere, somehow, perhaps not in any universe humans had ever imagined, but a planet nonetheless, dedicated to the suffering of all manner of sentient beings.

And Peter was one of them. Meaghan didn't like to think of him suffering, but she could not turn away. She consoled herself with the knowledge that if she and Lazarus had not come, Peter would never have been freed. Of course, that was getting a bit ahead of herself, but she had a blind faith that they would escape from this world.

"We're almost through," Lazarus said, smiling through the exhausted expression on his face. Meaghan did not reply, her mind too busy with other things. She thought again about time. Gauged by their need for blood, which was only now beginning to become a real problem, she and Lazarus had decided that the months which they had spent in Hell—though "on" Hell might have been a more appropriate expression—had not been even a single day on their own world. They were confident that if they could return, they could make a real difference in the battle against Mulkerrin. After all, surely the battle could not have been decided so quickly.

But what of Peter? If the months they had spent here were less than a day on their own world, how long had Peter been suffering inside his glass prison? He'd crossed over into Hell five years before Meaghan and Lazarus, according to their own timetable. On Hell, that had to be . . . Meaghan paused a moment in her work, but Lazarus didn't seem to notice. Peter had been the illegitimate son of the last Byzantine emperor. He'd become a predator, part of Karl Von Reinman's coven, but had renounced that path on the last night of the nineteenth century. Then he'd lived a new life, helping humans in small ways, hiding in plain sight.

And then he'd become the savior of his people, revealing the plot to destroy them, in time for a real defense, releasing them from mental restraints they had endured unaware for centuries. All that in five-and-a-half centuries of life and now he'd spent nearly twice that time in constant agony, completely alone, but aware. She knew that her own mind would not have been able to withstand such trauma. Was that the problem with Peter, the reason he did not respond to her attempts to communicate using their psychic rapport?

Was he insane?

"Meaghan!" Lazarus barked, stepping back from the glass. She looked at him, her own efforts to chip the glass given up for the moment. Lazarus's expression was one of complete disbelief, as he stared at Peter, inside the glass. Octavian's eyes moved from one of them to the other, and back again. He was naked, or apparently so under what looked to be a cloak of some kind over his shoulders and hanging down to cover his lap, where his arms lay crossed at the wrists.

She didn't see it.

"What?" she asked, ready to get back to work. They were so close to finishing, she just wanted it over, needed to know whether she would ever return to her home. Although, without Alexandra there, she didn't know if she could call it that anymore.

"What?" she said again, because Lazarus hadn't answered. Instead, he had moved toward, and then past, her peering in through the glass, trying to get a better look at something.

"Under the cloak, do you see it?" he said finally.

"What, that he's naked?" she asked, exasperated, but that was the wrong answer, and for the first time, Meaghan saw Lazarus get angry.

He snapped his neck to glare at her for just a moment, then growled, "Look!"

She moved to his side, her mind not really on what Lazarus was looking at. Instead, it was on everything else. Since begun their effort to free Peter, she could barely go ten minutes without wincing at the thought of the suffering that surrounded them, the burning beings on the mountainside above, the frozen agony all around them, the city of pain and glass. She wasn't paying much attention . . . but she saw it anyway.

"Oh, my sweet Lord," she whispered to herself, unaware of the rare prayer. For now she saw what had excited Lazarus so, and what had bewildered him as well. It had the same effect on her. Meaghan could not believe it, though she saw it with her own eyes. Resting on Peter's right thigh, nearly covered by his forearm where it lay across his leg, and hidden by the shrouded darkness of the cloak, was a book. *The Gospel of Shadows*. It could be no other. She asked the obvious question.

"How?"

"I don't know," Lazarus said, smiling, happy, hopeful. "Perhaps time is uncertain in traveling between worlds? Or, it could be that Octavian was put here only recently."

"If so, where was he before?" she asked, not giving that theory much credence.

"Does it matter?" Lazarus asked, and his smile was infectious.

"Okay," Meaghan said. "Let's get him out of there."

They redoubled their efforts, working at the glass, in silence more complete than before, if that were possible, and it wasn't more than an hour later that Meaghan's efforts had torn the ice away from Octavian's left shoulder nearly to the flesh.

"Lazarus," she said. "Over here. If we can get through to him, maybe we can pull from the inside rather than just chipping it away."

In seconds, it was done. Lazarus slowed as he got down to Peter's skin, but in no time they had a hole half an inch wide. Meaghan's hands returned to their human form—in truth the shape seemed almost unfamiliar to her—and she put her index finger to the hole and touched hot skin. It was something, but she despaired. At this rate it was still going to take them days to finish carving Peter out.

If they had to.

Meaghan stepped around Lazarus to be within Peter's line of vision. The frightening thing about looking at him was that despite the movement of his eyes, the rest of his face was frozen in place, a terrible mask of sadness and pain. He looked at her now, and she smiled, motioning to let him know that they'd broken through, in case he hadn't been able to feel her touch.

She knew he couldn't smile in return, so she went ahead.

"Peter," she said aloud, emphasizing the words with her lips. "Change. You've got to change form. Now that you've got an opening, you can escape!"

Nothing, Octavian didn't even blink.

Peter, Meaghan said in her mind. *Come on. Help us. We've got to get back and help the others. You've got the book but we've already been here too long. If you can change, you've got to try.*

Still nothing. Octavian just kept looking at her as if he hadn't heard a word. And maybe he hadn't.

"Shit."

"Maybe you're going about this the wrong way," Lazarus suggested.

And that was all it took. Making sure Peter was looking at her, Meaghan changed to mist, floated much closer to the glass prison that housed him, and changed back into her human form. *If that didn't work*, she thought, *they'd have to assume that his mind was gone.*

Nothing.

And then something. Slowly, beginning with his feet, which were tucked under him where he knelt, and working eventually up to his torso and finally his head, Peter followed Meaghan's lead. He turned to mist and, slowly, simply, seeped, like smoke from a lazy fire, through the hole they had scraped. Once outside, his change back to human form was even slower, and the agony of it was clear on his reappearing face.

Peter Octavian lay there, barely conscious, naked but for his cloak and wracked with pain. His body quivered and shook with convulsions, muscle contractions and a terrible healing. But he was free.

Meaghan knelt by her former lover, turning him over and cradling his head in her lap. Lazarus tore the hole in the crystal a bit larger, reached inside to retrieve *The Gospel of Shadows*, and began quickly flipping through it, attempting to find the spell to get them home.

"Oh, Peter," Meaghan said, the love she had once felt for him, the loss she had felt when he sacrificed himself for the world, and the loss of her one true love, Alexandra Nueva, who'd died searching for him, all coming back to her in a rush of emotion like nothing she'd felt before, as human or vampire.

"It's okay," she told him as his body twitched, his eyes fluttering open. "The pain is over now. We'll take you home now. We need you, Peter. All the shadows do."

He stared at her a moment, and then his body tensed, a growl rising from his throat, becoming a roar as he jumped up, tossing Meaghan aside.

"Peter," she pleaded, reaching out for him. And his right hand, curved and extended into a terrible weapon, lashed out and tore the flesh of her left cheek to the bone.

"Keep the fuck away from me, you bitch," he said, slowly, coldly. Sanely.

---------------------------- ✳ ----------------------------

17

U.S. Interstate 81, Glasgow,
Virginia, United States of America.
Wednesday, June 7, 2000, 4:04 A.M.:

"The secretary general of the United Nations has recalled the Japanese unit of the UN security force that was on its way to Salzburg. Meanwhile, local troops are evacuating civilians from what is apparently a twenty- to thirty-mile radius around the city. The Fortress Hohensalzburg, which the media and military had been unable to photograph, was apparently the scene of much of the battle. Once communications in the area had returned, a German cameraman was able to get this footage . . . As you can see, the fortress has been nearly destroyed, and the battle has moved out into the city proper. The number of combatants has dropped drastically, but Liam Mulkerrin, the man the UNSF came here to stop, is still on a rampage. The question now is, are the recent moves by the UN secretary general in preparation for a last-ditch nuclear attack?"

The CNN anchor droned on and on from the dashscreen of Joe Boudreau's car, and his chest felt cold and hollow If the UN persuaded the Americans to nuke Salzburg, which wouldn't take much after the President's assassination—come to think of it, the UN might be the only thing holding the new President back—if that happened, nobody in the city would survive, human or vampire.

"I'd love to wake up from this nightmare," George Marcopoulos said next to him, and Joe knew just what he meant. He'd led a simple life in Boston before he met Peter Octavian and Meaghan Gallagher. Joe had run a bookstore in Cambridge, last in a long series of occupations he had quit. But he couldn't ever quit being a vampire. In fact, if he didn't lose his cool, there was a good chance he would live as close to forever as any creature would ever get. But nukes. Uh-uh.

No, he couldn't quit anymore. Meaghan needed him. All the shadows did, and certainly George Marcopoulos, a human, would be dead without him. Joe felt good. For the first time in his life, he belonged somewhere, somebody wanted him around. His family had never given him any kind of encouragement, and he'd felt out of place with everyone he'd ever called a "friend." That was why he'd fallen so easily into the world of books, for the escape they offered, the endless new worlds in which to belong.

He didn't need books anymore. His life had a purpose, and he would not betray it. He'd driven quietly for the last hour, but George had come awake at the beginning of the current newscast and was even now listening intently to its discussion of the ascension of the new President and the battle in Salzburg. The media was trying its best to stay away from supernatural references to Mulkerrin and his power, was, in fact, concentrating on the villainous acts of the shadows who had gone to fight alongside the humans and then betrayed them. Or at least that's how it was made to seem.

"Joe," George said, "find someplace to pull off, will you?"

The old Greek doctor-turned-ambassador rubbed sleep out of his eyes, then stretched, never taking his eyes off the dash-screen.

"I've got to use the toilet, and make a phone call," George elaborated.

"Whatever you say," Joe replied, and began scanning the highway for a pit stop. They were still traveling along Route 81, and they'd been making excellent time. With mountains and forest rising up on either side of them, it would have been a beautiful trip during the day. Unfortunately, that hadn't been an option.

Joe saw a sign for the next town—"Buchanan, 5 mi."— and was surprised again at the time that they had made. Then again, the highway was completely deserted. Anyone awake at this hour was more than likely still at home, glued to CNN. By 7 A.M., they ought to have crossed into Tennessee. By 11:30, noon at the latest, they'd be passing through Georgia for about twenty minutes, and then it was across Alabama and a tiny corner of Mississippi. A long way to go, but they'd be spending the night in New Orleans, come hell or high water. After all, they only had to stop for gas, and for the old doc to pee.

Joe saw the flickering sign for a Mobil station up ahead, and slowed to pull off the highway. Slouched in the passenger seat, Marcopoulos grumbled something and punched a button, and the dash-screen went off. The car rolled to a stop in front of the pumps, and Joe pulled the keys from the ignition.

"Let's keep an eye on each other, shall we?" George said, and Joe nodded. As they were getting out of the car, a Virginia State Police cruiser slid into the station and parked. Joe and George shut their doors and watched as the trooper hopped out and went into the tiny convenience store portion of the station. The bell atop the glass door jingled as it shut.

"Be careful" was all George said as they walked up to the store, following the trooper in. George went directly down the hall to the left and disappeared into the men's room. The trooper held what looked to Joe like an enormous cup of coffee, and was shooting the breeze with the clerk who'd just handed it to him. The trooper didn't appear to have any plans to pay for his coffee, but what surprised Joe was that he didn't appear to get free doughnuts to go with it.

The man was lean, young but not a child, and his close-cropped hair promised a seriousness that his laughter did not make good on. When Joe laid two twenties on the counter and said, "Fillin' up the Buick," the trooper barely glanced at him. And why should he do more? Joe was a regular-looking guy, some might even call him a dweeb, geek, dork, nerd. *Whatever they were calling quiet outcast children these days*, he thought.

He sure didn't look like a vampire.

George Marcopoulos came out of the men's room with an attitude. The place was a pigsty, and he'd nearly slipped in a small puddle on the floor. He hoped it was water, because he'd gotten some on his pants leg. A man his age ought to be able to relieve himself in a relatively clean, safe and smoke-free environment. This place was none of those things, and George was particularly incensed about the cigarette butts on the floor. Smoking was, after all, illegal in public places, including gas station rest rooms!

And now, approaching the counter, he was even more annoyed. It was the clerk who smoked, and he was lighting up at that very moment. The nerve of the man, with the police officer standing right there, doing nothing. Though he'd been a pipe smoker for years, George was content to do so only in his own home, and the smell of cigarettes had always nauseated him. Perhaps he was a hypocrite after all, but in his lifetime, he felt, he'd earned a little hypocrisy.

"Do you have a videophone?" George asked, and the clerk looked at him as if he were insane.

"Not just yet, fella. Telephone's outside and to the right if you can handle that."

George harrumphed and turned to go, but glanced back to tell the clerk, in no uncertain terms, what he thought of the conditions in the bathroom . . . and caught something strange on the police officer's face. The man looked puzzled, as though his mind were reaching for something just out of range. The officer met his eyes, looking more closely at George now, getting a good, long look. The puzzled expression didn't leave his face as the clerk said, "Something else, mister?"

George's heart fluttered.

"You ought to clean that bathroom," he said finally. "It's disgusting."

He hurried out, realizing that he'd procrastinated long enough, that he really ought to have done something sooner to change his appearance. There might not be a "posse" after him, but certainly there must be a warrant for his arrest. They ought to get out of there, he knew, but he had to make this phone call. If the cop did realize who he was, George only prayed it was after they'd left the station. By then, his call would have been traced anyway. Once they got closer to their destination, George couldn't take that chance, but just this once . . .

He slipped his card through the slot, then punched in the number lodged in his head. Only one person would ever answer that phone. There was no answering service, no secretary or receptionist. It seemed to ring forever, and George was concerned that the man he was calling might not have the phone with him.

George heard a door open behind him, and Joe was going into the store to get his change. Good, now they had a full tank of gas. He continued to watch, and listen to the phone ringing on the other end of the line. The sky had been brightening for some time, but now he could see it start to burn, just at the horizon line. The sun would be up in no time. When Joe came out, the police officer was right behind him. Both men went and sat in their cars, and George looked from one to the other. Inside the police car, a blue light, like that from a dashscreen, came on, and wondering what the trooper was watching suddenly made George very nervous.

"Come on, you son of a bitch," he said into the receiver, "pick up the phone."

"What?" a startled voice said at the other end of the line.

"Oh, Rafe, thank God!"

"Who the hell is this?" Rafael Nieto, secretary general of the United Nations, barked over his private line.

"Who do you think?" George snapped back, annoyed. "We've got to talk."

"I can't believe you're calling me," Nieto said, recognizing George's voice now. "Are you out of your mind?"

"Listen," George said calmly, "I only have a minute, so pay attention. The shadows aren't what you think. Just like us, they have white hats and black hats, but mostly gray hats. I won't argue that with you now, but I have two things you've got to know."

Nieto was silent for a moment, then said, "Go on."

"First, that these creatures have been hunted too long. If you start it all over again, you're liable to drive the gray hats over the edge. Second, I don't know if this nuclear thing was your idea, but watch Bill Galin, Rafe. I mean. watch him very closely."

"What's that supposed to mean?" Nieto said, and suddenly George had the feeling that maybe the secretary general wasn't having the call traced after all.

"What it means is that the man is dangerously unstable. Perhaps even insane. After the President was killed, and that Agent Williams saved both our lives, Galin tried to murder me himself."

George couldn't even hear Nieto breathing on the other end. It occurred to him that, for the moment, the man might not be. Across the parking lot, the trooper was getting out of his car. George hadn't seen him on the police radio, and he hoped that was a good sign.

"I'm not going to try to convince you, Rafe," George said into the silence. "I don't have time. All I'll say is, you know me. You know some of these people, these vampires. Don't trust Galin, and please, for God's sake, don't use the nukes."

The cop was approaching the Buick. George couldn't see Joe's face inside, but the engine was running.

"I've got to go," George said.

"Be careful," Nieto said quietly on the other end.

"No, my friend," George replied. "It's in your hands now. *You* be careful. And be watchful. Hannibal will certainly want you dead too, but he's far from your only enemy."

George Marcopoulos hung up the phone, and heard the gunshot.

The car was running, and over it he could see Joe embracing the police officer, his mouth on the man's neck. The clerk opened the door of the station to get a better look, then shut it quickly, locking it behind him. George watched as the man stepped behind the counter and picked up the phone.

"Joe," George shouted, "we've got to go!"

But Joe ignored him. Pushing the cop away, Joe Boudreau stepped over the man where he fell, and ran across the parking lot so fast that George could barely follow him. By the time he reached the glass door, Joe had transformed himself into the form of a large wolf, and George couldn't help but note his reliance on the traditional vampiric forms—he was young, yet.

A crashing noise was followed by the sound of the clerk screaming, and then silence from behind the counter. George couldn't see either of them anymore. After a few moments, Joe reappeared in the window, human once again, and rifled the cash register. When he emerged from the station, he had a big bag of pretzels and two big bottles of Coke in his arms. He trotted across the lot, but George was already at the running car. In seconds, they were on the road.

George looked back at the police officer, sprawled on the pavement, then at Joe, and finally down at his hands.

"They'll both live," Joe said. "I won't kill anyone I don't have to."

It seemed important to him that George understand, and unfortunately, George did.

"And now at least you've eaten," he said, and Joe nodded in return.

"We've got to assume he'll identify me," George said, "but I don't think I'll be much of a priority."

"You don't think so?" Joe looked unsure.

"No," George sighed. "I've just realized that this is bound to be happening all over the world right about now, humans confronting vampires, and most with far less pleasant results than we left back there."

"Back to square one," Joe said, just as they crested a hill, and the sun truly broke over the horizon.

"No," George said sadly. "It's much worse than that.'

Salzburg, Austria, European Union.
Wednesday, June 7, 2000, 9:29 A.M.:

Martha was desperate. Her brother's blood-son, Isaac, was dead, consumed by a dark thing, a *Nachzehrer*, which Liam Mulkerrin had summoned to the fortress from *elsewhere*. Will Cody was buried beneath the rubble of an entire wall that Mulkerrin had dropped on him. Of the dozens of vampires who had stormed the fortress intending to destroy the sorcerer, less than half remained, led by the Shadow Justice System deputy she knew only as Stefan and by Martha herself.

Mulkerrin hovered, borne aloft by his hold on the ephemeral, essential tethers of the world around him, by magic, shielded from attack. Apparently, Will Cody had somehow become immune to the effect of magic on his person, but not on his surroundings, which was how he had come to be buried. Already quite mad when he escaped from his exile in Hell, Liam Mulkerrin appeared to be growing more insane with every passing moment. Martha only hoped that her brother Lazarus or John Courage would return soon with help.

Even as she and Stefan gathered their forces for another attack, Martha had to admit that they'd had some success. After all, they had battered at the madman's defenses until he could no longer control the ghost warriors who had taken over the bodies of tourists at the fortress, nor could he hold open the many doorways from Hell he had created. Mulkerrin was using all of his concentration to repel the vampires' attack, and he hadn't summoned any other creatures since Isaac had been killed. Martha thought that meant that such summonings drained the sorcerer. *He's weakening*, she told herself, and could only hope it was true. Otherwise, they would all be dead before help arrived.

"Come to me!" Mulkerrin called in a deep, less than human voice, which resounded within the crumbling walls of the fortress. "Come and be purified. Your kind must be cleansed from the Earth before the purification, and the redemption of humanity, may occur. It is inevitable. It is God's will. Come to me!"

From everything her brother had told her, Martha knew that Liam Mulkerrin had once been an extraordinarily evil man. But no longer. Now he was merely insane. She signaled to Stefan.

"Attack!" he yelled at her gesture, and the forty odd vampires left alive in the fortress surrounded Mulkerrin Those who had the ability to become fire did so, attempting with their great heat and less mass to penetrate his magical protection Those who could not blaze became bats and great birds of prey, battering against the field with their wings and bodies, doing their best to weaken the sorcerous shield at any cost. Martha admired their valiant efforts.

Meanwhile she met Mulkerrin's eyes, saw the fanatical fervor there, saw the mission that the former priest had set himself upon, and redoubled her efforts. She had seen such eyes before, and the memory frightened her.

"Yes! Come to me!" Mulkerrin shouted, and then more softly, he chanted: "*Gibil Gashru Umuna Yanduru; Tushte Yesh Shir Illani U Ma Yalki!*"

The sorcerer lifted his hands, and the greenish glowing sphere of magical influence that surrounded him, protected him, kept back the attacks by the vampire warriors burst into a green flame of its own. This blazing new fire leapt out and scorched hawks, bats and eagles, who burnt in the mid-morning sunlight falling on the debris-strewn courtyard. Several turned to mist, or returned to their human forms and fell to the broken stone ground in pain, but the rest wailed in agony as the green flames engulfed them. Then their own flames—yellow, orange and red—burned even brighter, and they exploded, one by one, a fireworks display, into a shower of cinders, which fell to the stone like blazing snow.

The shadows who were already fire when Mulkerrin's green blaze erupted were themselves engulfed. Most were driven back, away from the sorcerer, but several were absorbed into the green flame, their orange light winking out merging with the magic, creatures meant to destroy the sorcerer now part of his protection.

Martha held back from the attack, searching for vulnerabilities in the shield, in the sorcerer. The murder of half their number happened so quickly that she could not have helped even if she had an idea how to do so. In moments. Stefan and seventeen others stood with her, recovering from their struggle with the green flame, and she was at a loss as to their next move. Martha looked to Stefan for his help and suggestions, but he could only stare at the fireball that now hung in the air, with Liam Mulkerrin as its unburning center.

Amazingly, Martha thought, *they could still see him.*

And then there came a cry from behind her, quite unexpected. She whirled to see that a large portal had opened up, a doorway to Hell. Martha could see her own reflection in the silvery, shimmering vertical pool that led to a terrible fate. It was huge, the largest she had seen, and Martha knew then that they had no hope. If the sorcerer was still powerful enough to open such a portal, then they had merely distracted him before, rather than weakening him. His power had not diminished, only been distracted for a moment. *As soon as he felt like it*, Martha thought, *it was likely Mulkerrin could do it all again, anytime he wanted, anywhere he wanted—the ghostly soldiers, the hellish beasts, the earthquakes—all over the world.*

"No!" she shouted, but Mulkerrin was already rushing toward them, rushing toward the huge portal, which hung against the rubble where a wall had once stood, a wall which now lay on Will Cody, who might or might not still be alive underneath the debris. Trapped between the green fire that had killed most of their comrades and a doorway into Hell itself, Stefan and the others attempted to dive away, beyond the range of the portal. Martha did not move, knowing it was going to be too wide for such an escape.

Several vampires ran straight ahead, preferring to face the fire, to die while attempting to reach Mulkerrin, and they made it part of the way through the field before being nearly vaporized by the green flame. The rest were caught between the fire and the portal. Faced with certain death on one hand and the unknown on the other, they chose life and backed through the liquid silver of the door to Hell.

Knowing she could not dodge the flames, Martha simply lay down, just before the fire slammed into her, and dug her hands into the rubble, searching for some kind of grip. The green flames blasted over her, charring and cracking her skin. She shut her eyes tight, but they would not last long under that onslaught. There was terrible pain in her legs, as if one of them were being torn off from the knee down, and she turned back and opened her eyes to see that the force of the blow had pushed the lower half of her body through the portal. Her hands had dragged a pile of stones three feet as she tried to save herself.

And now something beyond that door was ravaging her. She was overwhelmed by the sadness of the knowledge that those of her people who had already passed through would be destroyed by what lay beyond. It yanked at her, began chewing on her, and Martha was dragged farther even as she screamed.

Then, finally, she found a solid handhold under the debris, between two large stones in the courtyard. She pulled herself forward, ignoring the gnawing tug on her leg from beyond the door. She had dragged herself out as far as her waist, when she remembered Mulkerrin . . . and then his shoes were there, in front of her, and she looked up to see him smiling. He had given up all but a glowing aura, which hung from him like a suit of armor, and now he sat on a rock to watch her struggle and suffer.

Martha was dragged back several inches by a terrible tug, and she felt the muscle tear away from the calf of her good leg. If she could turn to flame herself, she might escape the portal and destroy whatever it was that was preying upon her, but in all her pain, she did not have the concentration for it. If it was her time, she would accept it and gladly go to meet God. She only wished that she could have sent Mulkerrin on ahead of her, especially now, as the smile spread across his aging face.

And then she saw it, beyond him, a low mist rising from the rubble where Mulkerrin had tumbled a stone wall onto Will Cody. Martha knew what it meant, who it was. Will had survived, of course, and had allowed himself a few minutes to recover before turning to mist and floating back up through the rocks to rejoin the battle.

"Will!" Martha shouted in her pain, and Mulkerrin snapped his head around to see the mist floating toward them. "Get out of here! Retreat! Find Courage and return to destroy the madman when you have a hope of surviving!"

And Martha smiled as the mist became a hawk, and the hawk sped up and over the wall of the fortress. A tendril of green fire arched out from Mulkerrin's upraised palm, surrounding the hawk, but nothing happened. Cody was immune to the magic. Huge stones lifted from the floor of the fortress and shot after the hawk, but it was out of range. As it dropped below the wall of the fortress, out of sight Martha laughed.

"You will not prevail, madman," she said, even as something tore into her buttocks, pulling her back into the portal up to her breasts.

Mulkerrin glared at her, then the aura around him extended once again, and he rose from the ground, floating within the magical field, above the wall, preparing to pursue Cody. Martha winced with pain, but gritted her teeth against the scream that lodged in her throat as the sorcerer called over his shoulder to her.

"God's work is never done, Defiant One. At least, not until I say it is."

And then he was gone, and the portal closed, cutting Martha in two.

As the portal closed, Stefan's hiding place dissolved leaving him vulnerable. He had been the only one to escape the press between fire and Hell, and had jumped behind the shimmering portal, onto the crumbling wall. He stepped down now and went to Martha's side. Her already burnt flesh was beginning to char further in the sunshine and soon there would be nothing left of her but ashes.

Stefan shapeshifted into a black raven, a change reflecting his sorrow, and took flight. Far behind, he followed Mulkerrin's slow progress. He would rejoin the fight as soon as Cody did, and die if he must. For there was no place for the shadow people in a world with Mulkerrin as its master.

Hell.
One Hundred Sixty-Seven Days,
Fifty-Five Minutes After Departure:

"I'm sorry," Peter Octavian said softly, and fell to his knees, sticking his hands out to keep from landing on his face. He slumped back, took a deep breath, then looked up at Meaghan, his eyes empty of life, filled with despair.

"It's been . . . so long," he said, and Meaghan's heart crumbled.

"It's okay," she said, kneeling by him. "I can't claim to understand what you're feeling, but it's okay now. We're going to go home."

Peter nodded, not even attempting a smile, and then turned to where Lazarus was standing, flipping through *The Gospel of Shadows*, searching for the spell that could take them back to their world. Meaghan had expected Peter to have a lot of questions, especially for

Lazarus, who he had once hoped had all the answers. But the questions never came.

"Peter, this whole time I've been trying to talk to you, in my head, and I get nothing," she said as she helped him to his feet, partially supporting his weight. "Have the years taken that contact away from us, or were you blocking me?"

Peter shook his head slowly, then stretched, as if waking from a long sleep. Finally his eyes began to take on a small spark of life, a slowly dawning awareness of his situation.

"I don't . . . No, I wasn't purposely keeping you out," he said. "In fact, I wasn't sure it was really you, since I didn't hear you in my head."

Peter looked at her, then—the old Peter, though weak and haggard.

"How long were you trapped here?" Meaghan asked him as she stepped back, giving him room to stretch further, to test his strength. "Were you aware of the passing of time?"

She sensed a stirring from Lazarus, but he said nothing. Peter looked thoughtful, but confident again.

"I've been here nearly a thousand years."

Meaghan wanted to be shocked, stunned at least. But she had already whispered these things to herself, guessing Peter's fate based upon the time she and Lazarus had spent in Hell. Still, it was horrible to hear the truth of it, to sense even a tiny bit of the suffering. And yet Meaghan had long since acknowledged that, if they did find Peter alive, things would never be the way they were. Alexandra's death only widened the gulf between them. As such she gained some comfort from the elapsed time, knowing that Peter could not possibly feel about her the way he had when he had crossed over into Hell, so long ago.

And then she wondered again why he asked no questions. That wasn't like him. Once upon a time he had fancied himself a detective. Curiosity had led him into his first confrontation with Liam Mulkerrin. *Maybe after all this time*, Meaghan thought, *he doesn't care about anything anymore*.

"Peter," Lazarus spoke to him for the first time, "how did you come to have the book?"

He held it forward, to be certain Octavian understood him, but Peter did not respond.

"We arrived here just over five months ago," Lazarus said. "You can't have been here, trapped in the crystal, for longer than that, because we had the book up until then. Where did it come from?"

"I don't know," Peter said after a moment's consideration. "But we'll need it to get out of here."

Lazarus harrumphed, indicating that Octavian was stating the obvious, and wasn't helping matters any, then he when back to scanning the book.

"What's going on back home.?" Peter did finally ask.

Grateful for the question, Meaghan told him everything all that had happened in his absence, while they thought he was dead. She told him of the Shadow Justice System and the new world order, of Allison's new jobs and Cody's return to filmmaking and mass media shows, of their search for Lazarus and his timely arrival ... of Mulkerrin's return, with extraordinary new power. In the silence that followed, while he digested all of this new information, Meaghan also told him that she and Alexandra had become lovers, and that Alex was now dead.

"What?" he asked and blinked, then turned to face Lazarus, pushing the book from his hands to get the elder's attention.

"You son of a bitch," Peter said coldly. "You knew I was here, knew I was suffering, and you didn't do a fucking thing about it. Then your friend Father Mulkerrin returns, and suddenly you need me. So you drag the two people who are most important to me down into Hell with you and you let one of them die!"

Peter was furious, his lips drawn back, his teeth gleaming. But Lazarus only stood, staring passively back at him, as Meaghan came to his rescue.

"No, Peter, it wasn't like that. Lazarus didn't know, he only guessed because Mulkerrin had returned, and so we all hoped that meant you were still alive as well. And he couldn't have saved Alex; I was there."

"I don't give a damn!" he roared, turning on Meaghan now. "And why are you so chummy suddenly with this traitor?"

"Octavian," Lazarus said quietly, attempting to soothe, to calm, to command respect with his reserve. Peter wasn't having any of it.

"Listen, you bastard," Peter snapped, turning back to Lazarus, "we both know that your friend the Stranger knew I was down here, and didn't lift a finger, so don't even try to—"

Peter's voice trailed off as Lazarus held up a hand, a command really, to stop speaking. The older vampire's face became suspicious, his right eyebrow lifting as he turned his head.

"What do you know of the Stranger?" Lazarus asked. "You sent your loved ones on a worldwide search for me, to find out about our race, about me. You know nothing you did not learn here, in Hell. So I ask you plainly now what Meaghan would only dance around: what happened here when you and Mulkerrin arrived? What happened between you? How did he escape? Why haven't we been attacked while trying to rescue you? Where did Mulkerrin come by his new abilities and you your new knowledge?

"Who are you, now, Octavian? Who have we come to bring home?"

Meaghan was staring, slack-jawed at both of them.

"Don't you think this can wait until . . .," she began, but Lazarus shook his head before she was even through.

"He's changed," Lazarus said. "I want to find out how much."

"You've changed over the past thousand years, I'll wager," Meaghan said to Lazarus, unwilling to confess that she shared some of his anxiety. "And you haven't been suffering the entire time."

"Meaghan, it's all right," Peter said. "He doesn't have a right to ask, but you, blood-daughter, have a right to know."

Blood-daughter, she thought, *that's what I am to him now*. And she felt a little sadness for all they had lost.

"I will save the whole story for a more appropriate time and setting," Peter said, "but I'll answer the most important questions now. When Mulkerrin and I arrived, I was preparing to kill him, though his magic still allowed him to call some of the demon-slaves here to his aid. But Beelzebub, whose escape to Earth I had prevented by bringing Mulkerrin here, was there to stop us. Instead of killing us on the spot, which I have wished infinitely he had done, we were kept alive, made to suffer . . ."

He trailed off for a moment, and Meaghan wanted to go to him, to hold him, but she needed to hear more. Peter detailed much of the suffering he and Mulkerrin had endured side by side, how Lord Beelzebub had worked some kind of dark magic on the sorcerer to keep him from dying, to keep him suffering.

"Many times, the demon-lord mentioned his hatred of the Stranger, and in describing why vampires had no real mooring in our world, he revealed a little of our people's true history, though he vowed he would not do so. He could not help it, so enraged would he become. Of course, Mulkerrin did not believe a word of it, dealing as we were with the Prince of Lies. I will not tell you, now, of the other tortures and indignities he devised for me, and for the despicable sorcerer. Instead, I will say only that I had a moment of rationality during a particularly agonizing time, and realized that Mulkerrin was gone. Somehow I sensed that he was not only gone from me, but from Hell. Of new power, I know nothing. Of our people, and the Stranger, I know only what the devil told me."

"How can you trust what he has said?" Meaghan asked softly, pained by Peter's tale.

"Why shouldn't I?" he said. "He had no reason to think I would ever leave here."

"So what did he tell you?" she asked.

"That's for later," Lazarus said, and Meaghan now looked at him in a new light, a light of doubt and suspicion. But Peter continued speaking, and Meaghan forgot about Lazarus for the moment.

"I was moved here just after that time I mentioned, when I noticed Mulkerrin had gone. You may not believe it, but this prison, suffering in the searing heat of the crystal, was a relief in comparison to what I had already endured. I have not seen Beelzebub, or any other demon, lord or slave, pass through this place since then. But I do suggest we get out of here as quickly as possible, in case my escape is sensed somehow."

"I second that," Meaghan said sincerely. "Lazarus, let's get that spell going."

"Yes," Octavian said. "Let's go."

And so Lazarus began to recite the spell that would take them home. He had searched for exactly the right spell, he explained, one which would take them to the location of the latest such portal opened to Earth. If Mulkerrin were still on the loose, the spell would bring them right to him. If not, they would end up back in Boston, where they had begun, and life could begin anew for them.

Meaghan could not help but wonder what she would do without Alexandra in her life. She found no answers, but knew for certain that she could not stay in Boston. She would find another home.

At Lazarus's words, the portal shimmered to life before them . . . and the ground began to quake. A natural occurrence in this unnatural place, or a reaction to the magic, she didn't know. New crystal spires, filled with the damned shot up from the ground, stabbing the sky.

"Go, Meaghan!" Peter yelled, and pushed her toward the shimmering silver doorway. But when Lazarus moved forward, Peter said, "No, you're the spellcaster, you've got to be last!"

Half her body through the door, Meaghan turned and watched helplessly as a crystal spear shot up from the ground, impaling Lazarus, then quickly absorbing him and *The Gospel of Shadows* before he could even scream. She saw the pain and terror in his eyes, saw Peter diving for her, grabbing her around the waist, his momentum carrying them both completely through the shrinking portal.

Lazarus was not dead, Meaghan knew. He was a prisoner, as Peter had been. But this time the book was on the other side, and as far as Meaghan knew, only Mulkerrin knew the spells by heart that would allow them to return to Hell, to rescue Lazarus.

She knew that would never happen. Lazarus would be in agony among the damned for eternity.

18

Pongau Basin, Austria, European Union.
Wednesday, June 7, 2000, 10.24 A.M.:

They stood at the entrance to the Eisriesenwelt, ice caves that stretched for dozens of miles beneath the mountains of Austria. The entrance was cut into the western face of the Hochkogel, thousands of feet up from the Salzach Valley. Rolf and his four remaining SJS agents— Annelise, Sebastiano, Carlos and Erika—and Jared, who had led them there, prepared to enter.

In truth, Rolf was surprised the others had stuck by him, for he didn't know any of them that well. Except perhaps for Erika, who had tracked *him* down rather than the other way around. She looked sixteen, and probably wasn't more than twenty. She'd been a vampire only two years when she joined the SJS, and before that, part of a very angry crowd on the streets of Atlanta, Georgia. She was violent, pessimistic and outspoken, but she was on his side, not Hannibal's, and that gave him hope.

"Hey, Boss," she said, speaking up now, though she'd been unusually quiet. Rolf had a moment to realize how glad he was that she had survived.

So far, he reminded himself as he turned to acknowledge her inquiring tone.

"Anybody else notice we haven't seen hide nor hair of anyone?" she asked now. "No military, no civilians, nobody working this friggin' tourist attraction? What's going on?"

Rolf looked at Jared, who obviously didn't have more of an answer than he did, but then Sebastiano answered for them.

"Well, let's put a little thought into this now," he said precisely, fighting his Italian accent. "If you were America, and your President had been assassinated, and your troops were being wiped out, and most of the civilians were already dead or evacuated, and the most powerful evil you'd ever known was back from the dead, what would you do?"

And then they were all as silent as their mute leader. Rolf lifted a hand to his forehead and closed his eyes a moment. Nobody said a word as he motioned them forward, into the caves. They didn't want to think about Erika's question, or Sebastiano's theory. They only wanted to destroy Hannibal before he could do more damage to their kind.

Of course, Rolf also wanted to rescue his lover, Elissa Thomas, but he knew that for the others that was less of a priority. And he couldn't blame them. Perhaps only Jared with his strangely peaceful manner, would truly make the effort to keep Elissa alive. A quick glance at Annelise and Carlos, who entered the cave shoulder to shoulder, their faces etched with hate and thoughts of murder, and Rolf knew that he had a job ahead of him.

Hannibal's band of killers had a head start but the burden of carrying Elissa ought to have slowed them down. It was possible that Rolf's group was only a few minutes behind, but Hannibal had thirty miles of cave in which to hide—if he wanted to. Rolf was gambling that Hannibal wanted to tear him apart just as much as he wanted to see the white-haired animal dead. Oh, Hannibal was hiding all right, but only for the moment. All Rolf and the others needed to do was walk through the caves and wait to be ambushed.

A simple plan, when you thought about it.

And if America was indeed planning to hit Salzburg with a nuclear strike, Rolf's only concern was that he see Hannibal dead before the missiles arrived.

"This way," Jared said, and led them deeper into the caves. Ice formed enormous caverns and tunnels branching off; waterfalls were frozen in place, and had not run for millennia; nearly humanoid ice figures stood like statues along their way. And soon they were past the area where tourists were allowed. They arrived at a fork, and once more Jared chose their path, prompting Rolf to look at him quizzically once again.

"I hate to admit it," Jared said in response, "but I can hear every thought in his head."

Rolf's eyes widened. *Jared must be one of Hannibal's blood-sons*, he thought.

"I can't hear *your* thoughts," Jared said then, "but I know what you're thinking. And you're wrong. Courage can hear your thoughts, can communicate with you, because he is your, how did he put it, ancestor? Yes. And I am Hannibal's. Though it shames me, he is of my bloodline."

Salzburg, Austria, European Union.
Wednesday, June 7, 2000, 10:01 A.M.:

Liam Mulkerrin was dismayed. He had not heard God's voice in some time, and he worried that he might somehow have displeased the Lord, that perhaps he had been too slow in destroying those who would oppose Him early on, too slow in purifying this part of the world. He would have to change that. It would have to end as quickly as possible, so that His work could continue unobstructed. The souls of all humankind needed Mulkerrin's cleansing fire, the ecstatic pain of purification.

Now, as he floated above the decimated city of Salzburg, he surveyed his work thus far and was pleased. Huge fissures had opened in the streets and squares; homes and historical sites had crumbled; electrical and gas fires had burned out whole blocks, caused by his earthquakes. Black acrid smoke rose through the warm morning sunlight and was carried west by a light breeze. Though most of the demons had been destroyed, Mulkerrin thought he spotted one for just a moment on a street far away. He saw no people.

All in all, it was a beautiful day.

Will Cody fled before him, and Mulkerrin was glad. He could not afford to let the cowboy come close to him again. There was too much he did not understand about Cody's seeming immunity to his spells. He had never encountered such an immunity before . . . and then Liam was shamed. He knew he needn't worry, that God would not allow any harm to befall His right hand, His most terrible and wonderful servant.

Then, beyond Cody, Mulkerrin got a clear view of the forces remaining to oppose him. He could have laughed. They were far less than the number he had already dispatched since his return. Still, he would use every ounce of his strength, every nuance of his control and endurance, to destroy them as quickly as possible. His strategy before had been to allow them to attack, and then destroy them—simple, effective, but not as expedient as a direct assault. Mulkerrin suspected that the Lord was becoming impatient, and he could not bear a moment of God's displeasure.

"Here they come," Allison said, worried and hopeful at the same time. Courage had told her that the bird speeding toward them was Cody, and she shivered to think that they would finally be reunited, and felt nauseated when she considered that the real battle, the final battle, had yet to begin.

The humans were in front. The several hundred remaining soldiers of the United Nations security force, under the command of Roberto Jimenez, were no longer concerned about civilians. All the people of Salzburg were either dead, evacuated, or very well hidden. As soon as Will Cody had flown over their heads, they opened fire with everything they had, rifles loaded with the deadliest ammunition available, automatic weapons, CAMEL rockets. The guys with the flamethrowers would have to wait until Mulkerrin came closer, but the point was, they didn't want him any closer than necessary.

"Will!" Allison shouted, safe for the moment behind the gathered warriors, both human and shadow, with Courage at her side. Cody shifted back to human form as he landed, and she was stunned for a moment at the sight of him. Her lover looked like hell. His face was haggard, his clothes tattered, and the torn sweatshirt he wore was covered with blood.

He saw her, the look of alarm on her face, and smiled broadly.

"Blood's not mine, sweetheart," he said as she fell into his arms. He felt so good to her, she didn't care about the blood or anything else. She just wanted him to live, to stay alive through the rest of this thing.

"Oh, God, I was so scared for you," Allison said, letting it out for the first time; the fear, the frustration and anxiety. She was a strong, brave woman, but her confidence in the face of his captivity had been a front. Now that she had her arms around Cody, she didn't want to let him go again.

"Well, I'm here now. I'm back," he said, lifting her chin for a quick kiss and then looking up and around at the gathered vampires.

"Who are they?" Cody asked, but it wasn't Allison who answered.

"Charlemagne's personal guard," John Courage said, walking up to them. "Mulkerrin will find them a lot harder to kill than the SJS agents were. I'm glad to see you're healed. I wondered for a bit if you would survive."

The two vampires clasped hands, meeting each other's eyes, and Allison thought there was a similarity, and a familiarity, between them that she hadn't seen before. She wondered for what must have been the hundredth time that day just where the world was headed now.

"The others weren't so lucky," Cody said. "Martha and Isaac—"

"I know," Courage said. "We have a lot to talk about."

"That we do, sir," Cody said, a new respect, and a million questions, in his tone, "but not the time to do it."

Cody looked over his shoulder at the gathered warriors, but made no comment about John Courage's claims regarding their identity. Good idea, Allison thought. *We don't have time for that; that they're on our side is all that matters.*

Cody was catching his breath, getting his bearings, and he looked to see that the barrage that the human forces were launching at Mulkerrin was having little or no effect on the sorcerer's protective shield. Not that he'd thought it would, but one could always hope. Mulkerrin had seemed desperate at the end, when he'd destroyed all of his attackers at the fortress, just before Cody had abandoned the place. He had to remind himself that retreat was the only way he could have helped. If he could catch Mulkerrin occupied and unaware, he might be able to get close enough to him to . . .

"They're not going to last, John," Allison said to Courage, distracting Will. He knew she was right: the humans stood no chance.

"We should evacuate them now," Cody said. "Save those we can."

Courage only nodded and watched the humans continue their assault. Mulkerrin had stopped advancing, and seemed to be working some kind of spells within his magical, protective aura.

Will, you have a very intelligent, intuitive woman, here, John Courage said in his head, startling him.

No kidding, he thought, turning to meet Courage's gaze. *How are you doing this, and why not speak aloud?*

How is unimportant. I know you have your suspicions, as does Allison. And I don't speak aloud so she remains calm. I know what has happened to you, Will. Even I can't explain it, but it makes my decisions that much more difficult.

How do you mean? Cody thought, his eyes narrowing and he saw in his peripheral vision that Allison had stiffened, was aware that something was passing between them.

I mean to keep you alive, Courage began.

Well, that's my plan as well was Cody's cynical reply.

But you are the only one who can get close enough to Mulkerrin to destroy him. Even I can't get past that barrier of his, Courage admitted.

Yes, let's address that, Cody said. *Since you know everything, even what I'm thinking, are you who I think you are, and if so, why can't you simply end this now, kill Mulkerrin?*

I am and I am not, Courage said in Cody's mind. *What once lived in me has long departed, leaving only a trace of itself behind.*

Cody's eyes were wide, and he could not hide his shock from Allison.

"What is it, Will?" she asked, coming to his side in time to stop him from collapsing. He looked up at Courage, expecting a consoling, kindly smile but finding only a gravely serious face.

"Whatever you want me to do," Cody said, touching Courage lightly on the shoulder, then turning to Allison for a hug.

"What is it?" she asked again, but it was Courage who answered.

"Between you," John said, "you now have nearly all the pieces to the puzzle you have been trying to solve since Octavian disappeared, the mystery that has haunted our kind since the church first toyed with our minds. When this is over, you may put it together.

"But first we have to survive."

And then the ground began to shake, and Cody saw anger flash on John Courage's face as he looked up at Mulkerrin, who had just begun his third earthquake.

"You're right," Cody said quickly. "The humans don't have a chance."

Courage looked at them, the couple, one human, one vampire, and pointed at them each in turn, as they all struggled to keep their balance.

"Take care of each other, but stay here until I return," he said loudly, over the noise of the quake. "Cody has a part to play in this, but it is necessary for both of you to survive."

And then Courage was gone, rushing off to join Charlemagne's warriors, and to talk some sense into Roberto Jimenez.

"What was all that about?" Allison asked, holding her lover tight to keep herself from falling down. Not far from where they stood, a new, wide fissure had appeared, stretching halfway across the south end of Residence Plaza not far from the shattered dome of the cathedral.

Already the quake was subsiding, and though they could expect more tremors, Cody paid that particular danger little attention. He hugged Allison to him, filled with emotion, wanting to dance, to shout, to pray. John Courage had made him whole again, when he'd never realized that part of him was truly missing. But first, he sobered; first Mulkerrin must be destroyed, and then the true battle for the future of all shadows would begin in earnest.

"It's about what John is," Cody answered finally, kissing Allison on the forehead, "and what that makes the rest of us."

"What *does* it make you?" Allison asked, confused by her own suspicions regarding John Courage.

Cody only smiled.

"Concentrate all fire at the bastard's head!" Roberto Jimenez shouted into his collarcomm. The quake had lasted barely a minute, but it sent a solid signal to all of them: Mulkerrin had not been weakened at all. They were throwing everything they had at him, but the sorcerer had not so much as flinched. Even now, as Jimenez watched, he was moving forward again, closer and closer to the small army that opposed him.

Jimenez realized that their only shot would be hammering at one spot on whatever the hell kind of force shield the son of a bitch was generating. That was the purpose of his order. If all weapons were fired nearly simultaneously at one part of his body—Roberto had chosen the head for maximum damage—perhaps they could break through. If not, they were totally lost. And then it would be up to the vampires, and he hated that thought. He knew the old saying, the enemy of his enemy, and all that, but once Mulkerrin was gone . . .

"On my mark, all weapons fire on that target!" he shouted again. "Ready! Aim! *Fire!*"

Mulkerrin was hurled, end over end, thirty or forty yards before he was able to right himself in the air. Though Jimenez could tell from where he stood that the energy field had not been breached, the sheer force of the blast had knocked him back. Even now, a number of Charlemagne's warriors had taken to the air, some as birds, but others in human form, with wings sprouting from their backs and swords held high. Charlemagne himself was at the head, and from where Jimenez sat, it appeared as if the "king's" hands were made of the same metal as his weapon. In fact, Roberto thought that the swords, and Charlemagne's hands, might be silver. But he shook the idea from his head—he was fairly certain that was impossible. Still, he wasn't positive about anything anymore.

Well, perhaps one thing. Their firepower had been useless, and he doubted the vampires could do any better. They were welcome to try, though, and die trying as far as he was concerned.

And then Mulkerrin shouted something, fury carved into his face. Roberto wished he could hear the sorcerer's words, but over the noise of gunfire and the screaming of Charlemagne's warriors, he couldn't make them out. Mulkerrin moved his hands in a series of wild gestures that gave Jimenez an inexplicable chill . . .

And then the fourth quake began. But this wasn't an earthquake, really. Rather, it was a rip in the fabric of the world. Instead of a tremor shaking the entire city, only the plaza beneath the feet of the human soldiers shook. Sudden realization almost stunned him into silence, but Roberto shook it off.

"Retreat!" he shouted. "The ground is going to go!"

And go it did. Even as his men and women were trying to fall back, escape from the trembling earth, the cobblestones beneath their feet cracked wide open, a fissure fifty yards long and ten wide tore across the plaza, and half of his soldiers were gone in the space of seconds, falling away into a hole that seemed to have no bottom.

The ground continued to rumble around the hole though it stopped growing. Perhaps two-thirds of the survivors were on the southern side of the gorge, not far from where Charlemagne's troops were engaging Mulkerrin to no avail. The other one-third were making an effort to reform into some kind of cohesive unit, in case anything came out of the hole, a definite possibility where Mulkerrin was concerned.

"Withdraw," a voice said right next to Commander Jimenez, and with his nerves as taut as they were, he nearly fired on John Courage, who had come to stand next to him without a sound. Or perhaps, in all this insanity, Jimenez had lost the alarm systems his training had instilled in him.

"What?" he asked.

"Your people are dying, your weapons have no effect. You must withdraw," Courage said again.

He was so calm, his logic so clear, that Jimenez momentarily regretted not shooting him.

"What makes you think your people will do any better?" he snapped.

"We've defeated him before," Courage said. "We have a better chance, but if we all die, why would you care? You plan to kill us anyway, don't you? Withdraw your troops and let us have our shot. If we don't kill him, you'll have time to get reinforcements ready. Though I suspect there might be another alternative brewing, one which might destroy us all."

Jimenez knew exactly what Courage was talking about. He had wondered all along whether the nuclear fail-safe on this mission would really be used. Now he realized that it very well might.

"What about my people on the other side?" he asked.

"You'll have to leave them," Courage answered.

"Fuck that!" Jimenez said, turning back to survey their situation. He'd find a way to get those soldiers out of there.

And then a portal shimmered to life, and Roberto thought he understood Mulkerrin's plan. The reflective surface of the doorway sprang into being beyond the UN soldiers, separating them from Liam Mulkerrin. They were trapped between a deadly fall into that hole, and whatever was going to come out of this new portal. Or they would be in a moment.

"Surro!" Jimenez shouted into his collarcomm, seeing that the French commander was among those on the far side of the hole.

"Evac right now! Everybody fall back, head east to . . . ," Roberto mentally scanned the map he'd memorized, ". . . Rudolfsplatz. Diego, get the choppers moving."

There was no reply other than the chatter of several hundred retreating soldiers.

"Diego? What's the problem?"

Still nothing. Roberto's mind raced. It was possible, he supposed, that Diego and the rest of the Evac team had been attacked and killed by demons, by vampires, by something—but not very likely. They were out of the way, prepared to evac the troops in case a retreat became necessary. They should have been safe. It was possible, but Roberto knew better. Evac Unit had withdrawn; Operation: Jericho had been abandoned. Which left only one possible answer. And he wasn't about to let his soldiers in on it.

"Surro, if Evac hasn't arrived when you reach the river, swim the fucking thing! Go! Go! Go!"

But he didn't have to tell them again; they were going. Behind him, the troops on Roberto's side of the gorge were already heading east at a run, leaving the battle to the vampires. Across that terrible gash in the cobblestones, soldiers on the eastern edge of the plaza had already escaped. But Commander Jimenez could feel in his gut that time was short.

Before he could shout another command, even urge them to hurry, before he could turn back to John Courage for some reassurance, dark things began to emerge from the portal. They were very tall, thin creatures with black, leathery skin. From the side, they were nearly invisible, and gossamer, glistening wings hung under their arms. Their eyes burned with a terrible crimson glow visible even in the daylight, though it seemed to Roberto that the world had suddenly grown darker, as if thunderclouds had rolled in to block the sun. These new creatures, whatever they were, terrified him.

They had pointed ears, like animals', blood red on the vulnerable inside and black outside. Their hands were three-fingered, and would have looked delicate were it not for the impossibly long, red-tinged claws at the ends of the fingers. Rather than feet, their lower appendages were not quite hooves and not quite paws, but similar to each, hard like bone, with short, sharp nails that clicked on the stones of the plaza. Filled with glistening, red-black needle fangs, dripping bloody drool, their mouths were more like terrible snouts. And their eyes proclaimed the difference between these creatures and the other demons Mulkerrin had dredged from Hell—they were aware.

Intelligent.

And there were a lot of them.

The creatures poured from the doorway, moving with a fluid grace that was captivating, almost hypnotic, distracting those within range from the terrible smell the things gave off. Roberto's stomach roiled with displeasure, his nose wrinkled, and for a moment, he stopped breathing, then covered his face with one hand. And yet, the allure of the creatures' motion was such that he wasn't even aware of this reaction to the stench.

And then his soldiers, men and women, human beings under his command, began to scream and die, and the allure was gone.

"Fire on the godforsaken things!" he screamed into his collarcomm, his finger tightening on the trigger of his H-K auto. "But don't hit our people!"

"What the hell are they?" he wondered aloud.

"Vampires," a voice said behind him, and Jimenez snapped his head around quickly. He'd forgotten Courage was standing there, and once again he had almost fired on him.

"What are you doing here?" Jimenez asked. He wanted to ask for help, but couldn't, not from this . . . And then Courage's words sank in.

"Did you say these things were vampires?" He kept firing.

"Did I?"

And then Will Cody was there, with the woman from CNN, Allison whatever, and Jimenez couldn't think anymore. He turned back to the slaughter of his men, wincing at every scream, trembling with the sound of gunfire and the kick of the weapon in his hands. He ignored the chatter behind him for a moment. Reloading, he saw that the creatures were not harmed by bullets, not in the least. They were flesh, that was certain, and they could be blown apart, as more than one had been already. But they came back together.

The things seemed indestructible. They herded soldiers into the gorge, some even flying down after them, knowing the men and women would already be dead at the bottom, wherever that was. He saw Commander Surro, then, grabbed under the armpits by one of the creatures, its talons sinking deep into her flesh as its snout dug into Surro's throat and tore, and it tossed back its head to gulp down the flesh. And then the snout returned, dug in deep and began, it seemed, to drink.

As he slammed a new cartridge home into the H-K, Roberto knew.

"They *are* vampires!" he yelled, turning his auto on Courage, knowing it was useless but needing answers. "What the hell is going on?"

Apparently Courage had just been explaining it to Buffalo Bill and the girl, and from the look on their faces, Roberto wasn't sure he wanted to know.

"As I said," Courage answered, with a calm that almost made Jimenez's trigger finger twitch, "they are vampires. But none of their kind has set foot in this world for nearly two thousand years. In time, if enough of their bodies is left, the humans killed by these vampires will mutate into creatures precisely like them, creatures of utter and complete darkness."

"How do you know all this?" Cody asked.

"I killed the last one myself," he said. "Though it had already infected me with its essence before it died."

"Then why didn't you become one of them?" Allison asked him.

Courage looked at her with an indulgent smile, as if she'd asked a terribly stupid question, but Roberto couldn't read any more from it than that. He didn't think Courage was going to answer, but then the vampire's face became serious once again.

"I wasn't entirely human myself," he said. Jimenez didn't know what the hell he was saying, but Cody and Allison seemed to understand, and both their mouths hung open in astonishment.

"Now," Courage said, "enough of this foolishness. Cody, Charlemagne's remaining troops will engage these vampires while I assist him and the others in their direct assault on the mad priest. You, meanwhile, are going to come at him from behind, quickly, silently . . . and kill him."

"With what?"

John Courage reached inside his shirt and removed the silver crucifix whose bottom had been honed into a dagger, and which he had earlier taken from Commander Jimenez himself. Cody looked at it in silence, clearly remembering the last time he had seen such a weapon, and for some reason, though he was not a coward, Roberto Jimenez was glad that Will Cody didn't know where Courage had gotten the weapon.

Now, though, Roberto was terribly confused. If none of these other shadows could break through whatever force field Mulkerrin had erected, he didn't know how Cody was going to do it. He wanted to argue. But he didn't. At this point, whatever Courage had planned had better happen soon, and he wasn't about to stand in the way.

"Commander," Courage said, "gather your surviving troops and withdraw, just as you had ordered."

Jimenez looked at him, then across at where so many of his people were dying. His eyes closed before he knew they were going to.

"There is nothing you can do for them, Roberto. Work to save those still living."

Commander Roberto Jimenez met John Courage's eyes, and he found something there, a profound sadness, almost mourning, and a resolution to do whatever was necessary to save the lives of his people. Jimenez wondered if he didn't have something in common with this vampire, though the thought disturbed him greatly. His heart felt frozen, shattered by Gloria's terrible death, Mulkerrin's violation of her. Hannibal's defection and that entire catastrophe had enraged him, and now not more than two hundred members of the United Nations security force survived. Operation: Jericho was a complete failure. Only the vampires could do anything about it.

"I owe you this at least," he said. "I'm pretty sure that this battle is being observed very closely. If it looks like you're going to lose, they'll probably nuke the whole city."

"No way!" Allison couldn't believe it. "They wouldn't do that. There are too many people here, civilians, homes . . . and the radiation."

"Everyone's been evac-ed," Jimenez said. "There are no more civilians, and if we can't take out Mulkerrin, who can? And as for people, well, vampires just killed the President of your country, Allison. I don't think anybody considers them people anymore. Just the enemy."

She spun to look at Cody. *Let's get out of here*, she wanted to say, but wouldn't. Cody couldn't go. Whatever was happening here, he was a part of it, an integral part. And if he couldn't leave, she wouldn't either. She loved him, and the time they'd been separated, when she hadn't known if he was alive or dead, had been the worst time of her life.

But then Commander Jimenez took her by the arm.

"Let's go," he said. "You're the only civilian left to evacuate."

"Don't touch me!" she snapped, holding on to Cody. "I was there during the Jihad. I've dealt with demons before."

Cody's eyes were sad, doubtful.

"Shit," she said. "I gave my blood to wake Charlemagne to bring these reinforcements here. I'm in this thing, Will, all the way."

Nobody said a word. Allison's nostrils were filled with the smell of the vampires from the portal, and bile rose in her throat. She could see that Cody wasn't going for it, and she wanted to slap his face. Instead, she threw her arms around him and hugged him tight, and he returned the embrace. She was crying, and she buried her eyes in his shoulder so he wouldn't see it.

"I know you can take care of yourself, darlin'," Cody said. "But if you go down, chances are you won't get up again. I can't let you take that risk."

"So I'm not as good, not as brave, as you because I die easier?" she asked, angry, sad.

And now Cody was mad too, pushing her to arm's length, making sure their eyes met.

"Don't ever say that," he said gravely. "You're a hell of a lot braver, and a lot luckier than the rest of us. You're still human!"

Allison was stung; her face crumbled and the tears came in earnest. She hugged Cody again and whispered, "I love you" in his ear, and his face softened. He returned the words, and then Allison turned toward Commander Jimenez.

"Got another weapon?" she asked, and he produced a semi-auto Beretta handgun and passed it to her. She looked it over quickly and wiped at her tears.

"It'll do," she said. "Now let's get the hell out of here."

When they'd gone, Cody let out the breath he'd been holding. Whatever Jimenez was, he was honorable. Allison could take care of herself, but he wasn't going to take any chances. Jimenez would consider Allison his responsibility the same way the rest of his troops were, and if there were any way to get them all clear, he'd do it. And yet their departure didn't lighten his heart any. Rather, Cody felt more pressure now, to stay alive, to be with Allison again.

There was just this little matter of killing Mulkerrin to deal with.

Sure, Cody could pass right through Mulkerrin's magical protection. He was immune to magic. But if Mulkerrin could somehow sense him coming, well there were other ways the sorcerer could fight back. He could set these newly arrived "vampires" on him for one thing. And Cody was starting to think that if he didn't kill Mulkerrin, nobody would be able to.

And then what?

Did you know these creatures would come? Cody asked John Courage, in his mind.

No, Courage admitted. *And they frighten me. We can destroy them fairly simply. We are much more powerful, but they are so savage, so gleefully . . . evil.*

But you've faced them before, and won, Cody said. *You said yourself that you purged them from our world, after you had been tainted by their evil.*

Courage faced him. *You've figured everything out now, haven't you?*

Most of it, I think, he agreed. *You said before what once lived in you had left a trace of itself behind. Add to that the poison taint of the true vampire, and you have . . .*

"Yes," Courage said aloud. "Us."

There was silence, both verbal and mental, between them for a moment. Cody could not think of a thing to say, was completely overwhelmed by what he now believed to be true. He sensed movement behind him and turned to see that Stefan, the young vampire who had been Rolf's assistant while the SJS was still in operation, had come up behind him. Cody had liked Stefan immediately upon their first meeting, two years earlier, and was pleased, though curious, to see he had survived.

"I thought you were dead," Cody said to him, wondering how the other had escaped Mulkerrin's wrath at the fortress.

"A strange choice of words," the serious shadow said, "but as you can see, I yet survive to continue this battle."

Cody introduced Stefan to John Courage, and the two exchanged greetings. Behind them, the portal continued to allow the original vampires to escape Hell, to walk the earth again. Most of the soldiers left in the plaza had been drained or thrown into the gorge. Just above the portal, they could see where Charlemagne and his winged warriors continued to batter Mulkerrin's protective field, and the rest of Charlemagne's troops were crossing the gorge, engaging the black, Hellish creatures of death, the leeches that poured forth.

Their swords looked like silver. Cody started to ask Courage if that was the answer, if the weapons were indeed forged of the poisonous metal and the creatures more susceptible to it than their own kind.

And then a second portal appeared, midway across the plaza, almost at its center. This doorway was smaller, and its shimmering surface a reddish color. For a moment, nothing happened, and then, at the edges of the portal, hands appeared. Two pair. It was clear that whatever was on the other side was struggling to pull itself into the world. Cody didn't want that to happen.

"Come," Courage said, and he was already running at full speed across the plaza when Cody and Stefan began to move. Obviously, he and Cody had had the same thought.

But even before they got there, one pair of hands had become a head of long blond hair, an upper torso and finally legs, all of which were familiar to Cody.

"Meaghan!" he shouted as he rushed to help her up. She was running both hands through her hair, and her eyes were wide as she puffed out a breath. She smiled as she got to her feet and gave Cody a quick hug before turning to check on the progress of her companion.

"This is Meaghan Gallagher?" Courage asked, and Cody nodded.

"And that," Meaghan pointed to a crown of brown hair that had emerged from the portal, "is Peter Octavian. Who might you be?"

Cody introduced Meaghan to John and Stefan, then, bewildered, he asked her where she had been.

"Hell," Meaghan said soberly, and nothing more.

Meaghan took a moment to take in her surroundings: the black vampire things and the battle being fought against Mulkerrin in the sky. Cody knew that Charlemagne's people would keep Mulkerrin busy for a while, but not forever. He was glad Meaghan and Peter had arrived; they could use all the help they could get.

And Peter was alive! That was the best news of all. Other than Rolf, Peter Octavian was the only vampire Will Cody had ever been willing to call brother. As a human being, he had seen the passing of many brothers, both in blood and in philosophy. He was pleased not to have lost another.

"Maybe we should help him," Stefan suggested, and Cody felt foolish for not having suggested it already. Meaghan smiled despite all she must have been through, and the battle she had returned to.

Cody and Stefan each reached for one of Octavian's hands.

"Where's Alexandra?" Cody asked.

"Dead," Meaghan answered, and Cody did not want to dwell on the pain in her eyes, or in his own heart, for in regaining a brother, he'd lost a sister. Instead, they pulled even harder, and Peter screamed aloud as he slipped through the portal, like the wail of a baby being born. He lay on the ground and shuddered for a moment before Cody helped him up.

"And Lazarus?" John Courage asked. "What of him?"

At that, they all looked up. Cody had only been dimly aware that Courage and Lazarus were connected. Meaghan's face was a big question mark, for she didn't know Courage at all. And Peter was frowning, almost angrily.

"You're the Stranger," Octavian said, and now Meaghan looked even more confused. Cody didn't get it, didn't understand the reference, but it seemed that she did. She looked at John Courage, the Stranger, with new respect.

"I've been called that," Courage answered, one brow raised in surprise at Octavian's words.

"Well," Peter said, his face relaxing, his tone consoling. "I'm sorry to have to tell you that Lazarus didn't make it. He is now a prisoner of Hell, as I was. And *The Gospel of Shadows* with him."

"He'll never get out now," Meaghan said sadly. "Without the book, nobody can go back for him."

"We'll see about that," Courage said, and Cody wasn't certain, but he thought he caught a bit of hostility in Courage's tone, for the first time.

"Well, Peter," Cody said, breaking the moment, "what do you say we take another shot at Father Liam Mulkerrin? Put him down for good?"

"My pleasure," Octavian said, and smiled.

But Will Cody wasn't at all certain he liked that smile.

19

Washington, D.C., United States of America.
Wednesday, June 7, 2000, 4:47 A.M.:

In the minutes since George Marcopoulos had called in on his safe line, Rafael Nieto had received the latest intelligence report, and he was shaking. The safe line had an auto-trace, so that he always knew if not who was contacting him, at least where he was being contacted from.

UN Intelligence agents had arrived at the gas station in Virginia five minutes ago. Nieto held in his hand the fax that had just been transmitted on a closed line from Agent Perkins's car. The report was clear. A police officer had been attacked and bitten by an unidentified vampire. That vampire had a traveling companion whose description matched that of George Marcopoulos.

Only recently had the UN resorted to an Intelligence Division, as a part of the general expansion of the organization's worldwide role. The problem was that nearly every UN staffer had other loyalties as well, Intelligence agents included. So Nieto could be fairly confident that if the new President of the United States, William Galin, didn't have a copy of the report yet, he would have it soon.

And amid the furor surrounding the events in Salzburg and Washington, with the specter of the deaths of so many of his soldiers hanging over his head, it was that one fact that caused Rafael Nieto to shiver now. Bill Galin disturbed him, even frightened him. And though he had not needed George Marcopoulos's hastily whispered advice, it had certainly not helped to calm him. Nieto had always suspected Galin was unstable, and he was inclined to believe Marcopoulos's story, that Galin had tried to kill him.

And Galin didn't want to stop there. Oh, no. The man had a hard-on for nuclear destruction, and he wanted the vampires dead. Nieto didn't love vampires, and he had a hard time trusting them with anything. But he'd known several shadows whom he'd trusted, even admired. Galin, though, wanted to use a nuclear rag to wipe the slate clean, and he had the UN running scared. Rafael had long since ordered the evacuation, just in case, but damn it, he had soldiers in there—soldiers who had fought hard, been through hell and were lucky enough to have survived so far.

And that lunatic Galin wanted to use them as bait!

He'd been calling Bill Galin every five minutes for the past hour, interrupted only by Marcopoulos's call. Now the phone rang, and as he picked up, Rafael Nieto privately wished George godspeed to whatever safe haven he now sought. He only hoped the old man was smart enough not to get caught.

"Yes?" he said sharply as the video image came into focus.

"You've been looking for me, I'm told." Bill Galin seemed bored, lethargic, as if Rafael were at the bottom of his list of people to call back.

"You know damn well I have!" he snarled at the former vice president.

"Well?" Galin's face and voice were smug, taunting. "What can I do for you?"

"Don't even think about using nukes," Nieto said. "The consequences for you would be very ugly."

"Why you . . ." Galin sputtered. "Don't you dare presume to threaten me. You don't want to mess with me. Rafael. I'm the goddamn President of the United States!"

"That means less every year," Nieto spat, "and the President's dead; you're nothing but an understudy brought in until they find a new star!"

For a moment Galin was speechless, and Nieto thought the veins in the man's forehead would burst—all in all probably the least troublesome solution to their current dilemma—but no such luck. Finally, the new President hissed, venom in every word.

"We'll have this conversation again next year," Galin said, "and then we'll see how much my job title means. Until then, *muchacho del barrio*, don't presume to tell the U.S.A. what to do. From now on, that means me."

The man is insane, Nieto thought. Galin wanted to nuke Salzburg, and Rafael Nieto could almost see his point. In fact, he might be inclined to go along with the plan, as long as proper evacuation could be guaranteed, but the crazy fucker wouldn't hear of it. He wanted to get the missiles flying that moment, no later. And he didn't care whether it meant ejection from the UN, sanctions, even military repercussions.

"I've got to go now," Galin was saying, "I have a package to deliver."

"Wait!" Rafael barked.

"Oh," Galin said and smiled, "I'm through waiting, and I see I'm getting through to you. The U.S. Congress has already voted in an emergency session to go ahead with this action regardless of UN approval."

"Give me two hours," Nieto said finally. "I've got to try to get my people out of there. I—"

"Fraid not, Rafe," Galin said and chuckled obnoxiously. "See, if your boys run away, what's going to hold our target in place until the missiles get there? Besides, you're in no position to ask for favors."

Galin leaned forward, putting his face close up to the screen, getting intimate with the secretary general on the other end, a friend telling secrets.

"This was a courtesy call, Rafe," Galin sneered. "If Congress hadn't made it a condition, I wouldn't have bothered returning your messages."

Nieto was stunned. It wasn't just anger, or insult, or disbelief at the outrageous lunacy of the new President—it was all of that, but more.

It was the voice of defeat that had suddenly begun to speak in his mind, to issue from his mouth.

"But," he said, scrambling for words, "you've seen the media reports. The vampires are all over Mulkerrin now, our people would be gone before—"

Galin was shaking his head.

"I don't think so," he began and then looked up, almost seductively. "Of course, I could be persuaded."

"Persuaded how?" Nieto jumped at the opening, as he knew he was meant to. He couldn't help it. If Galin wanted him as a puppet, that was fine, as long as he had the time.

"Well, for starters, there's the obvious," Galin said, and Nieto nodded.

"UN approval of the nuclear strike."

"Correct," Galin nodded. "Secondly, I want the UN to revoke all the privileges of shadows, to announce that the creatures are no better than animals, and I want the United Nations to declare open warfare on all shadows."

"Impossible!" Nieto stood and turned his back to the videophone, so that Galin could not see his horrified face. He had no love for shadows, but this . . . "No." He turned back to glare at Galin. "Henry Russo and Julie Graham's assassinations must be treated like any other terrorist act. Other than Hannibal, we can't know whether any other known shadow is involved. Their entire race should not suffer for them. We are not Nazis!"

"I'm afraid I don't see the comparison," Galin said whimsically.

"No," Nieto said sadly, and sat down again, "you wouldn't."

"In any case," the American went on, "shadows are not a 'race,' as you put it. They are creatures, not people. They're vampires, for God's sake! And their ambassador, George Marcopoulos, a friend of yours, I believe, tried to kill me before escaping with the help of some of his cohorts. He was obviously involved. No, these animals must be destroyed, and the UN will declare war."

Rafael Nieto knew he was defeated, and he tried to hide.

"The powers of my position have greatly increased over the years," he said, "but even I can't do that alone. The Security Council would have to—"

"And with you and I recommending such a move, the rest of the council will most assuredly do so at the emergency meeting you will call for this afternoon," Galin sneered. "Unless, of course, you are also involved in this conspiracy with your friend George Marcopoulos? Oh, there would be media feeding frenzy if such information were to come to light."

Galin's tone was insinuating, a promise in itself, and though Rafael thought of saying something like *You wouldn't dare*, he didn't. He knew better.

"Two hours?" he said finally, more a plea than anything else.

"Yes, yes." Galin waved him off now. "You can have your two hours, and if Mulkerrin still lives, no matter who is there, the city of Salzburg will be vaporized."

U.S. Interstate 81, Salem, Virginia, United States of America. Wednesday, June 7, 2000, 4:54 A.M.:

"Slow down!" George snapped, and Joe Boudreau looked nervously, angrily around at him . . . and then the look turned sheepish and the speedometer slid down from seventy-five to a more comfortable sixty or so. That was good, George thought—not too slow or they'd look too suspicious. They'd been gaining speed gradually for the past twenty-five minutes, and his heart was still pounding from their run-in with the law back at the gas station in Buchanan.

"You okay?" Joe asked, and George nodded, taking a breath and trying forcibly to calm himself down.

"Yes," he answered, suddenly feeling his age more than ever. "It just seems like this trip is going to take forever."

"I know what you mean," Joe said and nodded, without taking his eyes off the road. "Time isn't the same for me, and it feels that way already. Maybe because we both know that even when we arrive in New Orleans, the trip is far from over. Nothing's ever going to be the same again."

George took that in, realizing then that innocent and simple as he might seem, Joe Boudreau was neither. And how could George have expected any less; the man was a vampire after all. The changes that caused in a being were not merely physical. Suddenly George was very happy he'd never accepted his friends' offers of immortality, of vampirism. For just a moment, he was glad that he was old, that he would surely not survive the battle ahead. And then he wondered whether or not that made him a coward. He hoped not, for he had too much pride for that.

"It was strange back there," Joe said, and George knew he meant the gas station. "But I guess that's life from here on in, huh? Even if they don't nuke Austria, the worst has happened, right? I mean, my people will be hiding in the shadows, hunted down. With technology, we'll be wiped out in no time."

George looked at him and shook his head, perturbed.

"Don't be such a damned pessimist, Joseph," he said. "It's not as if twenty-first century vampire hunters will be out there after sixteenth-century vampires. Your people are probably the single richest segment of society, even with all of the drifters. The technology is yours as well, and there will be people who aren't after you, who will, in fact, help you to use it, to defend yourselves. Yes, things have come full circle, and your people have been lured out of the safety of myth, out of their secret lives, by the promise of peace and a taste of what passes for normalcy. And now that has backfired, and once again humans fear the unknown, and kill what they fear.

"But at least there's a unity now, and new strength and all the world to hide in. And don't forget that there are groups of humans who are obsessed with vampires to the point of worship, all over the world, who will gladly donate their blood to keep you safe, your existence a secret."

"But the new order . . .," Joe began.

". . . will barely be remembered," George cut him off. "When history is written, it will say that vampires were 'discovered,' and only dealt with after the President of the United States was assassinated."

"That sucks!" Joe said.

"Yes, it surely does," George replied, with no trace of a smile.

"We've got to stop that from happening, make people see the truth."

"If you have any ideas," George said, somewhat cynically, "I'd be happy to hear them."

But Joe was quiet.

There were more cars on the road now, and George couldn't believe that some people were already on their way to work. He imagined they must have long commutes or odd hours, and no interest in or awareness of the world's status quo collapsing around them—not as long as their own livelihood was unaffected. Still, cars and all, it was very easy going, Joe's foot barely touching the brake.

"Do you think anyone's after us, really?" Joe asked after a while.

"Not really, no," George answered. "Like I said, the gypsies among you are going to be the hardest hit, and they'll be the first to answer Hannibal's call to violence. I'm sure right now they're wreaking havoc, and the authorities will be much more interested in them. Still, it wouldn't be a bad idea to stop in a couple of hours and pick up a razor, some scissors and maybe a hat and sunglasses. I don't want to invite trouble."

They were quiet a while longer, and then Joe cleared his throat and reached for the dash-screen TV controls.

"Do you want CNN back on?" he asked.

"God, no," George Marcopoulos said with a shiver. "Anything but that. I think we deserve a rest, an hour in the dark, so to speak. We may never have the luxury again."

Pongau Basin, Austria, European Union.
Wednesday, June 7, 2000, 10:42 A.M.:

"Hey, big guy," Erika began, barely able to control the sarcasm that usually tainted her words, "what's up with Junior Boy Scout over here? Seems to me we're just getting ourselves lost."

Rolf smiled at the girl's attitude, then tried to shake the word "girl" from his head. Erika was a vampire, just like him, and though she looked like a teenager, she'd been dead for several years. Annelise, a tall, attractive shadow of French descent, and Carlos, a Central American whose true age and heritage were something of a mystery, nodded their agreement with Erika's words, with her doubt. Only Sebastiano, a vampire who'd been born in Sicily and who, as a matter of weird vanity, allowed his appearance to reflect the sixty-two years old he'd been when he died, seemed perturbed by what Erika said. Strangely, the object of her complaint, the vampire known as Jared, did not seem upset at all.

"Erika," Sebastiano chided, "if Jared's guidance is satisfactory to Rolf, the rest of us should have no complaint."

"Says you, Yano," Erika said and sniffed. "The guy could be leading us right into a trap, and we'd never know it. Do any of you even know him?"

Rolf halted then, turning back to look down at the girl, his eyebrows knitting together in a deep frown. She stopped in her tracks, and the others behind her, but she was not intimidated by him. Erika put her hands on her hips.

"Do *you* know him?" she asked Rolf, and though he was irked, he shook his head to say no. Then he turned and tapped Jared, to bring his attention to the matter at hand.

Jared stopped short. They were entering a narrow passage of ice, sloping gently downward until it became more and more difficult to walk. Their vampiric eyes could see clearly in the dark, but there was some light just the same. Daylight filtered weirdly up from somewhere ahead, though they were descending, and reflected, was refracted, off the ice to give increasing illumination.

"I don't blame you for lacking faith," Jared said, not bothering to whisper, in light of Erika's loud voice, "but I have already told your chief marshall here that Hannibal is of my bloodline, descended from me, as it were. I can sense him not far ahead."

He looked pointedly at Erika.

"And if there were no trap before," Jared said sharply "you may rest assured that there will be one now."

Rolf motioned, indicating that the conversation was over, and Jared turned back and continued to lead the group toward their final conflict with Hannibal. He was suddenly certain that Elissa was already dead, and only the lack of any blood on the ice calmed him.

"Well done," Annelise said to Erika behind him. "Now Hannibal will be prepared for us."

"So sue me," she answered.

"Hannibal shall do more than that if . . . ," Carlos began, and Erika shot him the finger as Sebastiano shushed them all. But Jared had stopped again.

"Hannibal shall do nothing but die," he said. "Our people have suffered enough this morning. I lost my brother and my father's sister to this battle with Mulkerrin, and I might not have if Hannibal had fought for his people instead of against us."

Jared turned back and continued to descend the slippery ice path. The incline became more and more steep, and soon the six of them were laying their hands palms open on the walls in order to stay on their feet. It worked for a while, and then, looking down, Jared saw that, though the path cut away until it was nearly impossible to keep from sliding down, it also ended about twenty-five feet ahead.

He turned to look at Rolf, who understood the unspoken question immediately, and nodded. Jared took his hands off the wall and surrendered his balance, sitting down hard on the ice and sliding down into the passage. At the bottom, he looked around, then motioned for the rest of them to come down. Which they did, sliding one by one. All but Erika, who transformed, instead, to mist and floated down. Rolf was certain she would have claimed it had something to do with her integrity.

At the bottom, they discovered the source of the light that had filtered weakly through the caves and that now lit the cavern in which they stood fairly well. It was a round opening, high above their heads, about five feet in diameter.

"That's not natural," Jared said quietly, still nervously scanning the room for Hannibal's followers.

"It's also brand new," Erika said, and motioned toward a pile of ice and earth that was directly beneath the opening in the roof of the cave.

"Well, he's gone then," Annelise said, looking to Rolf for support.

"It looks like the showdown is cancelled," Carlos agreed.

"Time for us to go, then?" Sebastiano asked Rolf, who was looking only at Jared, and who now shook his head no, slowly, his mind occupied. Finally, Jared turned to face them.

"He's not gone," Jared said. "He knows now that I can sense him, and he's trying to block me out. But that, his shielding himself, is like a beacon to me. He's close. Very close."

"Oh, yes!" A familiar voice rang through the cavern. "Very close!"

Rolf and his comrades looked up, following the voice and saw a crowd of heads surrounding the hole above them. One leaned farther over into the hole, and the sunlight streaming down into the cave became a halo around his winter-white hair. At Rolf's side, Carlos tensed as if he were about to change, and the mute turned quickly toward him, slapping his hands together with a loud crack to get the other vampire's attention. Carlos looked at him, frustration coloring his face, but Rolf held up one hand as if to say, *Be patient.*

"Where is Commander Thomas?" Jared called up to the vampires clustered around the hole. Their forms blocked much of the sun from the cavern, and it had become significantly darker.

Hannibal did not answer, but Rolf sensed movement in the darkness around them and, glancing around, saw that his meager band of shadows was not alone in the cavern. Hannibal had escaped with a handful of his vampiric followers, and only now did Rolf realize that there were more heads outside the cavern than there ought to have been. Now, more of them slid wraithlike into the cavern from several openings, which must have led into other caves other icy tunnels. In moments, perhaps a dozen vampires Rolf had never seen before stood in a rough circle around the perimeter of the room. His own soldiers, the very few that were left, were on guard, ready to do battle though defeat was almost certain.

And Hannibal still had Elissa.

"*Rolf!*" she screamed, and then was cut off as the wind was knocked out of her. He looked up, ignoring the vampires in the cavern with them, as they didn't seem to be moving in, and saw that his lover was alive. For the moment. Elissa Thomas grappled at air as her arms and upper torso hung down into the cavern, her lower half held tight by Hannibal's followers.

Even with his enhanced senses, Rolf could not see Elissa's face past the sunlight on her hair, just as he knew she could not see the fear, the concern, in his features, or that his brow was furrowed with frustration, or his hatred for Hannibal. But he could smell her terror. He knew that Elissa was not afraid of falling, of the drop into the cavern that awaited her if they let her go. Rolf knew that his lover feared precisely what he did: that she would not be dropped.

He glanced around, meeting the eyes of each of his people in turn: Carlos, angry and anxious to begin the battle, regardless of its outcome; Annelise, quietly resigned to their predicament; Jared, looking to Rolf for their next move, though Rolf was sure the much older vampire was more than capable of escaping the cavern himself; Sebastiano, looking old because he allowed it and terrified because he could not help it; and Erika, whose face was a mask of grim determination, confidence and faith in her leader, her friend—him.

Rolf looked once more at Jared, motioning for the other vampire to act in his place, to do what he could not, to speak.

"Hannibal!" Jared called loudly, his voice echoing off the icy walls of the cavern. "You know me now, boy. You know I am responsible for your creation. Release the human and do honorable battle alone against your accuser, as your ancestors did."

There was a stunned pause, as all present took in a breath, with the exception of Elissa Thomas, whose hitched breathing became even louder. The sun had moved slightly, nearly overhead now, and its glare made the figures outside the hole more difficult to distinguish. It was clearer, though, how the hole had been made, torn through several feet of ice, dirt and snow by supernatural strength. The ice around its inner edge was sweating, melting, and Rolf took a moment to realize how long the arms must be that suspended Elissa so low through that hole.

And then Hannibal responded, not with a laugh, but with a horrible braying, which Rolf had never heard from him before. He'd expected a similar reaction, yet his last hopes crumbled as the butcher's laughter slowed to snuffling giggles, then an amused dry chuckle, and finally, nothing.

And then: "Oh, please, dearest ancestor," Hannibal sneered, "do not attack my nobility, for surely you must see that it is far more profound than your own, or that of any of these, hmm, vegetarians? You seek to draw me out by invoking our ancestors, and yet you are obviously the weak link in my bloodline, the skeleton in the family closet.

"How dare you?!" Hannibal raged. "How dare you question my loyalty to our ancestry! I am the true heir to all that we are, all that we were and can be again. Why do I not meet Rolf Sechs in personal battle? Because I am not certain of victory, and in the unlikely event of my defeat my plans would be crushed. I would deliver to our kind their birthright: the blood of humans running like beer from the tap, the thrill of the hunt and the power of fear. I will not gamble that future merely because you taunt me."

"I do not taunt, child," Jared said grimly. "The ancestors I refer to are those who existed in the beginning, before our legacy was perverted by those who instilled such repulsive traits in our kind. Come, now, and fight your speechless foe. Kill him if you can, or die with honor if that is your fate."

"For the sake of our people," Hannibal declared, "I cannot allow that to happen, just as I cannot suffer any vampire who stands against me to live. Any of you who wish to join me may do so now, may return to the glory of our kind and bathe in the blood of humanity.

"Come," he urged Rolf's comrades, "join me and be worshipped as a part of the new shadow kingdom. Or stay and die, as an act of mercy. For if I allow you to live, you will only be hunted down, alone and afraid, by humans without the courage to race the *real* vampires."

Rolf's mouth dropped open as he sensed the movement at his side, and as Sebastiano stepped slowly forward, he wished for the first time in decades that he had the power of speech. The Sicilian, his wrinkled face grave and white as his hair, refused to return the stares of his friends.

"A kingdom, you say?" Sebastiano asked. "Are you, then, the king of shadows, Hannibal?"

Hannibal leaned impossibly far into the hole above them, his white hair hanging straight down. He was face-to-face with Elissa now, but Rolf knew she dare not attempt anything, just as he would not make a move as long as she was Hannibal's prisoner.

"Oh," Hannibal hissed with a smile, "that I am. That, I most certainly am."

"Then I kneel to you, shadow king," Sebastiano began, but Erika rushed toward him, screaming as he knelt.

"Yano, no!" she cried and reached for his arm. "How can you do this?"

And Sebastiano, his apparent weakness as deceiving as her own, used his vampiric strength and Erika's own momentum and hurled her toward the far wall, where her head met the ice with a terrible crack. Rolf spun toward him, and Hannibal's shadows tightened their circle around the cavern, but did not attack. Rolf did not approach Sebastiano, who yet refused to meet his eyes, but instead went to Erika's side. She was, of course, alive, but would take a few minutes of healing. He looked up into Hannibal's smiling face, hanging there next to Elissa's blood-streaked neck, but when he saw that her eyes were closed tightly, as if awaiting a blow, he simply moved back to where he had been standing, holding Erika up at his side.

"You followed me once before, Sebastiano," Hannibal was saying. "You may follow me again. Come."

And Sebastiano shifted his form into that of a bat, *clearly an appeal to Hannibal's sense of tradition*, Rolf thought, and flew up and through the hole in the cavern's ceiling, to disappear beyond the heads of the gathered shadows. Then, one by one, Hannibal's other followers, who had remained in the cavern, transformed and followed him.

"Do something, Rolf," Carlos hissed at him. "He's going to kill that damn human anyway. My blood, she's only human. Just because you fucked her, doesn't mean—"

And then Rolf was standing over him, Carlos sprawled on the ice floor of the cavern wiping his fist across his mouth as bats escaped the chamber. Rolf wanted to hurt Carlos for his words, but knew that that would be playing by Hannibal's rules. Erika was next to him then, and Annelise on the other side.

"Asshole," Erika said to Carlos.

"If that's how you feel," Annelise added, "you ought to follow Sebastiano."

Rolf merely shook his head, then turned his attention back to the ceiling of the cavern, where Hannibal hung side by side with Elissa, and the last of the white-haired vampire's followers flew up and past them, out into the sunshine.

"Blasphemer," Jared said suddenly beside him, and Rolf turned to see the hatred on his face, as if the words had been building within him and were only now bursting forth. Jared stepped forward, and Rolf tensed, prepared to stop him from going after Hannibal, but he needn't have worried. Jared knew Elissa's life was at stake—though Rolf had begun to realize that the stakes were much higher than one woman's life.

"You are no king!" Jared barked at Hannibal, and his white-haired descendant merely smiled. "There is only one king of shadows, and even now he fights to protect all the people of this world from a terrible danger, not merely to further his own lustful ends. Only one king, and you will bow before him, or you will die!"

What? Was he speaking of Charlemagne?

He must be, Rolf told himself. The former emperor now returned to life, to leadership, Charlemagne must have been the king of shadows to whom Jared referred. But Rolf wasn't certain he would bow to anyone.

"What are you going to do now?" Carlos called up to Hannibal.

"You've obviously got us outnumbered," Annelise said, "but you don't need the woman."

"Let her go, Hannibal!" Erika demanded. "Whatever you have planned for us, she's not part of it."

"Planned for you?" Hannibal smiled down at them, and the sun had moved farther across the sly above, so that the glare no longer clouded their enhanced vision. Though shadowed, Hannibal's face made his intentions quite clear, though his words told another story.

"I have nothing planned for you," Hannibal insisted. "In fact, I intend to leave you all right here."

"This is far from over, blood-child!" Jared yelled, his patience long since disappeared, and Hannibal's placating tone only making him angrier.

The smile disappeared from Hannibal's lips.

"*Au contraire, mon père*," he breathed, "for all of you, it is, most certainly, over."

His right hand, elongated into a terrible razor-sharp claw, flashed out faster even than the other vampires' eyes could truly follow, and Elissa Thomas's scream had just begun when it lost its vigor. Her uniform, and her flesh beneath, was torn open from crotch to collarbone, and in the stunned half second before Rolf and the others could react, they were showered by her blood, pelted by wet, pink flesh and what had once been the vital organs of a woman.

With a wordless roar, Rolf was off the ground, transforming mid-leap into a blood-smeared eagle, speeding for the opening in the cavern. His senses were focused on Hannibal's withdrawing face, on Elissa's dangling corpse, dead before her viscera hit the ice below, yet he knew without seeing or hearing them that Jared, Erika and the others were right behind him.

Beyond Hannibal, Rolf could see a line of bats across the sunny sky, a picture that nature should never have allowed as the self-proclaimed vampire king's followers escaped . . . And then Elissa's corpse was falling, and he was hurtling straight toward her, and though he knew in his mind she was dead, his heart screamed at him to catch her, and the frightened, pleading stare of her dead eyes nearly stopped him cold.

He changed again, into something not quite a man and not quite an eagle, and he did his best to break her fall. Erika was right behind him, and as he fell with his dead lover in his arms, Rolf bore her down as well. The others moved out of the way of the falling corpse and the two shadows trying to slow its descent, toward the edges of the cavern, and by the time they started up after Hannibal again, only his single form remained outlined against the sunny sky. He held something in his hand, but in the glare, none of them could see what it was.

"When muscle will not suffice," Hannibal called down to them, and wings grew from his back, his body hunched over, becoming an ugly crimson color, and he took flight, a rough, snarling scream completing the thought as he sped away: ". . . technology shall triumph!"

Carlos and Annelise led the charge up through the hole in the ceiling, Jared right behind them, but too late, as the entire cavern, and ice caves and tunnels a quarter mile in every direction, were vaporized in a flash of thermite.

Salzburg, Austria, European Union.
Wednesday, June 7, 2000, 10:23 A.M.:

Liam Mulkerrin had no idea what he had called from the depths of Hell. He had opened the portal in a moment of panic when he'd thought a particularly harsh blow from Charlemagne was going to penetrate his force shield. He had reached out blindly with his magic and flipped a mental switch that had, due to the frequency of its use, replaced a long, spoken spell that had once been required for the creation of such portals. His mind had sought something vicious enough to destroy Charlemagne and his troops, and it seemed as though the creatures on the other side of the portal had reached out to him as well.

Yet he had no idea what they were. Not that it mattered now, as Charlemagne's warriors, so much more advanced than the vampires Mulkerrin had faced before, were forced to break away their attack to defend themselves against the new arrivals. Black and blood-red, the creatures were paper-thin but incredibly strong, and their insubstantial wings kept them aloft as they attacked, outnumbering Charlemagne's forces three to one.

But not for long. For all their viciousness, their talons and needle teeth, the death promised in their eyes, these pure vampires—for that was what Mulkerrin somehow sensed they were—were no match for Charlemagne's warriors, whose weapons were made, not of steel as they had first appeared to be, but of silver. The material was poison to all magical things, in greater and lesser degrees, but the more evil a thing, the more powerful a weapon silver became. These pure vampires were truly evil, and one good wound from a silver blade caused them to explode in a burst of pustulent black fluid, the stench of which penetrated even Mulkerrin's magical protection.

Still, he reveled in the power that had been given him by the Lord, to force these creatures to do his bidding . . .

Yes, Liam, you have done well for me, the voice of God boomed in his head, and tears sprang from Mulkerrin's eyes as he thanked his creator for the mission, the chance to serve.

Ah, but why do you tarry so with these creatures? the voice asked. *Surely I gave you more than enough power to choose from a thousand ways to wipe them out?*

"Yes, Lord," Mulkerrin said aloud, kneeling, hovering, eyes closed, protected, amid the aerial portion of the bloody battle. "But you see I am only human, and it is taking me some time to become acquainted with all that you have given me. It has been somewhat difficult to concentrate on understanding my new abilities since my return to this plane."

Did I choose wrong in freeing you from your Hellish prison? the voice asked.

"Oh, no Lord! Please, your will shall be done! I only needed a little time to grow accustomed to my—your power! Now," he cried, "I shall destroy them all."

"Oh, I think not, old enemy," a voice from Mulkerrin's past said, and he opened his eyes. Before him, Peter Octavian hovered, battling the air currents with enormous feathered wings, his body otherwise unchanged, and smiling a terrible, mocking smile.

The voice of his Lord was silent now, but Mulkerrin did not mind He would get on with God's work in a moment, but first . . .

"Finally," he said to Octavian, his eyes widening with glee, "you will die."

John Courage, the Stranger, fought side by side with Meaghan Gallagher, Will Cody and this newcomer from the SJS, Stefan.

Courage no longer bothered to hide many of his long-developed abilities. Like Charlemagne, one hundred yards away, Courage's hands had become talons of real silver, and a powerful swipe was enough to cause one of the true vampires to explode. The creatures' numbers were dwindling fast, and only moments before, Mulkerrin had allowed the portal to close. Somehow, his concentration had again been broken.

Nearly two millenia had passed since the Stranger had last battled these true vampires, and then he'd destroyed the last of them on Earth. That conflict had not been nearly as simple, but Courage was not complaining. Instead, he was worried. There was something not quite right about Octavian, something familiar, though they'd never met, and the Stranger became more and more curious as minutes ticked by. Courage had tried to contact him mentally, as he ought to have been able to do with any earth-spawned vampire, but all he got was static, white noise, with the essence of something evil behind it. It was possible that this was caused by Octavian's long imprisonment in Hell, but not likely.

Perhaps his time there had more of an effect on him than any of us suspected, Courage thought. There was the fact that Octavian knew him as the Stranger, merely because Lazarus had told the former detective of his existence. Too coincidental, and certainly not detective work. And finally, there was the current question.

Courage had to wonder why he and the others were being swarmed by the gnashing jaws and flapping wings of the true vampires, while Octavian had not had to fight off a single one of the creatures as of yet.

We are nearly victorious. Charlemagne's thoughts came into his head.

Over these creatures, yes, but the sorcerer yet lives. Try not to destroy all of the vampires yet. Give it a moment, Courage sent back to him. *Let's see if Cody can get the job done.*

And then Charles was gone from his mind, and he opened his thoughts to Cody and Gallagher, simultaneously. He felt Meaghan's surprise, as she had not yet experienced contact with him, but he also sensed her respect for him. In Hell, she had told him, she had been shown deference by demon-lords simply because she mentioned his name.

Only a few more feet, he sent to them, *and we will be directly behind Mulkerrin. He thinks himself invulnerable from attack but as soon as Octavian engages him, Meaghan and I will destroy these "vampires" and give Cody a clear shot at the sorcerer's back.*

What if I screw it up? Cody's question came into Courage's mind. As did Meaghan Gallagher's response: *Don't.*

Courage watched as Octavian confronted Mulkerrin, and he wished that he could see the look on the sorcerer's face. As it was, the smile on Peter Octavian's lips told quite a story, and forced John Courage to dispel his concerns regarding Octavian's strangeness. This was a shadow thoroughly enjoying the impending defeat of an enemy who had cost him a thousand years of torture. Courage was relieved.

Cody, now! he thought as he moved in sync with Gallagher, lashing out at the leathery skin of the vampires that surrounded them. Cody transformed himself into a hawk shrieking as the silver dagger was absorbed into his body. The old cowboy had a while to go before he could comfortably forge wings from his flesh while retaining his otherwise human form. It was a learned skill, and he hadn't had the time, the years.

Lord, Charlemagne's voice came into Courage's head, *the few true vampires that still live are fleeing. Shall we give chase?*

God, no! Courage thought, hoping Mulkerrin didn't notice that his creatures had lost the battle. *No, Charles, we'll track them later, if this gambit works.*

And then their hand was played, as Cody shifted back to human form twenty feet directly above Mulkerrin and dropped, dagger in hand, through the sorcerer's shield.

Liam Mulkerrin could not believe it, nor could he understand. Peter Octavian, who had thwarted his plans for vampiric genocide and for a new Catholic Church under his own leadership, who had been responsible for his imprisonment in Hell and had been imprisoned at his side, subject to the same tortures . . . Octavian was laughing at him.

The vampire taunted him, and try as he might, Mulkerrin was powerless to stop him.

When the other vampires had attacked, he had needed to learn his new abilities, and their numbers were such that, unless they angered him, he would not concentrate on those few whose assault was direct, but on the masses. With Octavian, it was different. Mulkerrin's pure hatred of the shadow made it impossible for him to see beyond their conflict. And yet, it seemed he could not harm the creature. He had attempted spells that simply did not work; he had tried to reach out, using his sorcerous influence, and strike at Octavian, to no avail. Mulkerrin knew something had happened to Will Cody that made him immune to magical influence, but this thing with Octavian was something completely different, something more.

With Cody, the spells worked; Mulkerrin's influence was there, but did not affect him. With Octavian, the spells failed. His sorcery was functional in all other ways, his protective shield intact, but each time he attempted to use it against Octavian, it was as though he were striking out with the ghost of an amputated limb.

"What's wrong, Liam?" Octavian asked with a smirk. "From omnipotent to impotent in just seconds—it's an awful feeling, isn't it?"

"I have the power of God in me!" Mulkerrin nearly shrieked in panic, as Octavian moved closer. He realized then that he truly feared Octavian, and then he pushed the truth away, pretended it had never existed. With God on his side, he had no need for fear, he was protected.

"God?" Octavian laughed. "Would God help a butcher like you, a madman whose only love is the creation of pain and suffering?"

"My only love is God!" Mulkerrin said without hesitation. "Once I reveled in the pain of others, inflicted in the name of God. A millenia of suffering at your side in Hell has shown me that my pleasure in the suffering of others was vain, that such suffering is for God's pleasure only. It is through pain and death that this world will be purified for him.

"And you will not stop me!"

Mulkerrin tried again to lash out at Octavian, but he felt nothing inside, at the source of his control over the magic. The vampire moved closer still, and Mulkerrin winced.

"Would God," Octavian asked softly, slowly, "give you the power to call up creatures of the darkness? Would He use such creatures for his own ends?"

"Since the days of his son Jesus Christ and the human Joseph the Carpenter, God's Church has controlled the creatures of darkness, as you put it," Mulkerrin said proudly, drawing himself up. "It is only right that they be put to use cleansing the world they would have liked to destroy. All creatures are God's creatures."

At that Octavian smiled.

"Not all creatures," he said, and something told Mulkerrin to look away, away from the vampire, his old enemy, whose broad wings held him aloft in the air currents around them. Octavian's comment seemed to refer to these new things, the pure vampires that Mulkerrin had called up from . . . well, not Hell, but elsewhere. Mulkerrin looked down, where the creatures ought to have been savaging Charlemagne and his troops.

And were not. Instead, the creatures, the pure vampires he had brought to Earth had either been killed or fled into the alleys of Salzburg. But rather than taking flight to press an attack on Mulkerrin, Charlemagne's troops were poised, prepared for battle, and doing absolutely nothing. But why?

Mulkerrin glanced quickly back at Octavian, whose smile said nothing, and everything. A setup of some kind, but from . . . Mulkerrin moved, as fast as his mind could pull the strings of his sorcerous influence on the world around him, back away from Peter Octavian. And he watched as Will Cody fell past him, scrabbling at air with a silver dagger, only a few feet away and well within his "protective" shield. A lot of good it would have done; he had not even felt Cody's violation of his shield.

"Son of a bitch!" Cody yelled as he dropped, and as Mulkerrin watched, the vampire buckled in the air, his face a rictus of pain, as ragged wings sprouted from his back, his legs shrinking, drawing up into a painful combination of human flesh and feathered talon. But his upper body remained human, his right hand filled with silver, and he moved toward Mulkerrin with agony carved into his features. Unlike Octavian, there was nothing graceful or beautiful about this difficult transformation for Cody, nothing angelic.

Mulkerrin looked back at Octavian, and saw that his face had broken into a grin so impossibly wide it must have been assisted by vampiric metamorphosis. It was a terrible grin, with murderous intent, and all thoughts of the angelic appearance of his wings were gone from Mulkerrin's mind, not that he ever would have admitted to such a thought.

"Die, you bastard!" Cody shouted, and Octavian did not move to assist the other vampire as Mulkerrin conjured a trio of mist-wraiths, creatures who had long been his slaves. In the days when he was nothing more than a sorcerer, he had bound them to him, their wills nearly nonexistent, and used them as his most common ally, often for emergency transportation. When he first encountered Octavian, he had used mist-wraiths. In Venice, during the Jihad, he had relied on them heavily. Now, with so much going strangely wrong around him, it was reflex to call on them to attack Cody, and he didn't have time for more.

In seconds, the three wraiths covered Will Cody, and he could not concentrate on holding the winged form he had assumed. To avoid falling, Cody turned to mist, and the silver dagger he had been holding fell, tumbling, to the bloody cobblestones far below. Out of the corner of his eye, Mulkerrin saw Meaghan Gallagher and a male shadow he did not know, almost too close, but he ignored them. Perhaps he could not attack Octavian directly, but thus far the vampire hadn't made a move, which indicated that unlike Cody, he could not pass through Mulkerrin's protective shell.

Stalemate. It was time to shake off these minor considerations and battles, to stretch his new abilities to their limits. He would begin with the destruction of the city below, and let them attempt to stop him. The only one capable was Cody, and Mulkerrin would not let that shadow out of his sight, would summon demons to keep him away whenever necessary. He would do . . .

Nothing! the voice of God boomed in his head. *You will do nothing more, Liam. You have failed, been distracted far too long by your petty angers, tiny fears.*

"No, Lord!" Mulkerrin said aloud. "Don't do this to me. I am your fire of purification, your weapon."

Not a weapon. You have never been more than a tool.

"Please," the sorcerer pleaded. "Do not say such things."

And then his shield was gone and he was falling, summoning two more mist-wraiths even as he fell, the extra strength granted him now gone. Despair cast a pall over his soul. Abandoned by his God, he was suddenly without any guidance. Still, he was a sorcerer, and had knowledge of many spells of power—he would survive.

And then Octavian was there, his hands clasped around Mulkerrin's head, tightly squeezing, and the mist-wraiths had dissipated as if they had never been there. A hundred feet above the ground, Mulkerrin was held aloft by those hands on his head, and Octavian's wings lifted them both higher, then higher still.

"Admit it," Octavian said, his face so close to Mulkerrin's that their noses almost brushed. He spoke softly, like a lover. "Admit it, Liam."

"What are you talking about?" Mulkerrin screeched, even as his mind fought to concentrate on spells despite the pressure on his skull.

"Admit that you know what the vampires are, who the Stranger is. Admit that you knew, all along, in your heart of hearts, that it wasn't God speaking to you," Octavian purred.

"My God," Mulkerrin cried to the sky, "why have you abandoned me?"

"Come now, priest," Octavian chuckled dryly, "he abandoned you long ago, and you knew it. You knew. You were never on the side of the angels. Admit it to me, now. Forget your petty angers, your tiny fears, and admit that which you knew, but feared to recognize!"

The words burned into Mulkerrin's mind, past the blinding pressure in his head. Petty angers. Tiny fears. And he knew. Knew who had been speaking to him all along, who had freed him from Hell, made him such a formidable weapon and sent him forth. Liam Mulkerrin knew whom he served. It was not God, never God. And it was not, most certainly, Peter Octavian.

You! Mulkerrin thought.

Oh, yes, the voice came back to him, in his head. And Octavian smiled, kissing him on the forehead.

"Don't worry, Liam," Octavian said. "You were already damned."

Octavian stopped rising, now more than three hundred feet above the ruined Residence Plaza, lifted the old priest above his head and slammed the man's body across his lifted knee, the shattering of bones audible in the terrible silence that had fallen over the entire city. Then he simply let go, and with life slipping from him, finally, Mulkerrin saw the pleasure on Octavian's face as he fell. His last thought was a fervent wish for mercy, a hope that he would die before he hit the ground.

And then he did hit, and the time for wishes was at an end.

Salzburg, Austria, European Union.
Wednesday, June 7, 2000, 10:36 A.M.:

"Let me go, you son of a bitch!" Allison Vigeant screamed, finally, losing it, and started slamming her elbow into Roberto Jimenez's chest. They had crossed the Salzach, and Roberto had been hustling her along, trying to get them all out of there, when one of his soldiers, a black woman, had shouted for them all to look. Dozens of heads turned toward the sky and watched as, high above the city, one lone shadow broke Liam Mulkerrin, and hurled him to his doom on the street below.

"They did it!" Roberto said, astonished, and Allison turned to go back, but Jimenez wouldn't let her. So she fought him.

"Let go!" she yelled again, and used all her strength to flip him onto the pavement in front of her. Jimenez was an expert fighter, and she'd only been able to do it because he hadn't expected her to be able to do anything of the sort. She wanted to laugh at the look on his face and the stunned silence of the soldiers in their immediate vicinity But it wasn't time for laughing.

She went to kneel by him, but Jimenez wasn't having any of it; he was up and in her face in seconds. Still, she wasn't about to back off.

"What the hell are you up to?" she asked. "It's over, don't you see? We've won."

"You've got it all wrong," he said sternly. "*They've* won. The vampires. If we went back there now, it would be two to one in our favor, and with vampires, that's shit for odds. I'm not going back there without an army of hunters, specially prepared to take out vampires. And then we'll go after them and Hannibal at the same time."

"They wouldn't attack you, you fool!" She shook her head. "They've always been on your side; you could go after Hannibal together!"

Jimenez didn't have to say a word; the look on his face was enough.

"You're not going to stop the nukes, are you?" she asked. "Once you're safe, you'll tell them to go ahead."

"Don't be an idiot!" he told her. "With Mulkerrin out of the way, they won't want to destroy the whole city just to kill some vampires. Don't worry. If I can get in contact with the secretary general fast enough, there won't be any nuclear attack."

Jimenez had motioned for his troops to move on, and that's what they were doing, searching for a phone that hadn't been knocked out by earthquake or fire. Now he and Allison Vigeant only looked at each other with disgust.

"I'm not a vampire," she said. "Are you going to hunt me?"

"I'm trying to save you," he answered, softening a moment, but Allison was having none of it. His tone only angered her more.

"Good hunting, asshole," she said, giving him the finger.

"Good riddance, traitor," he answered as she turned and began walking back the way they'd come, back to her lover and his people.

It had just begun, she realized, and at the same time she understood that her old life had come to an end. Allison knew she ought to have mourned that passing, the end of an era, but somehow she didn't have the energy.

Salzburg, Austria, European Union.
Wednesday, June 7, 2000, 10:35 P.M.:

"Oh, my God!" Courage said, and Cody would have agreed, but he was speechless. He had joined Meaghan, Courage and the nearly speechless Stefan on the ground as Peter soared skyward with Mulkerrin in tow, and had watched in astonishment as the sorcerer's body shattered wetly not far from where they stood.

"How in hell did he do that?" Stefan blurted finally.

All is not what it seems, John Courage's calm voice said in Cody's head, taking the edge off his own anxiety, though he knew from the Stranger's initial reaction that he was not as calm as he sounded.

"What's going on, Stranger?" Meaghan demanded of Courage, and Cody wondered if she was thinking the same thing he was, that this was not the Peter Octavian they knew. A thousand years in Hell explained a lot, but how much?

And then Cody saw that the answers would not be long in coming, because Octavian was descending, gliding down toward them even as Charlemagne's troops formed up in military fashion behind himself, Courage and Meaghan. Charlemagne himself had gone to inspect Mulkerrin's body, even as Octavian landed on the cobblestones twenty feet in front of the gathered vampires. In seconds, the sorcerer's death was confirmed.

It said something, Will Cody felt, that he and Meaghan did not immediately rush to Octavian's side, and he glanced over at her, nodding almost unconsciously as they made the decision not to approach him at all. Everything about Peter, his manner of moving, of speaking, had suddenly become alien to them. Certainly Courage had sent Meaghan, Alexandra and Lazarus to Hell to retrieve Peter because he'd thought Octavian could be of help. Peter had obviously shared his time in Hell with Mulkerrin, and if one had grown powerful, it was assumed the other might have benefited as well.

But what powers had Octavian gained, to so easily murder a madman they had fought so hard and so fruitlessly to overcome?

"Your time away from this world has changed you, Nicephorus Dragases," John Courage said, and Cody was only partially surprised that Courage knew Peter Octavian's birth name. After all, he knew about all his blood-children. On the other hand, Cody expected Octavian to be shocked by it, and perhaps Courage did as well. But such was not the case. Octavian merely smiled.

"Such a simple ploy, Stranger," Octavian said, his voice sounding harsh, guttural. "So you know my true name, and names have power, as we know. But I know you, as well. I know who and what you are, and I know your name. I know the games you play on this plane, with these creatures."

"You know nothing," Courage said flatly, his eyes not betraying either hostility or concern.

"On the contrary," Octavian said grimly, his eyes slitted now, mouth set in a line, "it is you who know nothing, are nothing."

Octavian took several steps toward them, and Cody and Meaghan automatically took up fighting stances, while Courage, Charlemagne and his one hundred soldiers did little more than blink.

"Charlemagne," Courage said, and Cody felt as if he'd been broken out of a trance. Here was a vampire, the first vampire and the true king of shadows if everything Cody believed were true, calling to battle one of the most powerful kings in Europe's history, also a vampire, against a shadow who had only five years earlier saved their race, not to mention the fact that Octavian and Cody were blood-brothers, and friends.

"Peter," Cody said, and caught Meaghan's warning look out of the corner of his eye. "What's the matter with you? What's going on here?"

He stepped away from the group, and toward Peter, even as Charlemagne came forward and drew his sword, a challenge to Octavian, only two yards away. But Cody was having none of it, stepping between that gleaming silver sword and his strangely acting friend.

"You've finally defeated Mulkerrin, and we may not have the answers, but it's what we all wanted," Cody said, meeting Peter's eyes and finding only ice there. "We're friends, brothers. Why are we suddenly at odds?"

He could see that his words were having no effect, so he reached out to lay a hand on Octavian's shoulder.

"Peter, please explain . . . ," Cody began, and then erupted into a terrible scream as his hand landed on Octavian's shoulder. His hand was burning, burning with a pain unlike anything he had ever experienced, nearly blinding him. And he couldn't let go.

"Dolt!" Octavian yelled. "Those who touch me, die!"

And Cody realized that, somehow, he was dying. As the burning began to spread up his arm from his hand, he knew its tendrils would reach his heart and brain, and immortal or no, he would die. Whatever Mulkerrin had, Peter had that and much more.

Then the pain was gone, and his hand with it. Cody found himself lying on the cobblestones, clutching at the place where his hand had been. He looked up to see Charlemagne bringing his sword down in a crushing sweep toward Octavian's neck, and Cody realized that the old king had cut off his hand, saving his life. Apparently, he was not invulnerable to all magic. Something told him that, whatever Octavian had done to him, it would be a while before he could grow his hand back.

Charlemagne's sword sliced toward Octavian's neck, and his soldiers were already moving in to back him up as Octavian reached up and stopped the blade with his bare hand then yanked it from Charlemagne's grip. Peter turned the blade on its owner then, with a lightning-fast thrust that skewered the bearded ancient before he could move out of the way, and long before any of his soldiers could defend him. Octavian pressed close, hugging Charlemagne to him, and pulled up on the hilt of the sword, ripping the old king's insides even as a half dozen of Charlemagne's warriors tore the two apart and drove Octavian to the ground.

Even as the warriors struggled with him, they screamed with the pain of the same fire that had burned Will Cody, and Courage yelled, "Leave him alone!" But it was too late for those six, as their bodies withered to grotesque husks in seconds and began crumbling into flaky ash.

"You son of a bitch, who are you?" Meaghan shrieked as she leapt forward, her right hand extended to become a metal claw which tore the flesh off the left side of Octavian's face.

Peter lashed out at Meaghan, and the blow hurled her, tumbling, twenty feet across the plaza, in the direction of the huge gash in the earth Mulkerrin's last earthquake had left.

"Stop!" Courage shouted, and Charlemagne's troops froze.

Cody struggled to his feet and went to help Meaghan, as two warriors knelt by Charlemagne's side and helped him up. Half of Octavian's face was torn away, and not healing. Cody noticed, but he merely stood, arms crossed, waiting for Courage to speak.

"You went to great lengths to arrive on this plane," Courage said to Octavian. "Don't think for a moment that you will be staying."

"Oh, I shall stay, and I fully expect you to stay out of my way," Octavian said reasonably. "In fact, I would suggest you abandon this plane altogether."

"Do you get any of this?" Cody asked Meaghan, completely confused.

"Unfortunately," she answered, "I think I'm beginning to. Though why they're standing there chatting and not going at it tooth and claw is beyond me."

"But that's Peter!" Cody said, bewildered.

Meaghan only looked down at where his hand used to be, as she held both arms over her chest, crushed from Octavian's blow, and then she looked back at Cody's face.

"Don't be stupid," she said.

Cody looked over to where John Courage and Peter Octavian squared off, and he stared hard at Octavian's face, at his eyes. And he could no longer deny the truth of what he saw.

"We've been set up," he groaned. "The whole fucking thing, just a setup!"

Movement blurred in front of him, as Courage's hands grew huge and impossibly long, each finger a razor-sharp silver blade, and he dove for Octavian—who didn't move as those blades passed through him and emerged out the other side. His face showed that the silver caused great pain, and he hung there, impaled ten times over, until Courage removed the blades and Octavian slumped to the ground.

"Oh," Octavian said breathlessly as he knelt, bent over his wounds, "you're going to have to do better than that."

"Kill him," Courage ordered. "Send him back where he came from."

Ninety old and powerful vampires moved in, their silver swords held high.

And then Octavian began to grow, his skin tearing away in strips from what was underneath.

21

Pongau Basin, Austria, European Union.
Wednesday, June 7, 2000, 10:53 A.M.:

Rolf Sechs lay in the ruins of the mountainside, at the edge of a crater
where ice caves had once stretched beneath tons of stone and soil. The
caves were still there, extending for miles on either side of the crater,
underground. But on a quarter-mile, roughly circular scar of land,
thermite had blasted down to bare stone. Ash and debris, by whatever
had not been vaporized and set free to the winds by the blast, floated
down to form a fine layer on the stone.

Rolf was in pain, but he was alive. That was pure, unadulterated
luck. He never would have guessed what Hannibal had in mind. Rolf
could not have known that the elder had prepared a retreat before he
betrayed the SJS, but he felt he should have known. Hannibal had not
only had a group of his followers stay behind, out of the battle, but
he'd had them set a trap in the ice caves, laying thermite charges in
that cavern. And it had worked, to a point.

Two things had conspired to keep Rolf alive: his feelings for Elissa
and Hannibal's ego. Flying up to attack Hannibal, even as Elissa's
gored body was dropped, another vampire might have dodged her
falling body in order to reach her killer. Rolf couldn't do that; the
human part of him wouldn't allow it. It was more important to slow
her fall, to see if there was any life left in her, to ease her passing
somewhat, if at all possible. And if she were dead, he still had to have

respect for her corpse. Besides, there had been four other vampires there to press the attack on Hannibal.

Still, Rolf would have died had not Hannibal, at the last moment, shown his savage hand. Jared, Carlos and Annelise were on the attack, nearing the hole in the ceiling to the cavern. Rolf and Erika lay sprawled in a pile on the ground with the corpse of Elissa Thomas on top of them. Rolf had looked up then and seen what Hannibal held in his hand. His reaction was instantaneous. Only in flight was survival possible; and only in survival, vengeance.

Leaving what he now knew was only the empty husk of his lover, and grabbing hold of Erika, he rushed with all his vampiric speed toward the tunnel through which they had entered. Even as Hannibal set off the thermite charges, Rolf had metamorphosed into a flaming ball of ash, and seeing this, Erika was in the process of doing the same as the explosion rocked the cavern.

Rolf had concentrated on keeping himself together as the heat of the blast obliterated the tunnel around them shooting him forward like a flaming bullet in the barrel of a gun. At the edge of the blast area, he'd managed to crawl up from the tunnel, and now, as he got to his knees, every atom in his body screaming from the pain of healing, he finally had time to wonder what had happened to the others. He was fairly certain that Annelise, Carlos and Jared could not have survived, but Erika? What had happened to her?

She was far younger than he, and though he'd shoved her in front of him just as he made his change, she might not have had the concentration to retain cohesion under the buffeting force of the blast. Her molecules might have been spread through the fire of the thermite explosion, becoming a part of it. She might very well be dead.

Several minutes passed before he could stand, but when Rolf managed it, he made his way back down into the crater. It would be useless to search the scorched earth, he knew, but if Erika had survived, there was only one place she could be. The tunnel. It was much wider now, ice melted away from stone, blasted and blackened even this far away from ground zero.

About thirty feet in, away from the crater, where not all of the ice had melted, he found Erika. Her flesh was charred, and her left leg seemed to be missing from the knee down. Rolf assumed that she had not completed her change when the thermite charges exploded, but however it had happened, that leg would take a long time to reconstruct itself. Still, Erika had survived, and that was more than he could say for the others.

When he lifted her head into his lap, Erika moaned. Rolf stroked the new growth of hair that had already sprung from her pink scalp, and she opened her eyes. Erika tried to talk then, seeing that she was in Rolf's hands, and barely managed "The others . . .?"

Rolf only shook his head, for he could give no other response, and Erika's eyes closed for a moment. When she opened them again, twin tears, pink with blood, streaked her flaking cheeks.

Don't worry, young one, Rolf thought as he cradled the girl in his arms, *you'll be better soon.*

And then we'll hunt the bastard down.

Salzburg, Austria, European Union.
Wednesday, June 7, 2000, 10:59 A.M.

Meaghan had seen the demon before, and now she stopped wondering why he hadn't attacked them when they had invaded his sanctuary in Hell. Even as Beelzebub grew, tearing his way out of Peter Octavian's flesh, which slapped the cobblestones as he shed it, Charlemagne's troops were on him. They kept a distance, respectful of the power the demon had already shown, yet slashed at him with silver swords. The demon was hurt by the silver, but laughed as he grew. One warrior got too close, and the demon's now huge hands lifted the man, tearing him in two, and when the halves of him hit the ground, they were no more than steaming bones.

And the same will be your fate. The thing's voice slithered into Meaghan's head, and she remembered it from those years ago in Venice. That was why she had not been able to mind-link with Peter; his mind, if it still existed, was not in control of his body.

Get out of my head, filthy creature! she thought, and put a hand to her scarred face.

I just wanted to say that your girlfriend was a very tasty morsel, that terrible voice said and filled her head with laughter, *but then, you knew that, didn't you?*

She didn't bother screaming her rage as she began to change, forcing herself into the winged human form that seemed so well suited for battle, coping with the pain of learning such a change. But just as she took wing, strong hands held her legs, pulling her back to earth. She spun to attack, only to find Will Cody and John Courage defending themselves from her blows.

"What are you doing?" she screamed at them. "It's taken everyone I loved from me! First one lover, then my real love. Cody, they were your brother and sister! We've got to destroy it."

She tried again, to pull away, but they wouldn't let her go. Instead, they both pressed closer to her, forcing her to do what she didn't want to, to look at their faces and see the reason there, all the reasons, she ought to stay back.

Charlemagne, Courage called out mentally, and Meaghan was surprised that she could hear it, *keep the damned thing occupied*!

"Play all you want, Stranger!" the thing's voice boomed. "But I've won, and you know it. Once I've destroyed this group, the game is over, and to the victor go the spoils!"

Meaghan tried not to look at it, but couldn't help herself. Even though she had recognized the demon, it did not look the same as it had that terrible night in Venice. It was perhaps thirty-five or forty feet tall, with reptilian flesh and hooves rather than feet. It was an awful gray-green, which seemed to absorb the sun rather than reflect it, and its head had more eyes and teeth than it seemed the thing ought to have been able to accommodate. Its horns and scaly, ridged back made it look more dinosaur than demon. Meaghan realized that it was hardly as ugly as many of the other creatures they had battled, but it was far more fearsome in its power, in its intellect, in its true evil.

The demon-lord Beelzebub met her eyes, and she thought it smiled before she looked away.

"Meaghan, snap out of it!" Cody was yelling at her. She shook her head, and knew she'd been over the edge for a minute. She touched her face and found that the scars had healed, then released a breath and nodded, telling him she was all right.

"So what do we do?" she asked. "What can we do?"

"We've got to send him back!" Stefan said loudly, and they both looked at him in surprise, having nearly forgotten he was there.

"We need the spell!" Cody swore loudly.

"It won't work," Courage said gravely, his face sculpted into a deep frown. "I know the spell that would send him back, if he had been summoned. Demons are only able to come to Earth through a summoning, but in this case, the way was opened by Lazarus, and Beelzebub wore the flesh of Peter Octavian to pass through the portal unscathed."

"But there must be another spell," Stefan continued. "If Lazarus opened the way here, we must be able to open the way back and force the demon through!"

Stefan was pleading, and Meaghan said a silent prayer that he was right, but the look on the Stranger's face when he turned to them was one of despair. She shivered as he spoke, sternly, so Stefan would stop pushing, and Cody put a hand on the young shadow's shoulder.

"There is a spell," Courage said with great sorrow. "And it might be able to force the demon to return to its home. But to use it would allow, would invite, other demon-lords into our dimension, and then what?"

Meaghan's mind was whirling with questions; how to destroy or banish the demon in their midst, and how John Courage could have known these spells in the first place were chief among them. It was clear to her that they needed *The Gospel of Shadows*, but Lazarus had had that book in his hands when he was trapped in Hell. She realized now that Beelzebub had somehow engineered that event, to keep the book on the other side. And now Courage seemed to be losing the confidence he had shown.

"Better the devil you know . . . ," Cody started to say, and shook his head. "So now what? Why aren't we up there fighting with Charlemagne and his men?"

"No offense," the Stranger said, "but there's little you three could do this time. Those warriors' abilities are far more developed than your own. And as for me, oh, I could stay alive if I concentrated like those warriors do, but we need another solution. I'm trying to figure out if there's a magical or natural solution to this problem that will leave some of us alive. I've died once before, and painfully. I'd like to avoid doing it again."

"We've got to stop it," Meaghan snapped. "No matter what."

The Stranger nodded. He was well aware of the stakes.

Though there had been ninety fully capable vampire warriors on the attack, each a master of his abilities, fully a third of that number had already been destroyed. Charred and blackened bones lay in heaps scattered all about the battleground. Still, the others fought on. Beelzebub howled in pain as the sword strokes of silver blades cut through his flesh, but the wounds were already healing, and fresh ones could not be inflicted fast enough to do any real damage.

"Mulkerrin's moving!" Cody pointed across the plaza.

"I thought he was dead," Meaghan said, but she looked over, and sure enough, the sorcerer was struggling to rise to his feet.

And then Stefan was moving.

"Wait!" Meaghan shouted, but it was too late. She didn't know much about this Stefan, except that Rolf trusted him. That was enough for her to worry for him.

"Mulkerrin is too powerful for him!" Cody said, meaning to go after Stefan, but Courage stopped him.

"Leave him, Will," John Courage said softly. "I will get help for him, but we have other things to attend to."

Charlemagne's sword was held high, and he fought with a savagery he'd long forgotten. There was nothing noble about this fight, nothing dignified or honorable. The demon-lord must be driven back to Hell. Its ploy had worked thus far, a gambit which would give it free access to Earth, and which conventional Earth defenses would not stop.

He knew that the man and woman—Cody and Gallagher, the

Stranger had called them—were not advanced enough for this struggle, but they might be needed despite their flaws. As for the Stranger,
Charlemagne only hoped that his holding back meant he was formu-
lating some kind of plan. Too many of his warriors had already died
from the weird magicks this demon controlled.

Charles. The Stranger's voice was in his mind. *The sorcerer is not
as dead as we thought. Correct that error quickly.*

Charlemagne broke off his attack on the demon-lord, leaving his
warriors to continue, and flew swiftly to where Mulkerrin struggled to
walk. A tall, slender vampire that he had not seen before also
approached, but Charlemagne waved him away.

"Stand back," he said in Spanish, hoping the other understood, and
apparently he did, for he moved no closer.

Charlemagne drew back his silver blade and thrust it into the once-
priest's stomach, determined that he stay dead this time. Whatever
magicks kept him moving, the silver would force them from him.

And then gibberish spouted from Mulkerrin's mouth.

*"How dare you! . . . Lord, why have you forsaken me? . . . We will
be free! . . . We will feast on your entrails . . . Dear God, let me die . . ."*

It went on like that even as Charlemagne used all his vampiric
strength to wrench his sword up through the dead sorcerer's chest
cavity. Then the voices stopped, the light of some sentience returned
to Liam Mulkerrin's eyes, and he looked right at the vampire who had
finally ended his life.

"Is it true?" Mulkerrin slurred as the light drained from him. "Is the
Stranger really . . . Is it true?"

And, though the human spoke English, this time Charles understood perfectly.

"Yes," he said to the talking corpse. "Yes."

"Then I truly am in Hell," Mulkerrin whispered, and the light disappeared completely from his eyes.

Charlemagne lifted his sword to be certain, once and for all, that the
dead sorcerer would not rise again, but the ancient emperor's blow
would never fall. Mulkerrin's chest burst open as an arm shot out of
his prone form and buried its fingers into the old king's belly. Getting

a grip somewhere in Charlemagne's guts, the arm pulled him down, so that his face was buried in the gore of the sorcerer's viscera. Behind the entrails, beyond them, he could see flames flickering off granite walls. The hand in his guts burned him, and Charlemagne was surprised to find that he was screaming.

Stefan watched in amazement as demonic claws tore into Charlemagne's stomach, latching onto whatever they found there and pulling the former emperor toward the corpse of Liam Mulkerrin. He was frozen for a moment, completely unable to move. He had found it difficult enough to overcome his awe of the shadows he had dealt with day to day, but this was the emperor Charlemagne!

The old king had worked his sword far enough around to thrust it past his own face into the gaping wound in Mulkerrin's belly, and apparently at the face of whatever had him in its devastating grip. A great shriek rose from inside the corpse, shattering Stefan's eardrums from fifteen feet away, and he didn't want to imagine what it had done to Charlemagne. His ears began to heal on their own, and he knew the shrieking continued, though Charlemagne was released and now began to back away. Stefan could see that he was unsteady, and he looked as if he were trying to concentrate on something without much luck.

And then a pair of hands thrust forth and grabbed Charlemagne by the head, pulling him down once again. Stefan knew he had to act as claws dug into the elder's face, tore at his white beard.

Charlemagne could not manage the change; the hands tearing at his face were burning him horribly. The agony was incredible as they yanked him down, further opening the hole in Mulkerrin's corpse, and then he was with them, wherever they were, and they were eating him. A terrible screeching filled the air, and Charlemagne realized that it was his own throat making the noise. He was being torn apart, for food.

And then he was being tugged again, and he heard a voice shouting.

"*Let him go!*" the voice shouted, and he was being pulled, stretched, mauled from below even as his arms were yanked up.

Charlemagne's mind came back to him suddenly, and his vision with it. Only then did he realize that he had momentarily lost both of them. Now, looking up, he saw the face of that young vampire, whose name he did not know, pulling on his arms, his head and upper torso bloody and hanging down through the wound in Mulkerrin's chest, into whatever netherworld that gate of death led to. Beneath him, demons savaged his legs, tearing them to ribbons with jaws and talons. One, whose head was split in two and filled with fire, tore a huge chunk from his thigh as he looked on.

And his decision was made.

"Pull, boy!" he screamed up to the vampire who held him.

"I'm fucking pulling!" the boy screamed back, and Charlemagne decided that he liked the rude creature.

Grimacing, he pulled his sword hand free of his would be savior's grasp and swung the blade down with all the strength that remained in him. But when the blade found its mark, it was not demon flesh that was torn asunder. It was his own. Charlemagne screamed out loud as the silver blade sliced through the meat and bone of his legs as if he were scything crops in the field.

John Courage heard Charlemagne scream, and then covered his ears as an ear-piercing shriek issued from the body of Liam Mulkerrin.

"What in the name of God is happening here?" Cody shouted in Courage's ear, and then Charlemagne screamed again.

It didn't even cross the Stranger's mind to transform as he rushed to Charlemagne's aid. The scene before him was like nothing he had ever encountered. Charlemagne, whom Courage had sent to dispatch Mulkerrin permanently, and to make sure Stefan did not get killed, was now being pulled out through a huge hole in Mulkerrin's guts by the very vampire he'd been intended to protect. Courage didn't know what to make of it, but when he saw Charlemagne's double amputation, the stumps of both legs bleeding profusely as Stefan hoisted him into his arms, he at least knew what the screaming had been about.

"Demons . . . ," Stefan said, his fear eloquent in itself, and John Courage had to think fast. Charlemagne would live, if allowed time to heal, but he needed to be removed from the scene as quickly as possible.

"Stefan," Courage said, the unmistakable tone of an order in his voice. "Take Charlemagne far away from here."

"But the battle . . ."

John Courage looked into the other's eyes, and knew that more than words were needed here.

Understand, he said in Stefan's mind. *This battle will be won or lost regardless of your presence. That is not meant to offend; it is only the truth. It is your fate, however, to survive this fight, and to help Charlemagne to survive it. Our people will need him alive.*

His eyes wide, Stefan only nodded, and John Courage watched as he hefted Charlemagne in his arms and moved away from the battle. It was heartening to Courage to know that at least those two would survive, would continue the battle elsewhere if their gambit here in Salzburg were to fail.

Courage was standing over the corpse of the sorcerer, and now he looked down into the huge, gaping hole in Mulkerrin's body, and the three-eyed, fiery, cloven-skulled face of the demon-lord Alhazred looked back at him.

"No," he whispered.

"Hello, Stranger!" Lord Alhazred said gleefully. "Long time no see!"

And then Alhazred was cackling wildly as it pulled itself out of Mulkerrin's body. John Courage knew a physical effort to prevent its coming through was useless, but he hoped he could remember the spell to bar the gateway.

"*Ia Athzothtu!*" the Stranger screamed. "*Ia Angaku ! Ia zi Nebo! Marzas zi fornias kanpa! Lazhakas shin . . .*"

"No!" Lord Beelzebub cried from behind and above the Stranger, stamping the stones of the plaza with its great hooves.

Courage spun toward it, nearly losing his balance, but saw that for the moment, Charlemagne's warriors were still keeping Beelzebub back. It was only a matter of time, though, because there were fewer and fewer of the winged swordsmen, less and less sharpened silver to hold the demon-lord.

"*Lazhakas shin talsas kanpa!*" Courage yelled as he continued the spell, but in that moment when he had looked at Beelzebub, Lord Alhazred had pulled himself completely from Mulkerrin's corpse, which had become a portal, a gateway in itself.

When John Courage, the Stranger, looked back around Alhazred was standing only inches away. It stood several feet taller than Courage, with arms that hung nearly to the ground. Sharp horns lined its spine, and between the cloven halves of its skull, fire burned red and orange. The demon's hand whipped out and slashed across Courage's face, obliterating his left eye and the orbit of the skull around it. Courage screamed, continuing the spell, and fell back.

"Hey, where you going?" Alhazred called. "It's not a party till someone loses an eye!"

Then Lord Alhazred turned toward the body of the dead sorcerer and began to help its brothers from the pit. Even as he scrabbled backward on the cobblestones, Courage mumbled under his breath, working his way to the end of the complicated spell. Alhazred pulled Lord Azag-Thoth from the pit then—the worm had a body like a serpent's, a face like a wolf's and the tail of a scorpion. Unlike Beelzebub, these brothers had little magic, but they were cruel and powerful.

Then Cody and Meaghan were at John's side, helping him to his feet even as he pressed one hand against his ruined left eye. It wasn't healing, and Courage realized that was one small magic all these demon-lords shared. The wounds they inflicted did not heal the way others did. Unless they could be destroyed, Courage might never grow another eye.

"Oh, shit!" Meaghan said even as Courage was finishing the spell to block the gate. "Pa-Bil-Sag!"

And she was right. Lord Pa-Bil-Sag now emerged, with a great deal of help from Alhazred, from the gory mess that had once been the body of Liam Mulkerrin. Its bluish skin was flaking, as usual, a fine dust falling from the demon with every move. The tentacles from

inside Pa-Bil-Sag's mouth were darting wildly around its face, latching on to its own skin and to that of the crown of flesh, of sexual
organs, that it wore on its head. The demon-lord was incredibly obese,
and whatever might have been left of Mulkerrin was torn apart as it
made its way into the world of humans. Its huge eyeballs hung in
sacks like testicles between its legs, and it loosed a phlegmy laugh as
it saw the three vampires at their mercy.

"*Ia gushe-ya*! *Ia inanna*! *Ia erninni-iya*!" Courage said sternly,
more calmly now. And then the gate was closed.

"Time enough to open the gate again when you're safely in our bellies!" Lord Pa-Bil-Sag called, and Courage saw Meaghan shiver.

"You know them?" he asked her.

"All of them," she answered. "They led us in circles, but eventually
to Peter."

"*You performed exactly as we wished*!" Beelzebub boomed behind
them, but this time Courage did not turn around, not in the face of the
demon-lords who now approached.

We might be able to kill them, Courage sent to Meaghan and Will,
*and I can try to send them back with magic, but I don't really under-
stand how they got here. Nevertheless, unlike Beelzebub, they can be
fought hand to hand, can be injured, killed. On my mark, split up and
get silver weapons from where the fallen warriors have left them.*

"You seem to forget, Stranger, that I . . . ," Alhazred began, but
Courage had already moved, and Cody and Meaghan with him, in different directions.

The demon-lords merely laughed, and Courage knew that the lords
didn't believe there was any way for the vampires to be victorious. He
feared they were correct. After all, even if they defeated the newly
arrived demons, they would still have Beelzebub to contend with.
After Lucifer, the First Fallen, he was the most powerful. In fact,
Charlemagne's warriors were doing no more and no less than keeping
the creature exactly where it was, at the cost of their lives, with no
apparent hope for victory. They were counting on their leader, John
Courage, the Stranger, to find a way to destroy the huge demon. They
were counting on him.

And he was losing hope, losing faith.

No! He scolded himself. *I will never lose faith, for l know there is a Heaven. With that knowledge, we can drive these fiends back to Hell.* And then he was selfish a moment, mourning lost friends. He would attempt the spell to drive back Pa-Bil-Sag, Alhazred and Azag-Thoth, and then there would be only one course of action left to them in order to destroy Beelzebub. Cody wasn't ready for it, but the Stranger thought that Meaghan might be.

As she picked up the silver sword of a fallen warrior gritting her teeth as its poison burned her hand, Meaghan found herself looking once again at Charlemagne's men. They believed their king was dead, but they fought on. There was something about the fighting that confused her. Beelzebub's touch was painful; sustained, it was fatal—so . . .

Why don't they turn to mist to avoid his touch? she asked John Courage in her mind.

His body will absorb the mist, or flame, like a million omnivorous mouths, Courage answered, reminding Meaghan of Alexandra's terrible death. With that memory, she resolved to die for her lover's pain, to do anything she could to destroy the demon, or return it to Hell.

Meaghan. Courage's thoughts were somber. *Lazarus taught you new forms in Hell, did he not?*

Yes, she answered, and then she was at his side as he grabbed a sword of his own.

"But how did you . . .?" she began aloud, and he waved her question away.

"Your hands, before, they were steel," he explained. "You saw Charlemagne do it, I know, but if you can stand the pain, if you can concentrate through it, you can do this as well."

And as Meaghan watched, a new and deadly alchemy transformed the Stranger's hands and arms into silver.

"All of Charlemagne's warriors are old enough to do this, and if not for Lazarus's tutoring, I would have thought you too young, but you'll have to try. Cody probably isn't able to, so he'll be most vulnerable."

Then they turned to face the demon-lords, with Beelzebub laughing above them, those opposing him quickly dwindling in numbers.

It's not hopeless, Meaghan told herself. *It's not!*

Have faith, Courage said in her mind.

She was trying.

Who are you, really? she asked in her mind.

Cody knows, he said, and though Meaghan tried to probe his mind further, to find the answer she sought, he blocked her out.

And then Beelzebub's voice rang out in the shattered square, louder than before, as if it were gaining in power rather than suffering from the vampires' attack. But it was the thing's words that startled Meaghan most.

"Something is amiss!" it said, and the ground rumbled, the huge crack across the plaza stretching even wider. *"You hide your plans from me, as if you might actually be able to hurt me?"*

And the demon leaned over, hands on its hips, ignoring the pain of the swords being thrust at it, and its face seemed to hang fifteen feet in the air, right above its smiling demon-lord brothers, and too close to where Meaghan, Cody and Courage stood.

"Don't flatter yourself, Stranger!" it roared. *"You don't have the power to hurt me now."*

And then Beelzebub rose up and began swatting at the warriors surrounding it, sending three more burnt skeletons crashing into the pavement. The other, smaller demon-lords had been slowly advancing on Courage and Meaghan, Alhazred smiling happily, confident that they had all the time in the world. And then Lord Beelzebub took a step toward them, and suddenly the other three were charging ahead.

Meaghan concentrated, suffered the pain, and the transformation Courage had promised was hers. Her hands were long and thin, the fingers elongated into daggers of silver. She was her own weapon. Still, she wielded the sword, and it had fused to her, joining with the silver that her flesh had become. She leapt over Azag-Thoth as it struck out at her with both snout and stinging tail. Slashing as she flew through the air, she tore through that stinger with her left hand, and the demon-lord bucked with the pain.

She landed only a foot away from Pa-Bil-Sag, who was slower than the other two, and even as the obese creature moved to attack her, she saw Courage struggling out of the corner of her eye, fighting to keep out of Azag-Thoth's path, fighting to get inside the long reach of Alhazred's talons. Silver flashed, and Meaghan heard Alhazred shriek as one of its arms was sliced off at the joint. And she could hear Courage loudly shouting yet another spell.

Pa-Bil-Sag leered at her, the tentacles in its mouth whisking out and one actually latching on and tearing a chunk of flesh from her face before she grabbed a handful of them, searing them with the silver of her hands. She barely felt the pain of the silver herself now, but the demon surely did. Meaghan hadn't been aware how far those tentacles could reach, but now she was more careful. She feinted to one side, then thrust to the other, trying to get behind Pa-Bil-Sag . . . and it worked.

Ducking down, Meaghan put all her strength into one 2-handed slash of her sword, low to the ground, and was rewarded with a piercing shriek. Like rotten melons, PaBil-Sag's huge scrotal eyes burst as the silver blade passed through them, spraying steaming ichor into the air. Totally blind now, the beast fumbled to turn toward Meaghan lashing out. But she was no longer there. She stayed behind the demon-lord now, slashing at its back and neck.

"*Tirrama shaluti Sha Kashshapti Sha Ruchi ye,*" John Courage yelled, beginning the spell that Meaghan hoped would send the demon-lords back to Hell. "*Shupu yi arkhish . . .*"

"*Enough with your words, Nazarene!*" Beelzebub boomed, then sloughed off the half dozen or so warriors who still opposed it and, grinning, moved in on John Courage, the Stranger, unopposed. It was clear the two would meet in battle at last, and Meaghan feared for John's life.

But what was it the demon-lord had called him?

No! That's impossible, Meaghan thought. *He can't really be . . .*

And then she had latched herself onto Lord Pa-Bil-Sag's back and dug all of her sharp silver fingers into its chest, searching for the hearts she knew were there, searching for the way to kill the thing. Her mind was reeling with the implications of what she'd heard. Only feet away from her, John Courage was bloody and battered, fighting a losing battle against Alhazred and Azag-Thoth, as Beelzebub stomped ever closer, and now leaned down toward them.

And then a thrashing, hacking sound filled the air—not a human sound, not a living sound, but a sound of Earth, a tenuous grip on reality. It was the sound of helicopter rotors, and gunfire.

Four UN Security Force choppers crested the tops of the buildings at the north end of the plaza. They had no markings, but Meaghan was certain of their identity just the same. Which meant that, regardless of his misgivings, Commander Roberto Jimenez must have seen or heard what was happening here and ordered his evacuation team to assist. And here they were.

And then Meaghan realized that assist might not be the right word, as the choppers fired everything they had at everything and everyone in the plaza. Automatic-weapons fire strafed the cobblestones all around them, and even as Meaghan felt several bullets rip through her flesh, she watched as Cody, John Courage and the demons were also hit. As she fell under Pa-Bil-Sag, she prayed, truly prayed, that the human fools would put their hatred aside and unload on the most obvious target, the biggest.

And they did.

Simultaneously, more than likely at Jimenez's order, all four choppers launched two missiles right at Lord Beelzebub's chest. Even as Meaghan was rolling on top of Pa-Bil-Sag, as her hands locked on the demon-lord's two hearts crushing them in her silver grasp, poisoning the demon's vital organs, the missiles hit home. Beelzebub had a smile on its face, but when the missiles exploded on contact, they blew it right off, even as they blew a hole eight feet across in the center of its chest.

It fell backward, across the ruins of the Salzburg Cathedral, and screamed as the back of its open wound landed on the holy ground. An arc of green flame shot after the choppers as they receded into the distance, toward the fortress, but it did not reach far enough.

Beneath Meaghan, Pa-Bil-Sag was dead. Beelzebub was already moving, struggling to rise after the blow it had been dealt. That was inevitable. Conventional weapons could hurt the demon-lord, but not

kill it. Meaghan didn't know if even silver could kill it, but they would
have to find out. Meanwhile Courage was still trying to defend himself against the other two demon-lords, and Meaghan rushed to his aid.

Thinking once again about what Beelzebub had called him.

Nazarene!

22

In a city empty of all life save those creatures gathered in the ruins of a beautiful plaza, which had seen near constant battle for hours upon hours, with the shattered dome of a cathedral only yards away, chaos reigned.

Will Cody picked up a silver sword that had fallen not far from where Peter Octavian lay, and he had much weighing on his mind, on his soul. He tried not to look at Peter's remains, his sadness at the demon's violation of his blood-brother nearly overwhelming, the disgust more so. Beelzebub had killed Alexandra, had used Peter, defiled them both. Cody would see the demon-lord dead if he could. But if that were impossible, he was certainly not going to allow it to remain on Earth, to defile his world the way it had done his family.

Courage and Meaghan had both found swords and were about to join together to face the demon-lords, and Will Cody would go to them, stand at their side to the death. But something held him back, worked at his mind, like a whisper, or some vital bit of information, barely forgotten but crucially so. He could smell the demon. The stench of it was fierce, and he realized that the wind must have shifted. That stink was awful, and he thought of Hell, wondering how Meaghan and Lazarus had dealt with the stench of demons there. And Peter had been there for a thousand years!

And what of Peter?

Cody finally looked around to where the remains of his friend, Peter Octavian, had been left behind when Beelzebub had shed his flesh-and-blood disguise. His heart ached as he looked at the gore-covered, barely recognizable form, but not only for Peter. In less than a day, the world they had carefully constructed in the wake of Octavian's original sacrifice had crumbled around them. Hannibal had betrayed them and had more followers than any of them had imagined.

They shouldn't have been surprised, Cody chided himself, for it had been Hannibal who originally organized a volunteer corps of humans who gave their blood and often their lives up for their vampire masters. Hannibal had once had a worldwide network of vampiric and human spies, and they had been foolish to think that the Jihad in Venice had changed any of that. They'd thought Hannibal would want to protect himself within the image of propriety, and he had. But they had overestimated his patience with such politics.

Mulkerrin had returned and, in the brief battle that ensued, taken thousands of human lives and destroyed hundreds of vampires, many of whom Cody had known. But Mulkerrin had been nothing more than a tool, a ploy to force the vampires, the shadow people of Earth, to search Hell for Peter Octavian, and bring him back . . . to smuggle a demon-lord across the border to Earth. Beelzebub could not be blamed for Hannibal's actions, but all the murders perpetrated by Mulkerrin might as well have been performed by the demon's own hand.

Cody sensed some movement in his peripheral vision and spun, on guard, to his left.

"Peter," he hissed, not wanting to call out, and in an instant he was by Octavian's side. Still covered with blood, a long tear up his back open enough to show a spinal column knitting itself back together, Octavian shivered, his eyes closed tight in a grimace of pain. But he was awake! Aware! Alive!

Will! Octavian's mental voice was weak, distant, though he lay at Cody's feet, but Will knew he would survive. Given time.

I'm here, Peter, he thought, sending not just the words, but feelings of comfort and reassurance along their mind-link. *You're going to be all right, Brother.*

And so this had been the whisper in the back of his mind, an open channel of communication with Peter's lonely and wounded soul. He looked at the torn muscles and skin of Octavian's back, legs and shoulders, and at his bloody, matted hair. In a few minutes, it might be possible to move him, but for the moment, John and Meaghan would have to fend for themselves. Cody would not abandon his brother again.

Will? Peter's thoughts came stronger now, and he was able to turn over slightly, his eyes open, pained, but looking at Cody's face. *Where's Meaghan?*

At that, Cody looked over to where Meaghan and John were fighting, in close with the demons, and then Beelzebub screamed at Courage and threw off his other attackers, finally able to go directly after his ancient enemy. And Cody knew that they needed him now.

Peter, I've got to go! Will sent desperately along their mind-link. *We've got to go; the others need our help. Can you walk?*

Need . . . to feed was all Octavian managed, and when Will looked down, he saw that Peter's eyes were closed again.

In his human lifetime, Will Cody had always tried to stay on the side of the angels, and he'd known many noble souls. Though he'd lived longer in his current state, he'd known far fewer since becoming a vampire. Peter Octavian was one of the noblest souls he'd ever known. Even before they'd met, it had been Octavian's goodness, his humanity, and the comfort he had achieved with his vampiric life, that had inspired Will to defy the wisdom of their people and try to hold onto what humanity he had left. And when they finally had met, it was the honesty in Octavian's lopsided grin that had convinced him to make amends with his blood-family.

That in mind, it was nothing for Will Cody to bite open his own wrist, weakened as he was, and share his blood with his friend, his brother, Peter Octavian. There was little enough time, and true healing would have to wait, but after only a few moments, Octavian was able to stand.

And then the choppers rose over the buildings and fired on everyone in the plaza, and Octavian was on the cobblestones again. But this time, Cody was with him. As Will watched the helicopters, he realized that they must be from Jimenez's team, and therefore Allison must be on board one of them, or away elsewhere with the UNSF. But wherever she was, he knew she must be safe.

Peter Octavian was reeling. He had suffered for so long that time had seemed to come to a halt. Madness had in truth overtaken him for a period, perhaps a century, but eventually his mind came back from that place of escape, back to the pain. For a thousand years, each time he thought Beelzebub could do nothing worse, nothing more, he had found he was wrong. The final violation had occurred a year ago by Hell's clock, when the demon itself had entered him, consumed him, possessed him. Like a dream, he had seen everything around him, but had been powerless to control his words or actions. And when Beelzebub shed him in pieces, Peter had hoped he would die there, on the cobblestones.

But he was old now, and grown powerful under the yoke of the demon. He had never learned magic, but he had become comfortable with his vampiric body, able to control its nearly unlimited potential. Forged in Hell, he'd become an almost unbreakable weapon. Beelzebub had assumed that possessing Octavian, and tearing his body apart upon leaving it, would destroy the vampire. It was not the first time the demon-lord had been wrong.

Weakened though he was, Peter Octavian vowed that it would not be the last.

"Let's move it, Peter. Pick up that sword." Will Cody pointed to a silver blade that had fallen to the ground.

Instead, Octavian merely held up his hands to show that he had his own silver weapons. Cody was surprised, but only for a moment. He knew how long Peter had been in Hell, how old a vampire he was now. Still, Peter thought, knowing something and understanding it are vastly different things. To Cody and the others, to Meaghan, Peter had been gone only five years, a heartbeat in the life of a vampire. Peter had lived more than five hundred years before going to Hell, and nearly twice that long in suffering. He was now one of the oldest shadows alive.

"We've missed you, Brother," Cody said, even as they hurried toward where Meaghan and Courage battled the two remaining demon-lords. Beelzebub was already rising from the ground, the huge hole in its chest large enough to walk through upright.

Peter smiled.

"I missed you, too, Will," he said, but he knew it wasn't the same. He had fond memories of all of them, but those memories were incomplete. It had been so long ago that much of what their true relationship had been was lost. Peter remembered how he felt about his friends, well enough. But he could not fully recall why. If they survived the day, he was looking forward to learning once again.

Still weak, he was shoulder to shoulder with his friend Will Cody as they pulled Lord Alhazred off John Courage. The demon-lord's third eye, in the center of its head, was swollen shut, and one of its long deadly talons had been slashed off, but still it was dangerous. A noxious stench rose from the flames of its skull, and Alhazred struggled in their grip.

Next to them, Meaghan now leapt to avoid a crushing blow from the tail of Lord Azag-Thoth. The great worm darted in with its wolfen head, missing her throat by a mile and instead tearing at her left breast. Meaghan cried out in pain, and Peter responded.

"Away from her, worm!" he shouted, digging his hard, sharp silver hands into the serpent's head and using all his strength to fling it away. Azag-Thoth flopped on the ground fifteen feet from them, but was already rising.

"Is it really you?" Meaghan asked, not understanding but happy just the same.

Peter only nodded, and then he could see confusion, hurt and doubt on Meaghan's face. He knew what she was thinking. It was the question she had already asked, though with a different tone. Was it really him? And by nodding, by saying yes, was he really being honest? He was Peter Octavian, true, but not the Octavian she'd known. It hurt him to think that she mistrusted him now, but more so that much of what she must have once meant to him was lost forever.

"Thank you," Meaghan said uncertainly, and Peter favored her with a lopsided grin that felt familiar to him. Then Meaghan was smiling, and he knew that grin must have been familiar to her as well.

"*A momentary respite!*" Beelzebub's voice boomed then, as it rose, staggering, to its feet. "*I feel . . . refreshed!*"

The demon's sarcasm was not lost on Peter. It was badly injured, much more so than the slowly healing wound would indicate. Over the time he had spent in agony due to this creature's whim, they had become as intimate as cruel lovers. And now Beelzebub saw that he was still alive.

"*Ah, Octavian lives!*" the demon-lord cried. "*I am grateful to have the pleasure of killing you one final time!*"

And then, weakened though it was, though they both were, Lord Beelzebub was coming for Peter Octavian, for a final confrontation with its plaything.

"Octavian!" John Courage shouted. "You three must destroy these vile lords. The time has come for me to clash with the architect of this invasion!"

"But . . . ," Octavian began, then was interrupted by Courage's voice, in his mind, filling his brain.

Ah, Peter, you have suffered so, and you would make the demon-lord pay for his sins against you, the Stranger's voice said, calming, soothing, strengthening Peter even as Azag-Thoth slithered back into the fray and Peter slashed at the worm-lord.

But you are too weak now, to do what must be done, Courage's voice said. *And my battle with this creature goes back farther even than your own. It can be killed, but there must be sacrifice. You will have to lead them from here, keep our people safe . . . find Hannibal and destroy him, for he has escaped yet again.*

If that is your wish, Peter said in his mind, knowing there could be no argument. And then he saw wings sprout from John Courage's back, and the Stranger flew up and away, to face Beelzebub alone.

"Stay back, brothers!" he called as he rose into the air, for some of

Charlemagne's warriors still lived and wished to come to his aid. "Your time is almost at hand!"

And when Beelzebub grabbed the Stranger from the air . . . nothing happened. Unlike the warriors of Charlemagne, he did not burn, did not cry out in agony. Instead, his face and arms turned to silver, and he began to rip and tear the demon's flesh. Still, it did not look promising.

Peter could not watch anymore, for with Courage's departure, only he, Meaghan and Cody were left to battle the two demon-lords who, though severely wounded, continued to fight savagely. Peter's face was slashed open by the remaining talon of Lord Alhazred, and the demon screamed at him now.

"You're not paying attention, Octavian. That's going to cost your life!"

Peter's only reply was a feint and then a slice of his own silver claws across the thing's leathery chest. Green, malodorous pus squirted from the wound, and Peter knew that the demon was truly wounded. This was its true blood.

Meaghan couldn't believe that Peter was alive, that it was really him. Nevertheless, he had been drastically changed by his time in Hell, and she felt the pain of what had been stolen from him. Her happiness at his survival was overshadowed by the pain of Alexandra's death. Though it had happened, for her, months before, only now, with Alex's murderer finally revealed and so close, killing so many others of her kind and responsible for so much mayhem, pain and sorrow—only now did the true rage and fury of her pain reach her.

Whatever she had once felt for Peter was now only the love she had for him as her blood-father. But Alexandra had been her one, true love. She knew that she would never have another like it, never another person like Alex. And when Courage had flown off to confront Beelzebub, she had wanted to follow. But first, they must destroy his little brothers.

Meaghan and Cody were on either side of Lord Azag-Thoth, its snake-like body whipping back and forth and making it difficult to wound it without receiving an injury in return. But for Meaghan, as she thought of Alex, the time for caution was long since gone.

Cody went to the right, and Azag-Thoth followed with its wolf's jaws snapping shut. Meaghan jumped up, even as the demon's poisonous tail slashed at the spot in which she'd been only a moment before, and she landed on the wide body of the huge worm-beast. She wrapped her silver arms around it, under the head, and pulled back as hard as she could. It did not have any bones to break, but she could stop its movement at least for a moment.

"Now, Will! Tear the bastard open!" she screamed hysterically, and Cody slashed down with his silver sword, along Azag-Thoth's body, slicing at least seven feet of its flesh before the demon-lord's tail whipped around and knocked Meaghan off its back.

She was lucky. She didn't know what the demon's poison would do, and she was battered by the beast's tail, but the stinging portion had missed her. Instead of falling to the ground, she held tight with both arms and slid around the front of the creature, its slavering jaws snarling in her face. With a searing sound and a terrible stench of fur, she took its face in both her silver hands and dug in. It could do no more than yelp now, and strike with that stinger, but she dodged it easily.

"Will, the heart!"

"Where?" Cody yelled. "Where do I cut?"

"Go in and find it, damn it!" she shouted, and though she knew he must have thought she was crazy, he dodged the wildly thrashing stinger again and transformed himself into fire, entering the huge wound he had slashed in the demon-lord's belly and simply burning the thing's vulnerable guts.

Will had done it. He was sure to get the thing's heart if he kept up the flames. Meaghan turned away then, to help Peter destroy Lord Alhazred, which would then leave only—

"Time to die, Nazarene!" Beelzebub screamed above them, and Meaghan looked up to see Courage being lifted toward the demon-lord's mouth. She knew he could not transform into flame or fire, for fear of being absorbed through the demon's skin and thus consumed. But there must be . . .

"Yes!" Courage shouted, and Meaghan was stunned as he broke the demon-lord's grip, finally. "But not for me!"

Meaghan watched, realizing Courage had only been waiting to get close enough to Beelzebub's face, and now he changed himself into a winged creature the likes of which she had never seen, with two legs and six arms, all with claws the size of a bear's—and formed completely of silver. John Courage had transformed his entire body into silver!

In this new form, the Stranger latched his legs and two arms into the face of the Lord Beelzebub, and with the other four arms, all of silver, he began to burrow a hole through the demon's face, tearing out its eyes even as the demon howled in a sound that shook the ground.

Silver was poison to vampires! Transforming a small portion of the body was painful. To change the entire body would likely be fatal. And then Meaghan realized that it would be fatal, and that that was part of the plan, the sacrifice of the Stranger. Of . . .

"The Nazarene!" she said loudly, to no one but herself.

And yet Peter was there, at her side, even as he tore first one and then another heart from the open chest cavity of Lord Alhazred. She saw the fire die in Alhazred's split skull and knew it was truly dead.

"You understand then," Peter said, slumping to the ground and cradling his face with his left hand. His right hand was little more than a stump, but already the fingers were regenerating. Meaghan wasn't really paying attention to any of that.

"No!" she shouted at him. "I don't understand. I can't understand."

And now Cody had joined them, standing over Alhazred's corpse, apparently having finally destroyed Azag-Thoth. He, too, was greatly weakened, and his wounds were healing slowly.

"You do understand," Cody said. "Even Allison understood, sort of, and she had no reason to."

"But he can't be *the* Nazarene!" she said.

And then they were running, scrambling to get out of the way as Beelzebub fell once again, off balance from pain and blindness, insane with hatred for John Courage, for them all. It scratched at its face, trying to pry Courage off, but it was painful for it even to touch the silver beast that now burrowed into the hole where its left eye had once been. At the north end of the plaza, a building crumbled, and Meaghan barely noticed.

"It's not what you think," Cody said, and his face was lit up with the pleasure of sharing the truth with her. "At least, not exactly. He's called the Stranger because that's what he is, to Heaven and to Hell. The body and the mind *are* the Nazarene, but there is nothing of God in him now."

"Nothing of God . . ." She shook her head. "How? And how did you . . .?"

"It was the only answer," he said. "All the clues led there, and Allison figured it out, or at least part of it, as well. John gave us enough clues. Plus, when I was almost dead, I was a part of the magic, of the power that exists in the nature of the world, that Mulkerrin tapped. I . . . I knew things, then. As to how it happened to him, it's also how we came to be."

"Will is correct," Peter said, and Meaghan had almost forgotten he was standing there. "I learned all about the Stranger under the demon's loving care. When the Stranger's body was still inhabited by the Spirit of Heaven, he did battle with all kinds of demonic things. It is with him that the magic in *The Gospel of Shadows* originated. But even that magic couldn't control the pure vampires, the things that you saw this morning. Instead, he destroyed them, every one, and they haven't existed on Earth until today.

"The last Hellish thing he fought, nearly two millennia ago, was a true vampire, and it wounded him badly. Only the Spirit, that which was divine in him, saved his life. But he had been tainted by the vampire's attack. After he was crucified, and finally died, the Spirit left him to continue its work.

"A normal human being killed by one of these vampires would eventually return to life as one of them, a mindless wraith. But the Spirit had also tainted him, his human shell. Whatever had been divine in him while he lived now merged with the taint of evil, of the vampire. He became a shadow of his former self, a shadow of humanity, and he lived in the shadows between Heaven and Hell. He was the first of us, forever and always. With an angel's soul and a devil's heart."

"But then, can we expect . . . divine help? Surely he must mean something . . . ," Meaghan began, and Will Cody only looked at Peter for the answer.

"No," Peter said with certainty. "I've thought about that a lot. Heaven has no special place for him, though he carried their greatest gambit to fruition. He's tainted by evil, as we all are, imperfect, like the humans we once were."

"But . . . ," she began, and then was interrupted by the Stranger's voice barking harsh orders in her brain, in all their brains, for though Beelzebub was down, and thrashing, he could not defeat the demon-lord alone.

Meaghan! the voice came into her head. *Warriors of Charlemagne! I need you now. The demon is at the edge of defeat, and you must follow my example. Change your forms, enter the wound in the demon's chest, and from there we will kill it!*

"I love you both," Meaghan said, and took off toward the demon.

"Meaghan!" Will called to her even as she grew wings for the first time. "You don't have to go! You can't make that change!"

She looked back, smiling, and called loudly, "I know what I am, Will, and what I have to do."

"She can make the change," Peter said. "Lazarus trained her, in Hell."

"What about us?" Cody asked quickly, but Peter Octavian was already pulling him away, dragging him to the north.

"We are incapable, right now, of doing what must be done. Our job is to survive," Peter grimly replied.

Salzburg, Austria, European Union.
Wednesday, June 7, 2000, 11:16 A.M.:

Allison Vigeant had seen the helicopters fly above her, and heard the gunfire and explosions they had rained down upon the battle. She prayed then, that Will was still alive. As she entered Residence Plaza from the northeast corner, where it led into Mozartplatz, Lord Beelzebub was falling for a second time. Though it looked different, still she remembered the demon from Venice, remembered its stench and its effect on the air around it. The impact as the demon hit the cobblestone plaza sent her flying to the ground, and Allison's face slammed hard into stone with a crack. Behind her, a building was crumbling, and a cloud of dust moved out to envelop her. Had she walked through that alleyway ten seconds later, she would have been crushed.

As it was, she thought her nose was broken. She held a hand up and touched it, and came away with sticky blood which gleamed bright red in the sunshine. It occurred to her again that events as dark as those unfolding in Salzburg had no right to occur in the light of day.

But for Allison, the day had lost its illusion of safety long ago.

She brushed herself off even as she picked up her steps. Scanning the plaza, she realized how many had died. Peter and Meaghan were standing over the corpse of some kind of demon, and John Courage had apparently fallen under Beelzebub, for she had seen him attacking the demon's face before it fell. And then, finally, she saw Cody, coming up behind Peter and Meaghan.

Thank God!

Over the noise of the demon's screeching, they would never hear her call out, so she picked up her pace. She watched as Meaghan took off, joining a few of Charlemagne's warriors who still lived, in their attack on the demon. And then Peter and Cody were headed toward her, practically holding each other up, it seemed. Whatever else had happened, Will Cody was alive, and Allison could survive any other tragedy.

They were not far away from her now, but still she had to call out several times to get Will to look up. Finally he did smiling despite his pain, despite all that had happened—was happening—around them. Allison kicked something heavy that clanged hard on the stones. It was a sword made of silver, and she reached down without thinking and picked it up. Beelzebub wasn't dead yet, after all.

She was perhaps ten feet from them when the black, dripping, lance-like thing rose from behind them. It wavered in the air above their heads, and Allison screamed even as she threw the sword toward them.

The scorpion sting tail of the demon-lord Azag-Thoth whistled as it shot down toward the heart of the demon-lord's murderer, Will Cody, but when it found its mark, slashing through Peter Octavian's arm on the way, Will was gone. Leaping to the side, he used all of his strength to bring the sword down across the tail of the torn-open serpent-thing, which had slithered behind them, leaving a trail of gore. Cody sliced off the stinger portion of the tail with a burst of green flame and a terrible spray of black fluid.

Peter had been wounded, and Allison and Will met over him where he lay in the street. Octavian's eyes were open.

"It's just a scratch," he said. "Poison, though, even to us. I'll be sick for a while, but I'll live. A youngster like yourself, however . . ."

Allison looked at Peter and saw that, though he was kidding Will, he was also serious. A sting from that creature might have killed the old storyteller.

"God!" she yelled. "Please just let this all end!"

Meaghan had the answers now, the answers she and Peter had fought so hard for, answers that Cody had searched for years to find, that Alex had died for. And she was proud. The Stranger had sacrificed himself once so that others might be cleansed of an evil taint, and now he was prepared to do it again.

Could she do any less?

Blind and screeching its pain, Lord Beelzebub had nevertheless understood its vulnerability, understood something of what the Stranger was doing. It rose unsteadily to its feet. John Courage had dug his way into the demon's face and disappeared there. He was completely inside the demon's head, and he had instructed them to enter the rapidly healing wound that was open on both sides of the thing's body, blown through its incredible hide by the missiles of a human army.

In the thing's pain, both external and internal, they backed it south. Now, blind, it teetered on the edge of the seemingly bottomless crevice that Mulkerrin's final earthquake had opened up.

And fell in.

Claws grasped the edge of the crack in the plaza, lodging themselves where shattered cobblestones had once lain. The demon pulled its head and shoulders out of the hole, a new, green-black mucous pouring from the hole where its face had been. Its roar of agonized fury resounded off the crumbling buildings on the edges of the plaza, even as vampire warriors closed in on the creature's back. Still it hauled itself out farther, until its chest was on the ground and it only needed to pull its legs out.

And that was when they struck, Meaghan and the six surviving warriors of Charlemagne. They flew, transforming themselves in the air, all seven of them screaming their pain as their bodies turned to the one thing that would most certainly kill them over time: the poison metal, silver.

Meaghan nearly lost consciousness as she slammed into the wound in the demon's back, but the voice of John Courage in her mind snapped her back to reality.

Now! it said. *Follow me*!

She realized then that he was there, inside the demon's chest cavity. He must have torn his own path from the creature's head to its chest, down its throat perhaps, and then out again before he could be consumed. Then the Stranger, who was no longer a stranger to her but someone she had known all her life, began to tear at the demon's guts from inside, ripping a hole large enough for all of them to fit inside, and revealing two huge, pulsing organs that Meaghan recognized immediately for the demon's two hearts.

And finally she understood John Courage's plan. If the demon could not be sent back to Hell, banished from Earth once and for all time, and they were not certain they could truly end its life, then they had to be certain that it would never threaten human or vampire again. If Lord Beelzebub did not die, it would wish it had. After the suffering the demon had put Peter and infinite others through, on infinite planes and dimensions, Meaghan could think of no end more fitting.

Come, take my hand, John Courage said, in the cramped confines of the demon's flesh, which burned and steamed at the touch of their bodies, melting from around them. The creature shuddered and bucked where it lay, half-in and half-out of the crevice in the plaza, but they were tightly packed inside it.

And Meaghan reached out and took John Courage's hand, then slid her other hand at an awkward angle until one of her vampire brothers could grasp it. They gave themselves over to him, to the Stranger, and with his mind leading them, they began to flow, quicksilver, a liquid metal that burned everything it touched.

They had become a virus, Meaghan realized, a deadly virus infecting the demon's system. Sharing Courage's knowledge, and each sharing the pain the others experienced by keeping the body of silver they had adopted, they flowed into one enormous pool, then split into two groups, each surrounding one of the demon's hearts.

And, in the heat and stench of evil that was the heart of the demon for all intents and purposes, seven vampires including Meaghan Gallagher and the shadow king, a stranger known as John Courage, made the ultimate sacrifice.

Meaghan was dying; she knew that. When the poison they had become had killed them all, the silver would cool and the demon's hearts would be preserved, would burn forever in the shell of its body.

Meaghan! John Courage's voice called out to her mind, and through her pain, Meaghan Gallagher managed to feel pleasure. *I'm sorry it came to this. You were too young. Had I thought of it sooner . . .*

But you didn't, she thought, hoping that he could understand her still. *It doesn't matter. It's done now, and I can feel the pain of vengeance, the pleasure of sacrifice.*

And I'll be with Alex again, won't I?

This very day, the Stranger thought. *I promise you that.*

And then Meaghan Gallagher died.

Without a howl, a scream, a cry, even a whisper, the demon-lord Beelzebub reared up on its hooves, which had little purchase in the depth of the crevice, and, sliding farther down, fell on its back on the other side of the hole. Its hands beat the air silently, then lay over the hole at the center of its chest. The demon began to pant, to strain against its pain, and then its hands leapt away from its chest as if burnt.

Cody knew when it was done because the demon stopped moving completely. Seconds later, it began to rot, and soon it was a dozen streams of viscous flesh and blood, which ran across the stones and joined together in the indentations its legs had made in the ground as it fell, running eventually into the crevice that Liam Mulkerrin's earthquakes had opened at the south end of Residence Plaza.

Cody's bones were already knitted, but he was in pain, and his flesh wounds would take longer to heal, especially his eye. He and Allison helped Peter to stand, and they made their way to the edge of the hole. Looking down, they could not see the bottom, could not see where the demon's remains would eventually rest, and Cody said a prayer to God, his first in a long time, that the humans would be smart enough to seal the crevice up tight somehow.

When he looked up, only puddles of blood remained of Beelzebub, that and two perfect ovals, each six feet long which looked for all the world like nothing more than huge eggs made of silver. But God forbid they should ever hatch.

And they wouldn't, for even now they were shrinking. The living silver that was his brothers and sisters was contracting as it cooled, crushing the demon's hearts, and small holes had appeared from which the essence of the creature, its last blood, sprayed in spurts, its acid so much stronger than the rest, eating its way down into the stone and soil of the plaza. And Cody knew it was also eating away at the silver, even as the silver poisoned it. The hearts were shrinking not simply because the living silver was contracting, crushing the hearts to a pulp, but because the silver itself was being eaten, consumed by the acid before it burst out through the tiny holes in the "eggs."

After a time, the hearts were completely gone, the silver melted down into two pools each three or four feet across. It cooled and hardened on the stones, and that was all that remained of those who had sacrificed themselves, one of whom had given himself up for his people a second time.

Cody looked at Allison and Peter then, his lover and his brother. Seeing them there, in the sunshine, his heart was a little lighter, and though tempted, he did not turn to look back at where the demon had died. Instead, he thought of the future, of the new world they must face. There would be more blood, more fighting. They would be forced to hide from the humans, and to hunt Hannibal and his new coven.

But they would not be alone. And they had the strength of faith now. So long ago, it seemed, Peter had said, "Find out what we are." Now they knew, and it was that knowledge that would sustain them. They could love one another now, without reserve, without the specter of an assumption of their own evil hanging over their heads.

There were still many vampires out in the world, and it would be a race now, between them and Hannibal, to gather those survivors. But Cody and his clan had a message of hope and truth. Though they were products of Heaven and Hell, they were, like the first among them, inherently good. The true vampire's bite had given the Stranger a devil's heart, but he would always have an angel's soul.

That was their legacy.

Peter was having a rough time walking, the demon's poison in his leg giving him quite a bit of pain. But Will and Allison held him up. It would be Peter who would lead them, Will knew that, and he was comfortable with the thought. Comforted, really. For even while he was in Hell, and they did not know whether he was dead or alive, still it was Peter's leadership they had followed, his quest they had embraced.

"We'll be on the run now," Allison said. "To the humans every shadow is like Hannibal."

"Not all humans," Cody reminded her for no matter what the dangers, Allison would live and die a human being.

"I love you," Allison said.

"Me too," Peter's voice cracked as he said it, and then all three of them were smiling.

"Now that's the Octavian I remember," Cody laughed.

"Will," Peter said, his face mock-serious, "I know how much you've enjoyed your vacation, but could we go home now?"

"Oh, yeah," Cody said and nodded. "Oh, yeah."

"Where is home now?" Allison asked.

"New Orleans," Cody answered.

As they made their way out of Residence Plaza, they could hear military helicopters over the city. Cody knew the choppers were returning for the cleanup, that they would try to destroy any vampire they found alive. But he also knew the city could be saved, that the nukes were not coming. Another block and they found Stefan, weeping by the white and bloodless form of the emperor Charlemagne. When Peter put a hand on his arm, Stefan looked up.

"I don't know if he'll make it," Stefan said. "I don't know if he wants to."

With Cody's help, Stefan managed to pick Charlemagne up again, and together they left.

Somewhere in the city, church bells rang, and Will realized that some of Salzburg's residents had never been evacuated, and yet had survived. He was happy for them and though he didn't quite understand why, proud of them as well.

Allison counted aloud as the bell rang twelve times.

High noon, William F. Cody thought, but the showdown was over.

Epilogue

The folks were white and stricken, and each tongue seemed
weighted with lead;
Each heart was clutched in hollow hand of ice;
And every eye was staring at the horror of the dead,
The pity of the men who paid the price.
They were come, were come to mock us, in the first flush of our
peace;
Through writhing lips their teeth were all agleam;
They were coming in their thousands—oh, would they never
cease!
I closed my eyes, and then—it was a dream.

There was triumph, triumph, triumph down the scarlet glittering
street;
The town was mad, a man was like a boy.
A thousand flags were flaming where the sly and city meet;
A thousand bells were thundering the joy.
There was music, mirth and sunshine; but some eyes shone with
regret;
And while we stun with cheers our homing braves,
O God, in Thy great mercy, let us nevermore forget
The graves they left behind, the bitter graves.

—ROBERT SERVICE, *The March of the Dead*

New York City, New York, United States of America.
Monday, June 12, 2000, 2:31 P.M.:

Roberto Jimenez was grim-faced as he prepared for his new assignment. In a well-guarded office of the United Nations building, he scanned hundreds of international military files, and thousands of résumés and letters already received on-line from civilians, mostly mercenaries, who were offering their services in the hunting of vampires.

And that, Roberto knew, was his new job description, the new definition of his life. He had become, sometime in the last week, the world's most powerful vampire hunter.

Upon his return from Salzburg, Roberto had been dogged by every media personality in the world. After that first day, he had disappeared. In modern times, you weren't supposed to be able to do that, but Roberto was not Commander of the UNSF for nothing. He had gone underground, and only the secretary general, Rafael Nieto, and the new President of the United States knew where. And even that had been a mistake. The two men had spent four days playing "Berto in the middle," as each vied for his political support.

He didn't know which of them he hated more. Secretary General Nieto was a pacifist, who had made extraordinary strides toward world peace during his tenure as the most powerful man in the world. He was personally repulsed by the vampires—even he wasn't calling them shadows anymore—but he insisted that, like humans, they were a basically decent race with an inordinate number of bad apples.

President Galin, on the other hand, was a madman. Every day that passed, Roberto became more and more incredulous that the world media hadn't picked it up yet. Galin was certifiable, and Nieto certainly thought so. But on the other hand, Galin wanted to wipe vampires from the face of the Earth, and Roberto couldn't argue with that philosophy. In Roberto Jimenez's mind, the Venice Jihad and the Massacre at Salzburg would not have happened if the vampires had not existed. He couldn't help but blame them.

Though he'd sensed a certain nobility in a couple of the vampires he'd dealt with, they were too dangerous to be allowed to survive, to multiply, and Hannibal had declared war, after all. Roberto thought the creatures should be taken out like rabid dogs, and Galin was the number one proponent of that side of the issue. Problem was, Galin was rabid, too, and Roberto didn't trust him at all. Luckily, politics had forced Nieto to at least meet Galin halfway, and that's where Jimenez had come in.

His new orders were to assemble an international tracking and investigation team to find vampires, as well as a corps of one hundred 8-member strike teams, eight hundred people whose job it would be to terminate individual vampires. They had assumed that most of the vampires would go back to their old patterns, mainly hiding in plain sight, alone. But some would gather in packs, or covens, as Allison Vigeant's book about the Venice Jihad explained. In that case, the strike teams could operate in hundreds of combinations.

According to Nieto, the whole thing had been set up just to track down Hannibal's coven and eliminate it, and him. But Galin had assured Roberto, and Nieto had quietly admitted, that this was merely the beginning. Commander Roberto Jimenez was setting up a world-wide search-and-destroy mission—a mission with no time constraints, few legal parameters.

Killing vampires had now become his life's work.

London, England, European Union.
Monday, June 12, 2000, 11:59 A.M.:

Marie Wilkins was looking for a new job. She was a pretty woman, though not as smart as most people thought. With her jet-black hair and formidable figure, she stuck out in a crowd of fair, thin British women. It had definitely helped her on interviews so far. So what if she couldn't type more than thirty-five words a minute. As far as she was concerned, with her legs, that wouldn't matter.

As she walked down Tottenham Court Road, still several blocks from her next interview, Marie's mind was on Kev, the new man in her life. He smoked too much and drank too much, he liked his sex rough and tumble, and his every word to her outside the sack was sharp and biting. They'd only met a couple of nights ago, but already Marie thought she was in love.

He was a big wanker, was Kev, and she liked them big. Strong. Bullies had always been her get, and that's the way she liked it. Oh, she didn't want them to hurt her, really. Not unless she asked for it. But she wanted to know they could if they wanted to. She wanted to be with a man who was a danger to her, who could overpower her and beat her bloody anytime he wanted.

That was why she'd gone after Rolf Sechs originally, and why she'd lost interest long before the vampire disappeared. When Marie had taken the job as receptionist/secretary for the Shadow Justice System offices in London, she liked the mute right away. It didn't matter that he couldn't speak, what thrilled Marie was that he was far stronger, far more dangerous than any man she'd ever been with. The pay hadn't been great, but she'd taken the job just the same, and Rolf had been an excellent lover.

If you went for that sensitive, gentle stuff.

Sure, he could have killed her in a flash, but Marie knew there was no chance of that ever happening. She'd lost interest in Rolf pretty quickly. At the same time, the office politics between him and Hannibal had been so interesting that she'd kept sleeping with Rolf just to infuriate the old man, who clearly wanted a poke at her himself.

And that wasn't going to happen. Hannibal didn't just feel dangerous. Marie liked men to be cruel to her; it made her feel wanted, needed. She was sure that had to do with Daddy. But she didn't want to die. And look how that had turned out. Hannibal and his flunkies had been blamed for hundreds of murders in the past five days alone. Office politics had become global politics. She'd been questioned by UN investigators and just about everyone else she'd ever heard of, not to mention plenty she hadn't. Most of those people had been mean to her, but not in any intimate way.

Ah, but Kev—she'd known the moment she'd seen him in the pub.

One look at the scowl on his face and she knew he'd be coming back to her place. Her friends were all uptight bitches, though she loved them still. But they couldn't understand her, in fact denied that she could truly enjoy being with men like Kev. They just didn't get it. These men were powerful, were dangerous and cruel. But when they were inside her, no matter how rough they were, no matter how she whimpered, she was in charge. They had to have her, and that was the real power.

Her girlfriends just didn't understand. In fact, some of them were ashamed of her. *Fuck 'em*, Marie thought, *I know what I like*.

The morning had started out sunny, but the clouds had rolled in almost right away, and now it had started to rain. It was just a drip drop at first, but she knew that it would be pissin' down in no time.

Heaven forbid I should take the tube!

Two blocks from the Mackeson Building, where she hoped to find a job, since they were paying better than the others, it did finally begin to pour, and now she tried to run in her heels without falling on her face. Only a block-and-a-half to go, and then she'd take a taxi home after. She put her leather bag on top of her head, trying to keep her hair as dry as possible under the circumstances. God, she was going to make a horrendous first impression, she thought. She could probably kiss the job good-bye.

Marie was dodging now, around other people who were trying to get in out of the rain. And then suddenly she couldn't dodge. There was a man in front of her and there was no way she could get around him. Instead, she plowed into the bastard and sent them both tumbling into the rain-filled gutter along the pavement.

"Uhhfff!" Marie gasped as she hit the ground, closing her eyes as the dirty water splashed into her face. She was soaked to the bone in half a second, and she shook her head to try to sort out her thoughts.

She could hear the chuckles over the clumsy scene even with the rain absorbing and replacing most of the sounds around her. Marie tried to sit up, wanting to be away from the water as quickly as possible, but she couldn't. The man she had run into, who was wearing a long raincoat, had landed with his legs across her lower torso. His hair was silver-gray—an old man, then? She worried for a moment that she might actually have hurt him. Even though she was furious about her clothes, about the interview she would now have to cancel, Marie felt guilty.

"Here, you," she said, tapping on the man's shoulder even as he pushed himself off the ground with both hands. "Are you all right, then? I didn't mean to—"

And then, rather than pulling his legs off her, the old man pushed himself over onto her, trapping her arms and legs, her body, beneath him, like so many of her lovers had done. She had enjoyed it then, but now . . .

Marie saw his face, finally, and she screamed as his teeth sank into her neck, there in the gutter, in the cold rainwater. People all around began to yell, rushing forward to punch and kick the man, but he did not move away. Marie Wilkins stared down into the ice-blue eyes of her own death, into the eyes of Hannibal. After a moment, her screaming stopped, and her eyes felt as if they were going to burst from her face as she watched the vampire drink her blood. She heard the whistle of a bobby on the way, but she knew he would come too late.

"I will never be denied again!" Hannibal told her triumphantly, the smile on his face terrible. Cruel.

He punched a clawed hand through her chest and crushed her heart.

Her brain could not understand, but her eyes still recorded the vampire's transformation to mist.

And then they were both gone.

New Orleans, Louisiana, United States of America.
Monday, June 12, 2000, 8:37 P.M.:

In a three-story home with terraces that hung out over Decatur Street, four blocks from Jackson Square in the French Quarter, a small group of humans and shadows crowded into their living room. They shared this home, living together, in peace, and if anyone on the streets of New Orleans knew that vampires lived on Decatur Street, they weren't saying. They were used to the presence of shadows, and not much interested in politics. As long as their sons and daughters didn't go missing in the middle of the night, they weren't about to start trouble with the neighbors.

The room was Old South, as befitted the house. Will Cody and Allison Vigeant snuggled together on the love seat. Peter Octavian looked at his reflection in the window and ran a hand through his long hair to flatten it, a familiar gesture which only reaffirmed his identity to those in the room. Erika Hunter shared the long couch with Rolf Sechs, and Joe Boudreau sat on the floor with his back against it. They all looked up as Stefan came down the stairs.

"How is he?" Peter asked, his eyebrows knitted with concern.

"Sleeping fitfully," Stefan said. "Even with the blood we've all given, his legs have barely begun to grow. I wonder . . ."

Stefan left the thought unfinished, but they all knew where he was going with it, for they had wondered as well. Charlemagne was to have been their leader now. If he had given up, if his will was not strong enough to heal him, to replace his amputated limbs, then Peter would lead them. And they all knew, as well, that Peter didn't really want the job. The mood in the house was somber.

Will, Peter and Allison had arrived only a few hours earlier, with Stefan and Charlemagne in their care. Erika and Rolf had been there a full day, and had been met by Joe Boudreau and George Marcopoulos, who had already begun to ready the house for them. It was a new beginning, set up for them by Meaghan Gallagher. Now that the others had arrived, and though George was not yet home from making a most important phone call, they finally had time to mourn, together, everything and everyone they had lost.

They mourned for Alexandra Nueva, for Meaghan Gallagher, and for Elissa Thomas. They mourned for Martha, Isaac and Jared, and for John Courage. They mourned for Lazarus, who might be dead or trapped forever in the bowels of Hell. They mourned for an old king who lived in agony, and his faithful warriors, who had been resurrected only to truly and finally die, but whose valor had been instrumental in their salvation. They mourned for Annelise and Carlo, whose last names Rolf and Erika were forced to admit they had never known. They mourned for all those nameless soldiers and civilians, humans and vampires, who had died at the hands of Hannibal and Mulkerrin and the lords of Hell. And they mourned for themselves, forced to live in a world where they would be hunted by both humans and vampires, trapped between two sides in a war, like all others, without a victor.

They rejoiced to have discovered the true nature of shadows, to know their history, to have obtained a foundation for the future. They planned for the future, together, and spoke excitedly about their proselytizing mission, to seek out shadows across the Earth and bring them to their cause, to enlighten them with the truth about themselves, to undermine Hannibal's barbaric efforts.

They worried about the new American President, his hatred for shadows, and George Marcopoulos's contention that the man was insane. They hoped that one day humanity's leadership would have more vision, better perception, and see that for all their power, vampires shadows—were more like humans than not like them. They wished they didn't have to hide, and secretly, sometimes, that they had remained hidden.

"If wishes were horses," Allison said when that was mentioned, and a light chuckle filled the room.

"There's no going back," Cody added. "We move forward or we die."

"I'm not prepared to die again," Octavian said.

"So what then?" Joe Boudreau asked. "We just hide out, wait for the humans to hunt us down?"

"We find Hannibal," Erika said gravely, "and we kill him. That's half our problem taken care of."

"I'm not so sure—" Stefan began, but Erika cut him off.

"I'm sure," she said.

"And then?" Allison asked, her eyes on her lover, Will Cody.

"And then, darlin'," Cody said and squeezed her hand, "we start chipping away at the world outside. But we start by taking care of each other. Our own coven, in a way, but the first made up of shadows *and* humans. We stick together, and watch out for one another, and we'll be just fine."

"I wish I could believe that," Erika said, and it was Rolf, next to her on the couch, who answered in his own way. He reached out and stroked her cheek and merely nodded, as if to say, *Believe it*.

They were quiet after that.

A few minutes later, George Marcopoulos came in, ready to tell them that the UN had joined the American declaration of war against all vampires, but before he got two sentences out of his mouth, he saw Allison and Will. And Peter.

Peter Octavian, his best friend, whom he had thought dead for five long years, whose survival he had been unaware of until that very moment. He couldn't say a word as Peter crossed the room and took him in his arms. Peter was gentle, for George was getting old, but they hugged each other tight. They were like father and son, though which was which had never been certain.

"Oh, my friend," George finally whispered into the silence of the room, "I missed you. We have so much to talk about."

And so George took his place in the high-backed chair that had been left empty for him, put his feet up on the ottoman while Joe went to get him a cup of tea, and told them all that the stakes had risen higher still. And he told them of the death of his wife, Valerie, the only woman he had ever loved, who had apparently missed him too much.

Once again they mourned, they remembered, they cried. Later, they laughed and talked and dreamed. Finally, when it was far past George's bedtime and they admitted that they all needed rest, they prayed.

Together.